✔ KT-421-432

HIS ILLEGITIMATE HEIR

BY
SARAH M. ANDERSON

MILLS & BOON

First Published in Great Britain 2016
By Mills & Boon, an imprint of HarperCollins*Publishers*
1 London Bridge Street, London, SE1 9GF

© 2016 Sarah M. Anderson

ISBN: 978-0-263-91881-6

51-1016

Our policy is to use papers that are natural, renewable and recyclable products and made from wood grown in sustainable forests. The logging and manufacturing processes conform to the legal environmental regulations of the country of origin.

Printed and bound in Spain
by CPI, Barcelona

Sarah M. Anderson may live east of the Mississippi River, but her heart lies out West on the Great Plains. Sarah's book *A Man of Privilege* won an RT Reviewers' Choice Best Book Award in 2012.

Sarah spends her days having conversations with imaginary cowboys and American Indians. Find out more about Sarah's love of cowboys and Indians at www.sarahmanderson.com and sign up for the new-release newsletter at www.eepurl.com/nv39b.

To Lisa Marie Perry,
who never ceases to shock and amaze me.
We'll always have Jesse Williams!

One

"You ready for this?" Jamal asked from the front seat of the limo.

Zeb Richards felt a smile pull at the corner of his mouth. "I was born ready."

It wasn't an exaggeration. Finally, after all these years, Zeb was coming home to claim what was rightfully his. The Beaumont Brewery had—until very recently—been owned and operated by the Beaumont family. There were a hundred twenty-five years of family history in this building—history that Zeb had been deprived of.

He was a Beaumont by blood. Hardwick Beaumont was Zeb's father.

But he was illegitimate. As far as he knew, outside of the payoff money Hardwick had given his mother, Emily, shortly after Zeb's birth, no one in the Beaumont family had ever acknowledged his existence.

He was tired of being ignored. More than that, he

was tired of being denied his rightful place in the Beaumont family.

So he was finally taking what was rightfully his. After years of careful planning and sheer luck, the Beaumont Brewery now belonged to him.

Jamal snorted, which made Zeb look at him. Jamal Hitchens was Zeb's right-hand man, filling out the roles of chauffeur and bodyguard—plus, he baked a damn fine chocolate chip cookie. Jamal had worked for Zeb ever since he'd blown out his knees his senior year as linebacker at the University of Georgia, but the two of them went back much farther than that.

"You sure about this?" Jamal asked. "I still think I should go in with you."

Zeb shook his head. "No offense, but you'd just scare the hell out of them. I want my new employees intimidated, not terrified."

Jamal met Zeb's gaze in the rearview mirror and an unspoken understanding passed between the two men. Zeb could pull off intimidating all by himself.

With a sigh of resignation, Jamal parked in front of the corporate headquarters and came around to open Zeb's door. Starting right now, Zeb was a Beaumont in every way that counted.

Jamal looked around as Zeb stood and straightened the cuffs on his bespoke suit. "Last chance for backup."

"You're not nervous, are you?" Zeb wasn't. There was such a sense of rightness about this that he couldn't be nervous, so he simply wasn't.

Jamal gave him a look. "You realize you're not going to be hailed as a hero, right? You didn't exactly get this company in a way that most people might call *ethical*."

Zeb notched an eyebrow at his oldest friend. With Jamal at his back, Zeb had gone from being the son of a hairdresser to being the sole owner of ZOLA, a private equity firm that he'd founded. He'd made his millions without a single offer of assistance from the Beaumonts.

More than that, he had proven that he was better than they were. He'd outmaneuvered and outflanked them and taken their precious brewery away from them.

But taking over the family business was something he had to do himself. "Your concern is duly noted. I'll text you if I need backup. Otherwise, you'll be viewing the properties?"

They needed a place to live now that they would be based in Denver. ZOLA, Zeb's company, was still head-quartered in New York—a hedge just in case his owner-ship of the Beaumont Brewery backfired. But buying a house here would signal to everyone that Zeb Richards wasn't going anywhere anytime soon.

Jamal realized he wasn't going to win this fight. Zeb could tell by the way he straightened his shoulders. "Right, boss. Finest money can buy?"

"Always." It didn't really matter what the house looked like or how many bathrooms it had. All that mattered was that it was better than anyone else's. Spe-cifically, better than any of the other Beaumonts'. "But make sure it's got a nice kitchen."

Jamal smirked at that bone of friendship Zeb threw him. "Good luck."

Zeb slid a sideways glance at Jamal. "Good luck hap-pens when you work for it." And Zeb? He *always* worked for it.

With a sense of purpose, he strode into the corporate headquarters of the Beaumont Brewery. He hadn't called to announce his impending arrival, because he wanted to see what the employees looked like when they weren't ready to be inspected by their new CEO.

However, he was fully aware that he was an unfamiliar African American man walking into a building as if he owned it—which he did. Surely the employees knew that Zebadiah Richards was their new boss. But how many of them would recognize him?

True to form, he got plenty of double takes as he walked through the building. One woman put her hand on her phone as he passed, as if she was going to call security. But then someone else whispered something over the edge of her cubicle wall and the woman's eyes got very wide. Zeb notched an eyebrow at her and she pulled her hand away from her phone like it had burned her.

Silence trailed in his wake as he made his way toward the executive office. Zeb fought hard to keep a smile off his face. So they did know who he was. He appreciated employees who were up-to-date on their corporate leadership. If they recognized him, then they had also probably read the rumors about him.

Zebadiah Richards and his private equity firm bought failing companies, restructured them and sold them for profit. ZOLA had made him rich—and earned him a reputation for ruthlessness.

He would need that reputation here. Contrary to some of the rumors, he was not actually heartless. And he understood that the employees at this brewery had undergone the ouster of not one but two CEOs in less than a year. From his reports on the company's filings, he understood that most people still missed Chadwick Beaumont, the last Beaumont to run the brewery.

Zeb had not gotten Chadwick removed—but he had taken advantage of the turmoil that the sale of the brewery to the conglomerate AllBev had caused. And when Chadwick's temporary replacement, Ethan Logan, had failed to turn the company around fast enough, Zeb had agitated for AllBev to sell the company.

To him, of course.

But what that really meant was that he now owned a company full of employees who were scared and desperate. Employee turnover was at an all-time high. A significant percentage of top-level management had followed Chadwick Beaumont to his new company, Percheron Drafts. Many others had taken early retirement.

The employees who had survived this long were holding on by the skin of their teeth and probably had nothing left to lose. Which made them dangerous. He'd seen it before in other failing companies. Change was a constant in his world but most people hated it and if they fought against it hard enough, they could doom an entire company. When that happened, Zeb shrugged and broke the business up to be sold for its base parts. Normally, he didn't care if that happened—so long as he made a profit, he was happy.

But like he told Jamal, he was here to stay. He was a Beaumont and this was his brewery. He cared about this place and its history because it was his history, acknowledged or not. Not that he'd wanted anyone to know that this was personal—he'd kept his quest to take what was rightfully his quiet for years. That way, no one could preempt his strikes or lock him out.

But now that he was here, he had the overwhelming urge to shout, "Look at me!" He was done being ignored by the Beaumonts and he was done pretending he wasn't one of them.

Whispers of his arrival must have made it to the executive suite because when he rounded the corner, a plump older woman sitting behind a desk in front of what he assumed was the CEO's office stood and swallowed nervously. "Mr. Richards," she said in a crackly voice. "We weren't expecting you today."

Zeb nodded his head in acknowledgment. He didn't explain his sudden appearance and he didn't try to reassure her. "And you are?"

"Delores Hahn," she said. "I'm the executive assistant to the—to you." Her hands twisted nervously in front of her before she caught herself and stilled them. "Welcome to the Beaumont Brewery."

Zeb almost grinned in sympathy. His assistant was in a tough spot, but she was putting on a good face. "Thank you."

Delores cleared her throat. "Would you like a tour of the facilities?" Her voice was still a bit shaky, but she was holding it together. Zeb decided he liked Delores.

Not that he wanted her to know that right away. He was not here to make friends. He was here to run a business. "I will—after I get settled in." Then he headed for his office.

Once inside, he shut the door behind him and leaned against it. This was really happening. After years of plotting and watching and waiting, he had the Beaumont Brewery—his birthright.

He felt like laughing at the wonder of it all. But he didn't. For all he knew, Delores had her ear to the door, listening for any hint of what her new boss was like. Maniacal laughter was not a good first impression, no matter how justified it might be.

Instead, he pushed away from the door and surveyed his office. "Begin as you mean to go on," Zeb reminded himself.

He'd read about this room, studied pictures of it. But he hadn't been prepared for what it would actually feel like to walk into a piece of his family's history—to know that he belonged here, that this was his rightful place.

The building had been constructed in the 1940s by Zeb's grandfather John, soon after Prohibition had ended. The walls were mahogany panels that had been oiled until they gleamed. A built-in bar with a huge mirror took up the whole interior wall—and, if Zeb wasn't mistaken, the beer was on tap.

The exterior wall was lined with windows, hung with heavy gray velvet drapes and crowned with elaborately hand-carved woodwork that told the story of the Beaumont Brewery. His grandfather had had the conference table built in the office because it was so large and the desk was built to match.

Tucked in the far corner was a grouping of two leather club chairs and a matching leather love seat. The wagon-wheel coffee table in front of the chairs was supposed to be a wheel from the wagon that his great-great-grandfather Phillipe Beaumont had driven across the Great Plains on his way to Denver to found the brewery back in the 1880s.

The whole room screamed opulence and wealth and history. Zeb's history. This was who he was and he would be damned if he let anyone tell him it wasn't his.

He crossed to the desk and turned on the computer—top-of-the-line, of course. Beaumonts never did anything by halves. That was one family trait they all shared.

He sat down in the leather office chair. From as far back as he could remember, his mother, Emily Richards, had told him this belonged to him. Zeb was only four months younger than Chadwick Beaumont. He should have been here, learning the business at his father's knee, instead of standing next to his mother's hairdressing chair.

But Hardwick had never married his mother—despite the fact that Hardwick had married several of his mistresses. But not Emily Richards—and for one simple reason.

Emily was black. Which made her son black.

Which meant Zeb didn't exist in the eyes of the Beaumonts.

For so long, he had been shut out of half of his heritage. And now he had the one thing that the Beaumonts had valued above all else—the Beaumont Brewery.

God, it felt good to come home.

He got himself under control. Taking possession of the brewery was a victory—but it was just the first step in making sure the Beaumonts paid for excluding him.

He was not the only Beaumont bastard Hardwick had left behind. It was time to start doing things his way. He grinned. The Beaumonts weren't going to see this coming.

He pressed the button on an antique-looking intercom. It buzzed to life and Delores said, "Yes, sir?"

"I want you to arrange a press conference for this Friday. I'm going to be announcing my plans for the brewery."

There was a pause. "Yes, sir," she said in a way that had an edge to it. "I assume you want the conference here?" Already Zeb could tell she was getting over her nervousness at his unannounced arrival.

If he had to guess, he'd say that someone like Delores Hahn had probably made the last CEO's life miserable. "Yes, on the front steps of the brewery. Oh, and Delores?"

"Yes?"

"Write a memo. Every employee needs to have an updated résumé on my desk by end of business tomorrow."

There was another pause—this one was longer. Zeb could only imagine the glare she was giving the intercom right about now. "Why? I mean—of course I'll get right on it. But is there a reason?"

"Of course there is, Delores. There is a reason behind every single thing I do. And the reason for the memo is simple. Every employee needs to reapply for their own job." He exhaled slowly, letting the tension build. "Including you."

"Boss?"

Casey Johnson jerked her head toward the sound of Larry's voice—which meant she smacked her forehead against the bottom of tank number fifteen. "Ow, dammit." She pushed herself out from under the tank, rubbing her head. "What?"

Larry Kaczynski was a middle-aged man with a beer gut, which was appropriate considering he brewed beer for a living. Normally, he was full of bluster and the latest stats on his fantasy football team. But today he looked worried. Specifically, he looked worried about the piece of paper in his hand. "The new guy... He's here."

"Well, good for him," Casey said, turning her attention back to her tank. This was the second new CEO in less than a year and, given recent history, he probably wouldn't make it past a couple of months. All Casey had to do was outlast him.

That, of course, was the challenge. Beer did not brew itself—although, given the attitude of the last CEO, some people thought it did.

Tank fifteen was her priority right now. Being a brewmaster was about brewing beer—but it was also about making sure the equipment was clean and functional. And right now tank fifteen wasn't either of those things.

"You don't understand," Larry sputtered before she'd rolled back under the tank. "He's been on the property for less than an hour and he's already sent this memo…"

"Larry," she said, her voice echoing against the body of the tank, "are you going to get to the point today?"

"We have to reapply for our jobs," Larry said in a rush. "By the end of the day tomorrow. I don't—Casey, you know me. I don't even have a résumé. I've worked here for the last thirty years."

Oh, for the love of everything holy… Casey pushed herself out from under the tank again and sat up. "Okay," she said in a much softer voice as she got to her feet. "Start from the beginning. What does the memo say?" Because Larry was like a canary in a coal mine. If he kept calm, the staff she was left with would also keep calm. But if Larry panicked…

Larry looked down at the paper in his hands again. He swallowed hard and Casey got the strangest sensation he was trying not to crack.

Crap. They were screwed. "It just says that by end of business tomorrow, every Beaumont Brewery employee needs to have an updated résumé on the new CEO's desk so he can decide if they get to keep their job or not."

Son of a… "Let me see."

Larry handed over the paper as if he'd suddenly discovered it was contagious, and he stepped back. "What am I going to do, boss?"

Casey scanned the memo and saw that Larry had pretty much read verbatim. Every employee, no exceptions.

She did not have time for this. She was responsible for brewing about seven thousand gallons of beer every single day of the year on a skeleton staff of seventeen people. Two years ago, forty people had been responsible for that level of production. But two years ago, the company hadn't been in the middle of the never-ending string of upstart CEOs.

And now the latest CEO was rolling up into *her* brewery and scaring the hell out of *her* employees? This new guy thought he would tell her she had to apply for her job—the job she'd earned?

She didn't know much about this Zebadiah Richards—but he was going to get one thing straight if he thought he was going to run this company.

The Beaumont Brewery brewed beer. No beer, no brewery. And no brewmaster, no beer.

She turned to Larry, who was pale and possibly shaking. She understood why he was scared—Larry was not the brightest bulb and he knew it. That was the reason he hadn't left when Chadwick lost the company or when Ethan Logan tried to right the sinking ship.

That was why Casey had been promoted over him to brewmaster, even though Larry had almost twenty years of experience on her. He liked his job, he liked beer and as long as he got regular cost-of-living increases in his salary and a year-end bonus, he was perfectly content to spend the rest of his life right where he was. He hadn't wanted the responsibility of management.

Frankly, Casey was starting to wonder why she had. "I'll take care of this," she told him.

Surprisingly, this announcement made Larry look even more nervous. Apparently, he didn't put a lot of faith in her ability to keep her temper. "What are you going to do?"

His reaction made it clear that he was afraid she'd get

fired—and then he'd be in charge. "This Richards guy and I are going to have words."

Larry fretted. "Are you sure that's the smart thing to do?"

"Probably not," she agreed. "But what's he going to do—fire the brewmaster? I don't think so, Larry." She patted him on the shoulder. "Don't worry, okay?"

Larry gave her a weak smile, but he nodded resolutely.

Casey hurried to her office and stripped off her hairnet. She knew she was no great beauty, but nobody wanted to confront a new boss in a hairnet. She grabbed her Beaumont Brewery hat and slid her ponytail through the back. And she was off, yelling over her shoulder to Larry, "See if you can get that drainage tube off—and if you can, see if you can get it flushed again. I'll be back in a bit."

She did *not* have time for this. She was already working ten-to twelve-hour days—six or seven days a week—just to keep the equipment clean and the beer flowing. If she lost more of her staff...

It wouldn't come to that. She wouldn't let it. And if it did...

Okay, so she'd promised Larry she wouldn't get fired. But what if she did? Her options weren't great, but at least she had some. Unlike Larry, she did have an updated résumé that she kept on file just in case. She didn't want to use it. She wanted to stay right here at the Beaumont Brewery and brew her favorite beer for the rest of her life.

Or at least, she had. No, if she was being honest, what she really wanted was to be the brewmaster at the old Beaumont Brewery, the one she'd worked at for the previous twelve years—the one that the Beaumont family had run. Back then the brewery had been a family business and the owners had been personally invested in their employees.

They'd even given a wide-eyed college girl the chance to do something no one else had—brew beer.

But the memo in her hand reminded her that this wasn't the same brewery. The Beaumonts no longer ran things and the company was suffering.

She was suffering. She couldn't remember the last time she'd strung together more than twenty-four hours of free time. She was doing the job of three people and, thanks to the hiring freeze the last CEO implemented, there was no relief in sight. And now this. She could not afford to lose another single person.

She was a thirty-two-year-old brewmaster—and a woman, at that. She'd come so far so fast. But not one of her predecessors in the illustrious history of the Beaumont Brewery had put up with quite this much crap. They'd been left to brew beer in relative peace.

She stormed to the CEO suite. Delores was behind the desk. When she saw Casey coming, the older woman jumped to her feet with surprising agility. "Casey—wait. You don't—"

"Oh, yes, I do," she said, blowing past Delores and shoving open the door to the CEO's office. "Just who the hell do you think you...are?"

Two

Casey came to a stumbling stop. Where was he? The desk was vacant and no one was sitting on the leather couches.

But then a movement off to her left caught her eye and she turned and gasped in surprise.

A man stood by the windows, looking out over the brewery campus. He had his hands in his pockets and his back turned to her—but despite that, everything about him screamed power and money. The cut of his suit fit him like a second skin and he stood with his feet shoulder-width apart, as if he were master of all he saw.

A shiver went through her. She was not the kind of girl who went for power suits or the men who wore them but something about this man—this man who was threatening her job—took her breath away. Was it the broad shoulders? Or the raw power wafting off him like the finest cologne?

And then he turned to face her and all she could see were his eyes—*green* eyes. Good Lord, those eyes—they held her gaze like a magnet and she knew her breath was gone for good.

He was, hands down, the most handsome man she'd ever seen. Everything—the power suit, the broad shoulders, the close-cropped hair and most especially the eyes—it was a potent blend that she felt powerless to resist. And this was her new boss? The man who'd sent out the memo?

He notched an eyebrow at her and let his gaze travel over her body. And any admiration she had for a good suit and nice eyes died on the vine because she knew exactly what he saw. Underneath her lab coat, she had on a men's small polo shirt with Beaumont Brewery embroidered over the chest—and she'd sweat through it because the brew room was always hot. Her face was probably red from the heat and also from the anger, and she no doubt smelled like mash and wort.

She must look like a madwoman.

A conclusion he no doubt reached on his own, because by the time he looked her in the eyes, one corner of his mouth had curved up into the kind of smile that said exactly one thing.

He thought she was a joke.

Well, he'd soon learn this was no laughing matter.

"Congratulations," he said in a voice that bordered on cold. "You're first." He lifted his wrist and looked down at a watch that, even at this distance, Casey could tell was expensive. "Thirty-five minutes. I'm impressed."

His imperious attitude poured cold water on the heat that had almost swamped her. She wasn't here to gawk at a gorgeous man. She was here to protect her workers. "Are you Richards?"

"Zebadiah Richards, yes. Your new boss," he added in a menacing tone, as if he thought he could intimidate her. Didn't he know she had so very little left to lose? "And you are?"

She'd worked in a male-dominated industry for twelve years. She couldn't be intimidated. "I'm Casey Johnson—your brewmaster." What kind of name was Zebadiah? Was that biblical? "What's the meaning of this?" She held up the memo.

Richards's eyes widened in surprise—but only for a second before he once again looked ice-cold. "Forgive me," he said in a smooth voice when Casey glared at him. "I must say that you are not what I was expecting."

Casey rolled her eyes and made no attempt to hide it. Few people expected women to like beer. Even fewer people expected women to brew beer. And with a name like Casey, everyone just assumed she was a man—and usually, they assumed she was a man like Larry. Middle-aged, beer gut—the whole nine yards. "It's not my problem if you made a set of erroneous assumptions."

The moment she said it, she realized she'd also made some erroneous assumptions herself. Because she had not anticipated that the new CEO would look quite like him. Oh, sure—the power suit was par for the course. But his hair was close-cropped to his head and his eyes... Damn, she just couldn't get past them.

He grinned—oh, Lord, that was not good. Well, it was—but in a bad way because that grin took everything hard and cold about him and warmed him up. She was certainly about to break out in another sweat.

"Indeed. Well, since you're the first person to barge into my office, I'll tell you the meaning of that memo, Ms. Johnson—although I'd hope the employees here at the brewery would be able to figure it out on their own. Everyone has to reapply for their jobs."

She welcomed his condescending tone because it pushed her from falling into the heat of his eyes and kept her focused on her task. "Is that a fact? Where'd you learn that management technique? Management 'R' Us?"

Something that almost looked like amusement flickered over his gaze and she was tempted to smile. A lot of people found her abrasive and yeah, she could rub people the wrong way. She didn't pull her punches and she wasn't about to sit down and shut up just because she was a girl and men didn't like to have their authority challenged.

What was rarer was for someone to get her sense of humor. Could this Richards actually be a real man who smiled? God, she wanted to work for a man she wouldn't have to fight every step of the way. Maybe they could get along. Maybe...

But as quickly as it had appeared, the humor was gone. His eyes narrowed and Casey thought, *You're not the only one who can be condescending.*

"The purpose is twofold, Ms. Johnson. One, I'd like to see what skill sets my employees possess. And two, I want to see if they can follow basic instructions."

So much for a sense of humor. Men as hot as he was probably weren't allowed to laugh at a joke. Pity. On the other hand, if he smiled, it might kill her with handsomeness and the only thing worse than a CEO she couldn't work with would be a CEO she lusted after.

No lusting allowed. And he was making that easier with every single thing he said.

"Let me assure you, Mr. Richards, that this company did not spring fully formed from your forehead yesterday. We've been brewing beer here for—"

"For over one hundred and thirty years—I know." He tilted his head to the side and gave her a long look. "And you've only been doing it for less than a year—is that correct?"

If she weren't so pissed at him, she'd have been terrified, because that was most definitely a threat to her job. But she didn't have time for unproductive emotions and anger was vastly more useful than fear.

"I have—and I earned that job. But before you question how a woman my age can have possibly surpassed all the good ol' boys who normally brew beer, let me tell you that it's also because all the more experienced brewers have already left the company. If you want to maintain a quality product line, you're stuck with me for the foreseeable future." She waved the memo in front of her. "And I don't have time to deal with this crap."

But instead of doing anything any normal boss would do when basically yelled at by an employee—like firing her on the spot—Richards tilted his head to one side and looked at her again and she absolutely did not shiver when he did it. "Why not?"

"Why not what?"

"Why don't you have time to respond to a simple administrative task?"

Casey didn't want to betray any sign of weakness but a trickle of sweat rolled out from under her hat and into her eye. Dammit. He better not think she was crying. She wiped her eyes with the palm of her hand. "Because I'm operating with a bare-bones staff—I have been for the last nine months. I'm doing the work of three people—we all are. We're understaffed, overworked and—"

"And you don't have time for this 'crap,' as you so eloquently put it," he murmured.

Was that a note of sympathy? Or was he mocking her? She couldn't read him that well.

Not yet, a teasing voice in the back of her mind whispered. But she pushed that voice away. She wasn't interested in reading him better. "Not if you want to fulfill production orders."

"So just hire more people."

Now she gaped at him. "What?"

He shrugged, which was an impossibly smooth gesture on him. Men should not be that smooth. It wasn't good for them, she decided. And it definitely wasn't good for her. This would be so much easier if he were at least 70 percent less attractive. "Hire more people. But I want to see their résumés, too. Why let the new people off easy, right?"

This guy didn't know anything, did he? They were screwed, then. This was the beginning of the end. Now she would have to help Larry write a résumé.

"But…there's been a hiring freeze," she told him. "For the last eight months. Until we can show a profit."

Richards stepped forward and traced a finger over the top of the conference table. It was an oddly intimate motion—a caress, almost. Watching his hand move over the wood…

She broke out in goose bumps.

"Tell me, Ms. Johnson, was it Chadwick Beaumont who put on the hiring freeze? Or Ethan Logan?"

There was something about his voice that matched his caress of the conference table. Casey studied him. She had the oddest feeling that he looked familiar but she was sure she would remember seeing him before. Who could forget those eyes? Those…everything?

"Logan did."

"Ah," he said, shifting so he wasn't silhouetted

against the window anymore. More light fell on him and Casey was startled to realize that the green eyes were set against skin that wasn't light but wasn't exactly deep brown, either. His skin was warm, almost tan, and she realized he was at least partly African American. Why hadn't she seen that right away?

Well, she knew why. First off, she was mad and when she was mad, she didn't exactly pay attention to the bigger picture. She hadn't noticed the fullness to his frowning lips or the slight flare of his nostrils. Second off, his eyes had demanded her total attention. They were striking, so gorgeous, and even…familiar?

His hand was still on top of the conference table. "So what you're telling me is that the only non-Beaumont to run this company instituted a series of policies designed to cut costs and, in the process, hamstrung the operations and production?"

"Yes." There was something about the way he said *the only non-Beaumont* that threw her for a loop.

And then—maybe because now she was paying more attention—it hit her like a ton of bricks.

This guy—this Zeb Richards who wasn't quite black and wasn't quite white—he looked vaguely familiar. Something in the nose, the chin…those eyes…

He looked a little bit like Chadwick Beaumont.

Sweet merciful heavens. He *was* a Beaumont, too.

Her knees gave in to the weight of the revelation and she lurched forward to lean on the coffee table. "Oh, my God," she asked, staring at him. "You're one of them, aren't you?"

Richards snatched his hand back and put it in his pocket like he was trying to hide something. "I can neither confirm nor deny that—at least, not until the press conference on Friday." He moved away from the conference table and toward his desk.

If he was trying to intimidate her, it wasn't working. Casey followed him. He sat behind the desk—the same place she had seen Chadwick Beaumont too many times to count and, at least three times, Hardwick Beaumont. The resemblance was unmistakable.

"My God," she repeated again. "You're one of the bastards."

He leaned back in his chair and steepled his fingers. Everything about him had shut down. No traces of humor, no hints of warmth. She was staring at the coldest man she'd ever seen. "The bastards?"

"Beaumont's bastards—there were always rumors that Hardwick had a bunch of illegitimate children." She blinked. It all made sense, in a way. The Beaumonts were a notoriously good-looking group of men and women—far too handsome for their own good. And this man… He was gorgeous. But not the same kind of blond handsomeness that had marked Chadwick and Matthew Beaumont. She knew he would stand out in a crowd of Beaumonts. Hell, he would stand out in *any* crowd. "He was your father, wasn't he?"

Richards stared at her for a long time and she got the feeling he was making some sort of decision. She didn't know what—he hadn't fired her yet but the day wasn't over.

Her mind felt like it was fizzing with information. Zeb Richards—the mysterious man who was rumored to have single-handedly driven down the brewery's stock price so he could force AllBev to sell off the company—was a Beaumont? Did Chadwick know? Was he in on it or was this something else?

One word whispered across her mind. *Revenge.*

Because up until about thirty-seven seconds ago, Beaumont's bastards had never been anything but a rumor. And now one of them had the company.

She had no idea if this was a good thing or a very, *very* bad thing.

Suddenly, Richards leaned forward and made a minute adjustment to something on his desk. "We've gotten off track. Your primary reason for barging into my office unannounced was about résumés."

She felt like a bottle of beer that had been shaken but hadn't been opened. At any second, she might explode from the pressure. "Right," she agreed, collapsing into the chair in front of his desk. "The problem is, some of my employees have been here for twenty, thirty years and they don't have a résumé ready to go. Producing one on short notice is going to cause nothing but panic. They aren't the kind of guys who look good on paper. What matters is that they do good work for me and we produce a quality product." She took a deep breath, trying to sound managerial. "Are you familiar with our product line?"

The corner of Richard's mouth twitched. "It's beer, right?"

She rolled her eyes at him, which, surprisingly, made him grin even more. Oh, that was a bad idea, making him smile like that, because when he did, all the hard, cold edges fell away from his face. He was the kind of handsome that wasn't fair to the rest of humanity.

Sinful. That was what he was. And she had been too well behaved for too long.

She shivered. She wasn't sure if it had anything to do with the smile on his face or the fact that she was cooling off and her sweat-soaked shirt was now sticking to her skin. "That's correct. We brew beer here. I appreciate you giving me the go-ahead to hire more workers but that's a process that will take weeks. Training will also take time. Placing additional paperwork demands on my staff runs the risk of compromising the quality of our beer."

Richards didn't say anything. Casey cleared her throat. "You *are* interested in the beer, right?"

He gave her another one of those measured looks. Casey sighed. She really wasn't so complicated that he had to stare at her.

"I'm interested in the beer," he finally said. "This is a family company and I'd like to keep it that way. I must say," he went on before Casey could ask about that whole "family" thing, "I certainly appreciate your willingness to defend your staff. However, I'd like to be reassured that the employees who work for this brewery not only are able to follow basic instructions," he added with a notch of his eyebrow that made Casey want to pound on something, "but have the skills to take this company in a new direction."

"A new direction? We're…still going to brew beer, right? We're not getting into electronics or apps or anything?"

"Oh, we'll be getting into apps," he said. "But I need to know if there's anyone on staff who can handle that or if I'm going to need to bring in an outside developer— you see my point, don't you? The Beaumont Brewery has been losing market share. You brew seven thousand gallons a day—but it was eleven thousand years ago. The popularity of craft breweries—and I'm including Percheron Drafts in that—has slowly eroded our sales."

Our sales? He was serious, she realized. He was here to run this company.

"While I understand Logan's cost-cutting measures,"

he went on, oblivious to the way her mouth had dropped open, "what we need to do at this point is not to hunker down and hope for the best, but invest heavily in research and development—new products. And part of that is connecting with our audience." His gaze traveled around the room and Casey thought there was something about him that seemed…hopeful, almost.

She wanted to like her job. She wanted to like working for Zeb Richards. And if he was really talking about launching new products—new beers—well, then she might like her job again. The feeling that blossomed in her chest was so unfamiliar that it took a second to realize what it was—hope. Hope that this might actually work out.

"Part of what made the Beaumont Brewery a success was its long family traditions," Richards went on in a quiet voice. "That's why Logan failed. The employees liked Chadwick—any idiot knows that. And his brother Phillip? Phillip was the brewery's connection with our target market. When we lost both Phillip and Chadwick, the brewery lost its way."

Everything he said made sense. Because Casey had spent the last year not only feeling lost but knowing they were lost. They lost ground, they lost employees, they lost friends—they lost the knowledge and the tradition that had made them great. She was only one woman—one woman who liked to make beer. She couldn't save the company all by herself but she was doing her damnedest to save the beer.

Still, Richards had been on the job for about two hours now—maybe less. He was talking a hell of a good game, but at this point, that was all it was—talk. All talk and sinful handsomeness, with a hearty dollop of mystery.

But action was what this company needed. His mesmerizing eyes wouldn't right this ship all by themselves.

Still, if Richards really was a Beaumont by birth—bastard or not—he just might be able to do it. She'd long ago learned to never underestimate the Beaumonts.

"So you're going to be the one to light the path?"

He stared her in the eyes, one eyebrow gently lifted. God, if she wasn't careful, she could get lost in his gaze. "I have a plan, Ms. Johnson. You let me worry about the company and you worry about the beer."

"Sounds good to me," she muttered.

She stood because it seemed like a final sort of statement. But Richards stopped her. "How many workers do you need to hire?"

"At least ten. What I need most right now is maintenance staff. I don't know how much you know about beer, but most of what I do is automated. It's making sure to push the right button at the right time and checking to make sure that things come together the right way. It doesn't take a lot of know-how to brew beer, honestly, once you have the recipes." At this statement, both of his eyebrows lifted. "But keeping equipment running is another matter. It's hot, messy work and I need at least eight people who can take a tank apart and put it back together in less than an hour."

He thought about that for a moment. "I don't mean to be rude, but is that what you were doing before you came in here?"

She rolled her eyes again. "What gave it away?"

He grinned. Casey took another step back from the desk—away from Zeb Richards smiling at her. She tried to take comfort in the fact that he probably knew exactly how lethal his grin could be. Men as gorgeous as he was didn't get through life without knowing exactly what kind of effect they had on women—and it usually made them jerks. Which was fine. Gorgeous jerks never went for women like her and she didn't bother with them, either.

But there was something in the way he was looking at her that felt like a warning.

"I'll compromise with you, Ms. Johnson. You and your staff will be excused from submitting résumés."

That didn't sound like a compromise. That sounded like she was getting everything she asked for. Which meant the other shoe was about to drop. "And?"

"Instead…" He paused and shot her another grin. This one wasn't warm and fuzzy—this one was the sharp smile of a man who'd somehow bought a company out from under the Beaumonts. Out from under his own family. "…you and your team will produce a selection of new beers for me to choose from."

That was one hell of a shoe—and it had landed right on her. "I'm sorry?"

"Your point that the skills of some of your employees won't readily translate into bullet points on a résumé is well taken. So I'd like to see their skills demonstrated in action."

She knew her mouth was open, but she didn't think she could get it closed. She gave it a shot—nope, it was still open. "I can't just…"

"You do know how to brew beer, don't you?"

He was needling her—and it was working, dammit. "Of course I know how to brew beer. I've been brewing Beaumont beer for twelve years."

"Then what's the problem?"

It was probably bad form to strangle your boss on his first day on the job. Tempting, though. "I can't just produce beer by snapping my fingers. I have to test new recipes—and some of them are not going to work—and then there's the brewing time, and I won't be able to do any of that until I get more staff hired."

"How long will it take?"

She grasped at the first number that popped into her mind. "Two months. At least. Maybe three."

"Fine. Three months to hire the workers and test some new recipes." He sat forward in his chair and dropped his gaze to the desk, as if they were done.

"It isn't that simple," she told him. "We need to get Marketing to provide us with guidance on what's currently popular and two—"

"I don't care what Marketing says." He cut her off. "This is my company and I want it to brew beers that I like."

"But I don't even know what you like." The moment the words left her mouth, she wished she could take them back. But it was too late. He fixed those eyes on her. Heat flushed down her back, warming her from the inside out. "I mean, when it comes to beer," she quickly corrected. "We've got everything on tap…" she added, trying not to blush as she motioned to the bar that ran along one side of the wall.

Richards leaned forward on his elbows as his gaze raked up and down her body again. Damn it all, he was a jerk. He only confirmed it when he opened his mouth and said, "I'd be more than happy to take some time after work and show you exactly what I like."

Well. If that was how it was going to be, he was making it a lot easier *not* to develop a crush on him. Because she had not gotten this job by sleeping her way to the top. He might be the most beautiful man she'd ever seen and those green eyes were the stuff of fantasy—but none of it mattered if he used his power as CEO to take advantage of his employees. She was good at what she did and she wouldn't let anyone take that away from her.

"Mr. Richards, you're going to have to decide what kind of Beaumont you are going to be—*if* you really are one." His eyes hardened, but she didn't back down. "Because if you're going to be a predator like your father instead of a businessman like your brother, you're going to need a new brewmaster."

Head held high, she walked out of his office and back to her own.

Then she updated her résumé.

Three

Zeb did not have time to think about his new brew-master's parting shot. It was, however, difficult not to think about *her*.

He'd known full well there would be pushback against the memo. He hadn't lied when he'd told her he wanted to see who could follow directions—but he also wanted to see who wouldn't and why. Because the fact was, having the entire company divert work hours to producing résumés was not an efficient use of time. And the workers who already had up-to-date résumés ready to go—well, that was because they were a flight risk.

He couldn't say he was surprised when the brewmaster was the first person to call him on it.

But he still couldn't believe the brewmaster was a young woman with fire in her eyes and a fierce instinct to protect her employees. A woman who didn't look at him like he was ripe for the picking. A woman who took one look at him—okay, maybe more than one—and saw the truth.

A young woman with a hell of a mouth on her.

Zeb pushed Casey Johnson from his mind and picked up his phone. He started scrolling through his contacts until he came to one name in particular—Daniel Lee. He dialed and waited.

"Hello?"

"Daniel—it's Zeb. Are you still in?"

There was a pause on the other end of the line. Daniel Lee was a former political operative who'd worked behind the scenes to get several incumbents defeated. He could manipulate public perception and he could drill down into data. But that wasn't why Zeb called him.

Daniel—much like Zeb—was one of *them*. Beaumont's bastards.

"Where are you?" Daniel asked, and Zeb didn't miss the way he neatly avoided the question.

"Sitting in the CEO's office of the Beaumont Brewery. I scheduled a press conference for Friday—I'd like you to be there. I want to show the whole world that they can't ignore us anymore."

There was another pause. On one level, Zeb appreciated that Daniel was methodical. Everything he did was well thought-out and carefully researched, with the data to back it up.

But on the other hand, Zeb didn't want his relationship with his brother to be one based solely on how the numbers played out. He didn't know Daniel very well—they'd met only two months ago, after Zeb had spent almost a year and thousands upon thousands of dollars tracking down two of his half brothers. But he and Daniel were family all the same and when Zeb announced to the world that he was a Beaumont and this was his brewery, he wanted his brothers by his side.

"What about CJ?" Daniel asked.

Zeb exhaled. "He's out." Zeb had tracked down two illegitimate brothers; all three of them had been born within five years of each other. Daniel was three years younger than Zeb and half-Korean.

The other brother he'd found was Carlos Julián Santino—although he now went by CJ Wesley. Unlike Zeb and Daniel, CJ was a rancher. He didn't seem to have inherited the Beaumont drive for business.

Two months ago, when the men had all met for the first time over dinner and Zeb had laid out his plan for taking control of the brewery and finally taking what was rightfully theirs, Daniel politely agreed to look at the numbers and weigh the outcomes. But CJ had said he wasn't interested. Unlike Zeb's mother, CJ's mother had married and he'd been adopted by her husband. CJ did not consider Hardwick Beaumont to be his father. He'd made his position clear—he wanted nothing to do with the Beaumonts or the brewery.

He wanted nothing to do with his brothers.

"That's unfortunate," Daniel said. "I had hoped..."

Yeah, Zeb had hoped, too. But he wasn't going to dwell on his failures. Not when success was within his grasp. "I need you by my side, Daniel. This is our time. I won't be swept under the rug any longer. We are both Beaumonts. It's not enough that I've taken their company away from them—I need it to do better than it did under them. And that means I need you. This is the dawn of a new era."

Daniel chuckled. "You can stop with the hard sell— I'm in. But I get to be the chief marketing officer, right?"

"I wouldn't have it any other way."

There was another long pause. "This had better work," Daniel said in a menacing voice.

Which made Zeb grin. "It already has."

It was late afternoon before Zeb was able to get a tour of the facilities. Delores, tablet in hand, alternated between leading the way and falling behind him. Zeb couldn't tell if she was humoring him or if she really was that intimidated.

The tour moved slowly because in every department, Zeb stopped and talked with the staff. He was pleased when several managers asked to speak to him privately and then questioned the need to have a résumé for every single person on staff—wouldn't it be better if they just turned in a report on head count? It was heartening, really. Those managers were willing to risk their necks to protect their people—while they still looked for a way to do what Zeb told them.

However, Zeb didn't want to be seen as a weak leader who changed his mind. He allowed the managers to submit a report by the deadline, but he still wanted to see résumés. He informed everyone that the hiring freeze was over but he needed to know what he had before he began to fill the empty cubicles.

As he'd anticipated after his conversation with Casey, the news that the hiring freeze was over—coupled with the announcement that he would prefer not to see his staff working ten-to twelve-hour days—bought him a considerable amount of goodwill. That was not to say people weren't still wary—they were—but the overwhelming emotion was relief. It was obvious Casey wasn't the only one doing the job of two or three people.

The brewhouse was the last stop on their tour. Zeb wasn't sure if that was because it was the logical conclusion or because Delores was trying to delay another confrontation with Casey.

Unsurprisingly, the brewhouse was warm, and emptier than he expected. He saw now what Casey had meant when she said most of the process was automated. The few men he did see wore white lab coats and hairnets, along with safety goggles. They held tablets and when Zeb and Delores passed them, they paused and looked up.

"The staffing levels two years ago?" Zeb asked again.

He'd asked that question at least five times already. Two years ago, the company had been in the capable hands of Chadwick Beaumont. They'd been turning a consistent profit and their market share was stable. That hadn't been enough for some of their board members, though. Leon Harper had agitated for the company's sale, which made him hundreds of millions of dollars. From everything Zeb had read about Harper, the man was a foul piece of humanity. But there was no way Zeb ever could've gotten control of the company without him.

Delores tapped her tablet as they walked along. The room was oddly silent—there was the low hum of machinery, but it wasn't enough to dampen the echoes from their footfalls. The noise bounced off the huge tanks that reached at least twenty feet high. The only other noise was a regular hammering that got louder the farther they went into the room.

"Forty-two," she said after several minutes. "That was when we were at peak capacity. Ah, here we are."

Delores pointed at the floor and he looked down and saw two pairs of jeans-clad legs jutting out from underneath the tank.

Delores gave him a cautious smile and turned her attention back to the legs. "Casey?"

Zeb had to wonder what Delores had thought of Casey bursting into his office earlier—and whether or not Casey had said anything on her way out. He still hadn't decided what he thought of the young woman. Because she did seem impossibly young to be in charge. But what she might have lacked in maturity she made up for with sheer grit.

She probably didn't realize it, but there were very few people in this world who would dare burst into his office and dress him down. And those who would try would rarely be able to withstand the force of his disdain.

But she had. Easily. But more than that, she'd rebuffed his exploratory offer. No, that wasn't a strong enough word for how she'd destroyed him with her parting shot.

So many women looked at him as their golden ticket. He was rich and attractive and single—he knew that. But he didn't want to be anyone's ticket anywhere.

Casey Johnson hadn't treated him like that. She'd matched him verbal barb for barb and *then* bested him, all while looking like a hot mess.

He'd be lying if he said he wasn't intrigued.

"...try it again," came a muffled voice from underneath the tank. This was immediately followed by more hammering, which, at this close range, was deafening.

Zeb fought the urge to cover his ears and Delores winced. When there was a break in the hammering, she gently tapped one of the two pairs of shoes with her toe. "Casey—Mr. Richards is here."

The person whose shoe she'd nudged started—which was followed by a dull *thunk* and someone going, "Ow, dammit. What?"

And then she slid out from under the tank. She was in a white lab coat, a hairnet and safety goggles, just like everyone else. "Hello again, Ms. Johnson."

Her eyes widened. She was not what one might call a conventional beauty—especially not in the hairnet. She had a small spiderweb scar on one cheek that was more noticeable when she was red in the face—and Zeb hadn't yet seen her *not* red in the face. It was an imperfection, but it drew his eyes to her. She was maybe four inches shorter than he was and he thought her eyes were light brown. He wasn't even sure what color her hair was—it had been under the hat in his office.

But she was passionate about beer and Zeb appreciated that.

"You again," she said in a tone that sounded intentionally bored. "Back for more?"

He almost laughed—but he didn't. He was Zeb Richards, CEO of the Beaumont Brewery. And he was not going to snicker when his brewmaster copped an attitude. Still, her manner was refreshing after a day of people bowing and scraping.

Once again, he found himself running through her parting shot. Was he like his father or like his brother? He didn't know much about either of them. He knew his father had a lot of children—and ignored some of them—and he knew his half brother had successfully run the company for about ten years. But that was common knowledge anyone with an internet connection could find out.

Almost everyone else here—including one prone brewmaster with an attitude problem—would have known what she meant by that. But he didn't.

Not yet, anyway.

Delores looked shocked. "Casey," she hissed in warning. "I'm giving Mr. Richards a tour of the facilities. Would you like to show him around the tanks?"

For a moment, Casey looked contrite in the face of Delores's scolding and Zeb got the feeling Delores had held the company together longer than anyone else.

But the moment was short. "Can't. The damned tank won't cooperate. I'm busy. Come back tomorrow." And with that, she slid right back under the tank. Before either he or Delores could say anything else, that infernal hammering picked up again. This time, he was sure it was even louder.

Delores turned to him, looking stricken. "I apologize, Mr. Richards. I—"

Zeb held up a hand to cut her off. Then he nudged the shoes again. This time, both people slid out. The other person was a man in his midfifties. He looked panic-stricken. Casey glared up at Zeb. *"What."*

"You and I need to schedule a time to go over the product line and discuss ideas for new launches."

She rolled her eyes, which made Delores gasp in horror. "Can't you get someone from Sales to go over the beer with you?"

"No, I can't," he said coldly. It was one thing to let her get the better of him in the privacy of his office but another thing entirely to let her run unchallenged in front of staff. "It has to be you, Ms. Johnson. If you want to brew a new beer that matches my tastes, you should actually know what my tastes are. When can this tank be back up and running?"

She gave him a dull look. "It's hard to tell, what with all the constant interruptions." But then she notched an eyebrow at him, the corner of her mouth curving into a delicate grin, as if they shared a private joke.

He did some quick mental calculating. They didn't

have to meet before Friday—getting the press conference organized had to be his first priority. But by next week he needed to be working toward a new product line.

However, he was also aware that the press conference was going to create waves. It would be best to leave Monday open. "Lunch, Tuesday. Plan accordingly."

For just one second, he thought she would argue with him. Her mouth opened and she looked like she was spoiling for a fight. But then she changed her mind. "Fine. Tuesday. Now if you'll excuse me," she added, sliding back out of view.

"I'm so sorry," Delores repeated as they hurried away from the hammering. "Casey is…"

Zeb didn't rush into the gap. He was curious what the rest of the company thought of her.

He was surprised to realize *he* admired her. It couldn't be easy keeping the beer flowing—especially not as a young woman. She had to be at least twenty years younger than nearly every other man he'd seen in the brewhouse. But she hadn't let that stop her.

Because she was, most likely, unstoppable.

He hoped the employees thought highly of her. He needed people like her who cared for the company and the beer. People who weren't constrained by what they were or were not supposed to be.

Just like he wasn't.

"She's young," Delores finished.

Zeb snorted. Compared to his assistant, almost everyone would be.

"But she's very good," Delores said with finality.

"Good." He had no doubt that Casey Johnson would fight him at every step. "Make sure HR fast-tracks her hires. I want her to have all the help she needs."

He was looking forward to this.

Four

"Thank you all for joining me today," Zeb said, looking out at the worried faces of his chief officers, vice presidents and departmental heads. They were all crammed around the conference table in his office. They had twenty minutes until the press conference was scheduled to start and Zeb thought it was best to give his employees a little warning.

Everyone looked anxious. He couldn't blame them. He'd made everyone surrender their cell phones when they'd come into the office and a few people looked as if they were going through withdrawal. But he wasn't about to run the risk of someone preempting his announcement.

Only one person in the room looked like she knew what was coming next—Casey Johnson. Today she also looked like a member of the managerial team, Zeb noted with an inward smile. Her hair was slicked back into a neat bun and she wore a pale purple blouse and a pair of slacks. The change from the woman who'd stormed into his office was so big that if it hadn't been for the faint spiderweb scar on her cheek, Zeb wouldn't have recognized her.

"I'm going to tell you the same thing that I'm going to tell the press in twenty minutes," Zeb said. "I wanted to give you advance warning. When I make my announcement, I expect each and every one of you to look supportive. We're going to present a unified force. Not only is the Beaumont Brewery back, but it's going to be better than ever." He glanced at Casey. She notched an eyebrow at him and made a little motion with her hands that Zeb took to mean *Get on with it*.

So he did. "Hardwick Beaumont was my father."

As expected, the entire room shuddered with a gasp, followed by a rumbling murmur of disbelief. With amusement, Zeb noted that Casey stared around the room as if everyone else should have already realized the truth.

She didn't understand how unusual she was. No one had ever looked at him and seen the Beaumont in him. All they could see was a black man from Atlanta. Very few people ever bothered to look past that, even when he'd started making serious money.

But she had.

Some of the senior employees looked grim but not surprised. Everyone else seemed nothing but shocked. And the day wasn't over yet. When the murmur had subsided, Zeb pressed on.

"Some of you have met Daniel Lee," Zeb said, motioning to Daniel, who stood near the door. "In addition to being our new chief marketing officer, Daniel is also one of Hardwick's sons. So when I tell the reporters," he went on, ignoring the second round of shocked murmurs, "that the Beaumont Brewery is back in Beaumont hands, I want to know that I have your full support. I've spent the last week getting to know you and your teams. I know that Chadwick Beaumont, my half brother," he added, proud of the way he kept his voice level, "ran this company with a sense of pride and family honor and I'm making this promise to you, here, in this room—we will restore the Beaumont pride and we will restore the honor to this company. My last name may not be Beaumont, but I am one nonetheless. Do I have your support?"

Again, his eyes found Casey's. She was looking at him and then Daniel—no doubt looking for the family resemblance that lurked beneath their unique racial heritages.

Murmurs continued to rumble around the room, like thunder before a storm. Zeb waited. He wasn't going to ask a second time, because that would denote weakness and he was never weak.

"Does Chadwick know what you're doing?"

Zeb didn't see who asked the question, but from the voice, he guessed it was one of the older people in the room. Maybe even someone who had once worked not only for Chadwick but for Hardwick, as well. "He will shortly. At this time, Chadwick is a competitor. I wish him well, as I'm sure we all do, but he's not coming back. This is my company now. Not only do I want to get us back to where we were when he was in charge of things, but I want to get us ahead of where we were. I'll be laying out the details at the press conference, but I promise you this. We will have new beers," he said, nodding to Casey, "and new marketing strategies, thanks to Daniel and his extensive experience."

He could tell he didn't have them. The ones standing were shuffling their feet and the ones sitting were looking anywhere but at him. If this had been a normal business negotiation, he'd have let the silence stretch. But it wasn't. "This was once a great place to work and I want to make it that place again. As I discussed with some of you, I've lifted the hiring freeze. The bottom line is and will continue to be important, but so is the beer."

An older man in the back stepped forward. "The last guy tried to run us into the ground."

"The last guy wasn't a Beaumont," Zeb shot back. He could see the doubt in their eyes. He didn't look the part that he was trying to sell them on.

Then Casey stood, acting far more respectable—and respectful—than the last time he had seen her. "I don't know about everyone else, but I just want to make beer. And if you say we're going to keep making beer, then I'm in."

Zeb acknowledged her with a nod of his head and looked around this room. He'd wager that there'd be one or two resignations on his desk by Monday morning. Maybe more. But Casey fixed them with a stern look and most of his employees stood up.

"All right," the older man who had spoken earlier repeated. Zeb was going to have to learn his name soon, because he clearly commanded a great deal of respect. "What do we have to do?"

"Daniel has arranged this press conference. Think of it as a political rally." Which was what Daniel knew best. The similarities were not coincidences. "I'd like everyone to look supportive and encouraging of the new plan."

"Try to smile," Daniel said, and Zeb saw nearly everyone jump in surprise. It was the first time Daniel had spoken. "I'm going to line you up and then we're going to walk out onto the front steps of the building. I'm going to group you accordingly. You are all the face of the Beaumont Brewery, each and every one of you. Try to remember that when the cameras are rolling."

Spoken like a true political consultant.

"Mr. Richards," Delores said, poking her head in the room, "it's almost time."

Daniel began arranging everyone in line as he wanted them and people went along with it. Zeb went back to his private bathroom to splash water on his face. Did he have enough support to put on a good show?

Probably.

He stared at the mirror. He *was* a Beaumont. For almost his entire life, that fact had been a secret that only three people knew—him and his parents. If his mother had so much as breathed a word about his true parentage, Hardwick would've come after her with pitchforks and torches. He would've burned her to the ground.

But Hardwick was dead and Zeb no longer had to keep his father's secrets. Now the whole world was going to know who he really was.

He walked out to find one person still in the conference room. He couldn't even be surprised when he saw it was Casey Johnson. For some reason, something in his chest unclenched.

"How did I do?" The moment the words left his mouth, he started. He didn't need her approval. He didn't even want it. But he'd asked for it anyway.

She tilted her head to one side and studied him. "Not bad," she finally allowed. "You may lose the entire marketing department."

Zeb's eyebrows jumped up. Was it because of him or because he brought in Daniel, another outsider? "You think so?"

She nodded and then sighed. "Are you sure you know what you're doing?"

"Can you keep a secret?"

"If I say yes, is that your cue to say, 'So can I'?"

Zeb would never admit to being nervous. But if he *had* been, a little verbal sparring with Ms. Johnson would have been just the thing to distract him. He gave her a measured look. "I'll take that as a no, you can't keep a secret. Nevertheless," he went on before she could protest, "I am putting the fate of this company in the hands of a young woman with an attitude problem, when any other sane owner would turn toward an older, more experienced brewmaster. I have faith in you, Ms. Johnson. Try to have a little in me."

She clearly did not win a lot of poker games. One second, she looked like she wanted to tear him a new one for daring to suggest she might have an attitude problem. But then the compliment registered and the oddest thing happened.

She blushed. Not the overheated red that he'd seen on her several times now. This was a delicate coloring of her cheeks, a kiss of light pink along her skin. "You have faith in me?"

"I had a beer last night. Since you've been in charge of brewing for the last year, I feel it's a reasonable assumption that you brewed it. So yes, I have faith in your abilities." Her lips parted. She sucked in a little gasp and Zeb was nearly overcome with the urge to lean forward and kiss her. Because she looked utterly kissable right now.

But the moment the thought occurred to him, he pushed it away. What the hell was wrong with him today? He was about to go out and face a bloodthirsty pack of reporters. Kissing anyone—least of all his brewmaster—should have been the farthest thing from his mind. Especially considering the setdown she'd given him a few days ago.

Was he like his father or his brother?

Still, he couldn't fight the urge to lean forward. Her eyes widened and her pupils darkened.

"Don't let me down," he said in a low voice.

He wasn't sure what she would say. But then the door swung open again and Daniel poked his head in.

"Ah, Ms... Johnson, is it? We're waiting on you." He looked over her head to Zeb. "Two minutes."

Ms. Johnson turned, but at the doorway, she paused and looked back. "Don't let the company down," she told him.

He hoped he wouldn't.

Casey knew she should be paying more attention to whatever Zeb was saying. Because he was certainly saying a lot of things, some of them passionately. She caught phrases like *quality beer* and *family company* but for the most part, she tuned out.

He had faith in her? That was so disconcerting that she didn't have a good response. But the thing that had really blown her mind was that she had been—and this was by her own estimation—a royal bitch during the two times they'd met previous to today.

It wasn't that no one respected her. The guys she'd worked with for the last twelve years respected her. Because she had earned it. She had shown up, day in and day out. She had taken their crap and given as good as she got. She had taken every single job they threw at her, even the really awful ones like scrubbing out the tanks. Guys like Larry respected her because they knew her.

Aside from those two conversations, Zeb Richards didn't know her at all.

Maybe what he'd said was a load of crap. After all, a guy as good-looking as he was didn't get to be where he was in life without learning how to say the right thing at the right time to a woman. And he'd already hit on her once, on that first day when she'd burst into his office. So it was entirely possible that he'd figured out the one thing she needed to hear and then said it to soften her up.

Even though she wasn't paying attention, she still knew the moment he dropped his big bomb. She felt the tension ripple among her coworkers—but that wasn't it. No, the entire corps of reporters recoiled in shock. Seconds later, they were all shouting questions.

"Can you prove that Hardwick Beaumont was your father?"

"How many more bastards are there?"

"Did you plan the takeover with Chadwick Beaumont?"

"What are your plans for the brewery now that the Beaumonts are back in charge?"

Casey studied Richards. The reporters had jumped out of their chairs and were now crowding the stage, as if being first in line meant their questions would be answered first. Even though they weren't shouting at her, she still had the urge to flee in horror.

But not Richards. He stood behind his podium and stared down at the reporters as if they were nothing more than gnats bothering him on a summer day. After a moment, the reporters quieted down. Richards waited until they returned to their seats before ignoring the questions completely and moving on with his prepared remarks.

Well, that was impressive. She glanced at the one person who had thrown her for a loop this morning—Daniel Lee. The two men stood nearly shoulder to shoulder, with Daniel just a step behind and to the right of Richards. Richards had two inches on his half brother and maybe forty pounds of what appeared to be pure muscle. The two men shouldn't have looked anything alike. Lee was clearly Asian American and Richards wasn't definitively one ethnicity or another. But despite those differences—and despite the fact that they had apparently not been raised together, like the other Beaumonts had been—there was something similar about them. The way they held their heads, their chins—not that Casey had met all of the Beaumont siblings, but apparently, they all shared the same jaw.

As Richards continued to talk about his plans for restoring the Beaumont family honor, Casey wondered where she fit in all of this.

In her time, when she'd been a young intern fresh out of college and desperate to get her foot in the door, Hardwick Beaumont had been…well, not an old man, but an older man. He'd had a sharp eye and wandering hands. Wally Winking, the old brewmaster, whose voice still held a faint hint of a German accent even though he'd been at the brewery for over fifty years, had told her she reminded him of his granddaughter. Then he'd told her never to be alone with Hardwick. She hadn't had to ask why.

Three days ago, Richards had made a pass at her. That was something his father would have done. But today?

Today, when they'd been alone together, he'd had faith in her abilities. He made it sound like he respected her—both as a person and as a brewmaster.

And that was what made him sound like his brother Chadwick.

Oh, her father was going to have a field day with this. And then he was going to be mad at her that she hadn't warned him in advance. To say that Carl Johnson was heavily invested in her career would be like saying that NASA sometimes thought about Mars. He constantly worried that she was on the verge of losing her job—a sentiment that had only gotten stronger over the last year. Her dad was protective of his little girl, which was both sweet and irritating.

What was she going to tell her father? She hadn't told him about her confrontational first meeting with Richards—or the second one, for that matter. But she was pretty sure she would be on the news tonight, one face in a human backdrop behind Zeb Richards as he completely blew up everything people thought they knew about the Beaumont family and the brewery.

Well, there was only one thing to do. As soon as Daniel Lee gave her phone back, she had to text her dad.

Oh, the reporters were shouting again. Richards picked up his tablet to walk off the platform. Daniel motioned to the people in front of her as they were beginning to walk back up the front steps. The press conference was apparently over. Thank God for that.

Richards appeared to be ignoring the reporters but that only made the reporters shout louder. He'd almost made it to the door when Natalie Baker—the beautiful blonde woman who trafficked in local Denver gossip on her show, *A Good Morning with Natalie Baker*—physically blocked Zeb's way with her body. And her breasts. They were really nice ones, the kind that Casey had never had and never would.

Natalie Baker all but purred a question at Richards. "Are there more like you?" she asked, her gaze sweeping to include Daniel in the question.

It must've been the breasts, because for the first time, Richards went off script. "I've located one more brother, but he's not part of this venture. Now if you'll excuse me."

Baker looked thrilled and the rest of the crowd started shouting questions again. *That was a dumb thing to do*, Casey thought. Now everyone would have to know who the third one was and why he wasn't on the stage with Richards and Lee.

Men. A nice rack and they lost their little minds.

She didn't get a chance to talk to Richards again. And even if she had, what would she have said? *Nice press conference that I didn't pay attention to?* No, even she knew that was not the way to go about things.

Besides, she had her own brand of damage control to deal with. She needed to text her dad, warning him that the company would be in the news again but he shouldn't panic—her boss had faith in her. Then she had to go back and warn her crew. No, it was probably too late for that. She had to reassure them that they were going to keep making beer. Then she had to start the hiring process for some new employees and she had to make sure that tank fifteen was actually working properly today...

And she had to get ready for Tuesday. She was having lunch and beer with the boss.

Which boss would show up?

Five

Frankly, he could use a beer.

"Did you contact CJ?" Daniel asked. "He needs to be warned."

Here, in the privacy of his own office with no one but Daniel around, Zeb allowed himself to lean forward and pinch the bridge of his nose. Make that several beers.

"I did. He didn't seem concerned. As long as we keep his name and whereabouts out of it, he thinks he's unfindable."

Daniel snorted. "You found him."

"A fact of which I reminded him." Zeb knew that CJ's refusal to be a part of Zeb's vision for the brothers wasn't personal. Still, it bugged him. "I think it's safe to say that he's a little more laid-back than we are."

That made Daniel grin. "He'll come around. Eventually. Has there been any other…contact?"

"No." It wasn't that he expected the acknowledged

members of the Beaumont family to storm the brewery gates and engage in a battle for the heart and soul of the family business. But while the rest of the world was engaged in furious rounds of questions and speculation, there had been radio silence from the Beaumonts themselves. Not even a *No comment*. Just…nothing.

Not that Zeb expected any of them to fall over themselves to welcome him and Daniel into the family. He didn't.

He checked his watch.

"Do you have a hot date?" Daniel asked in an offhand way.

"I'm having lunch with the brewmaster, Casey Johnson."

That got Daniel's attention. He sat up straighter. "And?"

And she asked me if I was like my father or my brother and I didn't have an answer.

But that wasn't what he said. In fact, he didn't say anything. Yes, he and Daniel were in this together, and yes, they were technically brothers. But there were some things he still didn't want to share. Daniel was too smart and he knew how to bend the truth to suit his purposes.

Zeb had no desire to be bent to anyone's purposes but his own. "We're going over the product line. It's hard to believe that a woman so young is the brewmaster in charge of all of our beer and I want to make sure she knows her stuff."

His phone rang. He winced inwardly—it was his mother. "I've got to take this. We'll talk later?"

Daniel nodded. "One last thing. I had four resignations in the marketing department."

Casey had not been wrong about that, either. She had a certain brashness to her, but she knew this business.

"Hire whoever you want," Zeb said as he answered the call. "Hello, Mom."

"I shouldn't have to call you," his mother said, the steel in her voice sounding extra sharp today.

How much beer could one man reasonably drink at work? Zeb was going to have to test that limit today, because if there was one thing he didn't want to deal with right now, it was his mother.

"But I'm glad you did," he replied easily. "How's the salon?"

"Humph." Emily Richards ran a chain of successful hair salons in Georgia. Thanks to his careful management, Doo-Wop and Pop! had gone from being six chairs in a strip-mall storefront to fifteen locations scattered throughout Georgia and a small but successful line of hair weaves and braid accessories targeted toward the affluent African American buyer.

Zeb had done that for his mother. He'd taken her from lower middle class, where the two of them got by on $30,000 a year, to upper class. Doo-Wop and Pop! had made Emily Richards rich and was on track to make even more profit this year.

But that *humph* told Zeb everything he needed to know. It didn't matter that he had taken his mother's idea and turned it into a hugely successful woman-owned business. All that really mattered to Emily Richards was getting revenge on the man she claimed had ruined her life.

A fact she drove home with her next statement. "Well? Did you finally take what's yours?"

It always came back to the brewery. And the way she said *finally* grated on his nerves like a steel file. Still, she was his mother. "It's really mine, Mom."

Those words should have filled him with satisfaction.

He had done what he had set out to do. The Beaumont Brewery was his now.

So why did he feel so odd?

He shook it off. It had been an exceptionally long weekend, after all. As expected, his press conference had created not just waves but tsunamis that had to be dealt with. His one mistake—revealing that there was a third Beaumont bastard, unnamed and unknown—had threatened to undermine his triumphant ascension to power.

"They'll come for you," his mother intoned ominously. "Those Beaumonts can't let it rest. You watch your back."

Not for the first time, Zeb wondered if his mother was a touch paranoid. He understood now what he hadn't when he was little—that his father had bought her silence. But more and more, she acted like his siblings would go to extreme measures to enforce that silence.

His father, maybe. But none of the research he'd done on any of his siblings had turned up any proclivities for violence.

Still, he knew he couldn't convince his mother. So he let it go.

There was a knock on the door and before he could say anything, it popped open. In walked Jamal, boxes stacked in his hands. When he saw that Zeb was on the phone, he nodded his head in greeting and moved quietly to the conference table. There he began unpacking lunch.

"I will," Zeb promised his mother. And it wasn't even one of those little white lies he told her to keep her happy. He had stirred up several hornets' nests over the last few days. It only made good sense to watch his back.

"They deserve to pay for what they did to me. And you," she added as an afterthought.

But wasn't that the thing? None of the Beaumonts who were living today had ever done anything to Zeb. They'd just…ignored him.

"I've got to go, Mom. I have a meeting that starts in a few minutes." He didn't miss the way his Southern accent was stronger. Hearing it roll off Mom's tongue made his show up in force.

"Humph," she repeated. "Love you, baby boy."

"Love you, too, Mom." He hung up.

"Let me guess," Jamal said as he spread out the four-course meal he had prepared. "She's still not happy."

"Let it go, man." But something about the conversation with his mother was bugging him.

For a long time, his mother had spoken of what the Beaumonts owed *him*. They had taken what rightfully belonged to him and it was his duty to get it back. And if they wouldn't give it to him legitimately, he would just have to take it by force.

But that was all she'd ever told him about the Beaumont family. She'd never told him anything about his father or his father's family. She'd told him practically nothing about her time in Denver—he wasn't all that sure what she had done for Hardwick back in the '70s. Every time he asked, she refused to answer and instead launched into another rant about how they'd cut him out of what was rightfully his.

He had so many questions and not enough answers. He was missing something and he knew it. It was a feeling he did not enjoy, because in his business, answers made money.

His intercom buzzed. "Mr. Richards, Ms. Johnson is here."

Jamal shot him a funny look. "I thought you said you were having lunch with your brewmaster."

Before Zeb could explain, the door opened and Casey walked in. "Good morning. I spoke with the cook in the cafeteria. She said she hadn't been asked to prepare any— Oh. Hello," she said cautiously when she caught sight of Jamal plating up what smelled like his famous salt-crusted beef tenderloin.

Zeb noted with amusement that today she was back in the unisex lab coat with Beaumont Brewery embroidered on the lapel—but she wasn't bright red or sweating buckets. Her hair was still in a ponytail, though. She was, on the whole, one of the least feminine women he'd ever met. He couldn't even begin to imagine her in a dress but somehow that made her all the more intriguing.

No, he was not going to be intrigued by her. Especially not with Jamal watching. "Ms. Johnson, this is Jamal—"

"Jamal Hitchens?"

Now it was Jamal's turn to take a step back and look at Casey with caution. "Yeah... You recognize me?" He shot a funny look over to Zeb, but he just shrugged.

He was learning what Zeb had already figured out. There was no way to predict what Casey Johnson would do or say.

"Of course I recognize you," she gushed. "You played for the University of Georgia—you were in the running for the Heisman, weren't you? I mean, until you blew your knees out. Sorry about that," she added, wincing.

Jamal was gaping down at her as if she'd peeled off her skin to reveal an alien in disguise. "You know who I am?"

"Ms. Johnson is a woman of many talents," Zeb said, not even bothering to fight the grin. Jamal would've gone pro if it hadn't been for his knees. But it was rare that anyone remembered a distant runner-up for the Heisman who hadn't played ball in years. "I've learned it's best not to underestimate her. Ms. Johnson is my brewmaster."

It was hard to get the drop on Jamal, but one small woman in a lab coat clearly had. "What are you doing here?" Casey sniffed the air. "God, that smells good."

Honest to God, Jamal blushed. "Oh. Thank you." He glanced nervously at Zeb.

"Jamal is my oldest friend," Zeb explained. He almost added, *He's the closest thing I have to a brother*—but then he stopped himself. Even if it was true, the whole point of this endeavor with the Beaumont Brewery was to prove that he had a family whether they wanted him or not. "He is my right-hand man. One of his many talents is cooking. I asked him to prepare some of my favorites today to accompany our tasting." He turned to Jamal, whose mouth was still flopped open in shock. "What did you bring?" Zeb prodded.

"What? Oh, right. The food." It was so unusual to hear Jamal sound unsure of himself that Zeb had to stare. "It's a tasting menu," he began, sounding embarrassed about it. It was rare that Jamal's past life in sports ever intersected with his current life. Actually, Zeb couldn't remember a time when someone who hadn't played football recognized him.

Jamal ran through the menu—in addition to the salt-crusted beef tenderloin, which had been paired with new potatoes, there was a spaghetti Bolognese, a vichyssoise soup and Jamal's famous fried chicken. Dessert was flourless chocolate cupcakes dusted with powdered sugar—Zeb's favorite.

Casey surveyed the feast before her, and Zeb got the feeling that she didn't approve. He couldn't say why he thought that, because she was perfectly polite to Jamal at all times. In fact, when he tried to leave, she insisted on getting a picture with him so she could send it to her father—apparently, her father was a huge sports fan and would also know who Jamal was.

So Zeb took the photo for her and then Jamal hurried away, somewhere between flattered and uncomfortable.

And then Zeb and Casey were alone.

She didn't move. "So Jamal Hitchens is an old friend of yours?"

"Yes."

"And he's your…personal chef?"

Zeb settled into his seat at the head of the conference table. "Among other things, yes." He didn't offer up any other information.

"You don't really strike me as a sports guy," she replied.

"Come, now, Ms. Johnson. Surely you've researched me by now?"

Her cheeks colored again. He liked that delicate blush on her. He shouldn't, but he did. "I don't remember reading about you owning a sports franchise."

Zeb lifted one shoulder. "Who knows. Maybe I'll buy a team and make Jamal the general manager. After all, what goes together better than sports and beer?"

She was still standing near the door, as if he were an alligator that looked hungry. Finally, she asked, "Have you decided, then?"

"About what?"

He saw her swallow, but it was the only betrayal of her nerves. Well, that and the fact that she wasn't smart-mouthing him. Actually, that she wasn't saying whatever came to mind was unusual.

"About what kind of Beaumont you're going to be."

He involuntarily tensed and then let out a breath slowly. Like his father or his brother? He had no idea.

He wanted to ask what she knew—was it the same as the public image of the company? Or was there something else he didn't know? Maybe his father had secretly been the kindest man on earth. Or maybe Chadwick was just as bad as Hardwick had been. He didn't know.

What he did know was that the last time he'd seen her, he'd had the urge to kiss her. It'd been nerves, he'd decided. He'd been concerned about the press conference and Casey Johnson was the closest thing to a friendly face here—when she wasn't scowling at him. That was all that passing desire had been. Reassurance. Comfort.

He didn't feel comfortable now.

"I'm going to be a different kind of Beaumont," he said confidently because it was the only true thing he *could* say. "I'm my own man."

She thought this over. "And what kind of man is that?"

She had guts, he had to admit. Anyone else might have nodded and smiled and said, *Of course.* But not her. "The kind with strong opinions about beer."

"Fair enough." She headed for the bar.

Zeb watched her as she pulled on the tap with a smooth, practiced hand. He needed to stop being surprised at her competency. She was the brewmaster. Of course she knew how to pour beer. Tapping the keg was probably second nature to her. And there wasn't a doubt in his mind that she could also destroy him in a sports trivia contest.

But this was different from watching a bartender fill a pint glass. Watching her hands on the taps was far more interesting than it'd ever been before. She had long fingers and they wrapped around each handle with a firm, sure grip.

Unexpectedly, he found himself wondering what else she'd grip like that. But the moment the thought found its way to his consciousness, he pushed it aside. This wasn't about attraction. This was about beer.

Then she glanced up at him and a soft smile ghosted across her lips, like she was actually glad to see him, and Zeb forgot about beer. Instead, he openly stared at her. Was she glad he was here? Was she able to look at him and see not just a hidden bastard or a ruthless businessman but...

...him? Did she see *him*?

Zeb cleared his throat and shifted in his seat as Casey gathered up the pint glasses. After a moment's consideration, she set down one pair of glasses in front of the tenderloin and another in front of the pasta. Zeb reached for the closest glass, but she said, "Wait! If we're going to do this right, I have to walk you through the beers."

"Is there a wrong way to drink beer?" he asked, pulling his hand back.

"Mr. Richards," she said, exasperated. "This is a tasting. We're not 'drinking beer.' I don't drink on the job—none of us do. I sample. That's all this is."

She was scolding him, he realized. He was confident that he'd never been scolded by an employee before. The thought made him laugh—which got him some serious side-eye.

"Fine," he said, trying to restrain himself. When had that become difficult to do? He was always restrained. *Always.* "We'll do this your way."

He'd told Jamal the truth. He should never underestimate Casey Johnson.

She went back behind his bar and filled more half-pint glasses, twenty in all. Each pair was placed in front of a different dish. And the whole time, she was quiet.

Silence was a negotiating tactic and, as such, one that never worked on Zeb. Except...he felt himself getting twitchy as he watched her focus on her work. The next thing he knew, he was volunteering information. "Four people in the marketing department have resigned," he announced into the silence. "You were right about that."

She shrugged, as if it were no big deal. "You gave a nice talk about family honor and a bunch of other stuff, but you didn't warn anyone that you were bringing in a new CMO. People were upset."

Was she upset? No, it didn't matter, he told himself. He wasn't in this business for the touchy-feely. He was in it to make money. Well, that and to get revenge against the Beaumonts.

So, with that firmly in mind, he said, "The position was vacant. And Daniel's brilliant when it comes to campaigns. I have no doubt the skills he learned in politics will apply to beer, as well." But even as he said it, he wondered why he felt the need to explain his managerial decisions to her.

Evidently, she wondered the same thing, as she held up her hands in surrender. "Hey, you don't have to justify it to me. Although it might have been a good idea to justify it to the marketing department."

She was probably right—but he didn't want to admit that, so he changed tactics. "How about your department? Anyone there decide I was the final straw?" As he asked it, he realized what he really wanted to know was if *she'd* decided he was the final straw.

What the hell was this? He didn't care what his employees thought about him. He never had. All he cared about was that people knew their jobs and did them well. Results—that was what he cared about. This was business, not a popularity contest.

Or it had been, he thought as Casey smirked at him when she took her seat.

"My people are nervous, but that's to be expected. The ones who've hung in this long don't like change. They keep hoping that things will go back to the way they were," she said, catching his eye. No, that was a hedge. She already *had* his eye because he couldn't stop staring at her. "Or some reasonable facsimile thereof. A new normal, maybe. But no, I haven't had anyone quit on me."

A new normal. He liked that. "Good. I don't want you to be understaffed again."

She paused and then cleared her throat. When she looked up at him again, he felt the ground shift under his feet. She was gazing at him with something he so desperately wanted to think was appreciation. Why did he need her approval so damned bad?

"Thank you," she said softly. "I mean, I get that owning the company is part of your birthright, I guess, but this place..." She looked around as her voice trailed off with something that Zeb recognized—longing.

It was as if he were seeing another woman—one younger, more idealistic. A version of Casey that must have somehow found her way to the Beaumont Brewery years ago. Had she gotten the job through her father or an uncle? An old family friend?

Or had she walked into this company and, in her normal assertive way, simply demanded a job and refused to take no for an answer?

He had a feeling that was it.

He wanted to know what she was doing here—what this place meant to her and why she'd risked so much to defend it. Because they both knew that he could have fired her already. Being without a brewmaster for a day or a week would have been a problem, but problems were what he fixed.

But he hadn't fired her. She'd pushed him and challenged him and…and he liked that. He liked that she wasn't afraid of him. Which didn't make any sense—fear and intimidation were weapons he deployed easily and often to get what he wanted, the way he wanted it. Almost every other employee in this company had backed down in the face of his memos and decrees. But not *this* employee.

Not Casey.

"Okay," she announced in a tone that made it clear she wasn't going to finish her earlier statement. She produced a tablet from her lab-coat pocket and sat to his right. "Let's get started."

They went through each of the ten Beaumont beers, one at a time. "As you taste each one," she said without looking at him, "think about the flavors as they hit your tongue."

He coughed. "The…flavors?"

She handed him a pint glass and picked up the other for herself. "Drinking beer isn't just chugging to get drunk," she said in a voice that made it sound like she was praying, almost. She held her glass up and gazed at the way the light filtered through the beer. Zeb knew he should do the same—but he couldn't. He was watching her.

"Drinking beer fulfills each of the senses. Every detail contributes to the full experience," she said in that voice that was serious yet also…wistful. "How does the color make you feel?" She brought the glass back to her lips—but she didn't drink. Instead, her eyes drifted shut as she inhaled deeply. "What does it smell like—and how do the aromas affect the taste? How does it feel in your mouth?"

Her lips parted and, fascinated, Zeb watched as she

tipped the glass back and took a drink. Her eyelashes fluttered in what looked to him like complete and total satisfaction. Once she'd swallowed, she sighed. "So we'll rate each beer on a scale of one to five."

Did she have any idea how sensual she looked right now? Did she look like that when she'd been satisfied in bed? Or was it just the beer that did that to her? If he leaned over and touched his fingertips to her cheek to angle her chin up so he could press his lips against hers, would she let him?

"Mr. Richards?"

"What?" Zeb shook back to himself to find that Casey was staring at him with amusement.

"Ready?"

"Yes," he said because, once again, that was the truth. He'd thought he'd been ready to take over this company—but until right then, he hadn't been sure he was ready for someone like Casey Johnson.

They got to work, sipping each beer and rating it accordingly. Amazingly, Zeb was able to focus on the beer—which was good. He could not keep staring at his brewmaster like some love-struck puppy. He was Zeb Richards, for God's sake.

"I've always preferred the Rocky Top," Zeb told her, pointedly sampling—not drinking—the stalwart of the Beaumont product line. "But the Rocky Top Light tastes like dishwater."

Casey frowned at this and made a note on her tablet. "I'd argue with you, but you're right. However, it remains one of our bestsellers among women aged twenty-one to thirty-five and is one of our top overall sellers."

That was interesting. "It's the beer we target toward women and you don't like it?"

She looked up at him sharply and he could almost

hear her snapping, *Women are not interchangeable.* But she didn't. Instead, in as polite a voice as he'd ever heard from her, she said, "People drink beer for different reasons," while she made notes. "I don't want to sacrifice taste for something as arbitrary as calorie count."

"Can you make it better?"

That got her attention. "We've used the same formula for... Well, since the '80s, I think. You'd want to mess with that?"

He didn't lean forward, no matter how much he wanted to. Instead, he kept plenty of space between them. "There's always room for improvement, don't you think? I'm not trapped by the past." But the moment he said it, he wondered how true that was. "Perhaps one of your experiments can be an improved light-beer recipe."

She held his gaze, her lips curved into a slight smile. It was disturbing how much he liked her meeting his challenges straight on like that. "I'll do that."

They went through the rest of the beers and, true to her word, Zeb couldn't have said that he'd drunk enough to even get a slight buzz. Finally, as they'd eaten the last of their cupcakes, he leaned back and said, "So what are we missing?"

She surprised him then. She picked up what was left of her Rocky Top and took a long drink. "Look—here's the thing about our current product line. It's fine. It's... serviceable."

He notched an eyebrow at her. "It gets the job done?"

"Exactly. But when we lost Percheron Drafts, we lost the IPA, the stout—the bigger beers with bolder tastes. We lost seasonal beers—the summer shandy and the fall Oktoberfest beers. What we've got now is basic. I'd love to get us back to having one or two spotlight beers that we could rotate in and out." She got a wistful look on her face. "It's hard to see that here, though."

"What do you mean?"

"I mean, look at this." She swept her hand out, encompassing the remains of their lunch. "*This*. Most people who drink our beer don't do so in the luxury of a private office with a catered four-course meal. They drink a beer at a game or on their couch, with a burger or a brat."

Suddenly, a feeling he'd gotten earlier—that she hadn't approved of the setup—got stronger. "What about you? Where do you drink your beer?"

"Me? Oh. I have season tickets to the Rockies. My dad and I go to every home game we can. Have you done that?" He shook his head. "You should. I've learned a lot about what people like just standing in line to get a beer at the game. I talk with the beer guys—that sort of thing."

"A ball game?" He must have sounded doubtful, because she nodded encouragingly. "I can get a box."

"Really?" She rolled her eyes. "That's not how people drink beer. Here. I'll tell you what—there's a game tomorrow night at seven, against the Braves. My dad can't go. You can use his ticket. Come with me and see what I mean."

He stared at her. It didn't sound like a come-on— but then, he'd never gotten quite so turned on watching another woman drink beer before. Nothing was typical when it came to this woman. "You're serious, aren't you?"

"Of course."

He had a feeling she was right. He'd spent years learning about the corporate workings of the brewery from a distance. If he was going to run this place as his own— and he was—then he needed to understand not just the employees but their customers.

Besides, the Braves were his team. And beyond that, this was a chance to see Casey outside work. Suddenly, that seemed important—vital, even. What was she like when she wasn't wearing a lab coat? He shouldn't have wanted to know. But he did anyway. "It's a da—" Casey's eyes got huge and her cheeks flushed and Zeb remembered that he wasn't having a drink with a pretty girl at a bar. He was at the brewery and he was the CEO. He had to act like it. "Company outing," he finished, as if that was what he'd meant to say all along.

She cleared her throat. "Covert market research, if you will." Her gaze flickered over his Hugo Boss suit. "And try to blend, maybe?"

He gave her a level stare, but she was unaffected. "Tomorrow at seven."

"Gate C." She gathered up her tablet. "We'll talk then."

He nodded and watched her walk out. Once the door was firmly closed behind her, he allowed himself to grin.

Whether she liked it or not, they had a date.

Six

Casey really didn't know what to expect as she stood near the C gate at Coors Field. She'd told Richards to blend but she was having trouble picturing him in anything other than a perfectly tailored suit.

Not that she was spending a lot of time thinking about him in a perfectly tailored suit. She wasn't. Just because he was the epitome of masculine grace and style, that was no reason at all to think about her boss.

Besides, she didn't even go for guys in suits. She usually went for blue-collar guys, the kind who kicked back on the weekend with a bunch of beer to watch sports. That was what she was comfortable with, anyway. And comfort was good, right?

And anyway, even if she did go for guys in suits—which she did not—she was positive she didn't go for guys like Richards. It wasn't that he was African American. She had looked him up, and one of the few pictures of him on the internet was him standing with a woman named Emily Richards in Atlanta, Georgia, outside a Doo-Wop and Pop! Salon. It was easy to see the resemblance between them—she was clearly his mother.

No, her not going for guys like Richards had nothing to do with race and everything to do with the fact that he was way too intense for her. The way he'd stared at her over the lip of his pint glass during their tasting lunch? Intensity personified, and as thrilling as it had been, it wasn't what she needed on her time off. Really. She had enough intensity at work. That was why she always went for low-key guys—guys who were fun for a weekend but never wanted anything more than that.

Right. So it was settled. She absolutely did not go for someone like Richards in a suit. Good.

"Casey?"

Casey whipped around and found herself staring not at a businessman in a suit—and also not at someone who was blending. Zeb Richards stood before her in a white T-shirt with bright red raglan sleeves. She was vaguely aware that he had on a hat and reasonably certain that he was wearing blue jeans, but she couldn't tear her eyes away from his chest. The T-shirt molded to his body in a way that his power suit hadn't. Her mouth went dry.

Good God.

That was as far as her brain got, because she tried to drag her eyes away from his chest—and made it exactly as far as his biceps.

Sweet mother of pearl was the last coherent thought she had as she tried to take in the magnitude of those biceps.

And when thinking stopped, she was left with nothing but her physical response. Her nipples tightened and her skin flushed—*flushed*, dammit, like she was an innocent schoolgirl confronted with a man's body for the first time. All that flushing left her shaken and sweaty and completely unable to look away. It took all of her self-control not to lean over and put a hand to that chest and feel what she was looking at. Because she'd be willing to bet a lot of money that he *felt* even better than he looked.

"...Casey?" he said with what she hoped like hell was humor in his voice. "Hello?"

"What?" Crap, she'd been caught gaping at him. "Right. Hi." Dumbly, she held up the tickets.

"Is there something wrong with my shirt?" He asked, looking down. Then he grasped the hem of the shirt and pulled it out so he could see the front, which had a graphic of the Braves' tomahawk on it. But when he did that, the neck of the shirt came down and Casey caught a glimpse of his collarbones.

She had no idea collarbones could be sexy. This was turning out to be quite an educational evening and it had only just begun. How on earth was she going to get through the rest of it without doing something humiliating, like *drooling* on the man?

Because drooling was off-limits. Everything about him was off-limits.

This was not a date. Nope. He was her boss, for crying out loud.

"Um, no. I mean, I didn't actually figure you would show up in the opposing team's shirt." Finally—and way too late for decency's sake—she managed to look up into his face. He was smiling at her, as if he knew exactly what kind of effect he had on her. Dammit. This was the other reason she didn't go for men like him. They were too cocky for their own good.

"That's all," she went on. "You don't exactly blend." She was pretty sure she was babbling.

"I'm from Atlanta, you know." He smirked at her and suddenly there it was—a luscious Southern accent that threatened to melt her. "Who did you think I was going to root for?" His gaze swept over her and Casey felt each and every hair on her body stand at attention. "I don't have anything purple," he went on when his gaze made it back to her face with something that looked a heck of a lot like approval.

She fought the urge to stand up straighter. She would not pose for him. This was not a date. She didn't care what he thought of her appearance. "We could fix that," she told him, waving at the T-shirt sellers hawking all sorts of Rockies gear. He scrunched his nose at her. "Or not," she said with a melodramatic sigh, trying to get her wits about her. "It's still better than a suit. Come on. We need to get in if we want to grab a beer before the game starts."

He looked around. People in purple hats and T-shirts were making their way inside and he was already getting a few funny looks. "This is literally your home turf. Lead on."

She headed toward the turnstiles. Zeb made a move toward one with a shorter line, but Casey put her hand on his arm. "This one," she told him, guiding him toward Joel's line.

"Why?"

"You'll see." At this cryptic statement, Zeb gave her a hard look. Oddly enough, it didn't carry as much weight as it might have if he'd been in a tie, surrounded by all the brewery history in his office. Instead, he looked almost...adorable.

Crap, this was bad. She absolutely couldn't be thinking of Zebadiah Richards as adorable. Or hot. Or... anything.

There might have been some grumbling following that statement, but Casey decided that she probably shouldn't get into a shouting match with him before they'd even gotten inside the stadium.

The line moved quickly and then Joel said, "Casey! There's my girl."

"Hey, Joel," she said, leaning over to give the old man a quick hug.

"Where's Carl?" Joel asked, eyeing Zeb behind her.

"Union meeting. Who do you think's going to win today?" She and Joel had the same conversation at nearly every game.

"You have to ask? The Braves are weak this season." Then he noticed Richards's shirt behind her and his easy smile twisted into a grimace of disapproval. He leaned over and grabbed two of the special promotion items—bobblehead dolls of the team. "Take one to your dad. I know he collects them."

"Aw, thanks, Joel. And give my best to Martha, okay?"

Joel gave a bobblehead to Richards, as well. "Good luck, fella," he muttered.

When they were several feet away, Richards said, "I see what you mean about blending. Do you want this?" He held out the bobblehead.

"I'm good. Two is my personal limit on these things. Give it to Jamal or something." She led him over to her favorite beer vendor. "Speaking of, where is Jamal? I thought you might bring him."

Honestly, she couldn't decide if she'd wanted Jamal to be here or not. If he had been, then maybe she'd have been able to focus on *not* focusing on Zeb a little better. Three was a crowd, after all.

But still...she was glad Zeb had come alone.

This time, he held back and waited until she picked the beer line. "He's still unpacking."

"Oh?" There were about six people in front of them. This game was going to be nowhere near a sellout. "So you really did move out here?"

"Of course." He slid her a side glance. "I said that at the press conference, you know."

They moved up a step in line. Casey decided that it was probably best not to admit that she hadn't been paying attention during the press conference. "So where are you guys at?"

"I bought a house over on Cedar Avenue. Jamal picked it out because he liked the kitchen."

Her eyes bugged out of her head. "You bought the mansion by the country club?"

"You know it?" He said it in such a casual way, as if buying the most expensive house in the Denver area were no biggie.

Well, maybe for him, it wasn't. Why was she surprised? She shouldn't have been. She wasn't. Someone like Zeb Richards would definitely plunk down nearly $10 million for a house and not think anything of it. "Yeah. My dad was hired to do some work there a couple years ago. He said it was an amazing house."

"I suppose it is." He didn't sound very convinced about this. But before Casey could ask him what he didn't like about the house, he went on, "What does your dad do? And I'm going to pay you back for his ticket. I'm sorry that I'm using it in his place."

She waved this away. "Don't worry about it. He really did have a union meeting tonight. He's an electrician. He does a lot of work in older homes—renovations and upgrading antique wiring. There's still a lot of knob-and-tube wiring in Denver, you know."

One corner of his mouth—not that she was staring at his mouth—curved up into a smile that was positively dangerous.

"What?" she said defensively—because if she didn't defend herself from that sly smile... Well, she didn't know what would happen. But it wouldn't be good.

In fact, it would be bad. The very best kind of bad.

"Nothing. I've just got to stop being surprised by you, that's all." They advanced another place in line. "What are we ordering?"

"Well, seeing as this is Coors Field, we really don't have too many options when it comes to beer. It's—shockingly—Coors."

"No!" he said in surprise. "Do they make beer?"

She stared at him. "Wait—was that a joke? Were you trying to be funny?"

That grin—oh, *hell*. "Depends. Did it work?"

No—well, yes, but *no*. No, she couldn't allow him to be a regular guy. If this "company outing" was going to stay strictly aboveboard, he could not suddenly develop a set of pecs *and* a sense of humor at the same time. She couldn't take it. "Mr. Richards—"

"Really, Casey," he said, cutting her off, "we're about to drink a competitor's beer outside of normal business hours at a game. Call me Zeb."

She was a strong woman. She was. She'd worked at the Beaumont Brewery for twelve years and during that time, she'd never once gotten involved with a coworker. She'd had to negotiate the fine line between "innocent flirting" and "sexual harassment" on too many occasions, but once she'd earned her place at the table, that had fallen away.

But this? Calling Richards by his first name? Buying beer with him at a ball game? Pointedly not staring at the way he filled out an officially licensed T-shirt? Listening to him crack jokes?

She simply wasn't that strong. This wasn't a company outing. It was starting to feel like a date.

They reached the cashier. "Casey!" Marco gave her a high five over the counter.

She could feel Zeb behind her. He wasn't touching her, but he was close enough that her skin was prickling. "Marco—what's the latest?"

"It happened, girl." Marco pointed to a neon sign over his head—one that proudly proclaimed they served Percheron Drafts.

Casey whistled. "You were right."

"I told you," he went on. "They cut a deal. You wanna try something? Their pale ale is good. Or is that not allowed? I heard you had a new boss there—another crazy Beaumont. Two of them, even!" He chuckled and shook his head in disbelief. "You think the Beaumonts knew their brother or half brother or whatever he is took over? I heard it might have been planned..."

It took everything Casey had not to look back over her shoulder at Zeb. Maybe she was reading too much into the situation, but she would put money on the fact that he wasn't grinning anymore. "I bet it was a hell of a surprise," she said, desperate to change the subject. "Give me the pale ale and—"

"Nachos, extra jalapeños?" He winked at her. "I'm on it."

"A *hell* of a surprise," Zeb whispered in her ear. The closeness of his voice was so unexpected that she jumped. But just then Marco came back with her order.

"Gotta say," Marco went on, ringing up her total, "it was good to see a brother up there, though. I mean...he was black, right?"

Behind her, Zeb made a noise that sounded like it was somewhere between a laugh and a choke. "It doesn't really matter," she said honestly as she handed over the cash, "as long as we get the beer right."

"Ah, that's what I like about you, Casey—a woman who knows her beer." He gave her a moony look, as if he were dazzled by beauty they both knew she didn't have. "It's not too late to marry me, you know that?"

Hand to God, Casey thought she heard Zeb growl behind her.

Okay, that was not the kind of noise a boss made when an employee engaged in chitchat with a— Well, Marco sold beer. So with a colleague of sorts. However, it was the sort of noise a man on a date made.

Not a date. *Not* a date.

For the first time, Marco seemed to notice the looming Braves fan behind her. "Come back and see me at the fifth?" Marco pleaded, keeping a cautious eye on Zeb.

"You know I will. And have Kenny bring me a stout in the third, okay?" She and Dad didn't have the super-expensive seats where people took her order and delivered it to her. But Kenny the beer vendor would bring them another beer in the third and again in the seventh—and not the beer he hawked to everyone else.

She got her nachos and her beer and moved off to the side. It was then she noticed that Zeb's eyes hadn't left her.

A shiver of heat went through her because Zeb's gaze was intense. He looked at her like…like she didn't even know what. She wasn't sure she wanted to find out, because what if he could see right through her?

What if he could see how much she was attracted to *him*?

This was a bad idea. She was on a date with her

brand-new CEO and he was hot and funny and brooding all at once and they were drinking their chief competitor's product and…

Zeb glanced over at her as he paid for his food and shot another warm grin at her.

And she was in trouble. Big, *big* trouble.

Seven

Zeb followed Casey to the seats. He tried his best to keep his gaze locked on the swinging ponytail that hung out the back of her Rockies hat—and not on her backside.

That was proving to be quite a challenge, though, because her backside was a sight to behold. Her jeans clung to her curves in all the right ways. Why hadn't he noticed that before?

Oh, yeah—the lab coat.

Which hadn't shown him the real woman. But this? A bright young woman with hips and curves who was friends with everyone and completely at home in the male bastion of a baseball stadium?

Who'd said—out loud—that it didn't matter if Zeb was black or not?

She turned suddenly and he snapped his gaze back up to her face. "Here," she said, notching an eyebrow at him and gesturing toward a nearly empty row. "Seats nine and ten."

They were eight rows off the first baseline, right behind the dugout. "Great seats," he told her. "I didn't bring my glove."

She snorted as she worked her way down the row. "Definitely keep your eyes on the ball here. You never know."

He made his way to seat nine. There weren't many people around, but he had a feeling that if there had been, they'd all have known Casey.

"What did you get?" she asked once they were seated.

"The Percheron lager."

"Oh, that's such a nice beer," she said with a wistful sigh.

"Yeah?" He held out his plastic collector's cup to her. "Have a drink."

She looked at him for a long moment and then leaned over and pressed her lips against the rim of his cup. Fascinated, he watched as her mouth opened and she took a sip.

Heat shot through his body, driving his pulse to a sudden pounding in his veins. It only got worse when she leaned back just enough that she could sweep her tongue over her lips, getting every last drop of beer.

Damn. Watching Casey Johnson drink beer was almost a holy experience.

Greedy was not a word he embraced. *Greedy* implied a lack of control—stupid mistakes and rash consequences. He was not a greedy person. He was methodical and detailed and careful. Always.

But right now he wanted. He wanted her lips to drink him in like she'd drunk the beer. He wanted her tongue to sweep over his lips with that slow intensity. God help him, he wanted her to savor him. And if that made him greedy, then so be it.

So, carefully, he turned the cup around and put his lips where hers had been. Her eyes darkened as he drank. "You're right," he said, the taste of the beer and of Casey mixing on his tongue. "It's a beautiful beer."

Her breath caught and her cheeks colored, throwing the spiderweb scar on her cheek into high relief. And then, heaven help him, she leaned toward him. She could have leaned away, turned away—done something to put distance between them. She could have made it clear that she didn't want him at all.

But she didn't. She felt it, too, this connection between them. Her lips parted ever so slightly and she leaned forward, close enough for him to touch. Close enough for him to take a sip.

The crack of a bat and the crowd cheering snapped his attention away. His head was buzzing as if he'd chugged a six-pack.

"Did they score?" Casey asked, shaking off her confusion. Then she did lean away, settling back into her chair.

Zeb immediately tamped down that rush of lust. They were in public, for God's sake. This wasn't like him. He didn't go for women like Casey—she was the walking embodiment of a tomboy. Women he favored were cultured and refined, elegant and beautiful. They were everything he'd spent his life trying to become.

Accepted. Welcomed. They belonged in the finest social circles.

Women he liked would never sit on the first-base side and hope to catch a fly ball. They wouldn't appreciate the finer points of an IPA or a lager. They wouldn't be proud of a father who was an electrician and they wouldn't be caught dead in a baseball hat—but Casey?

She was rough-and-tumble and there was a decent

chance she could best him in an arm-wrestling contest. There shouldn't have been a single thing about her that he found attractive.

So why couldn't he stop staring at her?

Because he couldn't. "Did you want to try mine? I helped develop it."

He leaned close to her and waited until she held the cup up to his lips. He couldn't tear his gaze away from hers, though. He saw when she sucked in a gasp when he ran his tongue over the rim before he reached up and placed his palm on the bottom of the cup, slowly tilting it back. The bitterness of the brew washed over him.

It wasn't like he'd never had an IPA before. But this was different. He could taste the beer, sure. But there was something about the brightness of the hops, the way it danced on his tongue—it tasted like...

Like her.

"It's really good," he told her. "You developed it?"

"I did. Percheron was, um..."

"It's all right," he said, leaning back. "I don't think if you say Chadwick's name three times, he magically appears. I understand the company's history."

"Oh. Okay." Damn, that blush only made her look prettier. "Well, Percheron was Chadwick's pet project and I'd been there for almost ten years by that point and he let me help. I was the assistant brewmaster for Percheron when he..." Her voice trailed off and she turned to face the field. "When he left."

Zeb mulled that over a bit. "Why didn't you go with him?"

"Because the brewmaster did and Chadwick wanted to actually make the beer himself. Percheron is a much smaller company."

He heard the sorrow in her voice. She'd wanted to go with her old boss—that much was clear.

Then she turned a wide smile in his direction. "Plus, if I'd left the brewery, I'd still be an assistant brewmaster. I'm the brewmaster for the third-largest brewery in the country because I outlasted everyone else. Attrition isn't the best way to get a promotion but it was effective nonetheless."

"That's what you wanted?"

She looked smug, the cat that had all the cream to herself. His pulse picked up another notch. "That's what I wanted."

Underneath that beer-drinking, sports-loving exterior, Zeb had to admire the sheer ambition of this woman. Not just anyone would set out to be the first—or youngest—female brewmaster in the country.

But Casey would. And she'd accomplished her goal.

Zeb took a long drink of his lager. It was good, too. "So, Percheron Drafts was your baby?"

"It was Chadwick's, but I was Igor to his Frankenstein."

He laughed—a deep, long sound that shocked him. That kind of laugh wasn't dignified or intimidating. Zeb didn't allow himself to laugh like that, because he was a CEO and he had to instill fear in the hearts of his enemies.

Except...except he was at a ball game, kicking back with a pretty girl and a beer, and his team was at the plate and the weather was warm and it was...

...perfect.

"So I want you to make Percheron—or something like it—your baby again."

Even though he wasn't looking at Casey, he felt the current of tension pass through her. "What?"

"I understand Chadwick started Percheron Drafts to compete with the explosion of craft breweries. And we lost that. I don't want to throw in that particular towel just yet. So, you want to try experimental beers? That's what I want you to do, too."

She turned to face him again, and dammit, she practically glowed. Maybe it was just the setting sun, but he didn't think so. She looked so happy—and he'd put that look on her face.

"Thank you," she said in a voice so quiet that he had to lean forward to hear it. "When you started, I thought…"

He smirked. She'd thought many things, he'd be willing to bet—and precious few of them had been good.

"Can you keep a secret?" he asked.

Her lips twisted in what he hoped was an amused grin. "How many times are you going to ask me that?"

"I'm not such a bad guy," he went on, ignoring her sass. "But don't tell anyone."

She mimed locking her lips and throwing the key over her shoulder.

Somewhere in the background, a ball game was happening. And he loved sports, he really did. But he had questions. He'd learned a little more about what kind of man his half brother was but that was just the tip of the iceberg.

But the spell of the moment had been broken. They settled in and watched the game. Sure enough, by the third inning, a grizzled older man came around with a stout for Casey. Zeb didn't warrant that level of personal service—certainly not in the opposing team's colors. As he sipped the flagship beer of his second-largest competitor, he decided it was…serviceable. Just as Casey had described their own beer.

A fact that was only highlighted when Casey let him sip her stout. "It's going to be tough to beat," he said with a sigh as she took a long drink.

For the first time, he had a doubt about what he was doing. He'd spent years—*years*—plotting and scheming to get his birthright back. He was a Beaumont and he was going to make sure everyone knew it.

But now, sitting here and drinking his half brother's beer...

He was reminded once again what he didn't have. Chadwick had literally decades to learn about the business of the brewery and the craft of beer. And Zeb—well, he knew a hell of a lot about business. But he hadn't learned it at his father's knee. Beer was his birthright—but he couldn't whip up his own batch if his life depended on it.

Casey patted his arm. "We don't have to beat it." She paused and he heard her clear her throat. "Unless..."

"Unless what?"

She looked into her cup. It was half-empty. "Unless you're out to destroy Percheron Drafts."

That was what she said. What she was really asking was, *Are you out to destroy the other Beaumonts?* It was a fair question.

"Because that's kind of a big thing," she went on in a quiet voice, looking anywhere but at him. "I don't know how many people would be supportive of that. At work, I mean." She grimaced. "There might be a lot of resignations."

She wouldn't be supportive of that. She would quit. She'd quit and go elsewhere because even though her first loyalty was to herself and then the beer, the Beaumont family was pretty high on her list.

Again, he wondered how she'd come to this point in

her life. The youngest female brewmaster at the third-largest brewery in the country. He might not know the details of her story, but he recognized this one simple truth: she was who she was in large part because the Beaumonts had given her a chance. Because she'd been Igor to Chadwick Beaumont's Frankenstein.

She'd give up her dream job if it came down to a choice between the Beaumont Brewery and Percheron Drafts.

This thought made him more than a little uncomfortable because he could try to explain how it was all business, how this was a battle for market share between two corporations and corporations were not people, but none of that was entirely true.

If he forced her to choose between the Beaumonts and himself, she'd choose them over him.

"There was a time," he said in a quiet voice, "when I wanted to destroy them."

Her head snapped up. "What?"

"I used to hate them. They had everything and I had nothing." Nothing but a bitter mother and a head for business.

"But..." She stared at him, her mouth open wide. "But *look* at you. You're rich and powerful and hot and you did that all on your own." He blinked at her, but she didn't seem to be aware of what she'd just said, because she went on without missing a beat, "Some of those Beaumonts— I mean, don't get me wrong— I like them. But they're more than a little messed up. Trust me. I was around them long enough to see how the public image wasn't reality. Phillip was a hot mess and Chadwick was miserable and Frances... I mean, they had everything handed to them and it didn't make them any happier." She shook her head and slouched back in her seat.

And suddenly, he felt he had to make her understand that this wasn't about his siblings, because he was an adult and he realized now what he hadn't known as a child—that his siblings were younger than he was and probably knew only what the rest of the world did about Hardwick Beaumont.

"Casey," he said. She looked at him and he could see how nervous she was. "I was going to say that I used to hate them—but I don't. How could I? I don't know them and I doubt any of them knew a thing about me before that press conference. I'm not out to destroy them and I'm not out to destroy Percheron Drafts. It's enough that I have the brewery."

She looked at him then—really looked at him. Zeb started to squirm in his seat, because, honestly? He didn't know what she saw. Did she see a man who made sure his mom had a booming business and his best friend had a good-paying job he loved? Did she see a son who'd never know his father?

Or—worse—would she see a boy rejected by his family, a man who wasn't black and wasn't white but who occupied a no-man's-land in the middle? Would she see an impostor who'd decided he was a Beaumont, regardless of how true it might actually be?

He didn't want to know what she saw. Because quite unexpectedly, Casey Johnson's opinion had become important to him and he didn't want to know if she didn't approve of him.

So he quickly changed the subject. "Tell me..." he said, keeping his voice casual as he turned his attention back to the field. He didn't even know what inning it was anymore. There—the scoreboard said fourth. The home team was at the plate and they already had two outs. Almost halfway done with this corporate outing. "Does that happen often?"

"What? Your boss admitting that he's not a total bastard?"

Zeb choked on his beer. "Actually, I meant that guy proposing to you."

"Who, Marco?" She snorted. "He proposes every time I see him. And since I have season tickets..."

"What does your dad think of that?"

That got him a serious side-eye. "First off, Marco's joking. Second off, my father is many things, but he's not my keeper. And third off—why do you care?"

"I don't," he answered quickly. Maybe too quickly. "Just trying to get a fuller picture of the one person responsible for keeping my company afloat."

She snorted as a pop fly ended the inning. "Come on," she said, standing and stretching. "Let's go."

Slowly, they worked their way out of the seats and back to the concession stands. He got a stout for himself and Casey got a porter. Marco flirted shamelessly but this time, Zeb focused on Casey. She smiled and joked, but at no point did she look at the young man the way she'd looked at him earlier. She didn't blush and she didn't lean toward Marco.

There was no heat. She was exactly as she appeared—a friendly tomboy. The difference between this woman and the one who'd blushed so prettily back in the seats, whose eyes had dilated and who'd leaned toward him with desire writ large on her face—that difference was huge.

With more beer and more nachos, they made their way back to their seats. As odd as it was, Zeb was having trouble remembering the last time he'd taken a night off like this. Yeah, they were still talking beer and competitors but...

But he was having fun. He was three beers in and even though he wasn't drunk—not even close—he was more relaxed than he'd been in a long time. It'd been months of watching and waiting to make sure all the final pieces of the puzzle were in place, and he was pretty sure he hadn't stopped to appreciate all that he'd accomplished.

Well, sort of relaxed. There was something else the beer vendor—Marco—had said that itched at the back of Zeb's mind.

"Did you mean what you said?" he blurted out. Hmm. Maybe he was a little more buzzed than he thought.

There was a longish pause before she said, "About?"

"That it didn't matter if I was black or not." Because it always mattered. *Always.* He was either "exotic" because he had an African American mother and green eyes or he was black and a borderline thug. He never got to be just a businessman. He was always a black businessman.

It was something white people never even thought about. But he always had that extra hurdle to clear. He didn't get to make mistakes, because even one would be proof that he couldn't cut it.

Not that he was complaining. He'd learned his lesson early in life—no one was going to give him a single damned thing. Not his father, not his family, not the world. Everything he wanted out of this life, he had to take. Being a black businessman made him a tougher negotiator, a sharper investor.

He wanted the brewery and the legitimacy that came with it. He wanted his father's approval and, short of that, he wanted the extended Beaumont family to know who he was.

He was Zebadiah Richards and he would not be ignored.

Not that Casey was ignoring him. She'd turned to look at him again—and for the second time tonight, he thought she was seeing more than he wanted her to.

Dammit, he should have kept his mouth shut.

"You tell me—does it matter?"

"It shouldn't." More than anything, he wanted it to not matter.

She shrugged. "Then it doesn't."

He should let this go. He had his victory—of sorts—and besides, what did it matter if she looked at him and saw a black CEO or just a CEO?

Or even, a small voice in the back of his mind whispered, *something other than a CEO? Something more?*

But he couldn't revel in his small victory. He needed to know—was she serious or was she paying lip service because he was her boss? "So you're saying it doesn't matter that my mother spent the last thirty-seven years doing hair in a black neighborhood in Atlanta? That I went to a historically black college? That people have pulled out of deals with me because no matter how light skinned I am, I'll never be white enough?"

He hadn't meant to say all of that. But the only thing worse than his skin color being the first—and sometimes only—thing people used to define him was when people tried to explain they didn't "see color." They meant well—he knew that—but the truth was, it *did* matter. He'd made his first fortune for his mother, merchandising a line of weave and braid products for upper-class African American consumers that had, thanks to millennials, reached a small level of crossover success in the mainstream market. When people said they didn't see color, they effectively erased the blackness from his life.

Being African American wasn't who he was—but it was a part of him. And for some reason, he needed her to understand that.

He had her full attention now. Her gaze swept over him and he felt his muscles tighten, almost as if he were in fight-or-flight mode. And he didn't run. He never ran.

"Will our beer suddenly taste black?" she asked.

"Don't be ridiculous. We might broaden our marketing reach, though."

She tilted her head. "All I care about is the beer."

"Seriously?"

She sighed heavily. "Let me ask you this—when you drink a Rocky Top beer, does it taste feminine?"

"You're being ridiculous."

That got him a hard glare. A glare he probably deserved, but still. "Zeb, I don't know what you want me to say here. Of course it matters, because that's your life. That's who you are. But I can't hold that against you, and anyway, why would I want to? You didn't ask for that. You can't change that, any more than I can change the fact that my mother died in a car accident when I was two and left me with this," she said, pointing to her scarred cheek, "and my father raised me as best he could—and that meant beer and sports and changing my own oil in my car. We both exist in a space that someone else is always going to say we shouldn't—so what? We're here. We like beer." She grinned hugely at him. "Get used to it."

Everything around him went still. He wasn't breathing. He wasn't sure his heart was even beating. He didn't hear the sounds of the game or the chatter of the fans around them.

His entire world narrowed to her. All he could see and hear and feel—because dammit, she was close enough that their forearms kept touching, their knees bumping—was Casey.

It mattered. *He* mattered. No conditions, no exceptions. He mattered just the way he was.

Had anyone ever said as much to him? Even his own mother? No. What had mattered was what he wasn't. He wasn't a Beaumont. He wasn't legitimate. He wasn't white.

Something in his chest unclenched, something he'd never known he was holding tightly. Something that felt like…

…peace.

He dimly heard a loud crack and then Casey jolted and shouted, "Look out!"

Zeb moved without thinking. He was in a weird space—everything happened as if it were in slow motion. His head turned like he was stuck in molasses, like the baseball was coming directly for him at a snail's pace. He reached out slowly and caught the fly ball a few inches from Casey's shoulder.

The pain of the ball smacking into his palm snapped him out of it. "Damn," he hissed, shaking his hand as a smattering of applause broke out from the crowd. "That hurt."

Casey turned her face toward him, her eyes wide. There was an unfamiliar feeling trying to make its way to the forefront of Zeb's mind as he stared into her beautiful light brown eyes, one he couldn't name. He wasn't sure he wanted to.

"You caught the ball bare-handed," she said, her voice breathy. Then, before Zeb could do anything, she looked down to where he was still holding the foul ball. She moved slowly when she pulled the ball out of his palm and stared at his reddening skin. Lightly, so lightly it almost hurt, she traced her fingertip over the palm of his hand. "Did it hurt?"

That unnamed, unfamiliar feeling was immediately buried under something that was much easier to identify—lust. "Not much," he said, and he didn't miss the way his voice dropped. He had a vague sense that he wasn't being entirely honest—it hurt enough to snap him out of his reverie. But with her stroking his skin…

…everything felt just fine.

And it got a whole lot better when she lifted his hand and pressed a kiss against his palm. "Do we need to go and get some ice or…?"

Or? *Or* sounded good. *Or* sounded great. "Only if you want to," he told her, shifting so that he was cupping her cheek in his hand. "Your call."

Because he wasn't talking about ice. Or beer. Or baseball.

He dragged his thumb over the top of her cheek as she leaned into his touch. She lifted her gaze to his face and for a second, he thought he'd taken it too far. He'd misread the signals and she would storm out of the stadium just like she'd stormed out of his office that first day. She would quit and he would deserve it.

Except she didn't. "I live a block away," she said, and he heard the slightest shiver in her voice, felt a matching shiver in her body. "If that's what you need."

What did he need? It should've been a simple question with a simple answer—her. Right now he needed her.

But there was nothing simple about Casey Johnson and everything got much more complicated when she pressed his hand closer to her cheek.

For the first time in a very long time, Zeb was at a loss for words. It wasn't like him. When it came to women, he'd always known what to say, when to say it. Growing up in a hair salon had given him plenty of opportunity to learn what women wanted, what they needed and where those two things met and when they didn't. *Smooth*, more than one of his paramours had called him. And he was. Smooth and cool and...cold. Distant. Reserved.

He didn't feel any of those things right now. All he could feel was the heat that flowed between her skin and his.

"I need to cool down," he told her, only dimly aware that that was not the smoothest line he had ever uttered. But he didn't have anything else right now. His hand was throbbing and his blood was throbbing and his dick—that, especially, was throbbing. Everything about him was hot and hard, and even though he was no innocent wallflower, it all felt strange and new. He felt strange and new because Casey saw him in a way that no one else did.

He didn't know what was going to happen. Even if all she did was take him back to her place and stick some ice on his hand, that was fine, too. He was not going to be *that* guy.

Still, when she said, "Come with me," Zeb hoped that he could do exactly that.

Eight

Was she seriously doing this? Taking Zeb Richards back to her apartment?

Well, obviously, she was. She was holding his not-wounded hand and leading him away from the stadium. So there really wasn't any question about what was happening here.

This was crazy. Absolutely crazy. She shouldn't be taking him back to her apartment, she shouldn't be holding his hand and she most especially shouldn't be thinking about what would happen when they got there.

But she was. She was thinking about peeling that T-shirt off him and running her hands over his muscles and…

His fingers tightened around hers and he pulled her a step closer to him. He was hot in a way that she hadn't anticipated. Heat radiated off his body, so much so that she thought the edges around his skin might waver like a mirage if she looked at him head-on.

She swallowed and tried to think of things she had done that were crazier than this. Walking into the brewery and demanding a job—that had been pretty bold. And there was that summer fling with a rookie on the Rockies—but he'd been traded to Seattle in the off-season and their paths didn't cross anymore. That had been wild and a hell of a lot of fun.

But nothing came close to bringing the new CEO of the Beaumont Brewery home with her. And the thing was, she wasn't entirely sure what had changed. One moment, they'd been talking—okay, flirting. They'd been flirting. But it seemed…innocent, almost.

And then she had told him about her mom dying in a car accident and he caught that ball before it hit her—she still didn't know how the hell he'd managed that—and everything had changed.

And now she was bringing her boss home with her.

Except that wasn't true, either. It was—but it also wasn't. She wasn't bringing home the ice-cold man in a suit who'd had the sheer nerve to call a press conference and announce that he was one of the Beaumont bastards. That man was fascinating—but that wasn't who was holding her hand.

She was bringing Zeb home. The son of a hairdresser who liked baseball and didn't look at her like she was his best friend or, worse, one of the guys.

She was probably going to regret this. But she didn't care right now. Because Zeb was looking at her and she felt beautiful, sensual, desirable and so very feminine. And that was what she wanted, even if it was for only a little while.

They made it back to her apartment. She led him to the elevator. Even standing here, holding his hand, felt off. This was the part she was never any good at. Sitting in front of the game with beers in their hands—yes. Then she could talk and flirt and be herself. But when she wanted to be that beautiful, desirable creature men craved…she froze up. It was not a pleasant sensation.

The elevator doors opened and they stepped inside. Casey hit the button for the fifth floor and the door slid shut. The next thing she knew, Zeb had pressed into the back of the elevator. His body held hers against the wall—but other than that, he didn't touch her and he didn't kiss her.

"Tell me I didn't read you wrong back there," he said, his voice low and husky. It sent a shiver down her spine and one corner of his mouth curved up into a cocky half smile. He lifted one hand and moved as if he were going to touch her face—but didn't. "Casey…"

This was her out—if she wanted it. She could laugh it off and say, *Gosh, how's your hand?* And that'd be that.

"You didn't," she whispered.

Then he did touch her. He cupped her cheek in his hand and tilted her head up. "Do I really matter to you?" he whispered against her skin. "Or are you just here for the beer?"

If Casey allowed herself to admit that she had thought of this moment before right now—and she wasn't necessarily admitting to anything—she hadn't pictured this. She assumed Zeb would pin her against the wall or his desk and seduce her ruthlessly. Not that there was anything wrong with being seduced ruthlessly—it had its place in the world and her fantasies.

But this tenderness? She didn't quite know what to make of it.

"At work tomorrow," she said, squinting her eyes shut because the last thing she wanted to think about was the number of company policies she was about to break, "it's about the beer." She felt Zeb tense and then there was a little bit of space between their bodies as he stepped away from her.

Oh, no. She wasn't going to let him go. Not when she had him right where she wanted him. She locked her arms around his neck and pulled him back into her. "But we're not at work right now, are we?"

"Right," he agreed. Her body molded to his and his to hers. "Nothing at work. But outside of work…"

Then he kissed her. And that? *That* bordered on a ruthless seduction because it wasn't a gentle, tentative touch of two lips meeting and exploring for the first time. No, when he kissed her, he *claimed* her. The heat from his mouth seared her, and suddenly, she was too hot—for the elevator, for her clothes, for any of it.

"Tell me what you want," he said again when his lips trailed over her jaw and down her neck.

This was crazy—but the very best kind of crazy. Carte blanche with someone as strong and hot and masculine as Zeb Richards? Oh, yeah, this was the stuff of fantasies.

She started to say what she always said. "Tell me—"

Just then, the elevator came to a stop and the door opened. Damn. She'd forgotten they weren't actually in her apartment yet.

Zeb pushed back as she fumbled around for her keys. Hopefully, that would be the last interruption for at least the next hour. Quickly, she led him down the hall. "It's not much," she explained, suddenly nervous all over again. Her studio apartment was certainly not one of the grand old mansions of Denver.

She unlocked the door. Zeb followed her in, and once the door was shut behind them, he put his hands on her hips. "Nice place," he said, and she could tell from the tone of his voice that he wasn't looking at her apartment at all. "Beautiful views," he added, and then he was pulling the hem of her shirt, lifting it until he accidentally knocked her hat off her head. The whole thing got hung up on her ponytail and, laughing, she reached around to help untangle it.

"What would you like me to tell you?" As he spoke, his lips were against the base of her neck, his teeth skimming over her sensitive skin.

She couldn't stop the shiver that went through her. "Tell me..." She opened her mouth to explain that she wanted to feel pretty—but stopped because she couldn't figure out how to say it without sounding lame, desperate even. And besides, wanting to feel pretty—it didn't exactly mesh with her fantasy about a ruthless seduction. So she hedged. She always hedged. "...what you're going to do to me."

In the past, that had worked like a charm. Ask for a little dirty talk? The cocky young men she brought home were always ready and willing.

But Zeb wasn't. Instead, he stood behind her, skimming the tips of his fingers over her shoulders and down her bare back. He didn't even wrench her bra off her, for crying out loud. All he did was...touch her.

Not that she was complaining about being touched. Her eyelids fluttered shut and she leaned into his touch.

"You still haven't told me what you want. I'm more than happy to describe it for you, but I need to know what I should be doing in the first place. For instance..." One hand removed itself from her skin. The next thing she knew, he wrapped her ponytail around his hand and pivoted, bringing her against the small countertop in her kitchen. "I could bend you over and take you hard and fast right here." He pulled her hair just enough that she had to lean back. "And I'd make sure you screamed when you came," he growled as he slipped his hand down over the seam of her jeans. With exquisite precision, he pressed against her most sensitive spot.

"Oh," she gasped, writhing against his hand. Her pulse pounded against where he was touching her and he used her ponytail to tilt her head so he could do more than skim his teeth over her neck. He bit down and, with the smallest movement of his hand, almost brought her to her knees. *"Zeb."*

And then the bastard stopped. "But maybe you don't like it rough," he said in the most casual voice she'd ever heard as he pulled his hands away from her ponytail and her pants. What the hell?

Then his hands were tracing the lines of her shoulders again.

"Maybe you want slow, sensual seduction, where I start kissing here…" he murmured against her neck. Then his lips moved down over her shoulder and he slid his hands up her waist to cup her breasts. "And there."

This time, both hands slid over the front of her jeans and maybe it was shameless, but she arched her back and opened for him. "And everywhere," he finished. "Until you can't take it."

And then he stopped *again*.

What was happening here? Because in the past, when she told someone to talk dirty to her, it got crude *fast*. And it wasn't like the sex was bad—it was good. She liked it. But it felt like…

It always felt like that was the best she could hope for. She wasn't pretty and she wasn't soft and she wasn't feminine, and so crude, fast sex was the best she could expect any man to do when faced with her naked.

And suddenly, she realized that wasn't what she wanted. Not anymore. Not from him.

"Maybe you want to be in charge," he went on, his voice so deep but different, too, because now there was that trace of a Southern accent coming through. It sounded like sin on the wind, that voice—honey sweet with just a hint of danger to it. He spun her around so he was leaning back on the counter and she had him boxed in. He dropped his hands and stared at her hungrily with those beautiful eyes. "Maybe I need to step back and let you show me what you want."

It was an intense feeling, being in Zeb Richards's sights.

"So what's it going to be?" But even as he asked it— sounding cool and calm and in complete control—she saw a muscle in his jaw tic and a tremor pass through his body. His gaze dipped down to her breasts, to her lucky purple bra that she wore to every home game, and a growl that she felt in her very center came rumbling out of his chest. He was hanging on to his control by the very thinnest of threads. Because of her.

He was waiting, she realized. It was her move. So that was what she did. She reached up and pulled his hat off his head and launched it somewhere in the middle of her apartment. He leaned toward her but he didn't touch her.

"What about you? What do you want?" she asked.

He shook his head in mock disappointment even as he smiled slyly at her. "I have this rule—if you don't tell me what you want, I won't give it to you. No mixed signals, no mind reading. I'm not going to guess and risk being wrong."

This wasn't working, she decided. At the very least, it wasn't what she was used to. All this…talking. It wasn't what she was good at. It only highlighted how awkward she was at things like seduction and romance, things that came naturally to other women.

She appreciated the fact that he wanted to be sure about her, about this—really, she did. But she didn't want to think. She didn't want each interaction to be a negotiation. She wanted to be swept away so she could pretend, if only for a little while, that she was soft and sultry and beautiful.

And she'd never get to hold on to that fantasy if she had to explain what she wanted, because explaining would only draw attention to what she wasn't.

Which left only one possible conclusion, really. She was done talking.

She leaned forward and grabbed the hem of his shirt. In one swift motion, she pulled it up and over his head and tossed it on the floor. And right about then, she not only stopped talking but stopped thinking.

Because Zeb's chest was a sight to behold. That T-shirt hadn't been lying. *Muscles*, she thought dimly as she reached out to stroke her hand over one of his packs. So many muscles.

"Casey…" He almost moaned when she skimmed her hand over his bare skin and moved lower. As she palmed the rippling muscles of his abs, he sucked in a breath and gripped the countertop so hard she could see his arms shaking. "You're killing me, woman."

That was better, she decided. She couldn't pull off seductive, but there was a lot to be said for raw sexual energy. That, at least, she could handle.

So she decided to handle it. Personally. She hooked her hands into the waistband of his jeans and pulled his hips toward her. As she did so, she started working at the buttons of his fly. His chest promised great, great things and she wanted to see if the rest of him could deliver on that promise.

"What do you want to hear?" he asked in that low, sensual voice that was summer sex on the wind.

Tell me I'm pretty.

But she couldn't say that, because she knew what would happen. She would ask him to tell her she was pretty and he would. He would probably even make it sound so good that she would believe him. After all, she thought as she pushed his jeans down and cupped him through his boxer briefs, what guy wouldn't find a woman who was about to sleep with him pretty?

She'd been here before, too. She might be pretty enough in the heat of the moment but the second the climactic high began to fade, so did any perceived beauty she possessed. Then she'd get her decidedly unfeminine clothes back on and before she knew it, she'd be one of the boys again.

She didn't just want him to tell her she was pretty or beautiful or sensual or any of those things. She wanted him to make her believe it, all of it, today, tomorrow and into next week, at the very least. And *that* was a trick no one had been able to master yet.

So she gave the waistband of his briefs a tug and freed him. He sprang to attention as a low groan issued from Zeb's throat.

Immediately, her jaw dropped. "Oh, Zeb," she breathed as she wrapped one and then the other hand around his girth, one on top of the other. Slowly, she stroked up the length of him and then back down. Then she looked up at him and caught him watching her. "I am *impressed.*"

He thrust in her hands—but even that was controlled. They were standing in her kitchen, both shirtless, and she was stroking him—and he wasn't even touching her. Sure, the look in his eyes was enough to make her shiver with want because she was having an impact. The cords of his neck tightened and his jaw clenched as his length slid in her grip.

But it wasn't enough. She needed more. "Feel free to join in," she told him.

"You're doing a pretty damn good job all by yourself," he ground out through gritted teeth. But even as he said it, he pried one hand off the countertop and gripped the back of her neck, pulling her into his chest. God, he was almost red-hot to the touch and all she wanted to do was be burned.

"Stop holding back." It came out as an order, but what was she supposed to do? If he was holding back out of some sort of sense of chivalry—however misguided—or consent or whatever, then she needed to get that cleared up right now.

She needed to tell him what she wanted—he'd already told her she had to, right? But she couldn't figure out how to say it without sounding sad about it, so instead, she fell back on the tried-and-true. "You've got what I want," she said as she gave him a firm squeeze. "So show me what you can do with it."

There was just a moment's hesitation—the calm before the storm, she realized. Zeb's eyes darkened and his fingers flexed against the back of her neck.

And then he exploded into movement. Casey was spun around and lifted up onto the countertop, her legs parted as he stepped into her. It happened so fast that she was almost dizzy. And *that* was what she needed right now. She needed his lips on her mouth, her neck, her chest. She needed his fingertips smoothly unhooking her lucky bra and she needed to hear the groan of desire when the bra fell to the ground.

"Damn, Casey—look at you," he said in a tone that was almost reverential.

Casey's eyes drifted shut as he stroked his fingertips over the tops of her breasts and then around her nipples.

"Yes," she whispered as he leaned down to take her in his mouth. His teeth scraped over her sensitive skin and then he sucked on her. "Oh, yes," she hissed, holding him to her.

His hand slid around her back and pulled her to the edge of the counter and then he was grinding against her, his erection hard and hot and everything she wanted— well, almost everything. There was the unfortunate matter of her jeans and the barrier they formed between the two of them.

"This is what you want, isn't it?" Zeb thrust against her. "You want me to take you here, on the countertop, because I can't wait long enough to get you into a bed?"

Every word was punctuated by another thrust. And every thrust was punctuated by a low moan that Casey couldn't have held if she'd tried.

"God, yes," she whimpered as her hips shimmied against his. This was better. Zeb was overpowering her senses, hard and fast. She didn't want to think. She just wanted to feel.

"I wonder," he said in a voice that bordered on ruthless, "if I should bite you here," he said as he traced a pattern on her shoulders with his tongue, "or here—" and he kissed the top of her left breast "—or...here." With that, he crouched down and nipped her inner thigh, and even though she could barely feel his teeth through the denim, she still shuddered with anticipation. This was better. This was things going according to script.

"D, all of the above." It was at that point that she discovered a problem. Zeb wore his hair close-cropped—there was nothing for her to thread her fingers through, nothing for her to hold on to as he rubbed along the seam of her jeans, over her very center.

But her hips bucked when he pressed against her. "Look at you," he growled as he came to his feet. "Just look at you."

She sucked in a ragged gasp when his hands moved and then he was undoing the button of her jeans and sliding down the zipper.

"I'd rather look at you," she told him as she lifted one hip and then the other off the countertop so he could work her jeans down. "You are, hands down, the most gorgeous man I've ever seen."

She let her hands skim over his shoulders and down his arms. It wasn't fair—there wasn't an ounce of fat on him. She was going to have to revise her opinion of men in suits, she thought dimly as he peeled her jeans the rest of the way off her legs.

"I can't wait," he growled in her ear, the raw urgency in his voice sending another shiver of desire through her body. He pulled the thin cotton of her panties to one side and then his erection was grinding directly against her. "Are you on something? Do you have something?"

"I'm on the Pill," she told him, her hips flexing to meet his. In that moment, she did feel desirable and wanted. His finger tested her body and she moaned into him. She might not be sensual or gorgeous, but she could still do this to a man—drive him so crazy with need that he couldn't even wait to get her undressed all the way.

"Now," she told him. "Now, Zeb. Please."

She didn't have to ask twice. He positioned himself at

her entrance. "You're so ready for me. God, just look at you." But he didn't thrust into her. Instead, it appeared he was actually going to look at her.

She pushed back against her insecurity as he studied her. She knew she couldn't measure up to his other lovers—a man that looked like him? He could have his pick of women. Hell, she wasn't even sure why he was here with her—except for the fact that she was…well, *available*. "Why are you stopping? Don't stop."

"Is that how you want it? Hard and fast?" Even as he asked, he moved, pushing into her inch by agonizing inch.

"Zeb." Even as she wrapped her legs around his hips and tried to draw him in farther. And when that worked only to a point, she wrapped her arms around his waist and dug her fingernails into his back.

That did the trick. With a roar of desire, he thrust forward and sank all the way into her. Oh, *God*. She took him in easily, moaning with desire. "Is that what you want?"

She heard his self-control hanging by a thread.

So she raked her nails up and down his back—not hard enough to break skin, but more than enough that he could feel it. He withdrew and thrust into her again, this time harder and faster.

"Yes," she whimpered. "More." She leaned her head back, lifting her chest up to him. "I need more."

Without breaking rhythm, he bent down and nipped at her breast again.

"More," she demanded because she was already so, so close. She needed just a little something to push her over the edge.

"I love a woman who knows what she wants." He sucked her nipple into his mouth—hard. There was just a hint of pain around the edges of the pleasure and it shocked her to her very core in the best way possible.

"Oh, God—" But anything else she would've tried to say got lost as his mouth worked on her and he buried himself in her again and again.

The orgasm snapped back on her like a rubber band pulled too tight, so strong she couldn't even cry out. She couldn't breathe—she couldn't think. All she could do was feel. It was everything she wanted and more. Everything she'd wanted since she'd stormed into his office that very first day and seen him. Ruthless seduction and mind-blowing climaxes and want and need all blended together into mindless pleasure.

Zeb relinquished his hold on her breast and buried his face in her neck, driving in harder and harder. She felt his teeth on her again, just as he promised. And then his hands moved between them and his thumb pressed against her sex as he thrust harder, and this time, Casey did scream. The orgasm shook through her and left her rag-doll limp as he thrust one final time and then froze. His shoulders slumped and he pulled her in close.

"God, Casey..." She took it as a source of personal pride that he sounded shaky. "That was *amazing*."

All she could do was sigh. That was enough. She'd take *amazing* every day of the week.

And then he had to go and ruin it.

He leaned back and shot her a surprised smile and said, "I should have guessed a girl like you would want it hard like that."

She didn't allow herself to be disappointed, because, really, what had she expected? She wasn't pretty or beautiful or sensual or sexy, damn it all. She was fun and cool, maybe, and she was definitely available. But beyond that? She was a good time, but that was it.

So she did what she always did. She put on her good-time smile and pushed him back so he was forced to withdraw from her body.

"Always happy to be a surprise," she said, inwardly cringing. "If you'll excuse me…"

Then she hurried to the bathroom and shut the door.

Nine

Jesus, what the hell had just happened? What had he just done?

Zeb looked down at Casey, mostly naked and flushed. Sitting on the edge of her kitchen counter. Staring at him as if she didn't know how they had gotten here.

Well, that made two of them. He felt like he was coming out of a fog—one of the thick ones that didn't just turn the world a ghostly white but blotted out the sun almost completely.

He had just taken her on her countertop. Had there even been any seduction? He tried to think but now that his blood was no longer pounding in his veins, he felt sluggish and stupid, a dull headache building in the back of his head. Hungover—that was how he felt. He didn't feel like he was in control anymore.

And he didn't like that.

He never lost control. *Ever.* He enjoyed women and sex, but this?

"If you'll excuse me," Casey said, hopping off the counter. She notched an eyebrow at him in something that looked like a challenge—but hell if he could figure out what the challenge was.

This was bad. As he watched her walk away, her body naked except for a pair of purple panties that might have matched her bra, his pulse tried to pick up the pace again. He was more than a little tempted to follow her back through her apartment, because if sex in the kitchen had been great, how good would sex in a bed be?

He was horrified to realize that he had not just had this thought but had actually taken two steps after her. He stumbled to a stop and realized that his jeans were still hanging off his butt. He tucked back into his boxer briefs and buttoned up, and the whole time, he tried to form a coherent thought.

What the hell was wrong with him? This wasn't like him. For God's sake—he hadn't even worn a condom. He had a dim recollection—she'd said she was on the Pill, right? How much had he had to drink, anyway? Three beers—that was all.

Even so, he'd done something he associated with getting plastered in a bar—he'd gone home with a woman and had wild, crazy, indiscriminate sex with her.

He scrubbed his hand over his face, but it didn't help. So he went to the sink and splashed cold water on his face. His hand—ostensibly the reason they'd come back to her place—throbbed in pain. He let the cold water run over it.

The indiscriminate sex was bad enough. But worse was that he'd just had sex with his brewmaster. An *employee*. An employee at the Beaumont Brewery, the very company he'd worked years to acquire. A company he was striving to turn around and manage productively.

And he…he couldn't even say he'd fallen into bed with Casey. They hadn't made it that far.

He splashed water on his face again. It didn't help.

He needed to think. He'd just done something he'd never done before and he wasn't sure how to handle it. Sure, he knew that employers and employees carried on affairs all the time. It happened. But it also created a ripple effect of problems. Zeb couldn't count the number of companies he'd bought that could trace their disintegration back to an affair between two adults who should have known better. And until this evening, he'd always been above such baser attractions. *Always.*

But that was before he'd met Casey. With her, he hadn't known better. And, apparently, neither had she.

Zeb found the paper towels and dried off his face. Then he scooped up his shirt and shrugged back into it. He had no idea where his hat had gone, but frankly, that was the least of his problems.

He'd lost control and gotten swept up in the moment with an employee.

It couldn't happen again.

That was the only reasonable conclusion. Yes, the sex had been amazing—but Zeb's position in the brewery and the community at large was tenuous at best. He couldn't jeopardize all of his plans for sex.

Hot, dirty, hard sex. Maybe the best sex he'd ever had. Raw and desperate and…

An involuntary shudder worked through his body. Jesus, what was *wrong* with him?

He heard the bathroom door open from somewhere inside the apartment. He could salvage this situation. He was reasonably sure that, before all the clothes had come off, she'd said…something about work. How they weren't going to do *that* at work. If he was remembering that right, then she also understood the tenuous situation they were in.

So he turned away from the sink to face her and explain, in a calm and rational way, that while what they shared had been lovely, it wasn't going to happen again.

He never got that far.

Because what he saw took his breath away and anything calm and rational was drowned out in a roar of blood rushing through his ears.

Casey had a short silk robe belted around her waist. Her hair was no longer pulled back into a ponytail—instead, it was down. Glorious waves brushed her shoulders and Zeb was almost overwhelmed with the urge to wind his fingers into that hair and pull her close to him again.

Last week, he wouldn't have called her beautiful. She still wasn't, not in the classic way. But right now, with the late-evening light filtering through the windows behind her, lighting her up with a glow, she was...

She was simply the most gorgeous woman he'd ever seen.

He was in so much trouble.

It only got worse when she smiled at him. Not the wide, friendly smile she'd aimed at every single person in the ballpark tonight. No, this was a small movement of the lips—something intimate. Something that was for him and him alone.

And then it was gone. "Can you hand me my bra?" she asked in the same voice she'd used when she'd been joking around with that beer guy.

"Sure," he said. This was good, right? This was exactly what he wanted. He didn't need her suddenly deciding she was in love with him or anything.

"Thanks." She scooped up her shirt and her jeans and

disappeared again. "Do you want to try and catch the end of the game?" she called out from somewhere deeper in the apartment. Which was *not* an invitation to join her.

Zeb stood there, blinking. What the hell? Okay, so he didn't want her to go all mushy on him. But she was acting like what had just happened…

…hadn't. Like they hadn't been flirting all night and hadn't just had some of the best sex of his life.

"Uh…" he said because seriously, what was wrong with him? First he lost control. Then he decided that this had to be a one-time-only thing. Then she appeared to be not only agreeing to the one-time thing but beating him to the punch? And that bothered him? It shouldn't have. It really shouldn't have.

But it did.

"I'll probably head back to the stadium," she said, reappearing and looking exactly the way she had when he'd first laid eyes on her this evening. Her hair was tucked back under her ball cap and she had his red cap in her hands.

It was like he hadn't left a mark on her at all.

But then he saw her swallow as she held his hat out to him. "This, um…this won't affect my job performance," she said with mock bravado.

Strangely, that made him feel better, in a perverse sort of way. He'd made an impact after all.

"It changes nothing," he agreed. He wasn't sure if his lie was any smoother than hers had been. "You're still in charge of the beer and I still want you to come up with a new product line."

And I still want you.

But he didn't say that part, because the signals she was sending out were loud and clear—no more touching. No more wanting.

"Okay. Good. Great." She shot him a wide smile that didn't get anywhere near her eyes.

In all his years, he'd never been in a postsex situation that was even half this awkward. Ever.

"I think I'm going to head home," he said, trying to sound just as cool as she did.

As his words hung in the air between them, something in her eyes changed and he knew that he'd hurt her.

Dammit, that wasn't what he wanted. At the very least, there'd been a moment when she'd made him feel things he hadn't thought he was capable of feeling and the sex had been electric. If nothing else, he was appreciative of those gifts she'd given him. So, even though it probably wasn't the best idea, he stepped into her and laced his fingers with hers.

"Thank you," he said in a low whisper. "I know we can't do this again—but I had a really good time tonight."

"You did?" Clearly, she didn't believe him.

"I did. The ball game and the beer and..." he cleared his throat. *And you.* But he didn't say that. "It was great. All of it." He squeezed her fingers and then, reluctantly, let go and stepped back. It was harder to do than he expected it to be. "I trust this will stay between us?"

That wasn't the right thing to say. But the hell of it was, he wasn't sure what, exactly, the right thing would be. There was no good way out of this.

"Of course," she replied stiffly. "I don't kiss and tell."

"I didn't—" He forced himself to exhale slowly. Attempting to bridge the divide between boss and lover wasn't working and he was better at being the boss anyway. "I look forward to seeing what you come up with," he said as he turned toward the door. "At work," he added stupidly.

"Right. See you at work," she said behind him as he walked out and shut the door behind him.

Just as the door closed, he thought he heard her sigh in what sounded like disappointment.

Well. He'd wondered what she'd seen when she'd looked at him.

He wished now he didn't know the answer.

All told, it could have been worse.

Her team had won and she'd gotten a bobblehead doll for Dad. She'd gotten to drink some Percheron Drafts, which were like memories in a cup. She'd gotten permission to do something similar—new, bold beers that would be hers and hers alone. None of that was bad.

Except for the part where she'd kind of, sort of, slept with her boss. And had some of the most intense orgasms of her life. And...and wanted more. She wanted more with him. More beers at the game, more short walks home, more time exploring his body with hers.

That part was not so good, because she was not going to get more.

Casey made sure to avoid the executive wing of the brewery as much as possible. It wasn't that she was avoiding Zeb, necessarily. She was just really focused on her job.

Okay, that was a total lie because she was avoiding him. But it was easy to do—in addition to overseeing the production lines, she was hiring new people and then training new people and resisting the urge to take a sledgehammer to tank fifteen because that damned piece of machinery had it coming and she had the urge to destroy something.

But underneath all of those everyday thoughts lurked two others that kept her constantly occupied. First, she had to come up with some new beers. She already had a porter in the fermenting tanks—she wanted to start with something that wasn't anywhere close to what the Beaumont Brewery currently had.

And then there was Zeb. He to be avoided at all costs. Besides, it wasn't like she wanted to see him again. She didn't. Really.

Okay, so the orgasms had been amazing. And yes, she'd had fun watching the game with him. And all right, he was simply the most gorgeous man she had ever seen, in or out of a suit.

But that didn't mean she wanted to see him again. Why would she? He had been everything she had expected—handsome, charming, great sex—and exactly nothing more than that.

She wanted him to be different. And he was—there was no argument about that. He was more intelligent, more ambitious and vastly wealthier than any other man she had ever even looked at. And that didn't even include the racial differences.

But she wanted him to be different in other ways, too. She felt stupid because she knew that, on at least one level, this was nothing but her own fault. The man had specifically asked her to tell him what she wanted—and she hadn't. Men, in her long and illustrious experience of being surrounded by them, were not mind readers. Never had been, never would be. So for her to have expected that Zeb would somehow magically guess what she needed was to feel gorgeous and beautiful and sultry— without her telling him—was unfair to both of them.

She didn't understand what was wrong with her. Why couldn't she ask for what she wanted? Why was it so hard to say that she wanted to be seduced with sweet nothings whispered in her ear? That instead of rough and dirty sex all the time, she wanted candlelight and silky negligees and—yes—bottles of champagne instead of beer? She wanted beautiful things. She wanted to *be* beautiful.

Well, one thing was clear. She was never going to get it if she didn't ask for it. Let this be a lesson, she decided. Next time a man said, *Tell me what you want*, she was going to tell him. It would be awkward and weird—but then, so was not getting what she wanted.

Next time, then. Not with her boss.

Casey wasn't sure what she expected from Zeb, but he seemed to be keeping his distance, as well. It wasn't that she wanted flowers or even a sweet little note…

Okay, that was another lie—she totally wanted flowers and the kind of love letter that she could hang on to during the long, dark winter nights. But the risk that came with any of those things showing up on her desk at work was too great. No one had ever sent her flowers at work before. If anything even remotely romantic showed up on her desk, the gossip would be vicious. Everyone would know something was up and there were always those few people in the office who wouldn't rest until they knew what they thought was the truth. And she knew damned well that if they couldn't get to the truth, they'd make up their own.

So it was fine that she avoided Zeb and he avoided her and they both apparently pretended that nothing had happened.

It was a week and a half later when she got the first email from him.

Ms. Johnson,
Status report?

Casey couldn't help but stare at her computer, her lips twisted in a grimace of displeasure. She knew she wasn't the kind of girl who got a lot of romance in her life, but really? He hadn't even signed the email, for God's sake. Four simple words that didn't seem very simple at all.

So she wrote back.

Mr. Richards, I've hired six new employees. Please see attached for their résumés. The new test beers are in process. Tank fifteen is still off-line. Further updates as events warrant.

And because she was still apparently mentally twelve, she didn't sign her email, either.

It was another day before Zeb replied.

Timeline on test beers?

Casey frowned at her email for the second time in as many days. Was he on a strict four-word diet or was she imagining things? This time, she hadn't even gotten the courtesy of a salutation.

This was fine, right? This was maintaining a professional distance with no repercussions from their one indiscretion.

Didn't feel any less awkward, though.

Still testing, she wrote back. It's going to be another few weeks before I know if I have anything.

The next day she got an even shorter email from him.

Status report?

Two words. Two stinking words and they drove her nuts. She was half-tempted to ask one of the other department heads if they got the same terse emails every day or so—but she didn't want to draw any attention to her relationship with Zeb, especially if that wasn't how he treated his other employees.

It was clear that he regretted their evening. In all reality, she should have been thankful she still had her job, because so far, she hadn't managed to handle herself as a professional around him yet. She was either yelling at him or throwing herself at him. Neither was good.

So she replied to his two-word emails that came every other day with the briefest summary she could.

Test beers still fermenting. Tank fifteen still not working. Hired a new employee—another woman.

But...

There were days when she looked at those short messages and wondered if maybe he wasn't asking something else. All she ever told him about was the beer. What if he was really asking about her?

What if *Status report?* was his really terrible way of asking, *How are you?*

What if he thought about her like she thought about him? Did he lie awake at night, remembering the feel of her hands on his body, like she remembered his? Did he think about the way he had fit against her, in her? Did he toss and turn until the frustration was too much and he had to take himself in hand—just like she had to stroke herself until a pale imitation of the climax he'd given her took the edge off?

Ridiculous, she decided. Of course he wasn't thinking about her. He'd made his position clear. They'd had a good time together once and once was enough. That was just how this went. She knew that. She was fun for a little while, but she was not the kind of woman men could see themselves in a relationship with. And to think that such a thing might be percolating just under the surface of the world's shortest emails was delusional at best. To convince herself that Zeb might actually care for her was nothing but heartache waiting to happen.

So she kept her mouth shut and went about her job, training her new employees, trying to beat tank fifteen into submission and tinkering with her new recipes. She caught evening games with her dad and added to her bobblehead collection and did her best to forget about one evening of wild abandon in Zeb Richards's arms.

Everything had gone back to normal.

Oh, no.

Casey stared down at the pack of birth control pills with a dawning sense of horror. Something was wrong. She hadn't been paying attention—but she was at the end of this pack. Which meant that five days ago, she should've started her period. What the hell? Why had she skipped her period?

This was *not* normal. She was regular. That was one of the advantages of being on the Pill. No surprises. No missed periods. No heart attacks at six fifty in the morning before she'd even had her coffee, for crying out loud.

In a moment of terror, she tried to recall—she hadn't skipped a dose. She had programmed a reminder into her phone. The reminder went off ten minutes after her alarm so she took a pill at exactly the same time every single day. She hadn't been sick—no antibiotics to screw with her system. Plus, she'd been on this brand for about a year.

Okay, so... She hadn't exactly had a lot of sex in the last year. Actually, now that she thought about it, there hadn't been anyone since that ballplayer a year and a half ago.

Unexpectedly, her stomach rolled and even though she hadn't had breakfast or her coffee, she raced for the bathroom. Which only made her more nervous. Was she barfing because she was panicking or was this morning sickness? Good Lord.

What if this was morning sickness?

Oh, God—what if she was…?

No, she couldn't even think it. Because if she was…

Oh, God.

What was she going to do?

Ten

"Anything else?" Zeb asked Daniel.

Daniel shook his head. "The sooner we know what the new beers are going to be, the sooner we'll be able to get started on the marketing."

Zeb nodded. "I've been getting regular status updates from Casey, but I'll check in with her again."

Which wasn't exactly the truth. He had been asking for regular status updates, and like a good employee, Casey had been replying to him. The emails were short and getting shorter all the time. He was pretty sure that the last one had been two words. *Nothing yet.* He could almost hear her sneering them. And he could definitely hear her going, *What do you want from me?*

Truthfully, he wasn't sure. Each time he sent her an email asking for a status report, he wondered if maybe he shouldn't do something else. Ask her how she was doing, ask if things were better now that she'd hired new people.

Ask her if she'd been to many more baseball games. If she'd caught any more foul balls.

He wanted to know if she ever thought of him outside the context of beer and the brewery. If he ever drifted through her dreams like she did his.

"Well, let me know. If you thought it would help," Daniel said as he stood and began to gather his things, "I could go talk to her about the production schedule myself."

"No," Zeb said too quickly. Daniel paused and shot him a hard look. "I mean, that won't be necessary. Your time is too valuable."

For a long, painful moment, Daniel didn't say anything. "Is there something I need to know?" he asked in a voice that was too silky for its own good.

God, no. No one needed to know about that moment of insanity that still haunted him. "Absolutely not."

It was clear that Daniel didn't buy this—but he also decided not to press it. "If it becomes something I need to know about, you'll tell me, right?"

Zeb knew that Daniel had been a political consultant, even something of a fixer—more than willing to roll around in the mud if it meant getting his opponent dirty, too. The thought of Daniel doing any digging into Casey's life made Zeb more than a little uncomfortable. Plus, he had no desire to give Daniel anything he could hold over Zeb's head. This was clearly one case where sharing was not caring, brotherly bonds of love be damned.

"Certainly," Zeb said with confidence because he was certain this was not a situation Daniel needed to know anything about. His one moment of indiscretion would remain just that—a moment.

"Right," Daniel said. With that, he turned and walked out of the office.

Zeb did the same thing he'd been doing for weeks now—he sent a short email to Casey asking for a status report.

She was exactly as she had been before their indiscretion. Terse and borderline snippy, but she got the job done and done well. He had been at the brewery for only about five weeks. And in that short amount of time, Casey had already managed to goose production up by another five hundred gallons. Imagine what she could do if she ever figured out the mystery that was apparently tank fifteen.

Then, just like he did every time he thought about Casey and the night that hadn't been a date, he forced himself to stop thinking about her. Really, it shouldn't have been this hard to not think about her. Maybe it was the brewery, he reasoned. For so long, taking his rightful place as the CEO of the Beaumont Brewery had occupied his every waking thought. And now he'd achieved that goal. Clearly, his mind was just at…loose ends. That was all.

This did not explain why when his intercom buzzed, he was pricing tickets to the next Rockies home game. The seats directly behind Casey's were available.

"Mr. Richards?" Delores's voice crackled over the old-fashioned speaker.

"Yes?" He quickly closed the browser tab.

"Ms. Johnson is here." There was a bit of mumbling in the background that he didn't understand. "She says she has a status report for you."

Well. This was something new. It had been—what— a little over three weeks since he'd last seen her? And also, she had waited to be announced by Delores? That wasn't like her. The Casey Johnson he knew would have stormed into this office and caught him looking at baseball tickets. She would've known exactly what he was thinking, too.

So something was off. "Send her in." And then he braced for the worst.

Had she gotten another job? And if so...

If she didn't work for him anymore, would it be unethical to ask her out?

He didn't get any further than that in his thinking, because the door opened and she walked in. Zeb stood, but instantly, he could see that something was wrong. Instead of the sweaty hot mess that she frequently was during work hours, she looked pale. Her eyes were huge and for some reason, he thought she looked scared. What the hell was she scared of? Not him, that much he knew. She had never once been scared of him. And it couldn't be the last email he'd sent, either. There hadn't been anything unusual about that—it was the same basic email he'd been sending for weeks now.

"What's wrong?" He said the moment the door shut behind her.

She didn't answer right away.

"Casey?" He came out from around the desk and began to walk to her.

"I have..." Her voice shook and it just worried him all the more. She swallowed and tried again. "I have a status report for you."

She was starting to freak him out. "Is everything okay? Was there an on-the-job accident?" He tried to smile. "Did tank fifteen finally blow up?"

She tried to smile, too. He felt the blood drain out of his face at the sight of that awful grimace.

"No," she said in a voice that was a pale imitation of her normal tone. "That's not what I have a status report about."

Okay. Good. Nothing had happened on the line. "Is this about the beers?"

She shook her head, a small movement. "They're still in process. I think the porter is going to be really good."

"Excellent." He waited because there had to be a reason she was here. "Was there something else?"

Her eyes got even wider. She swallowed again. "I—"

And then the worst thing that could have possibly happened did—she squeezed her eyes shut tight and a single tear trickled down her left cheek.

It was physically painful to watch that tear. He wanted to go to her and pull her into his arms and promise that whatever had happened, he'd take care of it.

But they were at work and Delores was sitting just a few feet away. So he pushed his instincts aside. He was her boss. Nothing more. "Yes?"

The seconds ticked by while he waited. It wasn't like whatever she was trying to tell him was the end of the world, was it?

And then it was.

"I'm pregnant," she said in a shattered voice.

He couldn't even blink as his brain tried to process what she had just said. "Pregnant?" he asked as if he had never heard the word before.

She nodded. "I don't understand... I mean, I'm on the Pill—or I was. I didn't miss any. This isn't supposed to happen." Her chin quivered and another tear spilled over and ran down the side of her face.

Pregnant. She was pregnant. "And I'm the…" He couldn't even say it. *Hell.*

She nodded again. "I hadn't been with anyone in over a year." She looked up at him. "You believe me, right?"

He didn't want to. The entire thing was unbelievable. What the hell did he know about fatherhood? Nothing, that's what. Not a single damned thing. He'd been raised by a single mother, by a collective of women in a beauty shop. His male role models had been few and far between.

He wasn't going to be a father. Not on purpose and not by accident.

In that moment, another flash of anger hit him—but not at her. He was furious with himself. He never lost control. He never got so carried away with a woman that he couldn't even make sure that he followed the basic protocols of birth control. Except for one time.

And one time was all it took, apparently.

"You're sure?" Because this was the sort of thing that one needed to be sure about.

She nodded again. "I realized yesterday morning that I was at the end of my month of pills and I hadn't had my…" She blushed. Somehow, in the midst of a discussion about one-night stands and pregnancy, she still had the ability to look innocent. "After work yesterday, I bought a test. It was positive." Her voice cracked on that last, important word.

Positive.

Of all the words in the English language that had the potential to change his life, he had never figured *positive* would be the one to actually do it.

"We…" He cleared his throat. *We.* There was now a *we.* "We can't talk about this. Here." He looked around the office—his father's office. The man who had gotten his mother pregnant and paid her to leave town. "During work hours."

She looked ill. "Right. Sorry. I didn't mean to use work hours for personal business."

Dimly, he was glad to see that she still had her attitude. "We'll…we'll meet. Tonight. I can come to you."

"No," she said quickly.

"Right." She didn't want him back in her apartment, where he'd gotten carried away and gotten her into this mess. He wanted to use a less painful word—*situation, predicament*—but this was a straight-up mess. "Come to my place. At seven." She already knew where he lived. Hell, her father had done work in his house at some point.

"I don't… Jamal," she said weakly.

"Come on, Casey. We have to have this conversation somewhere and I'm sure as hell not going to have it in public. Not when you look like you're about to start sobbing and I can't even think straight."

Her eyes narrowed and he instantly regretted his words. "Of course. It's unfortunate that this upsets me," she said in a voice that could freeze fire.

"That's not what I—"

She held up her hand. "Fine. Seven, your place." She gave him a hard look—which was undercut by her scrubbing at her face with the heel of her hand. "All I ask is that you not have Jamal around." She turned and began to walk out of his office.

For some reason, he couldn't let her go. "Casey?"

She paused, her hand on the doorknob. But she didn't turn around. "What?"

"Thank you for telling me. I'm sure we can work something out."

She glanced back at him, disappointment all over her

face. "Work something out," she murmured. "Well. I guess we know what kind of Beaumont you are."

Before Zeb could ask her what the hell she meant by that, she was gone.

Eleven

"Hey, baby boy."

At the sound of his mother's voice, something un-clenched in Zeb's chest. He'd screwed up—but he knew it'd work out. "Hey, Mom. Sorry to interrupt you."

"You've been quiet out there," she scolded. "Those Beaumonts giving you any trouble?"

"No." The silence had been deafening, almost. But he couldn't think about that other family right now. "It's just been busy. Taking over the company is a massive undertaking." Which was the truth. Taking over the Beaumont Brewery was easily the hardest thing he'd ever done. No, right now he had to focus on his own family. "Mom…"

She was instantly on high alert. "What's wrong?"

There wasn't a good way to have this conversation. "I'm going to be a father."

Emily Richards was hard to stun. She'd heard it all,

done it all—but for a long moment, she was shocked into silence. "A baby? I'm going to be a *grandma*?"

"Yeah." Zeb dropped his head into his hands. He hadn't wanted to tell her—but he'd needed to.

This was history repeating itself. "Just like my old man, huh?"

He expected her to go off on Hardwick Beaumont, that lying, cheating bastard who'd left her high and dry. But she didn't. "You gonna buy this girl off?"

"Of course not, Mom. Come on." He didn't know what to do—but he knew what he didn't want to happen. And he didn't want to put Casey aside or buy her off.

"Are you going to take this baby away from her?"

"That's not funny." But he knew she wasn't joking. Hardwick had either paid off his babies' mothers or married and divorced them, always keeping custody.

"Baby boy…" She sighed, a sound that was disappointment and hope all together. "I want to know my grandbaby—and her mother." Zeb couldn't think of what to say. He couldn't think, period. His mother went on, "Be better than your father, Zeb. I think you know what you need to do."

Which was how Zeb wound up at a jewelry store. He couldn't hope to make sense of what Casey had told him that morning but he knew enough to realize that he hadn't handled himself well.

Actually, no, that was letting himself off easy. In reality, he hadn't handled himself well since…the ball game. If he had realized that her getting pregnant was a legitimate outcome instead of a distant possibility…

He wanted to think that he wouldn't have slept with her. But at the very least, he wouldn't have walked out of her apartment with that disappointed sigh of hers lingering in his ears.

He'd hurt her then. He'd pissed her off today. He might not be an expert in women, but even he knew that the best solution here was diamonds.

The logic was sound. However, the fact that the diamonds he was looking at were set into engagement rings…

He was going to be a father. This thought kept coming back to him over and over again. What did he know about being a father? Nothing.

His own father had paid his mother to make sure that he never had to look at Zeb and acknowledge him as a son. Hardwick Beaumont might have been a brilliant businessman, but there was no way around the obvious fact that he'd been a terrible person. Or maybe he'd been a paragon of virtue in every area of his life except when it came to his mistresses—Emily Richards and Daniel's mother and CJ's and God only knew how many mothers of other illegitimate children.

"Let me see that one," he said to the clerk behind the counter, pointing to a huge pear-cut diamond with smaller diamonds set in the band.

Because this was where he'd come to in his life. He was going to be a father. He'd made that choice when he'd slept with Casey. Now he had to take responsibility.

He did not want to be a father like Hardwick had been. Zeb didn't want to hide any kid of his away, denying him his birthright. If he had a child, he was going to claim that child. He was going to fight for that child, damn it all, just like his father should have fought for him. His mother wanted to know her grandbaby.

He didn't want to have to fight Casey, though. Because the simplest way to stay in his child's life was to marry the mother.

Because, really, what were the alternatives?

He could struggle through custody agreements and legal arrangements—all of which would be fodder for gossip rags. He could pretend he hadn't slept with his brewmaster and put his own child through the special kind of hell that was a childhood divorced from half his heritage. He could do what Hardwick had done and cut a check to ensure his kid was well cared for—and nothing more.

Or he could ask Casey to marry him. Tonight. It would be sudden and out of left field and she might very well say no.

Married. He'd never seen himself married. But then, he'd never seen himself as a father, either. One fifteen-minute conversation this afternoon and suddenly he was an entirely different person, one he wasn't sure he recognized. He stared at the engagement ring, but he was seeing a life where he and Casey were tied together both by a child and by law.

No, not just that. By more than that. There was more between them than just a baby. So much more.

He'd spend his days with her watching baseball and discussing beer and—hopefully—having great sex. And the kid—he knew Casey would be good with the kid. She'd be the kind of mom who went to practices and games. She'd be fun, hands-on.

As for Zeb...

Well, he had two different businesses to run. He had to work. He'd made a fortune—but fortunes could be lost as fast as they'd been made. He'd seen it happen. And he couldn't let it happen to him. More than that, he couldn't let it happen to Casey. To their family.

He had to take care of them. Hardwick Beaumont had cut Emily Richards a check and the money had been enough to take care of him when he'd been a baby—but it hadn't lasted forever. His mother had needed to work to make ends meet. She'd worked days, nights, weekends.

There had been times when Zeb wondered if she was avoiding him. Emily Richards had always been happy to foist child care off on the other stylists and the customers. No one minded, but there'd been times he'd just wanted his mom and she'd been too busy.

He couldn't fault her drive. She was a self-made woman. But she'd put her business ahead of him, her own son. Even now, Zeb had trouble talking to her without feeling like he was imposing upon her time.

He didn't want that for his child. He wanted more for his family. He didn't want his baby's mother to miss out on all the little things that made up a childhood. He didn't want to miss them, either—but not only was the brewery his legacy, it would be his child's, as well. He *couldn't* let the brewery slide.

He'd work hard, as he always had. But he would be there. Part of his child's life. Maybe every once in a while, he'd even make it for a game or a play or whatever kids did in school. And he'd have Casey by his side.

"I'll take it," he said, even though he wasn't sure what he was looking at anymore. But he'd take that life, with Casey and their child.

"It's a beautiful piece." A deep voice came from his side.

Zeb snapped out of his reverie and turned to find himself face-to-face with none other than Chadwick Beaumont. For a long moment, Zeb did nothing but stare. It wasn't like looking in a mirror. Chadwick was white, with sandy blond hair that he wore a little long and floppy. But despite that, there were things Zeb recognized—the jaw-line and the eyes.

Zeb's green eyes had marked him as different in the African American community. But here? Here, stand-ing with this man he had never seen up close before, his eyes marked him as something else. They marked him as one of the Beaumonts.

Chadwick stuck out his hand. "I'm Chadwick."

"Zeb," he said, operating on autopilot as his hand went out to give Chadwick's a firm shake. "And who's this?" he asked, trying to smile at the little girl Chad-wick was holding.

"This is my daughter, Catherine."

Zeb studied the little girl. She couldn't be more than a year and a half old. "Hi there, Catherine," he said softly. He looked at Chadwick. "I didn't realize I was an uncle." The idea seemed so foreign to him that it was almost unrecognizable.

The little girl turned her face away and into Chad-wick's neck—then, a second later, she turned back, peek-ing at Zeb through thick lashes.

"You are—Byron has two children. Technically, Catherine is my wife's daughter from a previous re-lationship. But I've adopted her." Chadwick patted his daughter on her back. "I found that, when it comes to being a Beaumont, it's best to embrace a flexible defi-nition of the word *family*."

An awkward silence grew between them because Zeb didn't quite know what to say to that. He'd always thought that, at some point, he would confront the Beau-monts. In his mind's eye, the confrontation was not nearly this...polite. There wouldn't be any chitchat. He would revel in what he had done, taking the company

away from them and punishing them for failing to acknowledge him and they would…cower or beg for forgiveness. Or something.

There was a part of him that still wanted that—but
not in the middle of a high-end jewelry store and not in
front of a toddler.

So instead, he didn't say anything. He had no idea
what he was even supposed to say as he looked at this
man who shared his eyes.

Suddenly, Zeb desperately wanted to know what kind
of man this brother of his was. More specifically, he
wanted to know what kind of man Casey thought Chadwick was. Because Zeb still didn't know if he was like
his father or his brother and he needed to know.

"Who's the lucky woman?" Chadwick asked.

"Excuse me?"

Just then the clerk came back with the small bag that
held an engagement ring. Chadwick smiled. "The ring.
Anyone I know?"

It took a lot to make Zeb blush, but right then his face
got hot. Instead of responding, he went on the offensive.
"What about you?"

Chadwick smiled again, but this time it softened everything about his face. Zeb recognized that look—and
it only got stronger when Chadwick leaned down and
pressed a kiss to the top of his daughter's head. It was
the look of love. "My wife is expecting again and the
pregnancy has been…tiring. I'm picking her up something because, really, there's nothing else I can do and
diamonds tend to make everything better. Wouldn't you
agree?"

"Congratulations," Zeb said automatically. But he
didn't tell this man that he'd had the exact same thought.
He only hoped he wasn't wrong about the diamonds.

"Will there be anything else?" The clerk asked in a super-perky voice.

Zeb and Chadwick turned to see her looking at them with bright eyes and a wide smile. Crap. He needed to have a conversation with Chadwick—even if he wasn't exactly sure what the conversation should be about. But it couldn't happen here. How much longer before someone put two and two together and there were cameras or news crews and reporters or cell-phone-toting gossipmongers crowding them? Zeb didn't want to deal with it himself—he couldn't imagine that Chadwick wanted to put his daughter through it, either.

"No," he said just as another clerk approached and handed a small bag to Chadwick.

"Your necklace, Mr. Beaumont," the second clerk said. She and the first clerk stood elbow to elbow, grinning like loons.

They had to get out of here right now. "Would you like to…" *continue this conversation elsewhere?* But he didn't even get that far before Chadwick gave a quick nod of his head.

Both men picked up their small bags and headed out of the store. When they were safely away from the eager clerks, Zeb bit the bullet and asked first. "Would you like to go get a drink or something?"

"I wish I could," Chadwick said in a regretful voice. "But I don't think any conversation we have should be in public. And besides," he went on, switching his daughter to his other arm, "we probably only have another half an hour before we have a meltdown."

"Sure," Zeb said, trying to keep the disappointment out of his voice.

Chadwick stopped, which made Zeb stop, too. "You want answers." It was not a question.

Yes. "I don't want to intrude on your family time."

Chadwick stared at Zeb for a moment longer and his face cracked with the biggest smile that Zeb had ever seen. "You *are* family, Zeb."

That simple statement made Zeb feel as if someone had just gut-shot him. It took everything he had not to double over. This man considered *him* family? There was such a sense of relief that appeared out of nowhere—

But at the same time, Zeb was angry. If he was family, why hadn't Chadwick seen fit to inform him of that before now? Why had he waited until a chance meeting in a jewelry store, for God's sake?

Chadwick's eyes cut behind Zeb's shoulder. "We need to keep moving." He began walking again and Zeb had no choice but to follow. They headed out toward the parking lot.

Finally, Zeb asked, "How long have you known? About me, I mean."

"About six years. After my…" He winced. "I mean *our* father—"

Zeb cut him off. "He wasn't my father. Not really."

Chadwick nodded. "After Hardwick died," he went on diplomatically, "it took me a while to stabilize the company and get my bearings. I'd always heard rumors about other children and when I finally got to the point where I had a handle on the situation, I hired an investigator."

"Did you know about Daniel before the press conference?"

Chadwick nodded. "And Carlos."

That brought Zeb up short. CJ was not as unfindable as he liked to think he was. "He prefers CJ."

Chadwick smirked. "Duly noted. And of course, we already knew about Matthew. There was actually a bit of a break after that. I don't know if Hardwick got tired of paying off his mistresses or what."

"Are there more of us? Because I could only find the other two."

Chadwick nodded again. "There are a few that are still kids. The youngest is thirteen. I'm in contact with his mother, but she has decided that she's not interested in introducing her son to the family. I provide a monthly stipend—basically, I pay child support for the other three children." They reached a fancy SUV with darkened windows. "It seems like the least I can do, after everything Hardwick did." He opened up the back door and slid his daughter into the seat.

As he buckled in the little girl, Zeb stared at Chadwick in openmouthed shock. "You...you pay child support? For your half siblings?"

"They are family," Chadwick said simply as he clicked the buckle on the child seat. He straightened and turned to face Zeb. But he didn't add anything else. He just waited.

Family. It was such an odd concept to him. He had a family—his mother and the larger community that had orbited around her salon. He had Jamal. And now, whether she liked it or not, he had Casey, too.

"Why didn't you contact me?" He had so many questions, but that one was first. Chadwick was taking care of the other bastards. Why not him?

"By the time I found you, we were both in our thirties. You'd built up your business on your own, and at the time, I didn't think you wanted anything to do with us." Chadwick shrugged. "I didn't realize until later how wrong I was."

"What kind of man was he?" Zeb asked. And he felt wrong, somehow, asking it—but he needed to know.

He was getting a very good idea of what kind of man Chadwick was—loyal, dependable, the kind of man who would pay child support for his siblings because they were family, whether they liked it or not. The kind of man who not only cared about his wife but bought her diamonds because she was tired. The kind of man who knew how to put his own daughter into a safety seat.

Zeb knew he couldn't be like Chadwick, but he was beginning to understand what Casey meant when she asked if Zeb was like his brother.

Chadwick sighed and looked up at the sky. It was getting late, but the sun was still bright. "Why don't you come back to the house? This isn't the sort of thing that we can discuss in a parking lot."

Zeb just stared at the man. His brother. Chadwick had made the offer casually, as if it were truly no big deal. Zeb was family and family should come home and have a beer. Simple.

But it wasn't. Nothing about this was simple.

Zeb held up his small jewelry bag with the engagement ring that he somehow had to convince Casey to wear. "I have something to do at seven." He braced himself for Chadwick to ask about who the lucky woman was again, but the question didn't come.

Instead, Chadwick answered Zeb's earlier question. "Hardwick Beaumont…" He sighed and closed the door, as if he were trying to shield his daughter from the truth. "He was a man of contradictions—but then again, I'm sure we all are." He paused. "He was… For me, he was hard. He was a hard man. He was a perfectionist and when I couldn't give him perfection…" Chadwick grimaced.

"Was he violent?"

"He could be. But I think that was just with me, because I was his heir. He ignored Phillip almost completely, but then Frances—his first daughter—he spoiled her in every sense of the word." Chadwick tried to smile, but it looked like a thing of pain. "You asked me why I hadn't contacted you earlier—well, the truth is, I think I was a little jealous of you."

"What?" Surely, Zeb hadn't heard correctly. Surely, his brother, the heir of the Beaumont fortune, had not just said that he was—

"Jealous," Chadwick confirmed. "I'm not exaggerating when I say that Hardwick screwed us all up. I..." He took a deep breath and stared up at the night sky again. "He was my father, so I couldn't hate him, but I don't think I loved him, either. And I don't think he loved us. Certainly not me. So when I found out about you and the others, how you'd spent your whole lives without Hardwick standing over you, threatening and occasionally hitting you, I was jealous. You managed to make yourself into a respected businessman on your own. You did what you wanted—not what *he* wanted. It's taken me most of my life to separate out what I want from what he demanded."

Zeb was having trouble processing this information. "And I spent years trying to get what you have," he said, feeling numb. Years of believing that he had been cut out of his rightful place next to Hardwick Beaumont. It had never occurred to him that perhaps he didn't want to be next to Hardwick Beaumont.

Because he could see in Chadwick's eyes that this was the truth. His father had been a terrible man. Sure, Zeb had known that—a good man did not buy off his mistress and send her packing. A good man did not pretend like he didn't have multiple children hidden away. A good man took care of his family, no matter what.

Zeb suddenly had no idea if he was a good man or not. He took care of his mother, even when she drove him nuts, and he looked out for Jamal, the closest thing he'd had to a brother growing up.

But the Beaumonts were his family, too. Instead of looking out for them, he'd done everything he could to undermine them.

He realized Chadwick was staring. "I'm sorry," Chadwick said quickly. "You look like him."

Zeb snorted. "I look like my mother."

"I know." Chadwick moved a hand, as if he were going to pat Zeb on the shoulder—but he didn't. Instead, he dropped his arm back to his side. Then he waited. Zeb appreciated the silence while he tried to put his thoughts in order.

He knew he was running out of time. Chadwick's daughter would sit quietly for only so long—either that, or someone with a camera would show up. But he had so many questions. And he wasn't even sure that the answers would make it better.

For the first time in his life, he wasn't sure that knowing more was a good thing.

"I don't know how much of it was PR," Chadwick suddenly began. "But the press conference was brilliant and I wanted to let you know that we're glad to see that the brewery is back in family hands."

Really? But Zeb didn't let his surprise at this statement show. "We're still competitors," he replied. "Casey is formulating a line of beers to compete directly with Percheron Drafts as we speak."

Chadwick notched an eyebrow at him. "She'll be brilliant at it," he said, but with more caution in his voice. Too late, Zeb realized that he had spoken of her with too much familiarity. "And I expect nothing less—from both of you."

Inside the car, the little girl fussed. "I have to get going," Chadwick said, and this time, he did clap Zeb on the shoulder. "Come to the house sometime. We'll have dinner. Serena would love to meet you."

Zeb assumed that was Chadwick's wife. "What about the rest of your brothers and sisters?"

"You mean *our* brothers and sisters. They're...curious, shall we say. But getting all of us together in one room can be overwhelming. Besides, Serena was my executive assistant at the brewery. She knows almost as much about the place as I do."

Zeb stared at him. "You married your assistant?" Because that seemed odd, somehow. This seemed like something their father would've done. Well, maybe not the marrying part.

Had his brother gotten his assistant pregnant and then married her? Was history repeating itself? Was it possible for history to repeat itself even if Zeb hadn't known what that history was?

Chadwick gave him a look that might've intimidated a lesser man. But not Zeb. "I try not to be my father," he said in a voice that was colder than Zeb had heard yet. "But it seemed to be a family trait—falling for our employees. I married my assistant. Phillip married a horse trainer he hired. Frances married the last CEO of the brewery."

Oh, God. Had he somehow managed to turn into his father without ever even knowing a single thing about the man? He had gotten Casey pregnant because when he was around her, he couldn't help himself. She'd taken all of his prized control and blown it to smithereens, just as if she'd been blowing foam off a beer.

"Hardwick Beaumont is dead," Chadwick said with finality. "He doesn't have any more power over me, over any of us." He looked down at the small bag Zeb still clutched in his hand. "We are known for our control—both having it and losing it. But it's not the control that defines us. It's how we deal with the consequences."

Inside the car, the toddler started to cry in earnest. "Come by sometime," Chadwick said as he stuck out his hand. "I look forward to seeing how you turn the brewery around."

"I will," Zeb said as they shook hands.

"If you have any other questions, just ask."

Zeb nodded and stood aside as Chadwick got into his vehicle and drove away—back to the family home, to his assistant and their children. Back to where he could be his own man, without having to prove anything to his father ever again.

Hardwick Beaumont was dead. Suddenly, years of plotting and planning, watching and waiting for an opportunity to take revenge against the Beaumonts—was it all for nothing?

Because Zeb wasn't sure he wanted revenge—not on his brothers. Not anymore. How could he? If they'd known of him for only six years—hell, six years ago, Zeb had been just moving to New York, just taking ZOLA to the next level. What would he have done, six years ago? He wouldn't have given up ZOLA. He would've been suspicious of any overtures that Chadwick might've made. He wouldn't have wanted to put himself in a position where any Beaumont had power over him. And then he wouldn't have been in a position to take the brewery back from the corporation that bought it.

And now? Now Chadwick wanted him to succeed?

Even though they were competitors—and nowhere near friends—he hoped that Zeb would turn the brewery around?

It was damned hard to get revenge against a dead man. And Zeb wasn't sure he wanted revenge against the living.

He looked down at the small bag with an engagement ring in it.

What did he want?

Twelve

What did she want?

Casey had been asking herself that exact question for hours now. And the answer hadn't changed much.

She had no idea.

Well, that wasn't entirely the truth. What she wanted was... God, it sounded so silly, even in her head. But she wanted something romantic to happen. The hell of it was, she didn't know exactly what that was. She wanted Zeb to pull her into his arms and promise that everything was going to be all right. And not just the general promise, either. She wanted specific promises. He was going to take care of her and the baby. He was going to be a good father. He was going to be...

Seriously, they didn't have a whole lot of a relationship here. She didn't even know if she wanted to have a relationship—beyond the one that centered around a child, of course. Sometimes she did and sometimes she didn't. He was so gorgeous—too gorgeous. Zeb wasn't the kind of guy she normally went for; he was cool and smooth. Plus, he was a Beaumont. As a collective, they weren't known for being the most faithful of husbands.

That was unfair to Chadwick. But it wasn't unfair enough to Hardwick.

Fidelity aside, she had absolutely no idea if Zeb could be the kind of father she wanted her child to have. It wasn't that her own father, Carl Johnson, was perfect—he wasn't. But he cared. He had *always* cared for Casey, fighting for her and protecting her and encouraging her to do things that other people wouldn't have supported.

That was what she wanted. She wanted to do that for her and for this child.

Based on Zeb's reaction in the office earlier? She didn't have a lot of faith.

Casey had not been the best of friends with Chadwick Beaumont. They had been coworkers who got along well, and he'd never seen her as anything more than one of the guys. Which was fine. But she knew all of the office gossip—he had fallen in love with his assistant just as Serena Chase had gotten pregnant with someone else's baby. He had given up the company for her and adopted the baby girl as his own. Hell, even Ethan Logan—who had not understood a damned thing about beer—had given up the company for Frances Beaumont because they'd fallen in love.

Zeb's entire reason for being in Denver was the brewery.

Besides, she didn't want him to give it up. In fact, she preferred not to give it up, either. She had no idea what the company's maternity-leave policy looked like, though. She didn't know if Larry could handle the production lines while she was away. And after the leave was over, she didn't know how she would be a working mother with a newborn.

She didn't know if she would have to make it work herself or if she'd have help. And she still didn't know what she wanted that help to look like. But she didn't want to give up her job. She'd worked years to earn her place at the brewery's table. She loved being a brewmaster. It was who she was.

She was running a little bit late by the time she made it to the mansion where Zeb had set up shop. As she got out of her car, she realized her hands were shaking. Okay, everything was shaking. Was it too early to start blaming things on hormones? God, she had no idea. She hadn't spent a lot of time around babies and small children growing up. Other girls got jobs as babysitters. She went to work as an electrical assistant for her father. Small children were a mystery to her.

Oh, God. And now she was going to have one.

Stuck in this tornado of thoughts, she rang the bell. She knew she needed to tell Zeb what she wanted. Hadn't she resolved that she was going to do better at that? Okay, that resolution had been specifically about sex— but the concept held. Men were not mind readers. She needed to tell him what she wanted to happen here.

All she had to do in the next thirty seconds was figure out what that was.

It wasn't even thirty seconds before the door opened and there stood Zeb, looking nothing like the CEO she'd seen in the office just a few hours ago. But he didn't look like the sports fan that she'd gone on an almost date with, either. He was something in the middle. His loose-fitting black T-shirt hinted at his muscles, instead of clinging to them. It made him look softer. Easier to be around. God, how she needed him to be easier right now.

"Hi," she croaked. She cleared her throat and tried to smile.

"Come in," he said in a gentle voice. Which was, all things considered, a step up from this morning's reaction.

He shut the door behind her and then led her through the house. It was massive, a maze of rooms and parlors and stairs. He led her to a room that could best be described as a study—floor-to-ceiling bookcases, a plush Persian rug, heavy leather furniture and a fireplace. It was ornate, in a manly sort of way. And, thankfully, it was empty.

Zeb shut the door behind her and then they were alone. She couldn't bring herself to sit—she had too much nervous energy. She forced herself to stand in the middle of the room. "This is nice."

"Jamal can take the credit." Zeb gave her a long look and then he walked toward her. She hadn't actually seen him for several weeks—outside of this morning, of course. Was it possible she had forgotten how intense it was being in Zeb Richards's sights? "How are you?" he asked as he got near.

"Well, I'm pregnant."

He took another step closer and she tensed. Right about now it would be great if she could figure out what she wanted. "I don't mean this to sound callous," he said, lifting his hands in what looked a hell of a lot like surrender, "but I thought you said you were on the Pill?"

"I am. I mean, I was. I diagnosed myself via the internet—these things can…happen. It's something called breakthrough ovulation, apparently." He was another step closer and even though neither of them were making any broad declarations of love, her body was responding to his nearness all the same.

She could feel a prickle of heat starting low on her back and working its way up to her neck. Her cheeks were flushing and, God help her, all she wanted was for him to wrap his arms around her and tell her that everything was going to be all right.

And then, amazingly, that was exactly what happened. Zeb reached her and folded his strong arms around her and pulled her against the muscles of his chest and held her. "These things just happen, huh?"

With a sigh, she sank into his arms. This probably wasn't a good idea. But then, anything involving her touching Zeb Richards was probably a bad idea. Because once she started touching him, it was just too damn hard to stop. "Yeah."

"I'm sorry it happened to you."

She needed to hear that—but what killed her was the sincerity in his voice. Her eyes began to water. Oh, no—she didn't want to cry. She wasn't a crier. Really. She was definitely going to blame that one on the hormones.

"What are we going to do?" she asked. "I haven't seen you in weeks. We had one almost date and everything about it was great except that it ended...awkwardly. And since then..."

"Since then," he said as she could feel his voice rumbling deep out of his chest. It shouldn't have been soothing, dammit. She wanted to keep her wits about her, but he was lulling her into a sense of warmth and security. "Since then I've thought of you constantly. I wanted to see you but I got the feeling you might not have reciprocated that desire."

What? "Is that why you've been sending me emails every day?" She leaned back and looked up at him. "Asking for status reports?"

Oh, God, that blush was going to be the death of her. If there was one thing she knew, it was that an adorable Zeb Richards was an irresistible Zeb Richards. "You said at work that it was all about the beer. So I was trying to keep it professional."

Even as he said it, though, he was backing her up until they reached one of the overstuffed leather couches. Then he was pulling her down onto his lap and curling his arms around her and holding her tight. "But we're not at work right now, are we?"

She sighed into him. "No, we're not. We can't even claim that this is a corporate outing."

He chuckled and ran his hand up and down her back. She leaned into his touch because it was what she wanted. And she hadn't even had to ask for it. She let herself relax into him and wrapped her arms around his neck. "What are we going to do, Zeb?"

His hand kept moving up and down and he began rubbing his other hand along the side of her thigh. "I'm going to take care of you," he said, his voice soft and close to her ear.

God, it was what she needed to hear. She knew she was strong and independent. She lived her life on her own terms. She'd gotten the job she wanted and a nice place close to the ballpark. She paid her bills on time and managed to sock some away for retirement.

But this? Suddenly, her life was not exactly her own anymore and she didn't know how to deal with it.

"There's something between us," Zeb said, his breath caressing her cheek. She turned her face toward him. "I feel it. When I'm around you..." He cupped her face in his hands. "I could fall for you."

Her heart began to pound. "I feel it, too," she whispered, her lips moving against his. "I'm not supposed to go for someone like you. You're my boss and everything about this is wrong. So why can't I help myself?"

"I don't know. But I don't think I want you to."

And then he was kissing her. Unlike the first time, which had been hurried and frantic, this was everything she dreamed a kiss could be. Slowly, his lips moved over hers as he kissed the corner of her mouth and then ran his tongue along her lower lip.

If she'd been able to help herself, she wouldn't have opened her lips for him, wouldn't have drawn his tongue into her mouth, wouldn't have run her hands over his hair. If she'd been able to help herself at all, she wouldn't have moaned into his mouth when he nipped at her lip, her neck, her earlobe.

"I want you in a bed this time," he said when she skimmed her hands over his chest and went to grab the hem of his shirt. "I want to strip you bare and lay you out and I want to show you exactly what I can do for you."

"Yes," she gasped. And then she gasped again when he stood, lifting her in his arms as if she weighed next to nothing.

"Casey," he said as he stood there, holding her. His gaze stroked over her face. "Have I ever told you how beautiful you are?"

Thirteen

Whatever he'd just said, he needed to make sure he said it again. Often.

Because suddenly, Casey was all over him. She kissed him with so much passion he almost had to sit down on the couch again so he could strip her shirt off her and sink into her soft body and...

He slammed on the brakes. That wasn't what he'd promised her. Bed. He needed to get to a bed. And at the rate they were going, he needed to get there quickly.

It would be so tempting to get lost in her body. She had that ability, to make him lose himself. But it was different now. Everything was different. She was carrying his child. This wasn't about mindless pleasure, not anymore.

It wasn't like he wanted to be thinking about Chadwick Beaumont right now, but even as he carried Casey out of the office and up the wide staircase to his suite of rooms, he couldn't stop replaying some of the things his brother had said.

Casey took Zeb's hard-won control and blew it to smithereens, but that wasn't what made him a Beaumont. It was what he did after that.

He could turn her away. He could set her up with a monthly stipend and let her raise their child, just as Chadwick was doing with some of their half siblings.

But that was what his father would do. And Zeb knew now that he did not want to be like that man. And what was more, he didn't *have* to be like his father. He wasn't sure he could be as selfless as his brother was—but he didn't have to be that way, either.

He could be something else. Someone else. Someone who was both a Beaumont *and* a Richards.

A sense of rightness filled him. It was right that he take Casey to bed—a real bed this time. It was right that he make love to her tonight, tomorrow—maybe even for the rest of their lives. It was right that he become a part of the Beaumont family by *making* himself a part of it—both by finally taking his place as the head of the brewery and by starting his own family.

It was right to be here with Casey. To marry her and take care of her and their baby.

He kicked open the door to a suite of rooms and carried her through. Why was this house so damned big? Because he had to pass through another room and a half before he even got anywhere near his bed and each step was agony. He was rock hard and she was warm and soft against him and all he wanted to do was bury himself in her again and again.

Finally, he made it to his bed. Carefully, he set her down on top of the covers. He was burning for her as he lowered himself down on top of her—gently, this time. He knew that just because she was a few weeks along, didn't mean she was now some impossibly fragile, delicate flower who would snap if he looked at her wrong. But he wanted to treat her with care.

So, carefully, he slipped her T-shirt over her head. He smiled down at her plain beige bra. "No purple today?"

"I didn't wear my lucky bra, because I didn't think I was going to get lucky," she said in a husky voice. This time, when she grabbed at the hem of his shirt, he didn't stop her.

He wanted to take this slow, but when she ran her hands over his chest, her fingernails lightly grazing his nipples, she took what little self-control he had left and blew it away. Suddenly, he was undoing her jeans and yanking them off and she was grabbing his and trying to push them off his hips.

"Zeb…" she said, and he heard the need for him in her voice.

His blood was pounding in his veins—and other places—but he had to prove to her that he could be good for her. So instead of falling into her body, he knelt in front of the bed and, grabbing her by the hips, pulled her to the edge of it.

"I'm going to take care of you," he promised. He had never meant the words more than he did right now.

Last time, he hadn't even gotten her panties off her. Last time, he'd been more than a little selfish. This time, however, it was all about her.

He lowered his mouth to her sex and was rewarded as a ripple of tension moved through her body.

"Oh," she gasped as he spread her wide and kissed her again and again.

With each touch, her body spasmed around him. She ran her hand over his hair, heightening his awareness. Everything was about her. All he could see and taste and touch and smell and hear was her. Her sweetness was on his tongue and her moans were in his ears and her soft skin was under his hands.

Last time, he hadn't done this—taking the time to learn her. But this time? Every touch, every sigh, was a lesson—one he committed to memory.

This was right. The connection he felt with her—because that was what it was, a connection—it was something he'd never had before. He'd spent the last three weeks trying to ignore it, but he was done with that. He wasn't going to lie to himself anymore.

He wanted her. And by God, he was going to have her.

He slipped a finger inside her and her hips came off the bed as she cried out. "Zeb!"

"Let me show you what I can do for you," he murmured against her skin. "God, Casey—you're so beautiful."

"Yes, yes—don't stop!"

So he didn't. He stroked his tongue over her sex and his fingers into her body and told her again and again how beautiful she was, how good she felt around him. And the whole time, he got harder and harder until he wasn't sure he could make it. He needed her to let go so that he could let go.

Finally, he put his teeth against her sex—just a small nip, not a true bite. But that was what it took. Something a little bit raw and a little bit hard in the middle of something slow and sensual. She needed both.

Luckily, he could give her that. He could give her anything she wanted.

Her body tensed around him and her back came off the bed as the orgasm moved through her. Even he couldn't hold himself back anymore. The last of his control snapped and he let it carry him as he surged up onto the bed, between her legs. "You are so beautiful when you come," he said as he joined his body to hers.

Everything else fell away. His messy family history and their jobs, baseball and status reports—none of that mattered. All that mattered was that Casey was here with him and there was something between them and they couldn't fight it. Not anymore.

She cried out again as a second orgasm took her and he couldn't hold back anything else. His own climax took him and he slammed his mouth down over hers. If this was the rest of his life, he could be a happy man.

Suddenly exhausted, he collapsed onto her. She wrapped her arms around his back and held him to her. "Wow, Zeb," she murmured in his ear.

"I forgot to ask about birth control that time." She laughed at that, which made him smile. He managed to prop himself up on his elbows to look down at her. "Casey—" he said, but then he stopped because he suddenly realized he was about to tell her that he thought he was in love with her.

She stroked her fingertips over his cheek. "That..." she said, and he could hear the happiness in her voice. "That was everything I have ever dreamed." There was a pause. "And maybe a few things I hadn't thought of yet."

It was his turn to laugh. "Just think, after we're married, we get to do that every night." He withdrew from her body and rolled to the side, pulling her into his arms.

"What?" She didn't curl up in his arms like he thought she would.

"I'm going to take care of you," he told her again, pulling her into him. "I didn't have the chance to tell you, but I ran into Chadwick this afternoon and talking with him cleared up a couple of things for me."

"It...did?"

"It did. You've asked me if I'm like my father or my brother and I didn't know either of them. I only knew what was public knowledge. I knew that my father was not a good man, because he paid my mother to disappear. And I knew that everyone at the brewery liked Chadwick. But that didn't tell me what I needed to know."

"What did you need to know?" Her voice sounded oddly distant. Maybe she was tired from the sex?

That he could understand. His own eyelids were drifting shut but he forced himself to think for a bit longer. "When you asked me which one I was like, you were really asking me if I could be a good man. And not just a good man—a good man for you. I understand what that means now. You need someone who's loyal, who will take care of you and our child. You need someone who appreciates you the way you are."

Then she did curl into him. She slung her arm around his waist and held him tight. "Yes," she whispered against skin. "Yes, that's what I need."

"And that's what I want to give you." He disentangled himself long enough to reach over the side of the bed and retrieve his pants. He pulled out the small velvet-covered box with the ring inside. "I want to marry you and take care of you and our baby together. You won't have to struggle with being a single mother or worrying about making ends meet—I'll take care of all of that."

She stared at the box. "How do you mean?"

Was it his imagination or did she sound cautious? They were past that. He was all in. This was the right thing to do. He was stepping up and taking care of his own—her and their child.

"Obviously, we can't keep working together and you're going to need to take it easy. And your apartment was cute, but it's not big enough for the three of us." He hugged her. "I know I haven't talked about my childhood a lot—it was fine, but it was rough, too. My mom—she worked all the time and I basically lived at the salon, with a whole gaggle of employees watching over me. All I knew was that my dad didn't want me and my mom was working. And I don't want that kind of life for our baby. I don't want us to pass the baby off to employees or strangers. I want us to do this right."

"But…but I have to work, Zeb."

"No, you don't—don't you see? We'll get married and you can stay home—here. I'll take care of everything. We can be a family. And I can get to know Chadwick and his family—my family, I mean. All of the Beaumonts. I don't have to show them that I'm better than them. Because I think maybe…" He sighed. "Maybe they're going to accept me just the way I am, too."

He still couldn't believe that was possible. His whole life, he'd never felt completely secure in his own skin. He was either too light or too black, stuck in a no-man's-land in between.

But here in Denver? Chadwick wished him well and had invited him to be part of the family. And all Casey cared about was that he accepted her the exact same way he wanted to be accepted.

Finally, he had come home.

He opened the box and took the ring out. "Marry me, Casey. I know it's quick but I think it's the right thing."

She sat up and stared at him. "Wait— I— *Wait*."

He looked at her, confused. "What?"

A look of dawning horror crossed over her face—a look that was not what any man wanted to see after sex that good and a heartfelt offer of marriage. "You want to marry me so I can stay home and raise our kid?"

"Well…yes. I don't want to be the kind of father my own father was. I want to be part of my kid's life. I want to be part of your life. And I don't want you to struggle like my mom did. You mean too much to me to let that happen."

And then, suddenly, she was moving. She rolled out of the bed and away from him, gathering up her clothes.

"Are you serious?" she said, and he heard a decided note of panic in her voice. "That's not what I want."

"What do you mean, it's not what you want? I thought we agreed—there was something between us and you're pregnant and this makes sense."

"This does *not* make sense," she said as she angrily jabbed her legs into her jeans. "I am not about to quit my job so I can stay home and raise your baby."

"Casey—wait!" But she was already through the first door. She didn't even have a shirt on yet. She was running away as fast as she could.

Zeb threw himself out of bed, the engagement ring still in his hand. "Casey!" he called after her. "Talk to me, dammit. What is your problem here? I thought this would work. There's something here and I don't want to let that go." Unless...

Something new occurred to him. She had given him every indication that she wanted the baby, even if it was unexpected. But what if...?

What if she didn't? What if she didn't want to read stories at night and teach their kid how to ride a bike or throw a baseball? What if she didn't want to be the hands-on mom he'd imagined, coaching T-ball and playing in the park? The kind of mother he didn't have.

What if she was going to be like his mother—distant and reserved and...*bitter* about an unplanned pregnancy?

She swung around on him, her eyes blazing. "You don't know what you're talking about," she shot at him. The words sliced through the air like bullets out of a gun. "I don't want to quit my job. I've never wanted to be a stay-at-home mom."

"But you can't keep working," he told her, pushing against the rising panic in his chest. "You shouldn't have to."

That was the wrong thing to say. "I don't *have* to do anything I don't want to do. After I have this baby, I'm going to need help. If you think I'm going to give up my job and my life and fit myself into your world just because I'm pregnant with your baby, you've got another think coming."

She spun again and stalked away from him. "Casey!" He sprinted after her and managed to catch up to her—but only because she was trying to get her shirt on. "I'm trying to do the right thing here."

He was horrified to see tears spill over her eyelids. "Is this how it's going to be? Every time we're together, you make me feel so good—and then you ruin it. You just ruin it, Zeb." She scrubbed her hand across her face. "You'll be all perfect and then you'll be a total jerk."

What the hell was she talking about? "I'm trying not to be a jerk. I thought a marriage proposal and a commitment was the right thing to do. Obviously, we can't keep working together, because we can't keep our hands off each other." Her cheeks blushed a furious red. But then again, everything about her was furious right now. "So this is the obvious solution. I'm *not* going to raise a bastard. You *are* going to marry me. We *will* raise our child together and, damn it all, we *will* be a happy family. Unless…" He swallowed. "Unless you don't want me?"

She looked at him like he was stupid. Happiness seemed a long way off. She hadn't even put her bra on—it was hanging from her hand.

"You are trying so hard not to be like your father—

but this? Telling me what I want? Telling me what I'm going to do without giving me an option? You're essentially firing me. You're going to put me in this house and make me completely dependent upon you. You're going to hide me away here under the pretense of taking care of me because you somehow think that's going to absolve you of any guilt you feel. And that?" She jabbed at his chest with a finger. "That is *exactly* what your father would've done."

Her words hit him like a sledgehammer to the chest, so hard that he physically stumbled backward.

"I am not trying to hide anyone away. I'm not ashamed of you!" He realized too late he was shouting but he couldn't stop. "I just want my kid to have something I didn't—two loving parents who give a damn about whether he lives or dies!"

Her face softened—but only a little bit. She still looked fierce and when she spoke, it was in a low voice that somehow hurt all the more. "I am your brewmaster and I might be the mother of your child. I care about this baby and I could care very much for you—but not if you're going to spend the rest of our lives ordering me about. I am not your underling, Zeb. You don't get to decide that what you *think* you want is the same thing that I need. Because I'm only going to say this once. I'm sorry you had a miserable childhood. But it had nothing—not a damn thing—to do with the fact that you were raised by a single parent." A tear trickled down the side of her face and she scrubbed it away. "Don't you dare act like you're the only one raised by a single parent who had to work and sacrifice to survive."

"I never said that." But too late, he remembered her telling him how her mother had died in a car accident when she was two.

"Didn't you?" She moved in closer, and for a delusional second, he thought all was forgiven when she leaned in to kiss his cheek. But then she stepped back. "I give a damn, Zeb. Never think I don't. But I won't let your fears dictate my life."

She stepped around him, and this time, he didn't pull her back. He couldn't. Because he had the awful feeling that she might be right.

The door shut behind her, but he just stood there. Numbly, he looked down at the diamond ring in his hand. His father wouldn't have committed to the rest of his life with a woman he had gotten pregnant—he knew that.

But everything else?

He knew so little and the thing was, he wasn't sure he wanted to know more. He didn't know exactly what had happened between his parents. He couldn't be sure what made his mother the most bitter—the fact that Hardwick Beaumont had cast her aside? Or had it been something else? Had he forced her out of the company? Made her leave town and go back to Atlanta?

Why was this even a question? Hardwick had been married to a wealthy and powerful woman in her own right. Zeb was only four months younger than Chadwick. Of course Hardwick would've done everything within his power to hide Emily and Zeb.

And Zeb's mother…had she resented him? He was a living reminder of her great mistake—undeniable with his father's green eyes. Maybe she hadn't been able to love Zeb enough. And maybe—just maybe—that wasn't his fault.

Fourteen

She couldn't do this. Hell, at this point, she wasn't even sure what "this" was.

Could she be with Zeb? Could they have a relationship? Or would it always devolve into awful awkwardness? Could she work with him or was that impossible? If she didn't work at the brewery, what was she going to do?

It was hard enough to be a woman and a brewmaster. It wasn't like there were tons of jobs ripe for the picking at breweries conveniently located near her apartment. Plus, she was kind of pregnant. How was she supposed to interview at companies that might or might not exist and then ask for maternity leave after only a month or two on the job?

The entire situation was ridiculous. And she couldn't even think the whole thing over while drinking a bottle of beer. Somehow, that was the straw that was going to

SARAH M. ANDERSON 169

break her back. How was she going to brew beer without testing it?

There was a possible solution—she could go to Chadwick. He'd find a place for her at Percheron Drafts, she was pretty sure. And at least in the past, he had demonstrated a willingness to work around maternity leave. He knew what she was capable of, and frankly, his was the only brewery within the area that wouldn't force her to relocate. Plus...her child would be a Beaumont. Sort of. Chadwick would be her baby's uncle and the man was nothing if not loyal to the family name.

But even just thinking about going to Chadwick felt wrong. She wasn't six, running to her father to tattle. She was a grown woman. She'd gotten herself into this mess and she had to get herself out of it.

The worst part was, Zeb had been right. There *was* something between them. There had been since the very first moment she had walked into his office and locked eyes with him. There was chemistry and raw sexual attraction and the sex was amazing. And when he was doing everything right, he was practically... perfect.

But when he wasn't perfect, he *really* wasn't perfect.

Instead of going back to her apartment, Casey found herself heading toward her father's small ranch house in Brentwood. She'd grown up in this little house, and at one time, it had seemed like a mansion to her. She hadn't ever wanted to live in a real mansion. She didn't need to be surrounded by all the trappings of luxury—and she also did not need a diamond that probably cost more than a year's salary on her finger.

Instead, she wanted what she'd had growing up. A father who doted on her, who taught her how to do things like change a tire and throw a baseball and brew beer. A father who protected her.

She hadn't grown up with all the luxuries that money could buy. But she'd been happy. Was it wrong to want that? Was it wrong to *demand* that?

No. It wasn't. So that wasn't the right question.

The bigger question was, could she demand that of Zeb?

She was happy to see that the lights were on at home. Sometimes a girl needed her father. She walked in the house, feeling a little bit like a teenager who had stayed out past curfew and was about to get in trouble. "Daddy?"

"In the kitchen," he called back.

Casey smiled at that. Any other parent who was in the kitchen might reasonably be expected to be cooking. But not Carl Johnson. She knew without even seeing it that he had something taken apart on the kitchen table—a lamp or doorbell, something.

True to form, a chandelier was sitting in the middle of the table, wires strung everywhere.

The chandelier was a piece of work—cut crystal prisms caught the light and made it look like the room was glowing. It belonged in a mansion like Zeb's. Here, in her father's house, it looked horribly out of place. She knew the feeling.

It was such a comforting thing, sitting at this table while her father tinkered with this or that. Casey slid into her old seat. "How are you doing, Daddy?"

"Pretty good. How are you?" He looked at her and paused. "Honey? Is everything okay?"

No. Things were not all right and she wasn't sure how to fix them. "I think I've made a mistake."

He rested his hand on her shoulder. "Are you in trouble? You know I don't like you living in that apartment by yourself. There's still plenty of room for you here."

She smiled weakly at him. "It's not that. But I... I did something stupid and now I think I've messed everything up."

"Does this have something to do with work?" When Casey didn't reply immediately, her dad pressed on. "This is about your new boss?"

There was no good way to say this. "Yeah, it does. I'm... I'm pregnant."

Her father stiffened, his grip on her shoulder tight before he quickly released her. "Them Beaumonts—I never did trust them. Are you okay? Did he hurt you?"

Casey slumped forward, head in her hands and her elbows on the table. "No, it's not like that, Dad. I *like* him. He likes me. But I'm not sure that that's going to be enough." She looked at her father. He looked skeptical. "He asked me to marry him."

Her father sat straight up. "He did? Well, I guess that's the right thing to do—better than what his old man would've done." There was a long pause during which Casey went back to slumping against her hands. "Do you want to get married? Because you don't have to do anything you don't want to, honey."

"I don't know what to do. When he asked me, he made it clear that he expected me to quit my job and stay home and be a mother full-time." She sighed. It wasn't only that, though.

No, the thing that really bothered her had been the implication that she, Casey Johnson, wasn't good enough to be the mother to his child as she was. Instead, she needed to become someone else. The perfect mother. And what the hell did she know about mothering? Nothing. She'd never had one.

"And that's not what I want. I fought hard to get my job, Dad. And I like brewing beer. I don't want to throw that all away because of one mistake. But if I don't marry him, how am I going to keep working at the brewery?" Her father opened his mouth, but she cut him off. "And no, I don't think asking Chadwick for a job is the best solution, either. I have no desire to be the rope in Beaumont tug-of-war."

They sat quietly for a few moments, but it wasn't long until her father had picked up a few pieces of wire. He began stripping them in an absentminded sort of way. "This guy—"

"Zeb. Zeb Richards."

Another piece of copper shone in the light. "This Zeb—he's one of them Beaumont bastards, right?" Casey nodded. "And he offered to marry you so his kid wouldn't be a bastard like he was?"

"Yeah. I just… I just don't want that to be the only reason. I mean, I can see he's trying to do the right thing, but if I get married, I'd kind of like it to be for love."

Her dad nodded and continued to strip the wire. "I wish your mom were here," he said in an offhand way. "I don't know what to tell you, honey. But I will say this. Your mom and I got married because we had to."

"What?" Casey shot straight up in her chair and stared at him. Her father was blushing. Oh, *Lord.*

"I never told you about this, because it didn't seem right. We'd been dating around and she got pregnant and I asked her to marry me. I hadn't before then, because I wasn't sure I wanted to settle down, but with you on the way, I grew up—fast."

She gaped at him. "I had no idea, Dad."

"I didn't want you to think you were a mistake, honey.

Because you are the best thing that's ever happened to me." His eyes shone and he cleared his throat a few times—all while still stripping wire. "Anyway, that first year—that was rough. We had to learn how to talk to each other, how to live together. But you were born, and suddenly, everything about us just made more sense. And then when the accident came..." He shuddered. "The reason I'm telling you this," he went on in a more serious voice, as if he hadn't just announced that she was a surprise, "is that sometimes love comes a little later. If you guys like each other and you both want this kid, maybe you should think about it." He put down his wire trimmers and rested a hand on hers. "The most important thing is that you two talk to each other."

She felt awful because, well, there hadn't been a lot of talk. She'd gone over to his place tonight to do just that, and instead, they'd fallen into bed.

The one time she had sat down and had a conversation with the man had been at the ball game. She had liked him a great deal then—more than enough to bring him home with her. Maybe they could make this work.

No matter what Zeb had said, they didn't have to get married. Times had changed and her dad wasn't about to bust out a shotgun to escort them down the aisle.

She wasn't opposed to getting married. She didn't have anything against marriage. She just... Well, she didn't want their marriage to be on his terms only.

She knew who she was. She was a woman in her early thirties, unexpectedly pregnant. But she was also a huge sports fan. She could rewire a house. She brewed beer and changed her own oil.

She was never going to be a perfect stay-at-home

mom, baking cookies and wearing pearls and lunching with ladies. That wasn't who she was.

If Zeb wanted to marry her and raise their child as a family, then not only did he have to accept that she was going to do things differently, but he was going to have to support her. Encourage her.

That did not mean taking her job away under the pretext of taking care of her. That meant helping her find a way to work at the job she loved *and* raise a happy, healthy child.

She wanted it all.

And by God, it was all or nothing.

But men—even men as powerful as Zebadiah Richards—were not mind readers. She knew that. Hell, she was *living* that.

She needed to tell him what she wanted. Without falling into bed with him and without it devolving into awkward awfulness.

"I sure am sorry, honey," her dad went on. "I'd love to be a grandfather—but I hate that this has put you in an awkward position." He gave her fingers a squeeze. "You know that, no matter what you decide, I'll be here to back you up."

She leaned in to her dad's shoulder and he wrapped his arms around her and hugged her. "I know, Daddy. I appreciate it."

"Tell you what," Dad said when she straightened up. "Tomorrow's Friday, right? And the Rockies play a game at three. Why don't you play hooky tomorrow? Stay here with me tonight. We'll make a day of it."

She knew that this was not a solution in any way, shape or form. At some point, she was going to have to sit down with Zeb and hash out what, exactly, they were going to do.

Soon. Next week, she'd be an adult again. She would deal with this unexpected pregnancy with maturity and wisdom. Eventually, she needed to talk with Zeb.

But for right now, she needed to be the girl she'd always been.

Sometimes, fathers did know best.

Fifteen

"Where is she?"

The man Zeb had stopped—middle-aged, potbellied... He knew that he'd been introduced to this man before. Larry? Lance? Something like that. It wasn't important.

What was important was finding Casey.

"She's not here," the man said, his chins wobbling dangerously.

Zeb supposed he should be thankful that, since Casey was one of exactly two women in the production department, everyone knew which "she" he was talking about.

"Yes, I can see that. What I want to know," he said slowly and carefully, which caused all the blood to drain out of the guy's face, "is where she is now."

It wasn't fair to terrorize employees like this, but dammit, Zeb needed to talk to Casey. She had stormed out of his house last night and by the time he'd gotten dressed, she had disappeared. She hadn't been at her apartment—the security guy said he hadn't seen her. In desperation, Zeb had even stopped by the brewery, just to make sure she wasn't tinkering with her brews. But the place had been quiet and the night shift swore she hadn't been in.

Her office was just as dark this morning. He didn't know where she was and he was past worrying and headed straight for full-on panic.

Which meant that he was currently scaring the hell out of one of his employees. He stared at the man, willing himself not to shake the guy. "Well?"

"She said she wouldn't be in today."

Zeb took a deep breath and forced himself to remain calm. "Do you have any idea where she might be?"

He must not have been doing a good job at the whole "calm" thing, because his employee backed up another step. "Sometimes she takes off in the afternoon to go to a game. With her dad. But you wouldn't fire her for that, right?" The man straightened his shoulders and approximated a stern look. "I don't think you should."

The game. Of course—why hadn't Zeb thought of that? She had season tickets, right? She'd be at the game. The relief was so strong it almost buckled his knees.

"No, I'm not going to fire her," he assured the guy. "Thanks for the tip, though. And keep up the good work."

On the walk back to his office, he called up the time for the baseball game. Three o'clock—that wasn't her taking the afternoon off. That was her taking the whole day. Had he upset her so much that she couldn't even face him? It wasn't like her to avoid a confrontation, after all.

What a mess. His attempt at a marriage proposal last

night had not been his best work. But then, he had no experience proposing marriage while his brain was still fogged over from an amazing climax. He didn't have any experience in proposing marriage at all.

That was the situation he was going to change, though. He couldn't walk away from her. Hell, he hadn't even been able to do that before she had realized she was pregnant. There was something about her that he couldn't ignore. Yes, she was beautiful, and yes, she challenged him. Boy, did she challenge him. But there was more to it than that.

His entire life had been spent trying to prove that he was someone. That he was a Beaumont, that he belonged in the business world—that he mattered, regardless of his humble origins or the color of his skin.

And for all that Casey argued with him, she never once asked him to be anyone other than himself. She accepted him as who he was—even if who he was happened to be a man who sometimes said the wrong thing at the wrong time.

He had made her a promise that he would take care of her, and by God, he was going to do that.

But this time, he was going to ask her how she wanted him to take care of her. Because he should have known that telling her what to do was a bad idea.

Ah, the seats behind hers were still available for this afternoon's game. Zeb bought the tickets.

He was going to do something he had never done before—he was going to take the afternoon off work.

"You want me to go get you some more nachos, honey?" Dad asked for the third time in a mere two innings.

Casey looked down at the chips covered in gloppy

cheese. She was only kind of pregnant—wasn't it too soon for her stomach to be doing this many flips?

"I'm okay." She looked up and saw Dad staring at her. He looked so eager that she knew he needed something to do. "Really. But I could use another Sprite." Frankly, at this point, clear soda was the only thing keeping her stomach settled.

"I'll be right back," Dad said with a relieved smile, as if her problems could all be solved with more food. *Men*, Casey thought with another grin after he was gone.

Whereas she had no idea what she could do to make this better. No, it wasn't the most mature thing in the world to have skipped work today. It was just delaying the inevitable conversation that she would have to have with Zeb at some point or another.

There had been a moment last night—the moment before the kiss—where he'd told her that he was going to take care of her. That had been what she wanted. Hadn't that been why she'd gone to her dad after she had stormed out of Zeb's house? Because she wanted someone to take care of her?

But it wasn't a fair comparison. Her father had known her for her entire life. Of course he would know what she wanted—wasn't that why they were at this game today? It wasn't fair for her to hope and hope and just keep on hoping, dammit, that Zeb would guess correctly. Especially not when he'd gotten so close. There *was* a big part of her that wanted him to take care of her.

There was an equally big part of her that did not want to quit her job and be a stay-at-home mom. What if he couldn't see that? He was a hard-driving businessman who wasn't used to taking no for an answer. What if she couldn't convince him that she would be a better mom if she could keep her job and keep doing what she loved?

She was keeping her eye on the ball when she heard someone shuffling into the seat behind her. By instinct, she leaned forward to avoid any accidental hot dogs down the back of her neck. But as she did so, she startled as a voice came low and close to her ear. "It's a nice afternoon for baseball, isn't it?"

Zeb. She would recognize his voice anywhere—deep and serious, with just a hint of playfulness around the edge.

"Nice enough to skip work, even," he added when she didn't manage to come up with a coherent response.

Okay, now he was teasing her. She settled back in her chair, but she didn't turn around and look at him. She didn't want to see him in the suit and she didn't want to see him in a T-shirt. So she kept her eyes focused on the game in front of her. "How did you find me?"

"I asked Larry. I should've figured it out by myself. You weren't at your apartment and you weren't at work."

"I went home—I mean, my dad's home."

"I upset you. I didn't mean to, but I did." He exhaled and she felt his warmth against the back of her neck. "I shouldn't have assumed you would want to stay home. I know you and I know you're far too ambitious to give up everything you've worked for just because of something like this."

Now she did twist around. Good Lord—he was wearing purple. A Rockies T-shirt and a Rockies hat.

"You blend," she said in surprise. "I didn't think you knew how to do that."

"I can be taught." One corner of his mouth curved up in a small smile—the kind of smile that sent a shiver down her back. "I'm working on doing a better job of listening."

"Really?"

"Really. I have to tell you, I was frantic this morning when I couldn't find you at work. I was afraid you might quit on me and then where would I be?"

"But that's a problem, don't you see? How am I going to do my job? How am I going to brew beer if I can't drink it?"

Zeb settled back in his seat, that half smile still firmly on his face. "One of the things I've learned during my tenure as CEO of the Beaumont Brewery is that my employees do not drink on the job. They may sample in small quantities, but no one is ever drunk while they're at work—a fact which I appreciate. And I've also learned that I have extremely competent employees who care deeply about our brewery."

She stared at him in confusion. "What are you saying?"

He had the nerve to shrug nonchalantly. "I grew up in a hair salon, listening to women talk about pregnancies and babies and children. Obviously, we have to check with a doctor, but I think you taking a small sip every now and then isn't going to hurt anyone. And I don't want that to be the reason why you think you would have to leave a job you love."

She began to get a crick in her lower back. "Why are you here?" Because he was being perfect again and when he was perfect, he was simply irresistible.

"I'm here for you, Casey. I screwed up last night—I didn't ask you what you wanted. So that's what I'm doing now. What do you want to do?"

She was only vaguely aware that she was staring at him, mouth wide-open. But this was *the* moment. If she didn't tell him what she wanted right now, she might never get another chance.

"Come sit by me," she said. Obligingly, Zeb clambered down over the back of Dad's seat and settled in.

For a moment, Casey was silent as she watched the batter line out to right field. Zeb didn't say anything, though. He just waited for her.

"Okay," she said, mentally psyching herself up for this. Why could she defend her beer and her employees—but asking something for herself was such a struggle?

Well, to hell with that. She was doing this. Right now. "It's hard for me to ask for stuff that I want," she admitted. It wasn't a graceful statement, but it was the truth.

Zeb turned and looked at her funny. "You? Didn't you barge into my office and tell me off on my first day?"

"It's different. I defend my job and I defend my workers but for me to sit here and tell you what I want—it's... it's hard, okay? So just humor me."

"I will always listen to you, Casey. I want you to know that."

Her cheeks began to heat and the back of her neck prickled, but she wasn't allowing herself to get lost in the awkwardness of the moment. Instead, she forged ahead.

"The last time we were at a game together... I wanted you to tell me that I was beautiful and sensual and... and gorgeous. But it felt stupid, asking for that, so I didn't, and then after we..." She cleared her throat, hoping against hope that she hadn't turned bright red and knowing it was way too late for that. "Well, afterward, what you said made me feel even less pretty than normal. And so I shut down on you."

Now it was his turn to stare at her, mouth open and eyes wide. "But...do you have any idea how much you turn me on? How gorgeous you are?"

God, she was going to die of embarrassment. "It's not

that—okay, maybe it is. But it's that I've always been this tomboy. And when we were together in my kitchen, it was good. Great," she added quickly when he notched an eyebrow at her. "But I don't want that to be all there is. If we're going to have a relationship, I need romance. And most people think I don't, because I drink beer and I watch ball games."

She had not died of mortification yet, which had to count for something.

"Romance," he said, but he didn't sound like he was mocking her. Instead, he sounded…thoughtful.

A small flicker of hope sparked to life underneath the heat of embarrassment. "Yes."

He touched her then, his hand on hers. More heat. There'd always be this heat between them. "Duly noted. What else? Because I will do everything in my power to give you what you want and what you need."

For a moment, she almost got lost in his gaze. God, those green eyes—from the very first moment, they had pulled her in and refused to let her go. "I don't want to give up my job. And I don't want to quit and go some-place else. I've worked hard for my job and I love it. I love everything about making beer and everything about working for the brewery. Even my new CEO, who occasionally sends out mixed signals."

At that, Zeb laughed out loud. "Can you keep a secret?"

"Depends on the secret," she said archly.

"Before I met you, I don't think I ever did anything but work. That's all I've known. It's all my mom did and I thought I had to prove myself to her, to my father—to everyone. I've been so focused on being the boss and on besting the Beaumonts for so long that…" He sighed and looked out at the game. But Casey could tell he wasn't seeing it. "That I've forgotten how to be me. Then I met you. When I'm with you, I don't feel like I have to be something that I'm not. I don't have to prove myself over and over again. I can just be *me*." The look he gave her was tinged with sadness. "It's hard for me to let go of that—of being the CEO. But you make me want to do better."

"Oh, Zeb—there's so much more to you than just this brewery."

He cupped her face. "That goes for you, too—you are more than just a brewmaster to me. You are a passionate, beautiful woman who earned my respect first and my love second."

Tears begin to prick at Casey's eyes. Stupid hormones. "Oh, Zeb..."

"There's something between us and I don't want to screw that up. Any more than I already have," he added, looking sheepish.

"What do you want?" She felt it was only fair to ask him.

"I want to know my child. I want to be a part of his or her life. I don't want my child to be raised as a bastard." He paused and Casey felt a twinge of disappointment. It wasn't like she could disagree with that kind of sentiment—it was a damn noble one.

But was it enough? She wanted to be wanted not just because she was pregnant but because she was... Well, because she was Casey.

But before she could open her mouth to tell Zeb this, he went on, "That's not all."

"It's not?" Her voice came out with a bit of a waver in it.

He leaned in closer. "It's not. I want to be with someone who I respect, who I trust to pull me back to myself when I've forgotten how to be anything but the boss. I want to be with someone who sparks something in me, someone I look forward to coming home to every single night." Casey gasped, but he kept going. "I want to be with someone who's just as committed to her work as I am to mine—but who also knows how to relax and kick back. I want to be with someone who understands the different families I'm a part of now and who loves me because of them, not in spite of them." His lips were now just a breath away from hers. She could feel his warmth and she wanted nothing more than to melt into him again. "But most of all, I want to be with someone who can tell me what she wants—what she needs— and when she needs it. So tell me, Casey—what do you want?"

This was really happening. "I want to know you care, that you'll fight for me and the baby—and for us. That you'll protect us and support us, even if we do things that other people don't think we should."

Oh, God—that grin on him was too much. She couldn't resist him and she was tired of trying. "Like be the youngest female brewmaster in the country?"

He understood. "Yeah, that. If we do this, I want to do this right," she told him. "But I want to meet you in the middle. I don't know if I want to live in the big house and I know we can't live in my tiny apartment."

His eyes warmed. "We can talk about that."

"That's what I want—I want to know that I can talk to you and know that you'll listen. I want to know that everything is going to work out for the best."

He pulled back, just the tiniest bit. "I can't guarantee anything, Casey. But I can promise you this—I will love you and our baby no matter what."

Love. That was the something between them—the thing that neither of them could walk away from.

"That's what I want," she told him. She leaned into him, wrapping her hand around the back of his neck and pulling him in closer. "I love you, too. That's all."

"Then I'm yours. All you have to do is ask." He gave her a crooked grin. "I won't always get it right. I'm not a mind reader, you know."

She couldn't help it—she laughed. "Did the all-powerful Zebadiah Richards just admit there was something he couldn't do?"

"Shh," he teased, his eyes sparkling. "Don't tell anyone. It's a secret." Then he leaned in closer. "Let me give you everything, Casey. We'll run the brewery together and raise our kid. We'll do it our way."

"*Yes.* I want you."

Just as his lips brushed against hers, she heard someone clearing his throat—loudly.

Dad. In all the talk, she'd forgotten that he'd left to fetch a soda for her. She jolted in her seat, but Zeb didn't let her go. Instead, he wrapped his arms around her shoulders.

"Everything okay?" Dad asked as he eyed the two of them suspiciously. "You want me to get rid of him, honey?"

Casey looked up at her dad as she leaned back into Zeb's arms and smiled. "Nope," she said, knowing that this was right. "I want him to stay right here with me."

Everything she'd ever wanted was hers—a family, her job and Zeb. He was all hers.

All she'd had to do was ask for him.

* * * * *

The bedroom door swung open soundlessly and he didn't bother with lights.

Stripping out of his clothes, he slid between the Egyptian cotton sheets and rolled toward the center of his bed. Where he encountered a warm body.

His palm dipped into a nipped-in waist before smoothing over the curve of a hip. Tucker must have hustled to get him this coming-home present. He dipped his head and nuzzled the sweet spot behind the woman's ear.

The next thing he knew, the woman had rolled, tucked her feet into his chest and kicked. Chase flew off the bed and hit the carpeted floor with a soft thud.

"What the hell!" The woman scampered to the other side of the bed and turned on the lamp. "Who are you?"

He stood up, naked and unembarrassed. "I might ask you the same thing, wildcat."

"Oh, my God, you're naked. Get out!"

Before he could move, she nailed him in the chest with a boot. A Western boot. Covered in mud and... He sniffed the air.

"Get out of here, you pervert! I'm calling security."

"Good idea, since I'm throwing you out."

"What? You can't do that."

"Sure I can, kitten. This is my apartment."

Her jaw dropped and then her full lips formed a perfect O.

* * *

Convenient Cowgirl Bride
is part of the Red Dirt Royalty series:
These Oklahoma millionaires work hard and play harder.

CONVENIENT COWGIRL BRIDE

BY
SILVER JAMES

First Published in Great Britain 2016
By Mills & Boon, an imprint of HarperCollins*Publishers*
1 London Bridge Street, London, SE1 9GF

© 2016 Silver James

ISBN: 978-0-263-91881-6

51-1016

Printed and bound in Spain
by CPI, Barcelona

Silver James likes walks on the wild side and coffee. Okay. She LOVES coffee. A cowgirl at heart, she's been an army officer's wife and mum and worked in the legal field, fire service and law enforcement. Now retired from the real world, she lives in Oklahoma, spending her days writing with the assistance of two Newfoundlands, the cat who rules them all and the characters living in her imagination.

To every reader who is a cowgirl at heart,
to the man who taught me about the soul
of a horse and to the marvelous Harlequin
team who make it easy to let my imagination
gallop across the page.

One

Chasen "Chase" Barron needed a wife like he needed another hangover. Dark thoughts winnowed through his mind as he surveyed his world from the window of his Gulfstream jet. Below him, Las Vegas looked like a necklace of sparkling neon jewels strung on ribbons of car headlights. Vegas never slept. His kind of place.

His latest escapades had landed him back on the front page of the supermarket tabloids—much to his old man's disgust. Chase wasn't a bad guy. Not really. It was just that as head of Barron Entertainment, he was surrounded by beautiful women. And he was definitely a man who enjoyed beautiful women. Frequently. How was he to know the gorgeous actress—who'd told him she was separated—was still very much married to a powerful studio head? Or that she'd invited the paparazzi to record her tryst with Chase in order to… Just thinking about it made his head hurt.

He'd left LA for Nashville to deal with some problems in setting up Barron Entertainment's new country and Western record label, and there were two cute, young singers who wanted an edge. Being seen getting it on with the CEO of Barron Entertainment was their ticket to glory. Who knew those selfies they took would go viral? Yeah, he definitely should have confiscated their cell phones. Water under the bridge now. And lesson learned.

Despite the social media storm, his trip to Nashville had been productive. The new company, Bent Star Records, had launched, making headlines by signing superstar Deacon Tate, and his band, the Sons of Nashville, as the first act. That Deke was Chase's cousin was beside the point. Family did business with family. Which brought him back around to the situation at hand.

Waking up, predictably hungover, to his father's edict to marry the very disagreeable daughter of a business associate, Chase figured there was only one way out—head back to Las Vegas with all speed and ignore his father's demands. Besides, the old man hadn't called in his brothers for a family intervention, right? Or maybe dear old Dad was finally getting the message now that Chance, Cord and Clay had all defied the old jackass, married the women they loved and were living the lives they wanted without his permission.

Chase admired his older brothers. He'd fallen in with the old man's edicts during the family confrontations, but had secretly rooted for his siblings. Now if he could just figure out what was going on with his identical twin. Cash had been a coiled snake ready to strike every time Chase had seen him lately. And he was worried. They used to be so close they knew what the other was thinking. Not anymore.

But solving the mystery of his twin's behavior would have to wait. Chase had his own problems—mainly figuring out how not to get engaged to Janiece Carroll. While pretty enough, courtesy of a personal trainer and a skilled plastic surgeon, Janiece was High Maintenance, capitalized and trademarked. The former debutante had a voice like nails on a blackboard and the social skills of a spoiled toddler. Yeah, he needed to figure out a way to dodge this particular bullet.

On the ground, he traded the jet for his Jaguar F-type convertible. Once the top was down, he cranked up the sound system and the strains of Deacon's newest hit, "Heading Home," filled the hangar. He pulled out, maneuvered off airport property and headed into Las Vegas proper. The dazzling array of lights and throngs of people on the Strip felt like home.

Downshifting the powerful Jag, he coasted to a stop at a traffic light. Two women in spangly minidresses barely covering their butts sauntered by in the crosswalk in front of him. They watched him, their invitation plain in their expressions. Part of him was tempted. Part of him wanted only to hit his bed in the penthouse apartment at the Barron Crown Hotel and Casino. The light changed and the opportunity was lost. He wasn't disappointed. He'd had enough female manipulation for a while.

Chase cruised down the street debating whether to pull into the main entrance of the hotel or head around the block to the employees' parking garage. He hadn't shaken the headache so he decided to forgo the casino's clamor. The guard on duty at the garage nodded to him and opened the gate with a quiet "Good to have you back, sir."

After parking in his spot near the private elevators, he snagged his satchel and overnight bag. Having semipermanent residences in both LA and Nashville made for light travel. He rubbed his jaw as he rode up in the elevator.

Cash had upgraded security and it took Chase's thumbprint to get to any of the secured floors, including the top floor, where he resided. His card key was in his hand when he stepped into the beautifully appointed foyer. His apartment took up a third of the floor. Three suites—the smallest and cheapest going for ten grand a night—occupied the rest of the space.

Everything about the Crown was five-star, including

his apartment. He card-keyed the door and stepped inside, as soft lights slowly brightened. Motion detectors meant he never walked into a darkened room—except the master bedroom. The light switch in there was the old-fashioned kind.

He moved into the open living area and hit the wet bar. He skipped the bottles of top-shelf liquor and grabbed a cold bottle of beer from the fridge instead. Mail was stacked on his desk and he checked it with a bored eye. His vice president of operations would have already handled anything important. Tucker was his cousin and he trusted the man implicitly—again, it was that whole family-doing-business-together thing.

Wandering into the gourmet kitchen, Chase tried to decide if he was hungry. A plastic-wrapped tray of meat, cheese and a variety of artisan breads occupied one shelf in the Sub-Zero refrigerator. His pilot would have alerted Tuck of their pending arrival, and as usual, his cousin had taken care of him before shutting down for the night. The tray was perfect. He slid it out onto the granite top of the breakfast bar and hitched a hip onto the wrought iron bar stool. He ate and drank, watching the play of lights outside the floor-to-ceiling windows bracketing the living space.

A few minutes might have passed, or a few hours. He wasn't sure and didn't care. His headache had receded and he finally felt drowsy. He covered the tray and shoved it back into the fridge. As he stepped into the hallway leading to his bedroom, the lights behind him faded while the sconces in the hall flickered on. He'd left his briefcase at his desk and his overnight bag in the hallway. Housekeeping would deal with it in the morning, after he went to his business office on the third floor.

It was only one in the morning. He should have been fired up to hit the casino floor, or to check out one of the shows playing at the hotel. He should have hit his office, but he was tired. That fact might have worried him but he was too tired—or too bored—to care.

The bedroom door swung open soundlessly and he didn't bother with lights. He could navigate this room in the dark. After stripping out of his clothes, he slid between the 1200-thread-count Egyptian cotton sheets and rolled toward the center of the bed.

Where he encountered a warm body.

Reaching out, he found the soft cotton of a T-shirt. Chase wondered briefly if it was one of his. His palm dipped into a nipped-in waist before smoothing over the curve of a hip and down to the bare skin of a muscular thigh. Tucker must have hustled to get him this coming-home present. He dipped his head and nuzzled the sweet spot behind the woman's ear as his hand cupped her full breast.

The next thing he knew, the woman raked her nails down his arm, rolled, tucked her feet into his chest and kicked. Chase flew off the bed and hit the carpeted floor with a soft thud.

"What the hell!" The woman scampered to the other side of the bed and hit the on button for the lamp on the nightstand. "Who are you?"

He stood up, naked and unembarrassed. She was in his bed in his apartment in his hotel. He had nothing to be embarrassed about. "I might ask you the same thing, wildcat."

"Oh, my God, you're naked. Get out!"

Before he could move, she nailed him in the chest with a boot. A Western boot. Covered in mud and…he sniffed the air. Bending, he snatched the boot and stared at it, barely ducking in time when a second boot sailed toward his face.

"Get out of here, you pervert!" She snatched the phone and began dialing. "I'm calling Security."

"Good idea, since I'm throwing you out."

"What? You can't do that."

"Sure I can, kitten. This is my apartment."

Her jaw dropped and then her full lips formed a perfect O. Chase liked the looks of that. And it showed. Her eyes dropped and she flushed before tilting her chin to face him eye to eye. She stood on the far side of the bed and he got a good look at her.

She wasn't too tall—maybe five-six or five-seven—and while the baggy T-shirt covered most of her attributes, he could scope out her legs—long and muscular. Then he caught the saying emblazoned on her shirt: Sometimes A Cowgirl Has To Do What A Cowboy Can't. Reading the message stretched across her chest didn't help calm his libido. He dragged his gaze to her face, which was surrounded by a thick curtain of black hair, sleep tousled and begging for a man to run his fingers through it. Brown eyes bored into him from behind thick lashes that swept her high cheekbones with each blink.

"You're one of the Barrons," she murmured, her eyes still fastened on his face. Her tongue darted out from between her lips and he had to bite back a groan. "Can you, uh, put on some pants or something?"

He turned and walked to the chair where he'd dropped his jeans. Stepping into them commando, Chase glanced over his shoulder, only to catch her staring at his butt. His libido immediately whispered sweet nothings in his ear, but he'd already been burned twice in the past month. That shut up his libido and his body calmed down immediately.

"You wanna explain why you're in my bed?"

"I'm Savannah Wolfe."

She said it as though he should know the name. He didn't. "Yeah, and?"

"I… I have permission to be here. Kade—"

"No one has permission to be here."

"But—" Her face flushed as her temper flared. Chase discovered he liked putting that color in her cheeks.

"No one, wildcat, especially not you."

"Stop calling me that."

He showed her the four red marks on the inside of his forearm. "I think it fits. However, as much as I'd like to play, you're not staying. Get your stuff and get out."

"But—"

"We can do this like civilized people or I can call Security and have you arrested for trespassing."

"But—"

He pulled his cell from his hip pocket. "Tired of the *buts*, cat."

"I—"

He hit a button and she dropped her gaze.

"Fine. Get out so I can get dressed."

"Not happenin', girl." He snagged her boots and tossed them to her. She caught them easily.

"Fine. If you get off on watchin', then you are a big ol' pervert." She strode over to another chair and grabbed her jeans and a plaid shirt. An old canvas duffel bag slouched on the floor next to the chair. She had her shirt on but not buttoned and one leg in her jeans when Security hit the doorway.

"Problem, Mr. Barron?"

"Not anymore. Please escort this woman off the premises."

The dark-suited security officer didn't give Savannah a chance to get dressed. He snagged her bag, draped it over her shoulder, grabbed her boots and jammed them into her chest, gripped her arm and frog-marched her out. Sputtering and cussing, the girl did her best to get her jeans on. Chase followed them to the door and out into the foyer. He was grinning in the face of her scowl as the elevator doors closed. Pink polka-dotted panties. Now that was a sight he wouldn't forget any time soon.

Two

Savannah had never been so mortified in her life. She was going to kill Kaden Waite the next time she saw him.

"Chase is in Nashville until after the rodeo," Kade had told her, knowing money was tight and she'd probably be sleeping in her truck or in Indigo's stall. "No one will be there. I'll call the hotel and set it up."

He had. She'd checked in that night with no problem. The desk clerk had barely looked at her. Either Chase Barron had strange women asking for his card key all the time or Kade had totally smoothed the way. Before her ignominious exit, things had been great. She'd gotten Indigo settled into his stall at the Clark County Fairgrounds and had enough grain left to feed him well. She'd unhooked her horse trailer and parked it in the designated area near the barn before driving to the Strip.

She'd found a place in the Crown Hotel and Casino's parking lot and locked up her old truck. Not that it would take more than a twist of baling wire to pop the locks. Even with the odometer logging 200,000 miles, the old Ford still got her from rodeo to rodeo. She even had half a tank of gas—hopefully enough to last until she won the barrel event that weekend. And she had to win. She had a total of $175.00 in her checking account and twenty bucks in her pocket.

Then she'd woken up to a strange man in bed with her. The man who lived in that penthouse suite. Chase Barron. All six-plus feet of sexy male with his lean, I-run-on-the-treadmill-every-day body, his silky dark hair and those coffee-colored eyes. She jerked her thoughts back and remembered she'd nailed him in the chest with her boot. He deserved it. He was the world's biggest jerk.

The security guy mostly ignored her, but the walls of the elevator were polished to the point they might as well have been mirrors. She struggled into her jeans, got them buttoned and her belt buckled. He didn't give time to dig a pair of socks out of her duffel. Marching her barefoot across the lobby to the obvious entertainment of everyone they encountered just added to her now miserable night.

Security shoved her through the entrance, held open by a smirking doorman. Savannah stumbled a few steps, found her balance and moved to a granite planter. Plopping her butt on the edge of it, she glared at the man standing over her, ready to snatch her up to keep her moving. "Hold your frickin' horses, dude. I'm putting on my socks and boots."

It took her a minute to stamp her boots on. Straightening to her full height, chin up, she offered him her glaringest glare. "I can find my way out."

Turning on her heel, head still high, she stomped across the valet drive and headed into the crowded lot. Her truck was parked in the far corner. She kept walking, and about three rows in, her escort dropped back, then stopped altogether. She ducked behind an RV, and when she peeked back, he was returning to the hotel.

Still seething, she found her truck, only to discover the front tire was flat. That made her choice easy. Rather than driving back to the fairgrounds to sleep in Indy's stall, she'd sleep in the truck. She was too tired to change the tire tonight. Crawling inside, she swiped at her cheeks. She didn't have the spare time or energy to waste on tears. She *would* be back here in Las Vegas come December, competing in the Wrangler National Finals Rodeo, but that meant she had to be at her best for this week's qualifying rodeo. February was a late start but she was determined.

She pushed her duffel against the passenger door, stretched across the bench seat and jerked the Indian blanket off the back of the seat to cover her legs. She would deal with everything in the morning, including calling Mr. Kaden "I'll fix it" Waite to tell him not to do her any more favors.

Savannah sat straight up, cussing. She couldn't call Kade. She couldn't call anyone. Her phone was plugged in, charging on the nightstand, next to the bed belonging to the jackass who lived on the fiftieth floor of the monster hotel looming just beyond her windshield. Dammit. She would have to face the man again in the morning. With her luck, the jerk face would just throw her phone away when he found it, which would suck because she didn't have the money to get a new one.

Snatching a baseball cap off the headache rack behind the seat, she put it on and pulled the bill over her eyes. She had to sleep or she'd be sluggish tomorrow. She needed to work Indy in the arena because he'd been off training for three weeks. Her horse needed to settle and be in shape to get a good time for the first round. If her time wasn't fast enough, there wouldn't be a second round and she'd be in a world of economic hurt. She was already two rodeos behind on getting points and winnings.

Savvie thumped her duffel and sought a more comfortable position. She eventually drifted off.

Just before dawn, Chase found the woman's phone, when it buzzed on his nightstand. Irritated, he rolled over and grabbed it, ready to throw it against the far wall until he saw Kaden calling on the screen. It was the ranch manager of the Crown B. Curious, he answered.

"Yeah?"

"Uh…is Savannah around?"

"No."

"Where is she?"

"Why do you want to know?"

"Who is this?"

"Chase Barron."

Silence stretched for a long moment before Kade replied. "Chase? Kaden Waite. I thought you were in Nashville."

"I was until last night. Found someone in my bed, Kade."

"Damn. I'm sorry. Chance and Cord told me it'd be all right if Savvie stayed in your place while you were gone. They expected you to be in Nashville for at least another two weeks. The rodeo is over Saturday night and Sav would be back on the road Sunday."

"She your girlfriend?" Chase didn't expect the burst of laughter from the other man.

"Kissing her would be like kissing my sister. Our mothers were tight and we grew up practically next door to each other."

"So she's Chickasaw?" That would help explain the sleek, black hair, carved cheekbones and snapping brown eyes.

"Nope. Choctaw. Is that a problem?" Kade's voice took on an edge. "Look, Chase, I was trying to help the kid out. She's living on a shoestring and has big dreams about being the next All-Around Cowgirl. She was gonna sleep in her truck or her horse's stall, so I figured since you were gone and your brothers said—"

"Yeah, yeah. I rained on her parade by coming home early. Not a big deal, Kade. Look, she's out right now.

Forgot her phone. I'll have her call you." Chase was lying through his teeth. He wasn't about to explain he'd kicked her out last night.

"That's okay. She'll just get pissed because I'm checking up on her. I worry about her being out there alone, ya know?"

"Gotcha. Anything else? I gotta go, man." Yeah, he had to go find her before Kade found out.

"Thanks, Chase."

"Anytime, bro." And that last slipped out before he could catch it. Luckily, Kade hung up without comment. Chase was convinced Kade was a product of one of the old man's liaisons. The guy didn't act like he had a clue and he always kept an employer-employee barrier up between him and the Barron boys. Still, they all had their suspicions.

At the moment, though, figuring out Kade's parentage was less pressing than finding the girl Chase had tossed out like yesterday's garbage. He realized, belatedly, that she'd tried to explain her presence, and he never gave her the chance. Plus, he'd forced her into a walk of shame with Security—with everyone in the lobby there to witness every step. He could be a right bastard sometimes. He called Tucker about sending someone to the fairgrounds later to locate Savannah, and arranging a comped room for the girl.

A shower and a cup of coffee later, Chase dressed in an impeccable suit and custom black boots, then stood staring out the window. Activity in the parking lot below drew his attention. Red and blue flashing lights. Police. Members of hotel security. And a beat-up old truck. He slammed his mug on the counter and headed to the door at a trot.

Downstairs, the doorman got the heavy glass door open half a second before Chase would have slammed it open himself. He ignored the valet and strode into the parking lot. As he approached the knot of cops and security personnel, he heard the woman's indignant voice.

"But I wasn't soliciting that dude. He came on to me!" Her fisted hands hung stiffly at her sides and she had a smear of grease across one cheek. "I was just changing my tire."

Chase noticed the jack, the flat tire and the sorry state of the old Ford truck in general. Kade hadn't lied about her circumstances. And now that Chase wasn't pissed off and worried he was being set up again, he realized how gorgeous she looked, even in the same faded T-shirt from last night. She also had on a plaid shirt, faded jeans, muddy boots, and her face was dirty. She barely kept her temper in check, and Chase had the insane desire to find out what would happen when she snapped. Instead, he pushed into the group.

"I see you're still here, Miss Wolfe."

She glared, and he had to bite back a smile.

"You know her, boss?" Bart Stevens, head of hotel security, stepped up beside him.

"Kade called this morning," Chase said to her, without answering his security chief's question. He held out her phone. "You left this behind last night."

Savannah stared at him but didn't reach for the phone. Her expression reminded him of Miz Beth, the woman who'd helped raise the Barron brothers, staring at a rattlesnake—as if she didn't know whether to be afraid or take a hoe to his neck. He stepped closer, unsnapped the flap on the pocket over her left breast and slipped the phone inside. Turning to Stevens, he added, "Call the garage and have them send someone over to change the tire and move the truck."

"I can change my own tire," she growled at him, and he was reminded again of her wildcat tendencies.

"I'm sure you can, Savannah. But I'm paying people to change tires whether they are changing them or sitting on their butts. Grab your stuff and come with me."

"No." Her fists were now planted on her hips, her face

darkening as her eyes narrowed. "Don't do me any favors, Mr. Barron."

Oh, yeah, this was going to be fun. "Do you really want to do this in front of an audience?" He gestured toward the three uniformed security guards, his suited security chief and the four LVPD officers circling them.

"No. I just want to change my flat, get in my truck and get to the fairgrounds so I can work my horse."

"While the hotel garage is servicing your truck, I'll take you to the fairgrounds and you can work your horse."

Savannah glanced around before she stepped close to him and snarled into his ear. "Why are you being nice? You threw me out on my ass last night."

"I apologize." He said it quietly, his gaze covering the other men. "Long story. I'll explain later." He stepped back and said more loudly, "C'mon, Savannah, I'll buy you breakfast and then we'll head out to Clark County."

He offered his most appealing smile, the one most women begged to get. This woman just rolled her eyes, pivoted and reached into her truck to grab the duffel. She jerked her keys from her front pocket and dangled them from her fingers. Chase nodded to one of the guards to take the keys. A second guard reached for the duffel. Savannah relinquished it after a short tussle.

"I can carry my own stuff," she muttered.

"Yes, but this is my hotel and guests don't carry their own luggage."

She arched a brow at Chase. "Guest?"

"Come back to my apartment for breakfast and we'll talk."

Her gaze raked over him from his face to his boots and back to his eyes. "You don't impress me as a man who talks much, unless he's issuing orders."

Chase threw back his head and laughed. He dropped his arm across her shoulders and drew her along with him. "You think you have my number, wildcat. C'mon." When they had a modicum of privacy, he lowered his head closer to hers. "You can grab a hot shower and clean clothes while we're waiting for room service."

"Your bathroom better have a lock on the door."

He snorted and another deep belly laugh erupted as he squeezed her in a side hug. She tensed and tried to lean away, but he didn't let her. "I promise to be on my best behavior. Besides, Kade would probably beat me up if I tried anything."

The tension left her body. "You really did talk to him?"

"Yeah." He didn't say anything else until they crossed the lobby and entered the penthouse elevator. Chase took her duffel from the guard and the doors closed behind them. "I'm sorry I jumped the gun and didn't let you explain. I was coming off a situation that had to do with two girls and some selfies posted to social media and subsequently picked up by the press. That's why I came back to Vegas early. I also bypassed the front desk coming in, so they didn't have a chance to tell me I had a guest."

She turned her head and her lips quirked. A flash of heat washed over him as he watched her mouth. She stiffened beside him almost as if she'd read his mind. He needed to work on his poker face. Chase blinked to break the connection growing between them. She was a beautiful woman, sexy in a blunt, earthy way, and totally unlike his usual side dish. Still, the attraction remained—an attraction he wanted to explore. She'd be in town only a week. That was more than enough time.

Three

Chase leaned on the metal railing of the outdoor arena fence and watched Savannah ride the big black horse. The gelding loped around the perimeter, a rocking-chair gait that made the rider's hips undulate in a way that every part of Chase stood up and noticed. He'd grown up around horses, and cattle, but nothing had ever turned him on like watching Savannah simply ride in circles. Which was completely crazy. He wasn't a cowboy. He'd never hit the rodeo circuit like Cord and Chance, or Cash for that matter. He could ride. He'd grown up on the Crown B. But this? He shifted uncomfortably, and jerked when his phone buzzed in his hip pocket.

Tucker. Chase swiped his thumb across the phone to answer. "Yeah, bud. What's up?"

"I have her booked into a room with full comp."

"Thanks."

"You wanna explain what's going on?"

He would if he understood it himself. Instead, he went for the easy answer. "She's a friend of Kade's."

"A…friend."

"Get your mind out of the gutter, Tuck. Not that kind

of friend. They grew up together, sort of like brother and sister. She's here for the rodeo this weekend. I'm doing him a favor."

"Uh-huh."

Silence stretched between them before Chase finally broke it. "Say what's on your mind, Tuck."

"I got a look at the security footage, man."

"Ah."

"Yeah. The video has been deleted." The uncomfortable silence returned, but Tucker sliced through it this time. "She's not a stray dog, Chase. You can't toss her out, then leave food on the porch."

Chase thought fast because after talking to Kade, he did feel sorry he'd thrown her out, but there was something more—something he couldn't quite put his finger on. "If I'd known who she was, Tuck, I would have comped her a room last night. She's not a stray. She's Kade's friend."

"Whatever, cuz." Voices hummed in the background before Tuck continued. "When are you coming back?"

"What's up?"

"Not sure. Security thinks there might be something hinky going on out on the floor."

"Keep them on it. I'll be back after lunch."

"Okay."

He continued to silently watch Savannah exercise her horse, but when he noticed the animal's gait was off, he started to say something. She'd already realized there was a problem, reining the animal to a stop and slipping off his back. She checked his rear leg, then walked him to the gate. Chase met her there and took in her slumped shoulders and tight expression with one sweep of his gaze as he opened it for her.

"What's wrong?"

"Indy was kicked three weeks ago. I dropped out of that rodeo and didn't enter another to give him a chance to heal up. He seemed fine when we got here so I paid my entry. If I don't run him, I lose the fee."

"What's the vet say?"

She mumbled something Chase couldn't understand, so he touched her shoulder. Her muscles twitched but she didn't jerk away. "Savannah?"

"I don't have the money for a vet." She wouldn't meet his gaze, keeping her chin tucked in and her eyes downcast. "It's just a deep muscle bruise. I had someone look at it. Rest, heat, mild exercise."

"But…"

She pulled away from him and began leading the horse toward the long barn with the rental stalls. "But nothing. If he can't run, my season is over. I can't afford to buy another horse as good as Indy. Thing is, I have to win to keep going. I don't even know if I can get him back to Oklahoma and keep him long enough to heal. Grain isn't cheap." Snapping her mouth shut, she tucked her chin against her chest again. "I'm sorry. I didn't mean to dump my problems on you. It's none of your business. I'll deal with it." She moved away from him, putting the big horse between them when she added, "I need to cool Indy down, muck his stall and brush him. Can you stick around to give me a ride back to pick up my truck?"

"Yeah, I can do that."

When they entered the barn, and he figured out which stall was hers, Chase sent her off to cool down the horse. He took off his bespoke suit coat, stripped off his designer tie and rolled up his sleeves. Before he grabbed the shovel and hay fork, he placed a call to Tuck to get the best large-animal vet in Vegas to the fairgrounds to check out Savannah's horse.

While Chase shoveled manure out of the stall, then raked the dirt and clean straw into place, his internal dialogue was short and sarcastic. He didn't need to get wrapped up in this girl's problems. Not his style. At all.

But her tough-girl exterior and the flashes of vulnerability he glimpsed stirred something deep inside—something more than his libido.

Chase knew better than to examine that feeling too closely. He wasn't a white knight and this girl didn't need him riding to her rescue. Her clothes were old, her boots scuffed and run-down at the heels, her tack fixed so many times the repairs had repairs. She needed more than a quick roll in the hay and that was his standard operating procedure. He was definitely a love 'em and leave 'em kind of guy. Plus, he preferred his women sleek, designer and aware of the rules of his game. He didn't want—and definitely didn't need—a down-home cowgirl next door like Savannah Wolfe.

By the time Savannah returned with Indigo, Chase had bought fresh alfalfa hay and a bag of grain and filled the stall's manger and feed bucket.

He'd learned long ago it was better to ask for forgiveness than to ask for permission. Far fewer arguments that way. But he didn't quite manage to get her off the property before the vet showed up. They had that argument while the doctor examined her horse. When he delivered his prognosis—a deep muscle bruise, possibly bone chipping—all the fight went out of her. And Chase's heart went out to her—a wholly unexpected, and unusual, feeling.

Savannah didn't argue when he led her to his Jag. She looked defeated as he settled her into the passenger seat. He got behind the wheel and glanced at her before putting the sleek car into gear and driving off. "I'm sorry, Savannah. Indy will recover, though. That's good, right?"

"Yeah." She wouldn't look at him, and her flat tone didn't make him feel better.

They rode in silence for several miles. Savannah inhaled deeply and straightened her shoulders. She opened her mouth to speak, but the ringing of his phone interrupted. He hit the answer button on the steering wheel.

"Chase Barron."

"Where are you, Chase?"

"We're driving back to the hotel, Tuck. What's up?" He didn't like the tight sound of his cousin's voice.

"You need to pull over and take me off Bluetooth."

"Okay." He located a convenience store up ahead and pulled in. With a few deft motions, he disconnected the phone function and held his cell next to his ear. "Talk to me."

"I just got a request to free up two of the suites on the penthouse floor. For Uncle Cyrus and the Carrolls—father and daughter."

Chase glanced at Savannah, who was pretending she wasn't eavesdropping, not that she had a choice in the close confines of the sports car. "When?"

"They're arriving Friday." Tucker cleared his throat on a choked chortle. "I'm not supposed to tell you. Your old man is planning to ambush you."

"Ha. Thanks for the heads-up."

"What are you going to do?"

He cut his eyes to the passenger seat, an idea starting to form in his brain. A really bad idea. Or one that was utterly brilliant. Chase couldn't decide. "Not sure yet. I'll let you know."

Disconnecting the call, he put the Jag in gear and pulled back out into traffic. For the entire ride, until he turned into the valet lane at the Crown, he didn't give Savannah a chance to question him. With his hand gripping her arm just above the elbow, he guided her inside and to the VIP clerk at check-in to get a card key. In the private elevator, he punched in the number for her floor.

"We've comped you a room, and your things are already there. Grab a shower and clean clothes, then buzz me at extension seven star star one. I'll come down to get you, and we'll go back up to the apartment. We'll decide on lunch and order."

"Mr. Barron—"

"Chase. Please, Savannah? Just do this for me. We'll figure out something about your situation, okay?"

"Okay." The doors slithered open silently and she stepped out. He leaned against the panel, keeping the elevator open. "It'll be okay, Savannah."

She tilted her head and watched him through unblinking eyes. "Why are you being nice to me?"

The corner of his mouth quirked into a sardonic smile before he could stop himself. "I have no idea. I just know that I want to." He freed the door and it closed on her bemused expression.

Upstairs, he paced through the apartment, fitting pieces of a plan together. He had a crap ton of stuff to do and very little time to do it in.

Forty-five minutes later, he had a handle on almost everything. All he needed now was Savannah's cooperation. Considering the deal he'd put together, he figured it wouldn't be too hard to win her over, despite misgivings expressed by his brother Chance, and by Kade.

Savannah stood under the hot water pouring from the rainfall showerhead. Her room was like a little minisuite. There was a sitting area with a huge LED TV, and a small table for two next to the window that looked out over the Strip. The mattress on the king-size bed bounced her a little when she flopped on it, and then sucked her into its memory-foam goodness. The bathroom was…huge, sporting a whirlpool garden tub big enough for two and a separate granite-walled shower big enough for even more.

She pressed her hands against the stone wall and bowed her head. If some tears mixed in with the water, who would know? Besides her. She didn't cry. Didn't have the time or the inclination for it. But here she was, bawling twice in less than twenty-four hours. Letting go of a dream was hard, but she had no choice.

Indigo was hurt too badly to race. In fact, the vet had wanted to take him to the clinic for X-rays. Her horse was done. Out for at least three months, if not forever. The whole thing was so stupid. She'd been mounted, waiting her turn to run at a rodeo last month in Denver. Another competitor had ridden up beside her and within seconds, the other horse had freaked, whirled and nailed poor Indigo in the gaskin, the area between the thigh and hock. She'd checked Indy, but there was no broken skin. Thinking the flighty horse had missed, she'd run the barrels that night and Indy pulled up lame at the end of the run.

Guilt swamped her. One of the guys with the rodeo stock company had looked at Indy for her. He knew almost as much as a vet and had diagnosed a deep bruise. He'd recommended rest. Hot packs. Then alternate hot and cold packs. She didn't have money for a vet and she darn sure wasn't going to call home for a bailout. Her mother and Tom, Mom's latest loser boyfriend, would be all up in her face with the I-told-you-so's. Well, they'd told her so, and now she had no choice but to tuck her tail between her legs and sneak home. Her shoulders shook as she cried harder.

Maybe Kade would loan her enough money to get back to Oklahoma, though she didn't know what she'd do once she got there. Surely some of the restaurants or clubs in Oklahoma City were hiring. She'd need good tips to pay Kade back. She'd have to sell Indy. She couldn't afford to board him—or get him properly doctored by a vet— and with Tom living with her mom, she couldn't stay at the farm.

The thought of losing her horse hurt her heart. The first time she'd put him through his paces she knew she had a winner, and it had revived her dream of becoming the Champion All-Around Cowgirl at the Wrangler National Finals Rodeo.

And now that dream was dead, ground into the red dirt she'd never be able to shake off her boots.

Savannah twirled the shower handle and the water flow stopped. Braiding her hair while it was still wet, she didn't bother with makeup—not that she often wore any—and pulled on a pair of clean jeans, her boots and a T-shirt. She didn't want to see Chase Barron, sit in the same room with him, have lunch with him. Chase knew too much, saw too much. And with his dark hair, coffee-colored eyes and dimpled grin, he was far too dangerous for her to deal with when she was feeling this vulnerable.

Still, she picked up the phone and dialed his extension. While he'd been a major jerk in the beginning, he had stepped up to help when no one else had. Not that she needed help. She was just fine on her own—had proved that since she was twelve, when her mother brought that first scumbag home and he'd tried to get into bed with Savannah. She'd handled everything life had thrown at her so far. She would handle this, too. Because she had no choice.

When his phone beeped to announce Savannah was waiting, Chase was as ready as he could be. He went down in the elevator to retrieve her. Over hamburgers— her choice for lunch—he laid out his plan.

"I want to sponsor you."

She choked, grabbed the glass of expensive spring water he'd poured for her and chugged it. "Excuse me?" she sputtered once she could talk.

"You want to go to the National Finals, right?"

She nodded but didn't speak.

"I know Indigo is out of commission for now. I know you're on your last dime, almost literally. I know that piece-of-shit truck won't make another thousand miles, much less the ten thousand you'll need to drive to hit enough rodeos to qualify for Nationals."

Savannah just watched him, brow knitted, lips pursed. He really wanted to kiss those lips. Which was crazy, given what he was about to propose. When silence stretched between them, he pulled his eyes away from her mouth and refocused on her eyes.

"I'll sponsor you. Well, technically, Barron Entertainment will. The company will provide you with a new truck, a new trailer—both carrying our name. I've talked to Kade about a replacement horse. He has one in mind and can have it here before the first round Friday night. I'll pay your gas, all other travel expenses, entry fees, insurance, stall rentals and whatever rodeo-related expenses you have."

Her tongue darted out to wet her lips, her eyes wide now, and unbelieving. He wanted to chase her tongue with his lips. That could wait. He had to win her over to his plan first. "After Nationals, win, lose or draw, I'll pay you a bonus of two hundred and fifty thousand dollars."

"There has to be catch."

His little wildcat didn't trust easily. That was okay. He had every expectation he could convince her this was all to her benefit.

"What, besides barrel racing, do I have to do to receive this Barron bounty?"

"Marry me."

Four

"Marry you." Her voice was flat to her own ears, though she all but screeched her next question. "Are you out of your frickin' mind?"

"Maybe."

Savannah stared at Chase, wondering what bizarre thing would come out of his mouth next. "You're crazy. I'm not going to marry you. I… You…" She breathed through the tightness in her chest. He'd dangled her dream in front of her only to jerk it out of her reach. "No. You're completely nuts. Less than twenty-four hours ago you had Security perp walk me out of this hotel. Now you're all…" She fluttered her hands, at a loss for how to describe his actions. "Crazy. Just crazy."

"Please hear me out, Savannah."

She folded her arms across her chest, leaned back in the very comfortable chair and cocked a brow. "Fine. I'm listening."

"I find I'm in need of a wife."

"Uh-huh."

"A wife of my choosing, not my father's."

She leaned forward, curious despite her misgivings. This explanation was going to be a doozy.

"I'm fairly certain you're aware of my...reputation."

The snort escaped before she could hold it back. "Reputation? What? You mean the one that lands you on the front cover of every tabloid from LA to London? A different woman in your bed every night? Or do you mean the sex tapes floating around the internet? Yeah. I think the whole world is aware of your *reputation*, Mr. Barron."

He attempted to look contrite but she didn't buy it for a second.

"Call me Chase, please." He brushed a manicured hand through his expertly styled hair. "Look, Savannah, this is a win-win for you. And for me."

"You still haven't explained your reasons, Chase."

"My father has decided I need to settle down, and I need to get married in order to do that."

"So why me?"

"Because he has an acceptable wife picked out for me already."

She couldn't breathe for a moment, and her voice sounded slightly strangled as she pushed out words she didn't want to say. "An *acceptable* wife. And I'm not. You want to marry me because I'm a dirt-poor, Choctaw cowgirl and it will piss your old man off." Heat surged in her cheeks and her fingers tingled from adrenaline. She wanted to hit him. Or run. Anything but sit here and be embarrassed by this rich clown.

"No, Savannah. That's not true. Not really. Yes, I need to be legally married before he gets here Friday. Yes, you happen to be here and in a position where we can help each other out. But no, it didn't occur to me that you're...that you would be something to taunt him with. Well, beyond the fact that I'd be preemptively marrying you before he could try to force me to marry Janiece."

He sank onto the granite block that served as a coffee table, scrubbing at his face with the palms of his hands—hands, she reminded herself, with a better manicure than her own. There he sat in designer slacks, a starched cotton shirt with so many threads she probably couldn't count that high, his high-dollar haircut and boots that likely cost more than she'd made last year. And here she sat in faded jeans fraying at the back pockets, scuffed boots all but falling apart, a T-shirt advertising a boot company, and her hair semitamed into a braid.

"But I have to be honest, now that you've brought it to my attention. Yes, if you marry me, there will be flack. From the old man and probably from my family. I've already talked to my brother Chance. He's an attorney. I want him to draw up a prenuptial agreement."

She opened her mouth to protest, but Chase held up a hand to stay her argument.

"It's to protect you as much as me. I'm making certain promises to you. You have every expectation that I'll deliver. The prenup ensures that you'll be taken care of, as promised. I won't lie. Chance is not happy with me, but that's par for the course. I'm sort of the bad seed in the family." He offered a boyish grin meant to disarm her, and it succeeded—to a point.

"I'm not your type, Chase." She tried to meet his gaze head-on and add a glower, but she couldn't keep her eyes from sliding to the side as she spoke the truth. "I'm rough. I live from payday to payday. I don't wear heels or designer duds. I don't talk like you. Heck, I bet your hands are softer than mine. No one is going to buy this marriage as anything other than what it is—a marriage of convenience to get you out of trouble with your father."

Chase couldn't deny her words, nor would he do her the disservice of trying. She told the truth, but at the same time, there was something compelling about that. Most women—okay, every woman he'd ever dated—wanted something from him and would tell him whatever they thought he wanted to hear in order to get it. Savannah was different. She was…real. What he saw was what he'd get. And what he saw fascinated him.

She was prickly, stubborn, full of pride, curvy, tomboyish—all the things he stayed away from when it came to women. She'd be way more trouble than she was worth. She'd be a crimp in his social life. She'd bedevil him like crazy. And some perverse part of him looked forward to the challenge, actually craved it. He watched her struggle to meet his eyes, realized she was feeling exposed and didn't like the feeling.

Despite his social failings where the opposite sex was concerned, Chase understood people and their motivations on a visceral level. That made him extremely successful in the entertainment business. He sensed this woman would always speak the truth, at least as she perceived it. He'd appreciate that in the long run, if not always in the present. And despite her strength, there was a vulnerability shrouding her that stirred a deeply buried protective streak.

"I won't embarrass you, Savannah. I wouldn't do that to you. I'll take care of you for the length of the contract between us. You'll walk away at the end with what I've promised—new truck, the trailer, the horse we get from Kade, all your expenses. Clothes. Food. Hotels. Vets for the horse, including Indigo. I'll get Kade to bring your new horse out and he'll take Indigo back to the ranch to heal. You keep the money you win. You'll have enough to keep you going when we divorce. I'll even do something stupid so it's all on me. You can walk away free and clear with your head high."

"Why, Chase? I still don't get it. Why not just tell your father to go…" She stopped before using the word on the tip of her tongue and corrected it to "Uh…take a flying leap? You're an adult. Why let him control you?"

She had a point, but his reasons were so messed up, a battery of psychiatrists would have a field day trying to figure out his family dynamics. "Look up the term *dys-*

functional family in the dictionary. The definition will be two words. *The Barrons*." He lifted one shoulder in a negligent shrug. "But you deserve the truth. I'm weak, Savannah. And a coward, pretty much. My father is a right bastard, and he's ridden roughshod over every one of us. He's threatened to fire me. Chance fixed the family trust so I'll be taken care of, but I wouldn't be in charge of Barron Entertainment."

He pushed off the table and strode to the windows. Las Vegas and the desert beyond spread before him in a seemingly endless vista. "I *like* what I do. Hell, I love it. But more important, I'm good at it. I wasn't good at anything growing up."

Chase snapped his mouth shut and stiffened. What the hell was wrong with him? He never revealed his true thoughts to anyone. Not even Cash, especially not now. He wasn't smart like Chance. He wasn't a leader like Clay. He wasn't honorable like Cord. And he sure wasn't like his twin, always putting the family before his own needs. Quite the opposite, in fact.

"We're not consummating the marriage."

Thankfully, her words interrupted his reverie. He turned his head, and heat curled deep inside as he swept his gaze over her. She really was beautiful in a down-to-earth way. He didn't miss the widening of her eyes, the quick intake of breath that swelled her breasts or the delicate shiver that skittered over her skin as he watched her.

"But we are sleeping in the same bed," he countered.

"Whoa. What?"

"We have to convince my father we're married. That means you sleep in my bed—with me—while he's here. You'll be headed out on the circuit after the rodeo, right?"

She nodded, apprehension warring with something else in her expression. Was that interest? Maybe a touch of curious lust? He liked that idea.

"We won't necessarily be together under one roof. Except when you come back here and there's a long stretch between your appearances."

"Why can't I go home to Oklahoma?"

"Because you'll be my wife, and since this is my main residence, you'll come here. I'll arrange for permanent stable and training facilities for you." He walked back across the room and stopped in front of her so she had to crane her neck to look at him.

"We work together in public to make sure no one gets the wrong perception." He resisted the urge to cup her cheek. "We'll paint a picture of a happy couple in love. I'll have Tucker set up accounts for you at the hotel's boutiques. Buy whatever you need. I promise not to drag you to a fancy party unless absolutely necessary, and I'll prep you before that happens. We'll hold hands in public. Smile at each other. Do that sort of thing. Here in the apartment, when we're alone, we act as normal. My bed is huge. You can put pillows down the middle or whatever you need to feel comfortable. I promise not to put the moves on you."

He held out his hand. "Do we have a deal?"

Savvie's palm itched, and the muscles in her right arm contracted in preparation for the shake that would seal her fate—at least for the next year. A look crossed Chase's face as his gaze swept over her, much as it had when he stood across the room. This time, the impact was immediate. She couldn't ignore the thrill zinging through her. She couldn't help it. Despite being a royal jerk, he was sexy. And handsome. And charming. And she was a red-blooded Oklahoma cowgirl who knew prime breeding stock when she saw it. The guy had good genes—and jeans, or at least slacks. She shook her head to clear the sexual tension building in her middle. Getting involved with him was Trouble with a capital *T*.

But could she afford to walk away? He was offering her the chance to fulfill her dream. Making this deal with the devil would ensure she could keep Indy, and he'd get the treatment he needed. She wouldn't have to tuck tail and sneak home. All she had to do was live in a fishbowl for the next twelve months. She shouldn't trust this guy any farther than she could throw him but some twisted part of her urged her to accept him at face value. He was a scandal waiting to happen, but his boyish charm held a touch of uncertainty with a side helping of wistful desperation.

"Deal." She raised her hand and he clasped it. Had she been a romantic, she would have expected a bolt of energy or awareness or some mystical connection to surge between them at the touch of their hands. But she felt nothing beyond smooth skin, gentle pressure and a sense of relief.

"Excellent. We have a lot to do between now and Friday." He whipped out his phone and pressed a number. "Tucker, I need you in the apartment." He hung up and hit a second number. He listened for a moment, then left a message. "Chance, draw up the paperwork we discussed. Courier the originals out here. I'll have Tucker witness and notarize. Thanks, bro."

He paused to wink at her. "I'll have Security give you a code for the elevator. Tuck will take you downstairs to shop. In the meantime, call Kade. Tell him exactly what you need." He turned away, already keying in the next number on his cell.

"Uh… Chase?"

He refocused his attention her. "Yeah, kitten?"

Huh. She'd gone from *wildcat* to *kitten*. She wasn't quite sure how to process that. Instead, she pushed forward. "I… um… I don't mean to be greedy or anything, but could I talk to Kade about borrowing two horses? If I have a roping horse to go with a barrel horse, I can double up on my events and points. I won't keep them or anything, after… well…next year. I just want Indy. I'll ride the other horses, but they'll still belong to you. Okay?"

His gaze narrowed and then cleared as she babbled.

"Babe, whatever you need. Don't worry about expenses. I have money. Feel free to spend it. And those horses are yours. No matter what." With that, he moved away from her and into the recessed space that served as his office, his phone pressed to his ear.

She dug her cell phone out of her pocket and dialed Kade. She didn't expect the first words out of his mouth.

"Are you out of your freaking mind?"

"Uh, hi, Kade. I'm fine, thanks. How are you?"

"Pissed, little girl. You need to get as far away from Las Vegas as you can get."

"Nope. Can't do that."

"What have you done?"

"We shook on it, Kade." She huffed out a breath heavy enough to stir the thick strand of hair straggling over her forehead. "Look, this is a good deal for me. If I don't take it, I slink home so my mother and that jackass warming her bed can rub it in my face. I can't do that. I won't do it. Chase is offering me a deal I can't walk away from."

"You don't know him."

"Yeah, I do. I read the tabloids. I know he's a womanizing jerk face with entitlement issues."

An uncomfortable silence stretched between them before Kade's voice whispered in her ear. "*Itek soba*, he'll break your heart."

Sister of the horse. Kade hadn't called her that in a long time. Using the childhood Chickasaw nickname he'd given her brought home just how worried he was. "No, he won't. I'd have to love him first, and that is so not gonna happen, *anakfi*." She used the Choctaw word for *brother*. "There's paperwork so we're both covered. I have to do this, Kade. You know that. Are you going to help me?"

"Of course I am, Savvie. But I damn well don't have to like it."

"So… I need two horses."

"I figured you might. I have two Crown B bred horses

I think will work. Tansy Reed's been working Cimarron. He's rough and still needs seasoning but he's fast, and I think the two of you will work well. He has a soft mouth."

"Okay." Wow. Tansy Reed was *the* premier barrel racer and trainer. She'd retired from the rodeo circuit to raise her family and train horses. "What about a roping horse?"

"Have the perfect guy for you. I've been working Big Red myself. He's quick, responsive and I swear he knows where the calf is gonna be before I do. I've also done both heading and heeling with him in case you want to add team roping."

"I'll keep it in mind. Don't have a partner for that." She pursed her lips, considering. "Yet. I'll look around, see who's available."

"I'll load up and head that way today. I'll be there by Thursday morning. You'll have time to ride them both, and they'll have their ground legs back before the rodeo starts."

A knock on the door caught her attention. "Call me when you get here. I'll meet you at Clark County. Somebody's at the door. I gotta go, Kade."

His heavy sigh hung between them. "Are you sure, little girl?"

"Yeah. Everything is gonna be fine. You'll take care of Indy for me, right?"

"You don't even have to ask."

She ended the call, and when she caught Chase's attention, he waved her toward the door. She opened it, only to be confronted by a handsome man. He vaguely resembled Chase, except instead of sharp brown eyes, this man's were a startling blue and his hair was a dark russet brown instead of black.

"Huh." He stared at her, obviously not very impressed. "I can't wait until Uncle Cyrus gets a load of you. Let's go."

"Go?"

"Yeah. I'm Tucker, soon to be your cousin-in-law. I'm

taking you shopping. Clothes. Truck. Trailer. Sound familiar?"

"Before we sign the paperwork?"

"Nothing goes into your name until after the marriage."

"Oh." Savannah wasn't quite sure how she felt about that.

Tucker looked over the top of her head and called to Chase. "We'll stop by Security and get her into the system. See you for dinner."

He grabbed her arm and tugged, but she jerked free. "Wait. My purse."

Reaching around her, Tucker pulled the door closed. "You won't need it."

Five

Chase watched Tucker tease Savannah, surprised at the burn in his chest. His cousin and the woman he planned to marry had spent the previous afternoon picking out a pickup, a fancy horse trailer, getting her added to his credit accounts with a checking account of her own and into the hotel's security system so she could access his apartment. He'd spent the day auditioning some new showgirls, dealing with a situation on the casino floor and listening to his big brother rant about how stupid Chase was being. That was easy for Chance to say. He'd found and married the girl of his dreams. True, Dad had done his best to break them up, but Chance told the old man off and went merrily on his way. Chance didn't have the old man breathing down his neck, complete with a forced marriage looming.

If he had to take the plunge, Chase was darn sure he'd be doing it on his terms, not his dad's. He studied the woman he'd be marrying within the next twenty-four hours. This morning, he had a conference call with investors and the architect of the new hotel project in the Bahamas. He'd need to rent a car for Savannah to drive until the new pickup and trailer were ready. Kade was due to arrive in the morning, and she'd be out at the fairgrounds all day with the ranch foreman and the new horses.

He planned a fast trip to the Clark County Marriage License Bureau, an office open 24/7 due to Vegas's reputation for quickie weddings, for later in the afternoon. They'd get married Thursday night so it was a done deal before the old man hit Vegas on Friday.

"Hope you don't mind."

Chase pulled his head into the conversation and stared at Tucker. "Mind what?"

"That I'm taking Savannah to Leather and Lace."

Savannah choked and coffee spewed out her nose. She grabbed a napkin, coughing, while Chase thumped her on the back. "Can you breathe?" When she nodded, he still watched her to be sure, but answered Tucker. "I don't have a problem with that. See about getting her some custom boots. They won't have them ready before she heads out, but we'll have them here the first time she comes home."

"Uh, hello. Right here. I don't need boots. Or anything else…leather."

Both men glanced at her and Tucker chuckled. "L and L is the premier Western store in the area. The few things you found in the boutique downstairs won't go far."

Chase nodded. "We need to fill up your half of my closet. And Tuck's right. You need new clothes."

Her face turned red again, and she pushed out of her chair, all but spitting mad. "What's wrong with my clothes?"

It was totally perverse of him to enjoy her anger but dang if it wasn't fun. "Darlin', those jeans are nothing but holes held together with a prayer. You need new work boots. You need new boots for the arena and—" he propped one booted foot up on the table "—I know how comfortable custom boots are. As my wife, you need to upgrade. It's expected."

She sputtered and spit and shoved his foot off. "You

musta been raised in a barn, boy. Don't you know better'n to put your feet on a table with food?"

He grinned and was almost sorry she'd be taking off soon. He'd like the chance to get to know her better and do a whole lot more teasing. He liked her curves, and the way her expressions revealed her thoughts. Maybe he would do a little seducing along the way. Before he could think too deeply on that urge, Tucker's phone pinged.

"Courier from Chance is here." Tuck left to meet the person Security was escorting up.

Chase leaned back in his chair and studied Savannah. He hadn't missed her quick inhalation or the widening of her eyes at the mention of the arrival of the prenuptial paperwork. "Second thoughts, kitten?"

Her eyes wouldn't quite meet his when she replied. "No. Yes. A little." She squared her shoulders and met his gaze. "What about you? You can walk away and not be stuck with me."

"Something tells me I'm getting the better deal."

He realized he'd said that out loud when he saw the surprised look on Savannah's face. But before he could add anything, a very feminine squeal filled the air, and a bundle of feminine curves landed in his lap.

"Chase! I'm so glad Chance sent me. I've been wanting to see you for...like...forever." The girl in his lap cupped his cheeks and plastered kisses all over his face. He would kill his brother the next time he saw Chance. "I've never been to Vegas. I took some comp time so I can stay a couple of days, and you can show me around and we can—"

He cut off her babbling by clamping his hands around her waist and lifting her out of his lap. A glance at Savannah made him wince. She tried to hide her feelings, but she wasn't quick enough. He saw anger, and was that a little hurt, too? She definitely wasn't happy, and he couldn't blame her.

"Where's the paperwork from Chance, Debbie?"

"Darla. My name is Darla." The girl huffed in displeasure, one hand on her hip, the other holding a manila envelope.

"Oh, yeah. Right. Whatever."

Tucker relieved Darla of the sealed envelope. Using a pocket knife, he slit it open while Darla glowered. After a few moments, her eyes flicked to Savannah.

"Who're you?"

"This is my fiancée," Chase answered before Savannah could.

Savvie wasn't very happy when Darla bent over from the waist, laughing hard. She started to tamp down the remark on the tip of her tongue and then gave up on being circumspect. That wasn't really her style. Reaching over to take Chase's hand, she put her best snooty face on. "Chase, darlin', you really need to stop screwin' the hired help. They get so pushy and all uppity when you do."

Tucker lost it. He laughed so hard tears squeezed out from the corners of his eyes. Chase stared at her, biting his lips, but his eyes danced with amusement.

"Oh, my God. You can't be serious, Chase. She's… she's…"

Chase flicked his gaze to the girl, and Savannah was really glad he wasn't looking at her with that expression on his face. "She's the woman I'm marrying, Darla. You'd be wise to remember that. I'll call Chance about sending the papers back. For now, I suggest you head to the airport and catch the first flight back to Oklahoma City."

"But…but… I flew out here in the company jet."

"The company jet is reserved for family and employees. Effective as of right now, you are neither."

Savannah couldn't prevent her jaw from dropping. She squeezed Chase's hand and started to say something, but Chase shushed her with a look. She clamped her mouth shut and waited.

"I'll show you out, Darla." Tucker took the girl's arm

and tugged her toward the door. A few minutes later, he returned and shut the door. "Security has her. They'll escort her to the airport, and make sure she's on a plane. I'll call Chance, fill him in."

"Hey." Savannah quietly asked for Chase's attention. "You didn't need to fire her."

"Yeah, I did. You're going to be my wife, Savannah. Legally and binding. No one talks to you that way. No one makes that kind of assumption."

She studied his expression. He was serious and being truthful. Wow. Who knew the guy had some depth, and maybe a modicum of honor, after all? "Okay. But just so you know, I'm pretty good at taking care of myself."

Chase and Tucker exchanged looks, then both burst out laughing. "Hired help," Tucker sputtered.

"Pushy and uppity." Chase snorted, and laughed harder.

Savannah crossed her arms over her chest. "Dang. It wasn't even that snarky."

"Finish your breakfast, wildcat. Tucker wants to go all metrosexual and pick out a wardrobe for you. Let him."

"Okay." Savannah chewed on her bottom lip a moment. "What?"

"What what?"

Chase's gaze lasered in on her mouth. "You look like you want to ask something. What is it?"

"Oh. Just…uh…wondering what you'll be doing today while I go spend gobs of your money?"

"Running my empire." He leaned in to whisper in her ear. "And I doubt you'd spend my money at all if I weren't forcing it on you. Just be back by four this afternoon. We need to get the marriage license."

Her breath caught, and her body went a little haywire, not that she would let her reaction show—especially since they had an audience. She'd be smart to remember that Chase Barron was a rascal—a very sexy one who used women without a shred of guilt. Pushing back from the table, she retreated. The expression on his face told her he knew what she was doing. She didn't really care. She needed space.

"Before you go, we both need to sign the prenup."

"Oh, right."

Tuck watched her go through the racks. He was flirting with the salesclerk, but he also made note of what Savannah was doing. Every time she checked the price tag of an item, he snagged it and told the clerk to hang in it the dressing room.

"Stop doing that, Savannah. If you like something, try it on. If you want it, it's yours."

"Yeah, easy for you to say."

The negligent lift of one shoulder indicated he didn't care about her feelings on the matter. "Look, hon, my cousin very often leaps without considering the consequences. I read the prenup. I know what you're getting out of this deal. I've also spent time with you. You aren't comfortable with this. I don't know what your reasons are but they have nothing to do with Chase's money."

It was her turn to offer a desultory shrug. "People are still gonna talk."

"Yes, they will. You need to be prepared for that. Especially since Chase won't always be around to shield you."

"What does that mean?" she faced Tucker and asked. "Shield me from who?"

"His family. The media. Anyone familiar with the Barron name."

Chase would deal with his family so that wasn't a concern. The media? Yeah, that would suck. "Maybe I can fly under the radar. I won't use his name when I enter my events."

"Sorry, babe. That won't work. The Barron name will be plastered all over your truck and trailer. And Chase isn't exactly shy and retiring."

That got an eye roll. "No kidding." She closed her eyes and tilted her head back in an attempt to ease the tight muscles in her neck. After taking a deep breath, she opened her eyes and offered Tucker her I'm-gonna-do-this face. Then she spoiled it all by asking, "He's not going to be monogamous, is he?"

Tucker's expression was full of sympathy. "I doubt it. But you'll have to be."

She laughed at that. "I haven't had a date in two years." Heading to the dressing room, she left Tucker standing there with his mouth hanging open.

Four hours later, they walked out of Leather and Lace with bags and boxes and more clothes and pairs of boots than Savannah had owned in her entire life. Tucker had convinced her to change from her jeans and T into a dress that reminded her a little of traditional Choctaw garb. Embroidery, ribbons, a full skirt, all in natural colors that Tucker insisted set off her golden-brown skin and dark hair. And new boots. Expensive new boots that fit her feet like gloves. The boot maker in L and L had spent an hour measuring, drawing and discussing leathers, heels, colors and stitching designs. Tucker refused to let her see the bill but she'd seen the price tags. Who in their right mind dropped almost twenty thousand dollars on clothes? Oh, yeah. Chase Barron and the women he was used to dating, for sure, but not plain ol' Savannah Wolfe.

The last person she expected to see was Chase leaning up against Tucker's sleek Mercedes SUV, looking all fashion-model perfect in his tailored suit, starched shirt and designer tie. The slow grin lighting up his face did all sorts of things to her bits and pieces—which she needed to ignore because she was not letting Chase get under her skirts. Skin. She meant skin. And he was just slick enough that he could charm his way right there if she gave him any room at all.

"You buy the store out?"

Blushing, she tried to say something but only stammered out nonsense.

Chase was suddenly there, his hands gently gripping her waist. "Whoa, kitten. Breathe. I was joking."

Taking his advice, she inhaled several times. "I'm not a gold digger." She murmured it under her last deep breath, but he heard her.

"I know that, Savannah."

She stared into his eyes. "Do you? Do you really?"

Studying her face, Chase realized she was truly worried. "Yeah, kitten, I do." He dropped his head to place a kiss on her forehead. "You aren't Debbie."

"Darla."

"What? Oh, yeah, right. Darla. You aren't her, Savannah. You aren't that producer's wife. You aren't those two backup singers in Nashville. You're just…you. You're in a tight spot, and so am I. My money will help you out of yours. You marrying me gets my dad off my back. Trust me, I'd spend a small fortune to ensure that."

"You are definitely doing that—spending a fortune." She cocked her head to one side and studied him. He met her gaze without blinking. "Why me, Chase?"

"You've asked that before."

"I still don't get it. Why me?"

"Because you *are* you. You don't want my money. My wealth makes you uncomfortable. You're honest. In my world, that makes you pretty much one of a kind."

"Wow. I don't think I want to live in your world, if that's the case." She didn't smile at him and he could feel her sincerity.

"Not always a good place to be, but I have the feeling it's gonna be a little easier with you in it."

Tucker cleared his throat with a discreet cough. "Cuz, take your lady to a late lunch. I'll head back to the hotel with her stuff and see that it's put away in your apartment."

He off-loaded everything into his SUV and disappeared, leaving the two of them standing in the parking lot.

"What are you hungry for?" Chase's libido almost took him to his knees as Savannah stared up at him and licked her lips.

"Hungry for?"

He knew what he was hungry for. Keeping his hands-off promise might just kill him. He still couldn't pinpoint what drew him to this untamed cowgirl but something damn sure did. "Food, kitten."

"What are *you* hungry for?"

Her. He wanted to taste her—her mouth and other places. He willed his body to behave and plastered an easy smile on his face. Poker. They were playing emotional poker and he was a high-stakes player in this game. He made a quick decision and offered her a choice.

"Mexican or Chinese?"

"Mexican."

Hot and spicy. Just like her. He all but groaned at the direction his thoughts kept taking and gestured toward his Jag to cover his reaction to her.

Chase shared his favorite hole-in-the-wall taqueria with her. He didn't bring people here, except for Tucker, but his cousin didn't count as *people*. He'd never even brought his brothers here. It felt right to be sitting at the scarred wooden table with Savannah, sharing street tacos and listening to her talk about life on the rodeo circuit. Their conversation fell into an easy rhythm, and he found himself sharing anecdotes of his childhood and the scrapes he and his twin got into.

More at ease with her and his decision, Chase paid the bill, and they headed to the marriage license bureau. They shuffled through the line, with more than a few covert glances cast their direction. He'd hoped to keep things low-key but cell phones were not-so-surreptitiously pointed at them. Savannah appeared unruffled, and his admiration ratcheted up another notch. That was good. She'd need to be unflappable when word of their marriage leaked, and they faced his father. Cyrus didn't lose gracefully, and he'd do his damnedest to make them all pay.

Six

With license in hand, Chase steered the Jag toward the hotel. They hadn't driven even a block before his cell phone rang. He punched the Bluetooth button, but Tucker didn't give him a chance to speak.

"Mayday, Chase."

He exchanged a humorous glance with Savannah as he answered. "Can't be that bad, bud. What's up?"

"Wanna bet? Oh, wait. This is Vegas. I don't know if we have a spy or what, but your old man is on his way. Early."

Chase growled. "Debbie."

"Darla," Savannah corrected.

Watching the traffic ahead, Chase made a quick decision. "We'll get married now. I'm pulling into the Candelabra Wedding Chapel as we speak. When is the old man due to arrive?"

"My own spy says late tonight. After midnight."

"Okay. We'll stay out late."

"I'll cover."

"You always do, cuz. Thanks."

"Don't thank me. I'm keeping track, Chase. You owe me big-time." Tucker chuckled, then dead air hummed over the car's speakers.

Chase parked and cut the engine and swiveled to face Savannah. "Well, kitten, this is it. Your last chance to back out."

He didn't hold his breath, despite the inclination to do so. He was all sorts of a jerk for doing this, but standing up to his father without this pretense of a marriage wasn't something he felt capable of managing. Besides, Savannah needed help. It wasn't like she didn't benefit from this deal.

Her chest swelled as she breathed deeply. Her hands remained in her lap, clasped, and far more white-knuckled that he cared to see. Maybe she would cut and run. He wouldn't blame her if she did. Dealing with him, even on a limited basis, wouldn't be easy. He continued to watch her, waiting for her answer.

Savannah curled her lips between her teeth, straightened her shoulders and faced him. "Let's do this."

Whew! He'd dodged a bullet, and he knew it. Liking the woman he'd be tied to for a year even more, he winked and opened his door. "Yes, ma'am. Let's git 'er done."

They walked into what was essentially a lavender boudoir. Satin draped the walls, and there were plush velvet sofas and a dark purple runner that led them straight to a woman with swirls of silver curls—curls faintly tinged with purple. She greeted them with a fire-engine red smile. Her lace cocktail gown was the exact same tint as the walls.

"Welcome to the Candelabra Wedding Chapel!" Her eyes landed on the paper in Chase's hand. "Oh, excellent. You already have your license. So many young lovers don't, you know. Come, come." The woman clapped her hands in glee as she led them toward a long counter and an old-fashioned brass cash register. She slipped behind the counter and pushed a gold menu toward them. "We have many packages available and will happily create a custom experience for a slight extra charge."

Glancing at the list of services, Chase pointed to the bottom—and most expensive—package. "That one. How soon?"

"No waiting, dearie. That is our Stardust ceremony. Very romantic." The woman turned shrewd eyes on Savannah. "Do you need a wedding gown, lovey? We have a wide selection to choose from. Only a little added charge to rent."

Chase glanced over at Savannah. She looked fine to him. Her outfit—an airy skirt, beribboned blouse and a fringed shawl—would be considered Western chic. It'd do. "What she's wearing is suitable."

A flash of disappointment registered on the woman's face before her mask fell back into place. "Flowers? Rings?"

Oh, yeah. He studied the menu more closely. The package he'd picked came with a set of his and her gold wedding bands and a silk flower bouquet. That'd be enough. "We'll take the ones that come with the Stardust."

"Fine." The hostess sounded a bit snippy but she pulled out a velvet ring tray. "Pick any two on the bottom three rows."

He selected a band and held it out to Savannah to try on. Too small. He grabbed the next ring in the row. It was slightly too large, but again, it would suffice. Under the hawk-eyed gaze of the woman, he picked one for himself. He didn't wear jewelry so it would end up in his drawer later.

Moments later, the woman handed a bundle of white silk roses wrapped with satin ribbon to Savannah. "Do you have a witness?"

The front door opened with an electronic rendition of the opening notes of "Moonlight Serenade" and Tucker walked in.

"Yes," Chase told the woman. "We do."

"Will this be cash or credit card?"

Tucker reached into his pocket and pulled out a thick fold of bills. "Cash. How much?"

The woman punched the keys on the old cash register, muttering to herself. "That will be three hundred twenty-four dollars and twenty-nine cents, including tax."

She sorted the cash into the register drawer, then ushered them through a doorway. The room wasn't huge and carried on the purple theme. The hostess—called "Mother" by the officiant, a man with a lavender pompadour—seated herself at a linen-draped table and punched the button on a karaoke machine. She picked up a cheap digital camera and began taking pictures. A photo package was part of the deal.

Tucker offered to walk Savannah down the aisle—all six feet of it. She had never been a girlie-girl dreaming of her Prince Charming and a fairy-tale wedding, but this was pretty much a joke. Tucker's expression was studied, though he offered her hand a sympathetic pat where it rested just below the crook of his elbow. Means to an end, she reminded herself. That's all this was. Chase Barron wasn't a knight in shining armor, and while he might appear to be in distress—financially, anyway—she was no shy and retiring damsel in need of rescue. She'd rescue herself, thank you very much. Raising her chin, she squared her shoulders and focused on the man waiting about eight steps away.

The minister, dressed in a gray tux trimmed in violet and wearing a lilac-dyed fur cape, stood between two tall brass candelabras with electric candles flickering in time to the music. A medley of Liberace's music filtered over the minister's words. Loving and obeying were mentioned, richer, poorer, in sickness and health, and that whole death disclaimer. Twelve months. Fifty-two weeks. Three hundred and sixty-five days. If Savannah had a calculator, she'd figure the hours and minutes until she could return to Vegas and file for divorce.

"I do," she said when prompted.

"I do." When his turn came, Chase sounded about as enthusiastic as she did. He slid the too-big ring on her finger, and she made a mental note to get some tape to make it fit.

"You may now kiss the bride."

Her breath froze in her chest, and she couldn't even swallow. She'd been staring at the knot in Chase's tie during the recitation of their vows, but now she had to look up. Her gaze met his, and his heated expression thawed her paralysis. Before she could inhale, his mouth lowered to hers, capturing her lips. He nibbled on them, nipping her bottom lip before sweeping his tongue over it to ease the slight sting from his bite. One arm curved around her waist, pulling her hips tight against his. He was definitely happy to see her.

Her blood drained from her brain to parts more feminine as his free hand cupped her cheek and tilted her head so he could deepen the kiss. She locked her knees to keep them from shaking, and her eyelids fluttered to a close. Her nipples pebbled as her breasts encountered his chest, and she gripped his lapels in sheer self-defense.

Savannah had no clue how much time had elapsed before she surfaced from the sexual haze of that kiss. She blinked open her eyes, caught the smug satisfaction in Chase's expression and hated that she'd fallen for his ploy. The man was a player, plain and simple. And she'd entered into a marriage of convenience with him. Any feelings she might have purely complicated matters.

A discreet cough caused her to loosen her hands, give a push against Chase's muscled chest and step away. Tucker looked amused, and Mother and the faux Liberace appeared ready to proceed with pictures. Chase just preened. Savvie managed not to slap the smirk off his face.

They posed for pictures, her expression as fake as their marriage. In name only, she reminded herself. But what a name. Ten minutes later, she walked out with a CD of photos documenting essentially a marriage for hire, a gold-plated wedding band that didn't fit her finger and a bedraggled bouquet of fake flowers. That pretty much summed up everything about her. They should do a reality show about her: *My Big Fat Fake Wedding*.

In the parking lot, Tucker dropped a kiss on the top of her head and softly squeezed her shoulders. "I'll head back and cut Cyrus off at the pass when he arrives. I'd tell you to check into a suite at one of the other hotels, but that would be bad for business—the CEO of Barron Entertainment spending his wedding night somewhere other than his own resort? Yeah, no. I did, however, make reservations for a private dining room, lakeside, at Solstice. They've agreed to stay open—for a rather large fee—until the two of you leave."

Savvie shifted her gaze between the two men. "Solstice?"

"Five-star restaurant. Great steaks. And froufrou food," Chase explained. "The main thing is we'll have privacy and good food until Tuck calls to say the coast is clear."

Dinner was definitely a five-star affair. The room was lavish—like something from a Hollywood blockbuster. They'd been whisked through the line by the manager himself and escorted through the magnificently decorated restaurant to their "room." The place reminded her of a romance-book cover—something with sheikhs or barbarian princes. The man sitting across from her was certainly rich enough to be a prince, and handsome enough to grace the cover of a romance. She studied him over the rim of her champagne flute. She'd lost track of how many glasses Chase plied her with, but she admitted she liked the floaty feeling.

Chase retrieved her glass and set it on the table before taking her hand and urging her to stand. "Let's dance."

"Um…" She did her best not to stumble. "I'm not much of a dancer." Savvie could Texas two-step and do the Cotton Eyed Joe. Barely. But fancy dancing? Like waltzes or fox-trots or something?

"There's not much to it, kitten. We put our arms around each other and sway in time to the music."

"Oh. Okay. I can do that." She could, right?

He led her to the small dance floor, and a song that was vaguely familiar teased their feet to move. True to his word, he curled his arms around her waist and she put hers around his neck.

She was about five-eight in her boots and he stood almost a head taller. Her cheek nestled comfortably against the hollow of his shoulder and with her ear pressed against his chest, she could hear his heartbeat keeping time with the music.

Her fingers played with the fringe of black hair covering his collar. His hair was thick and soft, a little too long, but she liked the feel of it against her skin.

He was definitely handsome. Square jaw that was sculpted but not knife sharp. Straight nose, high cheekbones. Eyes the color of hot coffee. She stared into those eyes for a long moment, her hands dropping to his broad, muscular shoulders. She read humor there. Mischief. A hint of lust and…a secret. Chase Barron had secrets. He blinked and the moment passed.

Tall, dark, handsome—and rich to boot. The Barrons were Oklahoma royalty. A local paper once ran a cartoon depicting Cyrus Barron seated on a throne, wearing a cowboy hat with a tiara, like the ones rodeo queens wore. His five sons stood behind him, each a prince carrying the symbol of his specialty—government, law, oil, entertainment and security. A king wearing a "Midas" name tag along with caricatures of various world leaders lined up looking for handouts. Mr. Barron bought the paper in retaliation. Now that she'd been exposed to the reality of Barron wealth? Yeah, that cartoon was pretty much dead-on.

Chase Barron had everything going for him. What was

not to love? Her brain wanted to go there, figure out all the
cons, but it was foggy in her head and he smelled good.
The music was relaxing. Expensive champagne buzzed
in her blood.

Then he kissed her. The world pretty much stopped.
Her feet stopped moving as her hands tangled in his hair.
She pressed against him, her hips seeking the welcoming
hardness of his body. His tongue teased her mouth open,
swept inside, seduced her with a slow, sensual mating.

His phone buzzed. Chase didn't break the kiss but she
felt him pull out his cell. He whispered into the kiss, "All
clear, kitten. Time to go home."

Savvie shot straight up in bed, heart pounding and
ears aching from a high-pitched screech. She couldn't remember where she was, or what had happened last night.
Drunk. Chase had gotten her drunk on champagne. She'd
fallen asleep—okay, passed out—in his car. She didn't remember him carrying her to his apartment, barely remembered undressing in the bathroom, then falling into bed.
She panicked, but calmed when she realized she wore a
tank and sleep pants. That was good. The rest was bad. Her
mouth felt like it was stuffed with cotton, and her brain
hurt. A lot. The screaming didn't help. She squinted her
eyes closed, opened them, stared.

A blonde woman in a designer dress that probably cost
more than Savvie's entire wardrobe—well, her wardrobe
before yesterday, anyway—and wearing shoes looking like
they'd hurt to walk in stood in the doorway of the bedroom. The screams continued as the woman's face turned
red, and she jabbed her index finger in Savvie's direction.

"What are you doing in my fiancé's bed? Getoutgetout-
getout! How dare you!"

What the hell? Savvie's brain caught up with her hearing. Fiancé? Chase didn't mention having a fiancée when
he'd proposed this crazy arrangement. He'd mentioned a

woman his father wanted him to marry, but he'd said there was nothing finalized. Before she could say anything, the woman screeched again, and two men appeared—one tall, one shorter and rounder.

"Who are you?" the tall one demanded.

Savannah had to think a minute. This was obviously Cyrus Barron, Chase's father. The man had the same look—dark hair but with silver at the temples, piercing brown eyes the color of frozen coffee, high cheekbones and a sharp chin that was currently jutting in her direction. She threw back the covers and climbed out of bed. Better to face them standing on two feet. Luckily, she wasn't one for sexy lingerie. Her spaghetti-strap camisole and cotton sleep pants hid her assets from the appraising looks she received from the men.

"Yes, just who are you?" the woman repeated.

It was on the tip of her tongue to retort, "Savannah Wolfe," but she wasn't. Not anymore. For at least the next twelve months, she was Savannah Barron. So that's how she answered the question.

Seven

"Barron?" The three all spoke at once.

"Yes. Barron. Technically, I suppose I'm Mrs. Chase Barron." Where the hell was her so-called husband? If Chase had cut and run to leave her facing this alone she'd turn him into a steer just as soon as she got her hands on a knife.

"That's impossible." The woman looked both shocked and hurt, and her voice trembled.

"According to our marriage certificate, it's not only possible but true."

"But Chase is mine." The blonde turned to the slightly rotund man at her side and stamped her foot. "Daddy, you promised him to me."

Seriously? Savannah couldn't choke back the laughter bubbling in her throat. "Sorry to disappoint you, princess, but *I'm* married to Chase."

"But you can't be. Daddy, make her go away. Chase is mine. Write her a check or something."

Ouch. That hit a little too close to home, but while she didn't love Chase, Savvie couldn't really wish this bimbo on him. "Write me a check?" Her voice came out soft but clipped and coated in icicles.

"You just need to go away."

"Since I'm his wife that's not happenin'."

"No, you aren't. You can't be his wife."

"Want to see the license?" She hoped it had been legally filed. Maybe that's where Chase had gone. If so, she wouldn't fix him. Yet.

"It's a fake. It has to be. You trapped him into this. Do you have him tied up and drugged?"

Savvie stood there with her mouth hanging open. "Seriously? You think I drugged Chase Barron, dragged him off to marry me and even now have him tied up somewhere?" She gestured toward the bed behind them. "Are you stupid or something?"

"You can't talk to me that way."

"Sure I can."

Luckily, Chase picked that moment to slide into the room. She hadn't heard him come into the apartment.

He skirted his father, the other man and the woman, coming straight to Savvie's side. Chase curled his arm around her shoulder and dropped a kiss on her temple. "Morning, wildcat. Sorry I wasn't here when you woke up. Security called. We had a situation on the casino floor I had to take care of."

"No worries, hoss. I was just getting to know—" she waved her hand at the three other people "—them. We were discussing the status of our marriage."

"Yeah, I gathered that. You want to throw on some clothes? I'll order up breakfast."

"Works for me."

Chase turned her in his arms and dropped a kiss on her surprised mouth. His eyes twinkled as he winked at her. "Love ya, kitten," he murmured. Then he was gone, ushering their guests out of the bedroom by herding them in front of him and shutting the door.

She stood there, missing the warmth of his body and wondering what had just happened. His words were a throw-away, meant for their audience, but they still singed a spot next to her heart. Savvie had to be very careful from here on out. This man was proving to be most unexpected—in all the wrong ways.

Out in the living room, Chase dialed room service and ordered up a breakfast buffet. He was very careful to keep Janiece on the opposite side of any piece of furniture he could use to obstruct her from approaching him. Hopefully, Savannah wouldn't take long to appear. He hadn't meant for her to face down the old man alone. Chase would still have been in bed with her when his father arrived if the morning-shift pit boss hadn't alerted Security, who then alerted him and Tucker, about a card cheat on the floor. The guy had already taken the casino for half a million before they could verify he was cheating and then deal with the situation.

After their late-night arrival, Chase had figured his father and the Carrolls would sleep in. He'd figured wrong. Then it occurred to him that they'd accessed his apartment on their own. From the looks of things, Savannah had not gotten out of bed to answer the door. Tucker had been with him down in the casino. That meant his father had access to Chase's personal space. Whoever had given Cyrus the ability to get in was fired. Period. No second chances. Chase hired people who were loyal to him. Not to his father.

The door to the bedroom popped open and Savvie strolled out. Chase immediately forgot about the security problems. Dang, but the woman looked fine. She wore a new pair of jeans that sculpted her long, muscular legs and her very nice butt. The lacy T-shirt left just enough to his imagination, and he shifted uncomfortably, a move his father noted. Chase plastered on his happy groom face—which was far less difficult than it should be given the circumstances—and held his hand out for her to join him. He attempted to read her expression. This was the first huge test of their fabricated relationship, since getting his father to believe their marriage was real hinged on her actions.

Savannah approached with a smile and took his hand without hesitation. She sidled up to him, slipping under his arm like doing so was the most natural thing in the world. Chase let out a mental *whew*.

"Are you going to make introductions, hoss?" Her husky voice washed over him, and he had to resist kissing her again.

"Savannah, I'd like you to meet my father, Cyrus Barron, his business associate, Malcolm Carroll, and Mal's daughter, Janiece." Savvie acknowledged each with a dip of her head, but she stayed glued to his side and didn't speak. "Shall we get comfortable while we wait for breakfast?"

"Y'all pardon me a sec while I put some coffee on. My brain doesn't work until I've had that morning shot of caffeine." Savannah disengaged and ducked into the kitchen.

"Dad, Mal, Janiece, make yourselves comfortable. I'll give Savannah a hand." He followed her into the kitchen. The idea of being alone in uncomfortable silence with those three was totally unappealing. The thought of a few stolen moments with Savannah? Priceless.

He watched her set up the coffeemaker, then bustle around the kitchen, getting mugs, sugar and cream, and arranging a serving tray while the coffee dripped into the carafe. She paused to look at him. "What's the plan, Chase?" Her voice was a whisper.

"I meant to be here. Sorry." He'd wanted to kiss her awake but he couldn't admit that to her, especially with her hands-off policy in full force and effect. Still, he hadn't meant for her to face the old man on her own.

She lifted her shoulders in a forgiving shrug. "No biggie. Just FYI? That woman has the voice of a harpy and she was not happy to find me in your bed. Not the way I pictured waking up."

He stepped closer and pulled her into a hug. He couldn't help himself. Easier to plot, he figured, with her ear right there for him to whisper into. "*Our* bed, kitten," he corrected. "Sorry about the hangover. I ordered a bottle of champagne with the orange juice."

"Hair of the dog? No, thanks! I don't normally drink. Besides, that woman pretty much screeched the hangover out of me."

Chase choked back a laugh, then stiffened as his father came through the door and interrupted. "Really, Chase? You can't keep your hands off...*her* with your fiancée in the next room?"

"*Her* name is Savannah, Dad, and she's my wife. Unless you plan on me being a bigamist, I don't have a fiancée."

"Yo. Hello. Standing right here." Savvie pushed away, but didn't leave his side. "I know you're Chase's father, sir. For that you're due respect, but respect goes both ways. Don't talk down to me, and don't treat me like a bimbo. I assure you, I am not one."

Chase winced and wished she'd remained silent. Before he could get between her and his father, Cyrus cut him off.

"I believe you to be a calculating tramp who got her claws into my very impressionable son." The old man pulled a checkbook out of his suit pocket and flipped it open, pen in hand. "Your kind is always after the money. How much to get rid of you?"

Chase made a futile grab for Savvie's arm, but she was out of his reach and right up in his father's face before he could fully react.

"*My* kind? You mean female? Or Choctaw?"

"I will not stand here and allow Chase to make a fool of himself."

"The only person making a fool of himself is you. You walk into our home and make insinuations you have no right to make." She glanced at the checkbook and smiled. "You don't have enough zeros to buy me off, Mr. Barron. I'm married to your son and I intend to stay that way." She turned around and walked back to Chase.

Once again at his side, she confronted his father. "Just FYI? I didn't marry him for his money. If you believe that's the only reason a woman would marry Chase, then you're a sorry son of a buck and I pity you."

Wow. Chase didn't know whether to cringe, run or kiss her. No one had ever stood up for him like that. He certainly hadn't expected it from a woman he'd just met, whose loyalty he was basically buying. He straightened his shoulders and faced the old man. "We're married, Dad. For better or worse. Get used to the idea." He glanced at the TAG Heuer watch on his wrist. "Breakfast will be here any moment. You and the Carrolls are welcome to stay. Personally, I'd prefer you get the hell out so I can enjoy the small bit of honeymoon we've got left. Just know, if you stay, you will treat my wife with respect."

A loud knock sounded before Cyrus could answer. Chase dropped another kiss on Savvie's temple. "I'll go let room service in, kitten. Can you handle the coffee?"

"Got it, hoss."

He grinned, unable to help himself. "Yeah, you definitely got it, hon."

To say breakfast was strained would have been a huge understatement. Once Tucker arrived, Savvie kept her mouth shut and did her best to ignore Janiece's whining and pitiful attempts at flirting with Chase. He brushed his hand over Savvie's leg every time the other woman opened her mouth, an attempt to let her know things would be okay, she supposed. Cyrus continued to glare, which wasn't conducive to a healthy appetite. Maybe she should have kept her mouth shut. What had possessed her to take on the patriarch of the Barron clan? She needed to stay off Mr. Barron's radar big-time, and antagonizing the man was not the way to make that happen.

She managed to choke down some scrambled eggs and bacon, relying mostly on the strong coffee she'd brewed. Hardly anyone else ate. Just Chase. He shoveled food into his mouth like a bear stocking up for hibernation. Looking at him, one would think everything was hunky-dory. When he pushed his plate away, he reached for the champagne chilling in a bucket of ice, and popped the cork on it. He filled the crystal flutes on the tray next to the ice bucket and passed them around.

Remaining on his feet, he raised his glass in her direction. "Here's to my beautiful wife. She's already made my life better."

He extended his glass toward her, so Savvie carefully clinked hers against his. The fragile crystal pinged. She took a sip, then extended her glass. "And here's to my handsome husband, the man who surprises me constantly."

They clinked again, then touched glasses with the flute Tucker held out. The three of them each took a sip, while the others didn't move, the flutes sitting untouched next to their plates.

"I cannot believe you are participating in this travesty, Tucker." Cyrus turned on his nephew. "I mistakenly believed you were the one with some intelligence and sense."

Savvie's phone picked that moment to ring. She fished it out of her hip pocket, glanced at the screen and cringed inwardly. "I... Sorry. My mother. I need to take this call." She pushed away from the table before either Chase or Tucker could move to hold her chair. She ducked down the hallway as she answered and didn't stop walking until she was in the bedroom with the door shut.

"Mom?"

"You've been holding out on me, Savannah." Her mother's tone grated. Kayla Wolfe had been drinking.

"I don't know what you're talking about."

"Are you pregnant?"

"Excuse me?"

"You heard me. Did that SOB get you pregnant? I saw you and Chase Barron on that *Inside Celebrity* show. They said you got married. At least you were smart enough to get a ring on your finger. Not like some people."

Savannah closed her eyes and resisted the urge to bang her head against the wall. She knew exactly who that "some people" referred to. Every time the Barron name came up, her mother alluded to Kaden's mom, Rose, insinuating she'd had an affair with Cyrus Barron and Kaden was an illegitimate Barron son.

"No, Mom. I'm not pregnant."

"Good. Still, married to a Barron? You better get lots of money to send home to me, baby girl."

A soft rap on the door had her scrambling. "I have to go, Mom."

"Send money, baby. Tom needs a new truck."

Chase opened the door and peeked around its edge, a questioning expression on his face. She waved him in as she signed off. "Bye, Mom."

"Problem?"

She plastered a smile on her face. "No. She was just calling to congratulate us."

"Uh-huh." He brushed two fingers across her cheek. "Don't lie to me, kitten. And a word to the wise? Don't ever play poker with me. Especially strip poker. I'll have you naked before we finish one hand."

That made her laugh. "Pretty sure that's the truth."

"C'mon, babe. Talk to me."

She gave in to temptation and thunked her forehead against his chest. His arms came around her waist. "Yours isn't the only dysfunctional family in the world." She straightened and tried to smile, but figured it was more of a grimace, judging by Chase's expression. "Don't ever give my mother money. No matter what she says or does."

"Ah."

"Yeah, ah. I'm serious, Chase. She'll whine and wheedle and pull all sorts of crap to get it from you. And warn Tucker, too. Okay?"

"Sure, babe. We'll watch out for her."

"I'm sorry."

"For what?"

"For having a greedy mother. For letting your father get to me."

"Shh." He pulled her back to his chest and held her while he brushed his cheek over the top of her head. "You were pretty darn impressive. Not many people stand up him. Thank you for coming to my defense."

"You're welcome. Now, let's get back so we can make them all go away. We're supposed to be on our honeymoon."

Eight

Chase had hoped their guests would leave while he was in the bedroom with Savannah. Her words were still ricocheting through his brain. Her mother sounded like a piece of work, and he made a mental note to ask Kade about the woman. Savvie's reaction to the phone call left him feeling protective—and concerned. For a moment, he considered throwing money at the problem, then stopped cold. That's what his father would do, was trying to do with Savannah. No, he would follow Savannah's request. No money to her mother. Not without his wife's permission.

He almost tripped. *His wife. Needing—wanting—her permission.* Two totally new concepts for him. He liked the first, oddly enough. Holding her hand as they stepped into the living room, he stopped cold. His father was on the phone, yelling. Janiece looked smug, while her father appeared uncomfortable and was probably wishing he was anywhere but here. Chase seconded the feeling.

"You better fix this, Chance," Cyrus spit into his phone.

That explained the atmosphere. The prenup had been overnighted to Chance and was probably open on his desk at that very moment. While his big brother might think he was an idiot, he'd still cover Chase's ass.

His old man whirled and stabbed him with a glare as he threw the cell phone to the table. "You believe you're so smart, Chasen. We'll see how far you are willing to take this farce when I call a board meeting to have you ousted as CEO."

Chase didn't believe he was smart—he knew. Even so, the threat wasn't idle, but he could hold his own with the board. He'd taken Barron Entertainment from owning one hotel and three media outlets—print, television and radio—to a multibillion-dollar corporation with multiple five-star properties, an entire network of media companies and huge dividends for the very small pool of shareholders. Like all things under the Barron umbrella, the company was family held. That meant his brothers and cousins. They liked the money he made them.

"Well?" Cyrus prodded.

Chase squeezed Savannah's hand as he morphed his expression into one of bored amusement. "Well, what? Which of those nonquestions do you want me to answer?"

"Don't be flip with me, boy."

He bristled, the feeling unsettling. Everyone thought Cord was the easygoing brother, but Chase was the one who always went with the flow. Until now. "I'm not bein' flip, Dad. Just asking for clarification."

His father stared at him for a long moment, then another, before flicking his gaze to Savannah. "She worth losin' everything for?"

Without scrutinizing his actions for any deeper meanings, Chase tugged Savannah to him, embraced her and dipped his head to take her lips in a gentle kiss that quickly got heated. One hand went low, pressing her hips into his, while his other arm wrapped around her back. Her breath hitched in her lungs and he felt it in the deepest recesses of his existence. He was in trouble, and at the moment, he didn't care. He liked kissing this woman. Liked it a lot. And he decided then and there to woo her. Her hands-off policy? He fully intended to smash right through that.

The way she responded to his kisses assured him she was not immune to his charm. They were married. Married people made love. Oh, yeah, that was definitely on his agenda. As soon as he could convince her that they could have fun together for the yearlong length of their contract.

He broke the kiss and glanced at Tucker, then at his watch.

"Look, this has been all fun and games but I have a corporation to run, Savvie has a meeting and at some point, I plan to get back to our honeymoon."

Cyrus's eyes narrowed. "What's that supposed to mean?"

"It means that you are in the way, Dad. All of you. Unless you are here on a business matter? My personal life is off-limits. I never agreed to marry Janiece and frankly, if I were her, I'd be embarrassed that my father had to buy me a husband. Or in my case, a wife." Chase stared pointedly at Janiece before returning his gaze to Cyrus. "I'm quite capable of finding my own wife, Dad." He still held Savannah's hand, and he brought it to his lips, brushing a kiss over her knuckles before he continued. "As you can see."

Janiece, her eyes shiny bright with unshed tears, leaned against her father as he ushered her to the door. Mal glowered at Cyrus and muttered, "I've never been so embarrassed. You owe me, Barron." He patted Janiece's back as he said, "We're going home, girl. We're so done with this." They disappeared through the apartment door, slamming it behind them.

Chase faced off against his father, Tucker and Savvie by his side. "This conversation is done, Dad. You want a board meeting? Call it. I'm good at what I do. You know it. You think you can do it better? Go for it. I believe the board won't be very happy with your management style but if you're feeling lucky? No skin off my nose."

"This isn't over, Chasen." Cyrus pivoted, marched to the door, jerked it open and left it gaping after he passed through.

Tucker drifted after him, made sure his uncle had disappeared into his suite across the hall, then shut the door. He turned to face the couple. "Gee, that went well."

Savannah parked her brand-spanking-new Ford truck next to the equally new and shiny horse trailer in the long-term parking area of the Clark County Fairgrounds. She locked up the pickup and sighed as her fingers traced the emblem on the driver's door. What a difference a couple of days made. Shoving the keys into the front pocket of her jeans, she strolled toward the barn where Indigo's stall was located. As she approached, she recognized the silhouette of the big man framed in the doorway.

Her gait slowed and she inhaled deeply several times to settle her nerves. As soon as she was close enough, she noticed the disgruntled expression on Kade's face. He was not happy.

"What the hell were you thinking?" he asked as soon as she was close enough to hear. "Oh, wait. You weren't!"

"Gee. Hi, Kade. Happy to see you, too." She fought the urge to look away while digging the toe of her brand-new boot into the dirt.

"C'mere." He opened his arms, and she fell into them.

"Oh, Kade." She squiggled her nose against the burn of tears, and blinked moisture out of her eyes.

"What's wrong, baby girl?"

"His father."

"Cyrus?"

"Yeah."

"Crap. He's here?"

"Yes. He… Oh, lordy, Kade. That man is just evil. He…
The things he said. The threats. Poor Chase."

"Whoa. What? Poor *Chase*?"

She pushed off his chest and backed up a few steps.
"That man is despicable."

"Chase?"

"No. His father. Keep up here, Kade." He shook his
head, laughing, and Savvie breathed easier. "Chase is…
He's not what I expected."

"What's that mean?" Kade focused on her and she
smoothed out her expression.

"Later. Show me who you brought me?"

"No, sooner, but I'll let it go for now, hon. C'mon." He
turned on his heel and headed into the shadowy barn. "I
checked Indy. I think he'll be okay after treatment and
rehab. He'll get both at the Crown B."

The band around her chest eased a little as she caught
up to the man who was essentially her big brother—chosen by her heart, not by shared blood. "I was really worried, Kade. That's good."

He snagged her hand and squeezed, but didn't let go
as he led her toward the stalls at the end of the long aisle.
"You're gonna tell me all about the wild hair you got, but
first…" Kade stopped at a stall.

A black-and-white paint quarter horse dropped his head
over the gate and nickered softly. Her heart melted as she
gazed into the horse's big brown eyes. "Well, howdy there,
handsome."

"This is Barron's Cimarron River, Sav. He's your new
barrel racer."

She rubbed her knuckles against the horse's forehead
and he arched his neck to make it easier for her to reach.

"I should warn you, the beast is spoiled rotten. Miz
Beth took a shine to him and snuck him carrots when I
wasn't looking. He's especially fond of the baby variety."

That made Savannah laugh. "I'll be sure to carry a supply."

"That new trailer will make it easy. It's got a fridge in the dressing area."

"Yeah. I know." Savvie glanced over her shoulder. "Kade—"

"Not now. We'll sit down. Talk. Business first."

"Okay."

"Now, this fellow…" He pulled her away from Cimarron and nudged her toward the next stall. "This is Barron's Red River."

The horse that arched his head over the stall door was the color of his name—a bloodred sorrel with a slightly darker mane and tail. Savvie stroked his nose as Kade continued. "Big Red's a worker. And he's smart. You point him at a calf, he knows what to do. Team roping, he'll go either way like I said, but he's a better header."

She moved to stroke the horse's muscular neck. "Good to know." When team roping, one rider roped the steer's horns, and only the horns. There was a time penalty for catching the cow around the neck. The second rider basically dropped a loop on the ground to catch the steer's rear feet—his heels. Again, there was a penalty for catching only one hoof. "I prefer to head so it's all gravy."

"You found a partner yet?"

Glancing over her shoulder, she studied the man she'd known since she was a toddler. "Been a little busy."

"Yeah. Figured."

"Kade…"

"Later, babe. Where's your saddle? It's going in the trash."

"What?"

"Your tack is crap, Sav. I know that. You know that. Tucker told me to get the best. I went to The Saddlery in Cowtown. Rusty knows you so you now have the best. Saddles aren't quite custom fitted but close. I have a gear kit put together, too. S'already in your trailer. Let's get these boys saddled and exercised."

A grin split her face. As far as she was concerned, a bad day on a horse was better than a good day anywhere else. Except... Chase's kisses were pretty darn good. She caught a flash of dull gold on her left hand and looked down. Her fake wedding band. Her feelings dampened a bit. Yeah. The fake jewelry that left a dark band, as she'd discovered when she washed her hands, was symbolic of her fake marriage. It didn't matter that Chase was handsome. Funny. Charming. And could kiss. This was a business deal. And it was time to get down to business.

Nine

Chase needed to keep his thoughts on the business at hand. The Carrolls had checked out and returned to Oklahoma. His father was still occupying the suite across the hall. Chase had had Tucker change the security codes and fire the desk clerk who'd given his father access. From that moment on, no one got a card key to the apartment unless the order came directly from Chase or Tucker. It didn't matter who made the request. His hotel, his rules.

Savannah had gone to the fairgrounds to meet Kade, and Chase's thoughts kept wandering to the woman he'd taken as a bride. She surprised him. Continuously. He liked that. A lot.

He heard a throat being cleared. Tucker nailed his shin under the table. He jerked.

"What?"

"We cutting into your daydreams, Chase?"

He glared at his cousin before turning his gaze to the two businessmen from the United Arab Emirates. "I'm sorry, gentlemen. I admit my mind is elsewhere."

The two men exchanged knowing glances. "We understand congratulations are in order, Mr. Barron. I must admire a man who would leave his marriage bed to take care of business."

Okay, he could work with this. "I have a most understanding wife and as this meeting was already scheduled, I did not want to inconvenience you."

Chase glanced toward the architect and nodded. The man and his assistant rose, grabbed a cardboard tube and emptied it. In moments, the conference table was covered with floor plans and three-dimensional drawings. The Arab hoteliers were suitably impressed with the concept for the hotel and resort complex Barron Entertainment wanted to build in Dubai. This was Chase's project. One his father didn't know about. One that would make him and the company a desertful of money. He sat back in his chair, letting the artistic types use all the adjectives.

Catching Tucker's eye, he allowed a tiny twitch to curl the right side of his mouth into a hidden smile. His cousin's left eye lowered halfway. Yeah, they were on the same page and it felt good. Tuck always had his back, had since they were kids and thick as thieves. Chase, Cash, Tucker and Bridger Tate. The four musketeers. Now Bridge worked with Cash the way Tuck worked with him.

He made a note to call Cash to discuss the recent security breaches on the Crown's casino floor. His instincts screamed there was something more about the situation, but he couldn't put his finger on what troubled him. Security was Cash's baby. Chase felt secure in handing over the problem to his twin.

The Arabs were asking questions now. He continued to observe them, the nuances of their words, the exchanged glances and subtle body language. Oh, yeah. He had them hook, line and sinker. He'd get their signatures on the bottom line. Business first and then he'd track down his wife and commence with Operation Seduce Savannah.

* * *

Savannah, mounted on Cimarron, raced across the arena. Dirt flew behind the horse's hooves. Her heels rubbed Cim's sides, urging more speed. She kept her hands soft, the reins flapping against his neck. Then she pulled the big paint to a sliding stop with the barest lift and tug on the reins. The horse's mouth was just as sensitive as Kade had implied. She could work with that.

Easing the big animal around, she rode to the spot where Kade leaned against the fence, stopwatch in his hand.

"Well?"

"Thirteen point five." He grinned at her. "You'd be in the money with that time. Not bad, Sav. Not bad at all."

She grinned back, the smile so big her cheeks crinkled. "He has more to give, Kade. A lot more. Look at him!" She leaned forward and patted the horse's neck. "He's not even breathing hard. I can get under thirteen. Heck, I might even break twelve!"

"Yeah, I think you might." Kade reached through the fence and teased Cim's chin. "Let's get him cooled down and put up. I'm hungry. I'll buy you lunch."

Sav raised her arm to check her watch. "Two? It's already two o'clock? Dang. Yeah, I'm starved, too."

She urged Cim toward the gate and Kade met her there, opening then closing it behind her. She swung down from the saddle, loosened the girth and led the paint back to the barn, Kade keeping pace with her.

Before she could strip the saddle, Kade had already done so. While he carried it out to her trailer, she curried the horse, crooning to him and promising to bring carrots. Movement at the stall door caught her attention.

Kade braced his forearms on the top of the gate and watched her. She kept brushing, knowing he'd speak his mind sooner than later. He didn't disappoint.

"He's a player, Sav."

"Duh, Kade. I read when I'm standing in line at the grocery store."

"The headlines don't say it all."

"He's a Barron. That pretty much says the rest." It did, but it didn't. It didn't say Chase could be as sweet as he was clueless. It didn't say that the man could curl her toes with a kiss. It didn't say that now, after seeing Kade, Chase and old Mr. Barron up close, she could see what her mother saw. If Kade wasn't a Barron, there'd been gene splicing in his mother's womb.

"Have you two had sex?"

"Kade!" Heat rushed into her cheeks and she knew she was blushing furiously. "That is none of your business."

"I repeat, hon. Player."

"And I repeat, bro. I know. We have an agreement. This is a business arrangement."

"I've stayed in his apartment, Sav. He doesn't have a guest room."

"No. But."

"But what?"

"His bed is huge."

"And?"

"And I sleep on one side, he sleeps on the other." At least she hoped he did. She'd been passed out drunk last night and couldn't remember. Janiece's shrill voice had been such a shock to her system, Savvie didn't stop to consider things when she first opened her eyes. She'd woken up alone. That said volumes. Or so she thought.

"Hon, Chase attracts woman troubles like honeysuckle draws bees."

"I'm not sure of that, Kade." She reviewed what she thought she knew about Chase, and the things he'd said in passing. "I think maybe that sometimes he—"

"Sometimes I what?" Chase appeared next to Kade at the stall door and Savvie blushed.

"Y'all wanna explain why I'm the topic of conversation?" Chase was pissed.

Kade turned his head and gave him a lazy once-over before returning his attention to Sav.

"Didn't expect to see you out here, Chase. I thought you had a meeting," Savvie said.

"Had a meeting, babe. Now I'm here. Anything wrong with wanting to see my wife?" Her eyes widened and she opened her mouth to speak, but he cut her off. "Our business is our business, Savannah. You don't discuss it with employees."

Her nostrils flared, and her face colored beyond her previous blush. "Excuse me? You know what Kade is to me. And come to think of it, what am I? I'm your employee, too."

Chase felt Kade shift beside him, but he kept his gaze focused on Savannah. He liked that she had a temper. He liked that she was loyal, but she should be loyal to him, not… Chase cut that thought off. She considered Kade her family. After overhearing Sav's conversation with her mother that morning, he could understand why she was angry. While he should be thankful Kade was looking out for her, he was still pissed. She should be turning to him for that support. He was her husband. Only…not. She was right about that, too.

Chase reined in his emotions. What was it about this woman that sent him reeling from one extreme to another? He wimped out and completely changed the subject. "Good-lookin' horse, Kade."

The man beside him snorted. "Your cousin told me to bring the best."

He cut his eyes to Kade, then returned his gaze to Savvie. "I came to see if you wanted to go to lunch with me."

"No. I'm busy," she replied.

"Sav." The way he said her nickname got two pairs of eyes snapping to him.

"I'm doing lunch with Kade."

"He can join us."

"No."

"Sav." Chase said it again and gave her The Look. He recognized the moment she wavered, and pressed his point. "We'll take your new truck. You can drive." He was so intent on her reactions, he missed Kade shifting away and turning to face him.

"Yeah, Sav. Let's do lunch with the boss."

Chase watched Savannah's gaze dart between him and Kade. One part of him wondered what Kade was up to, while the other was glad the man appeared to agree with him. "We'll go to Cantina Del Sol."

"Is that where we ate the other day?"

Yup, he knew the way to her forgiveness. Food. "Yeah."

"Okay."

"Okay."

Chase ended up driving. She rode shotgun, but spent the trip twisted around in her seat talking to Kade. Every time Chase glanced at the rearview, Kade's eyes met his in the mirror. He and Kade would need to come to a meeting of the minds much sooner than later.

As he drove, Savvie filled the other man in on their arrangement, finishing with "So see? I'm not being dumb, Kade. I thought it through." She reached around her seat to grasp his hand. "Mom doesn't get to win. Not this time. And it's important to me. I've wanted the chance to compete on this level since I won my first belt buckle. You know that, Kade. You were sitting there on the fence cheering me on."

"Savvie, you were ten, and it was a kid's rodeo."

"And now I'm twenty-five. I had a good shot with Indigo. A really good shot. I got my hands on him by a fluke and a lot of horse trading. I have to stand on my own two feet."

As Chase watched in the mirror, Kade's tan skin darkened. "Your own two feet? How are you doin' that, baby girl? Chase is payin' your bills. Giving you the ways and means. What's he expect in payment?"

Before Chase could jump in to defend his actions, Savvie released Kade's hand and caught his. "Get your mind out of the gutter, Kaden Waite. You know me. We…" She gestured between herself and him before continuing. "Chase and me have an agreement. A contract. It's business. He gets advertising. I get a sponsorship."

"Then why are you married?"

"Because it was expedient," Chase interjected after a pause.

He didn't say anything else as he pulled into a parking lot and maneuvered the big vehicle into a pair of spaces. He retrieved Savannah's hand and twisted in the driver's seat so he could see both Sav and Kade.

"The old man was setting me up to get married, Kade. He even dragged Janiece Carroll and her father out here to force an engagement. Savannah needed a sponsor. I needed a wife. We have a prenup. She's covered. She'll get what she wants. This time next year, I'll do something stupid to give her grounds for divorce. She walks away with this truck, the trailer, all the gear you brought, plus the three horses. If she's as good as I think she is, she'll also have the All-Around Cowgirl Championship buckle, trophy and winnings. She walks away with two hundred and fifty thousand dollars over and above what I spend on her expenses. It's all a win for her."

"Except for spending nights in your bed."

Chase bit back a retort. Now was not the time to lose his temper, but Savannah beat him to a reply.

"He hasn't touched me, Kade. That's part of the contract. Yes, in public we act like newlyweds and a happily married couple. That's a show for his father."

"A show for Cyrus? Dammit, Savannah, do you know

what this makes you? A frickin' gold digger. I never thought—"

"Shut up, Kaden." Chase's voice was pure icy anger. No one disrespected Savannah. Especially not the man she considered family. "Nobody says that crap about Savannah. No one, not even you. My father stood there in my home—*our* home—this morning, a checkbook in his hand. You want to know what Savannah told him? She got toe-to-toe right up in his face and told him he didn't have enough zeroes to buy her off. She is *not* a gold digger, and you damn well will never say anything bad about her. Ever. You got me?"

Kade settled back against the seat, his gaze fixed on Chase. Emotion flickered across his expression, but Chase couldn't read its meaning.

"Okay, then."

Chase narrowed his eyes. "What's that mean?"

"You're right. I need to trust Savvie."

Chase jerked his chin down in acknowledgment. "Okay, then."

Ten

Kade stayed through Saturday. He was there cheering Savannah on, helping her with the horses and watching. Always watching. Before her runs on Saturday night, she approached him as he saddled Big Red for the roping event.

"Hey." She touched his arm and made sure she had his total attention. "I know what I'm doing."

"Does Chase?"

Kade's question threw her off stride. "What do you mean?"

"I see the way he looks at you, Savvie. He wants you."

His assertion should not have made her feel the way it did. She should not feel giddy and all, *OMG, he likes me!* Pushing those thoughts away, she considered Kade's statement and what she knew of Chase. He liked women. *Lots* of women. She was just one more notch on his bedpost. Right? Right! As long as she remembered that, she'd suffer through those searing kisses of his and resort to cold showers.

"I'm female, Kade. I'm not totally clueless, but we have an agreement. And I'll be gone first thing Monday morning. He's putting on a show for the cameras and his family. That's all."

Her best friend growled under his breath as he backed away to shake out her rope, removing the twists before looping it and dropping it over the saddle horn. She would not back down on this.

"Do you trust me?"

His head whipped around, and his sharp gaze stabbed her. "What kind of question is that, Sav?"

"The one you're forcing me to ask. Answer me."

"Of course I do."

"Then trust me. I know Chase. Yes, he's a player, but let's face it. I am *not* his type."

"You're female. That makes you his type."

She snorted out a laugh, catching Kade off guard if his scowl was any indication. "Hon, trust me. I am *not* his type. I don't have long legs, I have thunder thighs. I don't have melons, I have grapefruit. All my curves went south. He likes them runway thin, blonde and high maintenance. I am definitely not any of those things."

Kade stared at her for a long moment. "You don't have a clue, Savannah." He made a sweeping gesture with his hand. "There isn't a guy within a mile radius who wouldn't jump on you if you offered."

Sav rocked back on her heels, shocked but pleased. "Really?"

Tilting his head back, eyes to heaven, Kade sighed heavily. "You are clueless, babe. Totally clueless." He lowered his chin to look at her. "Yes. Really. You have any idea how many horny football players I beat up in high school?"

She giggled, then clapped her hand over her mouth. "No. You didn't!" At his slow nod, she bit her lips to get control before she continued. "No wonder I didn't have a date for prom."

"You had a date."

"With you! Not cool, Kade. You're like my brother."

She rolled her eyes and curled her lip into a disgusted snarl even as she fought laughter.

"Yeah. I am. And that's why we're having this conversation." He rubbed the back of his neck, then dropped a hand to her shoulder to get and keep her attention. "Look, I understand why you're doing this. I do. I don't like the way you're doing it, but I understand. Still, I'm worried. The guy is bad news. All the Barrons are." Some delayed emotion drifted across his features. "Well, the twins are. The others? They found good women, changed. But Chase and Cash? Not good, babe. Not good at all."

Chase stood close enough to hear their conversation, but was hidden in shadow. He should be angry that his employee was talking to Savannah and saying the things he said. At the same time, he was well aware of his reputation—one he'd somewhat fostered. One that was coming back to bite him in the ass now. He'd discovered something over the past several days spent with Savannah. He liked her. As a person. Granted, he found her sexy and enjoyed kissing her far more than he should, given the circumstances, but he was male. And she was very, *very* female. In all the right places.

He wasn't upset that Kade noticed, or that other men noticed how attractive Savannah was. As long as none of them tried to act on their urges and as long as she rebuffed them. She was Chase's wife. She had to stay beyond reproach to keep his old man off his back. At the same time, he was a little irate that Kade thought so little of him. He'd never done anything to Kade. None of his brothers had. The ranch foreman carried the Barron stamp, whether the guy knew it or not. Cyrus would never acknowledge an illegitimate son, which sucked for Kade, but Chase and his brothers had always treated him with respect. To find out now, under these circumstances, that Kade had so little respect for him stung.

The loudspeaker announced the next event—calf roping. He'd come back behind the chutes to wish Savannah good luck. She'd had good barrel racing runs and he thought she'd done okay with the calf roping so far, though she didn't have the best times. He didn't want to give away the fact he'd overheard them, so he faded farther back into the shadows and made his way to the box seat he'd bought. He'd managed to duck the gaggle of paparazzi they picked up every time they left the hotel, by slipping into the men's room. The photogs hadn't done their homework. There was a back exit that led to the competitors-only area.

Photos and stories were hitting the entertainment sites, along with tweets and Facebook postings. His cell phone had blown up with texts and voice mails. He was careful about sharing his number with most women, but a few had it. They were upset. He'd never made promises to them, nor had he thought about choosing any of them to get him out of this situation. Savannah had been in the right place at the right time, and she was the right woman.

Stopping at the concession stand, he grabbed a beer and returned to his seat. He sipped and reflected while waiting for Savannah's name to be called. The last couple of nights had been sheer torture. The night of their wedding, when she was so cutely drunk, Savvie had rolled into his side, snuggled in with her head on his shoulder and her arm draped across his bare chest. He tended to sleep nude but had kept his part of the bargain by wearing cotton sleep pants. She'd worn a tank that hid nothing and soft pants that slipped low on her hips.

He'd spent the whole night half-awake and totally aroused. Still, he'd kept his promise. He hadn't taken advantage. Once upon a time, he might have. Savannah had sought him out, wanting to sleep close. That said something about her feelings. But taking advantage of her hadn't been in the cards. She trusted him. Oh, he fully planned to seduce her, to make love to her, but he'd do it when she was sober—well, mostly sober. If she had a few beers or some wine to mellow out? He could work with that.

Thursday and Friday night she'd scrupulously stayed on her side of his California king bed. In a T-shirt. A long-sleeved T-shirt. And socks. He slept hot and tended to keep the room cooler at night, but her getup was ridiculous, and they both knew it was a futile attempt to keep him at bay.

He was so lost in his thoughts, he almost missed the announcer. "Here's a real show of dedication, folks. Next competitor is Savannah Wolfe Barron. She might be on her honeymoon but she's a real cowgirl because here she is."

That comment would generate more tweets and Insta-grams and news reports. Still, it fit the narrative he was building. Chase could live with the publicity, and he figured it wouldn't hurt Savannah's quest for the National Finals.

The calf burst from the chute and a second later, Savannah followed on Big Red. The sorrel was right on top of the calf in a few strides. Sav dropped her lasso over the animal's head, her arm whipping back to snug the loop as she twisted the rope around her saddle horn. Red slid to a stop even as Sav stepped from the saddle, dashed to the calf, grabbed, grounded and snugged in three legs while she tied them with the pigging string she'd carried in her mouth. She threw her arms up and the air horn sounded.

From the cheers, he figured she'd gotten a good time. He really needed to bone up on rodeo events. Sooner or later, some nosy reporter would ask. Plus, with Operation Se-duce Savannah in full force and effect, he needed the edge so he could celebrate and compliment her achievements.

After the calf roping ended, he headed back to the con-testant area. He'd take Savannah to a late dinner, take her home. There would be a hot bath. Maybe wine. The offer of a massage for tired muscles. He gave good rubdowns. Women enjoyed his hands.

He found Sav and Kade in the barn, rubbing down the

horses. He pitched in, putting out feed and hay, then carrying her saddles back to the trailer and locking it up. To be nice, he offered to include Kade in his dinner plans.

"Thanks, but no. I'm leaving at the butt crack of dawn, and I've got to swing by here to load Indigo before I go."

A look of concern washed over Savannah's face, and she focused on the stall where the black horse was stabled. Kade squeezed her shoulder.

"He'll be fine, Sav. I'll take care of him."

She offered Kade a tentative smile that seared Chase right down to his core. "I know you will. I just..." She drifted toward Indigo and the horse reacted by arching his head over the gate. Savvie rubbed his cheek and ears. "He's been good to me. I'll miss him."

Without thinking, Chase closed the distance between them and reached for her. He tugged her close for a hug. "I'll make sure Indy gets whatever he needs. And if you want to fly in to see him while you're on the road, do it. I'll cover the expense."

He physically felt Kade's stare burning into his back and raised his head to stare back. Chase was staking his claim, showing that Savannah's feelings were important to him, declaring that he understood what was important to her.

"I... Wow, Chase. That's..."

He returned his attention to the woman in his arms. "Shh. If you get the urge, fly home, kitten. Rent a car or I'll have someone pick you up at the airport." He glanced back to Kade. "Pretty sure Kade won't mind meeting you. You can stay in my room at the ranch. Though, fair warning. Miz Beth is nosy." He chuckled and felt Savvie's arms slip around his waist.

"I can handle Miz Beth."

He laughed outright at that. "I know you can, honey." He leaned back a little so he could see her face. "You can handle anything and everything, Savannah."

Eleven

After parting ways with Kade in the parking lot, Savannah folded into the passenger seat of Chase's Jaguar. She waited until he was settled and buckling his seat belt before speaking.

"I can drive the truck back to the hotel, you know. So you don't have to get up early and bring me back out here tomorrow morning."

"Kitten."

Those two syllables held layers of nuance and hidden meanings. "How do you do that?"

He glanced at her, amusement gleaming in his eyes. "Do what?"

"Guys. How do guys put so much into so little?"

He started the sleek vehicle, shifted into Reverse and backed out of the parking space. "I'm not following you, kitten."

"See? You did it again."

This time he laughed as he drove out of the lot. "Still not making sense."

"Men seldom do." She huffed a breath that ruffled the hair curving across her forehead. "Say it again."

"Say what?"

"Kitten."

She knew he was humoring her when he said it. "Kitten."

"See?"

"No, babe, I don't. Care to enlighten me?"

"Doesn't matter that it's only two syllables. When you say it—depending on how you say it—it says so much."

"Okay…" Chase drew out the word.

"I see you aren't following. Or maybe you are and there's some secret guy code that prevents you from explaining."

"Okay."

"Again! One word. And the way you said it just now makes it have completely different meanings."

"Okay."

"Stop it!" She slapped at his biceps and his laughter curled around her heart.

"I think I'm following. Sort of."

"Look, the first time you said *kitten*, there was a wealth of meaning there."

"What did I mean when I said it the first time?"

"I was making the point that you could sleep in rather than drag your butt out of bed to drive me out to the fairgrounds. Rodeo isn't your thing. There's no sense in you hanging around all day. So I say that. And you say *kitten*." She did her best to emulate the way he'd said it.

"And?"

"And what you said was that you were going to get up early, drive me out to the fairgrounds and hang around all day. That you *expected* to get up early, drive me and hang out. And that I should expect you to expect that."

"I said all that?"

"Well…yeah. Didn't you?"

"Sort of. What I actually said was that I'm a guy, I drive, you're my girl, so I'm going to drive you. And I'm expected to do those things and hang out all day because we just got married, are ostensibly on our honeymoon and that's what's expected of a newly married couple."

"See? That's exactly it. You said all that in a two-syllable word. A pet name. It's…" She sighed. "How do guys do that?"

He laughed again, but she didn't think he was laughing at her. He was simply enjoying the conversation. "Aren't guys supposed to be the strong, silent types?" She caught his glance and nodded. "So we have to learn to communicate in as few words as possible."

"Well, you do it well."

He offered her a three-quarter profile, an arched brow and a smug smile. "I do everything well."

"I've heard that." That got her a dimpled smile, which sent a little quiver shooting through her.

"You hungry?"

Savannah wanted to throw her hands in the air in frustration. Two words. Two innocuous words. He was asking if she'd like to get something to eat. She would. Her stomach was about a minute away from growling. But she wasn't thinking about food. She was thinking about him. And doing things to him. Him doing things to her. So yeah, she was hungry.

"I could eat."

That got her a sideways glance. "Want to go out or head home and order room service?"

She should remain in public with him. Definitely. "Let's do room service. I need a shower."

And dang if that didn't get her a full-face look and a slow, sexy grin. What was she thinking? And why wasn't her mouth obeying her brain?

"I can work with that."

Wisely keeping her mouth shut, she remained silent until they got to the hotel, rode up in the elevator and entered his apartment.

"Trust me?"

His question caught her off guard, and she gave him a narrow-eyed look. "Yeah…"

"Go grab your shower. I'll order up dinner."

"And what does any of that have to do with trust?" Oh, but he was devilish when his eyes twinkled like that. She breathed in deeply.

"Trust me to order something you'll like."

She wasn't expecting that answer, and she blinked a few times in order to catch up. "Oh. Uh, sure."

He flashed another smile, this one with only a hint of dimple, before he gripped her shoulders, turned her around and nudged her toward the hallway leading to the bedroom and master bath. "Take your time. In fact, if you'd like a bubble bath or—"

A snorting giggle escaped before she could smother it. "Uh, thanks, but I'm not really a bubble bath kind of girl."

He paused a couple of beats before he said, "That's too bad."

Oh, double dang damn. The way he uttered those words made her want to be that kind of girl—to be girlie and sexy and the type of woman Chase would take to his bed and do really sexy things with.

Chase watched her, doing his best to hide his smile. He'd seen her hesitation, and he couldn't help but notice the sudden added sway to her lush hips as she walked away. Definitely time to put his plan in action. He liked women. Understood them better than a lot of men. Savannah didn't want to be a notch on his bed. She wasn't. They were together for the next year. Married. Married people had sex. He'd make it good for her. Make her happy. Until it was time to make her unhappy so their split looked real.

A twinge of conscience nudged him, but he stuffed it away. Time for food and frolic. He wanted this woman. The more he got to know her, the more he wanted her. She knew who he was. What he was. She'd still signed on the dotted line. Was he cheating with this plan to get her in his bed for something more than sleep? Maybe. He refused to examine his motives too closely. Savannah Wolfe—Savannah Barron, he reminded himself—was intriguing. He wanted to solve the mystery of her, find out what made her tick. Find out what made her moan and beg, made her whisper his name in need.

Forty-five minutes later, he knocked on the closed—and locked—bathroom door.

"Yeah?"

"Food is on its way up, Sav."

"Be right out."

He'd taken the forty-five minutes to change clothes, stripping out of jeans, boots and Western shirt and getting comfortable in sweats and a T-shirt. This was his normal attire for a night in. Mostly. He was dressed as much for comfort as seduction. Wearing those sweats commando made stripping down easy.

Savannah strolled into the living area just as room service knocked on the door. She wore cotton drawstring pants and a slouchy pullover shirt with a wide neck. A spaghetti strap peeked out. Good. She was wearing the camisole tank she normally slept in. He liked the looks of her in that camisole. A lot.

"Grab me a beer, hon?" he called over his shoulder as he answered the door.

Ushering the waiter in, Chase waved him toward the couch and coffee table. "Set up there."

"Sure thing, Mr. B."

Something about the waiter's demeanor tripped alarms, and Chase watched him closely. It took a moment, but he found the miniature video camera the waiter hadn't hidden very well under the lapel of his jacket. Chase had his phone in his hand, texting Security while the guy off-loaded—rather clumsily—the service trolley. The fake waiter made another mistake when he held out the ticket for Chase's signature. Savannah hadn't come out of the kitchen yet and was still out of sight. The guy was lingering to catch a glimpse of her. That was good. It meant Security would be at the door when he walked out.

Chase's phone pinged. Security was in place, so Chase opened the door and shoved the paparazzo out. The man would be banned from all Barron properties. He'd be marched down to the security office, the camera footage erased. He'd be photographed, turned over to Las Vegas police and charged with trespassing.

When Savannah joined Chase, carrying two beers, she had no idea their privacy had been invaded. At some point, he'd need his security people to give her a briefing. Perhaps he should assign a bodyguard. He'd think on that. He didn't want to scare her, but he didn't want the tabloids getting too close. For now, though, it was all about beer, finger food he could feed her and then far more intimate pursuits. Chase had definite plans for his bride, and those plans meant she'd not only be sleeping in his bed, but she'd be *sleeping* with him. In other words, sleep didn't enter into the equation at all.

She settled into the deep cushions of his couch—close but not close enough to suit him. Still, he couldn't push. Wouldn't, truthfully. It was important she want him as much as he wanted her. He had a clue she did, given her reactions every time he kissed her. He enjoyed her breathless sigh when he broke off a kiss, the quick tensing of muscles before she relaxed into his embrace.

Putting his plan into motion, he filled a plate with cheese, crackers, meat and fruit. Leaning back into the soft leather of his couch, he held out a bite of sharp cheddar cheese. "Open up, kitten."

Her expression was distrustful. "I can feed myself."

"So?"

"So… I can feed myself."

He schooled the smile wanting to crease his cheeks

and tickled her lips with the point of the cheese wedge. "Take a bite."

She opened her lips and nibbled at the cheese before her jaw unclenched, and she allowed him to feed her. It wasn't wedding cake, but he got a thrill from feeding her. As she chewed and swallowed, he picked a slice of green apple. He took a bite, swallowed—crunchy tart with a hint of sweet. Then before she knew what he was doing, he kissed her. As he'd anticipated, the two flavors mixed on their tongues.

Her sharp inhalation caused one breast to collide with his arm. He cupped her jaw in his palm, caressing her cheek with his thumb. She watched him, her expression slightly dazed.

"What are you doing?" she whispered, her lips remaining parted and wet from his kiss.

"What does it look like I'm doing?"

"Chase."

Man, but the sound of his name sighing between those full lips of hers set him on fire. "Not gonna lie here, kitten. I want you. A lot. We're married. We sleep in the same bed. I'm yours for the next year. You're mine." He kissed the tip of her nose before shifting back a few inches so he could watch her without his eyes crossing. "Gonna be honest. I had every intention of keeping our bargain, of not touching you. But, baby? I gotta say, you're driving me crazy. You're beautiful. You're sweet. Waking up with you in my arms the other morning was…" Was what? he wondered. Perfect? Yes. Wonderful? Yes. Something he wanted more of? Most definitely. But he was not about to admit any of that to her.

He kissed her again, one arm slipping around her back, the other holding her head until she sank into the kiss. His hand dropped to her shoulder, then trailed lower to skirt the swell of her breast. When she sighed into his mouth, he moved to cup her, thrilled that the nipple under his fingers pebbled when she pressed into him.

"Bed," he murmured. "Want you in bed."

When she didn't argue, he sat up, taking her with him, then pushed off the couch, holding her cradled in his arms. He didn't quite run to the bedroom, but he was full speed ahead until he dropped onto the huge king, keeping her in his arms.

"Birth control?" he demanded, hoping she was on the pill. He wanted to take her bareback. He was clean and as he throbbed with the need for her, he didn't want to bother with a condom.

"No."

He inhaled around the breath he'd been holding.

"I…" She swallowed, and he got lost watching her throat. "I haven't dated in a while."

What? He didn't care if she had…oh. A part of his brain kicked in. Sort of. In her shy way, she was admitting she'd had no man in her bed. But no pill meant he needed to suit up. As he grew harder and his craving for her grew more intense, he almost forgot why it mattered. He rolled over her, jerked out the drawer in the nearest nightstand, grabbed a handful of foil packets.

"We're good." He wanted her and wanted her now, but he took the time to keep them both safe. Now naked and protected, he moved back over her.

In a long, slow movement, he rolled her onto her back. He kissed the soft hollow where her jaw met her throat. Trailing his lips down the slim column, he kissed his way along her collarbone. His hands skimmed up along her side and removed first her pullover shirt and then her camisole. Impatient at the sight of her breasts, rising and falling with her quickened breath, he stripped off her pants and panties. He pushed his thigh between hers, tangling their legs before settling between hers, his erection pressed against the heat at the V of her thighs. He could see her now, the shape of her face, the gleam in her eyes. He slid into her, and there was a quick hitch of her breath, followed by a slow exhale as he remained buried deep inside.

The moment stretched as he held still, watching her, waiting. Her eyes, at first wide and shocked, softened. Her expression followed, her lips curling at the corners, her jaw relaxing. He had her now. Had almost all of her. Before the night was done, he'd have everything.

He pulled back, watched her eyes narrow, hid his smile as her inner muscles clutched at him, working to keep him inside. He gave her what she wanted, pushing back in. Her eyes widened again, then her lashes fluttered closed to paint half-moon shadows on her high cheekbones.

"Don't." He murmured the entreaty. "Look at me, kitten. I want to see your eyes."

She did as he requested, hesitantly, her skin tingeing with embarrassment.

"Don't." An order this time. "This is just us, Savannah. Just you. Just me. Nobody intrudes here but us. You're beautiful. This is beautiful."

"I…" She swallowed hard, not finishing the sentence.

He watched her throat work, thinking of her mouth, and the part of his body currently buried inside her. That would come later. There were all sorts of things he wanted to do to and with this woman. She swiveled her hips, and he forgot to think at all.

Long, slow and deep. Over and over again. In. Out. He held her gaze, studied her, devoured the range of emotions disclosed there. Her body was rising toward him, his falling toward hers. She shuddered and groped for his hands. Their fingers linked, their mouths met, their breaths mingled.

He watched desire suffuse her face, felt his own climax climbing up his spine. "With me, baby," he ordered. "With me."

They exploded together, and the look in her eyes undid

him as he watched. Passion. Need. Want. Hope. Trust. Those last two froze him. What was he doing? This was business. Sex usually was for him, but this woman made him feel things—guilt, contentment, protectiveness. He had no room in his life for those things. Especially not with this woman.

He rolled away to divest himself of their protection. A moment later, he snugged her in close to his side, her head on his shoulder. "Go to sleep, kitten."

He listened as her breathing deepened, soft puffs of air teasing the hair on his chest. This was good. He liked this. He'd enjoy it tonight and tomorrow would take care of itself.

She was warm and naked, still soft from their love-making and sleep. Here in the dark, running his hands over her curves, he wondered if this was a dream. Touch. Fragrance. Sighs in the shadows of his darkened room. Savannah stretched, rolled into him, her lips leaving a damp trail across his skin. Fingers stroked over him, stirring him back to life.

He nudged her to lie across his body, her legs trapped between his. He cupped her face, stared into her eyes, looking for…something. He wasn't sure what. Acceptance? Desire? Maybe even a hint of love. She lowered her head, pushing against his palms. Her mouth sank to his, her body melting around him.

She sighed into the kiss, something wistful in the sound. Or maybe that was him. Maybe he wanted something more from this woman, from this relationship. Something he'd never have, never hoped to have. As she lay over him, he traced the curves of her heart-shaped butt, brushing his fingers up her spine, enjoying the shiver his action invoked. He cupped her shoulders—broader, stronger than those of the women who normally shared his bed. His hands swept down her back, the long, muscular line of it, until his hands once again cupped her. He smiled, remembering how he'd wanted to put his hands in her hip pockets to do just this. Skin to skin was infinitely better.

He hooked the backs of her thighs, repositioned her to straddle him, then reached for a condom. "Ride me, kitten," he commanded, once he was sleeved up.

"Yeah. I like that idea." She pushed off her knees, got him situated and sank down on him. Slow. Oh, so very slow. His hands gripped her thighs, her muscles bunched beneath them, giving her exquisite control. Lots of dirty words swirled in his brain. Crude words for what they were doing. He didn't say them. Not out loud. This moment between them was too divine for the vernacular.

She rode him slow. Rode him hard. Her heart galloped beneath his palm where he cupped her breast. He looked down, watching where their bodies remained connected. It was one of the sexiest sights he'd ever seen. Then his gaze traveled up her body. Golden tan skin, flushed with a tinge of pink. Dark hair tousled and playing peekaboo with her full breasts. Head thrown back, tongue kissing her lips and leaving them moist. He'd been wrong. *This* was the sexiest thing he'd ever seen.

They both came, again at the same time. She collapsed over him, her face buried against his neck and shoulder. He pushed one of her knees until she straightened her leg. Then he rolled them to their sides, holding her close, caressing her back with slow brushes of his fingertips. "Sleep, kitten. Sleep now."

When he awoke, sun teasing his eyes from the partially opened drapes, Savannah was still curled against him, and he liked it. Liked it a lot. Liked it maybe too much.

Twelve

Sunday afternoon, Savannah stood in the rodeo office, check in hand. She'd won all the go-rounds in the barrel racing and placed in the calf roping. Since she was out of practice at roping she was pleased. Kade hadn't lied about Big Red. The horse was cow savvy. The problem had been her inconsistencies with her loop. Well, that and Chase's presence in the stands cheering her on. Friday night. Saturday. Saturday night. And Sunday afternoon. He'd been sitting in a box right behind the chutes, cheering and whistling each time she competed. It had been distracting. But in a good way.

She offered the rodeo secretary a big smile over her shoulder as she pushed open the office door and walked into a barrage of camera flashes. She stopped dead, hand up to cover her eyes, blinking rapidly. When her vision cleared, she found Twyla Allan, the rodeo queen, draped across the chest of Savannah's husband, posing for photos. The urge to bang her head against the wall was almost overwhelming. Idiot. She was a complete idiot for getting involved with a player who attracted women like Chase did.

Mouth tight but her head high, she attempted to evade

the crowd of paparazzi. She got about four feet when Chase looked up and saw her. She was caught flat-footed when Chase disengaged from the sexy woman with her arms around his neck, strode directly to Savvie and folded her into his arms. He laid a big, fat wet one on her mouth, leaving her breathless and clutching at his shoulders when the kiss ended.

"Oh, wow." She blushed when a cocky grin spread across his face. She hadn't meant to say that aloud. Plus, she was supposed to be angry. He'd been flirting with that woman. After making love to her last night. For hours.

"Definitely wow, kitten." Chase murmured the words against her temple after he tipped her Stetson back. "Smile for the camera, darlin'. A few pics, then we're out of here. I'm taking my girl out for dinner to celebrate."

She did as he instructed, curling into his side and smiling as they were peppered with questions about their sudden marriage and other things. Savvie caught a glimpse of Twyla through the crowd. The girl stood on the edge of the group, hands fisted on her hips and an ugly expression on her face. A real beauty queen in her tight jeans and spangly top. Savvie understood why the girl stared daggers her direction. Sav was nothing to write home about.

"Give us another kiss, Chase!" one of the photographers yelled.

Chase obliged, sweeping her backward in a dip. His mouth fused to hers and her pulse galloped. Once again, she had to clutch his jacket front to keep her equilibrium. He held her like that for what seemed an eternity, then just as suddenly brought her back up to a standing position. His arm remained circling her waist—a good thing since her knees quivered to the point she wasn't sure she could stay upright without that assistance.

"Now, y'all forgive us. We're still on our honeymoon, and my girl has to head out in the morning for her next gig. I get one more night to celebrate with her, and we're going to do it up right." Chase winked at the media mob.

With that, he led her across the parking lot to his car and folded her into the passenger seat. He joined her moments later, the Jag purred to life and they drove away.

"Proud of you, babe. You did good," Chase said as he expertly maneuvered the slick car through traffic.

She caught a glimpse of his profile. He looked relaxed, happy and sincere. *Huh.* She felt a little ridiculous for feeling jealous of Twyla earlier.

"Thanks. I…" On impulse, she reached over and touched his thigh with her fingertips. "With Indy hurt, I couldn't have done this without you."

His eyes slid her direction, and the right corner of his mouth ticked up in a smile. "You'd have figured out a way, Savannah."

His faith in her made her feel warm inside. Without thinking, she squeezed the hard muscle beneath his jeans. Since sharing his apartment, she'd caught glimpses of him in various states of undress—not to mention naked. The man was seriously buff.

She reminded herself not to jump off that cliff. As casually as she could, Savvie withdrew her hand, only to have him grab it and wrap his fingers around hers. "Kinda like touching you, kitten."

"Uh…" Her brain went blank and he chuckled, a sound vibrating from deep in his chest all the way to where his hand held hers. "Uh…"

They caught a red light, and as the car idled, he turned to face her. "I surprised you."

"I… Yeah. A little." She inhaled and squiggled her nose and lips as she debated how much to reveal. "Kade's about the only person who ever believed in me. I'm…not used to compliments like that."

"Kitten."

Wow. The nuances in that one word. Kindness. Compassion. Understanding.

The light changed to green. He was still holding her hand, but his eyes were back on traffic, giving her the opportunity to study him. Getting emotionally involved with Chase Barron was a BAD IDEA, all in caps and followed with a whole line of exclamation points. She was better off remembering his public persona—the one she saw on the tabloid covers whenever she went through a checkout line.

No, she really needed to guard against his charm. One year. He'd given her one year. She'd take it to get her life on track, and when he pulled whatever stunt that made him the bad guy and her the injured party, they would divorce. Everyone would feel sorry for her. There was only one problem with that scenario. Chase was setting himself up to be a bad guy, but he wasn't a bad guy at all.

Lost in thought, she didn't realize they'd arrived at the Crown Casino until the doorman opened the passenger door and extended his hand to help her out. Scrambling, she got her feet under her and stood as Chase came around and joined her. He reclaimed her hand and all those warm feelings suffused her again. Until she realized they had an audience: no paparazzi, but tourists wielding cell phones were very much in evidence.

The scrutiny diminished slightly once they arrived in the lobby. Savannah felt her smile slipping, but Chase squeezed her to him with the arm draped around her shoulders. "We'll have dinner. Celebrate. And then we'll go hide upstairs. Sound like a plan?"

She gave him a tentative smile and nodded. "That works. I'm starved."

"Good. Barron House is famous for its steaks."

"Excuse me." A broad-shoulder man stopped in front of them. He wore a tailored suit but looked like he should be wearing army fatigues with bullet bandoliers draped across his shoulders.

"Problem?" Chase asked.

"Yes, sir. Mr. Tate asked me to send you to the security office as soon as you arrived."

Muttering under his breath, Chase dropped his mouth to Savannah's ear. "Gotta take care of this, kitten. Go on over to the restaurant and get seated. Tell the waiter I'll have my usual and I'll join you as quick as I can." He squeezed her shoulders again. "Sorry about this. Business first."

"I understand." She flashed him a tentative smile and glanced around the palatial lobby, looking for the steak-house entrance.

"Buck will show you the way, Sav."

She glanced at the man who was part of Chase's security staff. He definitely fit his name.

"Drop her off at Barron House before you come up."

"Yes, sir."

As Chase walked away without a backward glance, Savannah offered a shy smile to the big man still standing in front of her. "If you need to get back to work, I can probably find my way—"

Buck cut her off. "Not a problem, Mrs. Barron. If you'll follow me."

Savannah nodded and fell into step as Buck pivoted on his heel and marched through the lobby. Curious glances— some openly unfriendly—followed her. Shoulders square, head up, she did her best to ignore them.

It felt as though they walked several blocks, dodging the casino floor, trailing past the area she nicknamed "Boutique Row" with its high-end shops. They passed several restaurants—a froufrou café featuring French cuisine by some celebrity chef, a family-friendly diner decorated like something from the 1950s and a bar with art deco murals on the walls—before finally arriving at Barron House. Buck took his leave as soon as the entrance was in sight, and with a bit of trepidation, Savannah approached the imposing maître d'.

"Hi," she ventured. "Table for two?"

She got a snooty look and a cold "Do you have a reservation?"

"Uh…not exactly. At least I don't think so." Before she could mention Chase's name, the maître d' gave her a head-to-toe perusal, and she could tell she'd failed miserably.

"We also have a dress code," the man added, his tone snide.

She leaned a little to the side to glance into the restaurant. There were wood-paneled walls, low lights, white tablecloths and red linen napkins. A multisided fireplace blazed in the center of the space, flames leaping behind faceted glass. Waiters in starched white shirts, black leather vests and long black aprons bustled through the room. Women wore little black dresses. Men wore coats and ties.

Swallowing hard, she stammered, "Oh. I—I'll go change. I'm sorry. I didn't know." People seated nearby were starting to stare and murmur to each other.

Pivoting, she ran smack-dab into a warm body—a very warm and very muscular body. Her Stetson flew off her head but a hand grabbed it.

"Everything okay, kitten?" Chase eyed the maître d'. "Joseph, is there a problem with my table?"

"Mr. Barron, sir. I—I didn't know the young woman was with you. She didn't say."

"My wife shouldn't have to say, Joseph."

"Wife?"

The man sounded stunned, and when Savvie took the chance to look at him, his expression said it all. She was hardly the woman anyone would pick out in a crowd as being married to Chase Barron.

"Yes, Joseph. My wife."

The maître d' stepped closer and leaned in, his voice a low murmur as he said, "But the dress code, sir."

Sav stiffened and tried to pull away from Chase. "I'll go change. It's okay. I'm sorry. I've embarrassed—"

"No." Chase tightened his grip. "You won't change and you have nothing to apologize for." He eased back just a hair and tilted her chin up with two gentle fingers. "You're my wife, Savannah. You wear whatever you want wherever you want, especially in my hotel." His eyes searched hers. "Yeah?"

She nodded. She didn't know what else to do. She replied with a breathy, "Yeah."

"Good." He gave her a tight smile as his gaze slid to the officious man standing nearby, wringing his hands. "You will seat us now, Joseph, and you will report to my office first thing in the morning. We'll discuss your status then."

"Yes, sir. Of course, sir. Right this way, Mr. Barron."

They made it maybe five feet into the restaurant. Savannah's cheeks were burning under the stares of the other patrons, when she felt Chase's hand tighten against the small of her back. She froze when he stopped walking.

She glanced up. Cyrus stood there, seething. "Had you married Janiece, we would never suffer this embarrassment, Chasen. Your choice is unsuitable. This...*woman* is not and never will be good enough to be a Barron."

Thirteen

Chase didn't know how to respond so he hesitated. He realized his mistake the moment Savannah backed away. He glared at his father. "I'm not doing this here and certainly not in public. You need to pack up and go back to Oklahoma City, Dad. I'm married. End of discussion."

"No, you aren't. You're playing games, boy. Just like you always do. You don't love that woman. She's a handy piece to warm your bed while you thumb your nose at me. I know what's best for you, for this family."

Chase stepped closer and hissed out an angry whisper. "Keep your voice down. You complain every time I show up in the tabloids. Well, guess what? Every person in this restaurant has a cell phone, and you can bet they're taking our pictures and blasting them out to every social media outlet on the web."

Cyrus smoothed his expression just as he'd smooth a wrinkle in his suit coat. Chase saw his father's eyes flick behind him right before a self-satisfied smile settled on his face.

"It appears your new bride has cut and run. Come and sit down. We'll have dinner. Discuss things."

Glancing over his shoulder, Chase discovered his father was right. Savannah had disappeared. Anger flashed through him. So much for standing up with him. Fine. He shouldn't have expected loyalty from her, despite what they'd shared last night. He'd seen her expression when she'd come out of the rodeo office earlier. He'd explained that Twyla was a former employee, and that when she'd approached, he'd been cordial. It wasn't his fault the paparazzi were hanging around. And as soon as Savannah appeared, he'd disengaged and caught up to her.

The last thing he needed was his father thinking exactly what Chase was thinking. His marriage to Savannah had to appear real and solid. He'd done his bit, but at the first sign of trouble, she'd tucked her tail and run.

"Chasen? Are you coming?"

Fine. He'd sit. Have dinner. He needed to eat, anyway. Savannah could call for room service and hide. Whatever. "Yeah, Dad. Right behind you."

Savannah didn't run. She didn't cry, despite how much she wanted to. She kept her fists clenched at her sides, her chin up and her steps measured. She was so totally embarrassed—mortified, as her college English professor would say—but far too aware of the stares and the security cameras. She would not give the Barron staff any more reason for gossip. Backtracking through the maze of hallways, she finally found the correct bank of elevators. Her control was hanging by a thread. She stabbed the button. Then stabbed again. And again. Jabbing it with her thumb until a hand gentled her frantic motions.

"Easy, hon. Deep breaths."

Tucker stood beside her, partially shielding her from view. When she regained a little control, he led her to the last elevator. He punched in a code on a number pad and urged her on board.

She faced the back wall, chin tucked to her chest, staring at her boots. She couldn't face Tucker. He'd released her hand and turned toward the doors.

"I need to stop by the security office for a moment, then I'll escort you up to the apartment. Okay?"

Not trusting her voice, she lifted her shoulders almost to her ears.

"Savvie?"

She nodded, still unable to speak.

"Okay, hon." The elevator dinged and the doors opened. Tucker turned her and, keeping a gentle hand on her arm, propelled her down a long hallway. She caught enough in her peripheral vision to realize this was one of the executive floors. Tuck halted before a heavy wooden door, and she waited while he punched in another code, then placed his palm against a plate.

Why would the security to the security room be so secure? Her brain was caught on a hamster wheel of confusion—her way of ignoring the ache in her chest and stalling any sort of processing of what had happened downstairs.

The door opened to laughter and a female voice stating, "I mean, really? Wearing boots and jeans was bad enough, but that cowboy hat? The maître d' went off on her and she all but knocked Chase down."

The laughter died away as the people in the room became aware of who stood in the doorway.

Tucker's voice could freeze-dry steaks as he ordered, "Rack up that footage from Barron House for me. Now."

Savannah cringed and turned away. How soon before that footage hit social media? Anger wafted off Tucker in waves as he watched the exchange between Savannah and the maître d'.

His voice was clipped and hard when he ordered, "Erase it." He stood stock-still, and Savannah sensed movement behind her. "I'll be back as soon as I get Mrs. Barron settled. We'll have a little discussion. No one is off duty until I'm done. We clear?"

She heard a few mechanical squeaks, rustling paper, a couple of murmurs, but they exited to dead silence. Tucker kept his arm around her shoulders as he propelled her down the wide hallway back to the elevator. As soon as he punched in the code, the doors whispered open and they stepped in. With a whoosh she felt in her stomach, they shot upward to the penthouse floor. He walked her to the apartment, keyed the door and ushered her inside. He let the door close before he turned her to face him with his hands resting on her shoulders.

"I'm sorry, honey."

"You didn't do anything."

"No. But I will."

"Please, just let it go."

"Not gonna happen, Savannah. One, they disrespected you. I can't allow that to stand. You're Chase's wife, even under these circumstances. Employees—especially those who work in our security office—are given our absolute trust due to the confidentiality of the situations they often monitor. I will not allow what they were doing to continue. We clear on that?"

She swallowed around the lump in her throat and nodded.

"Good. Two, my cousin can be a total and complete jackass."

That shook her out of her stupor. "Please. Just let it go. We both know this whole thing is a sham. It's just pretend. He's not really—" Her voice hitched around the cold knot forming in her chest. She had to focus on breathing for a moment. "—not my husband." The words came out in a whisper.

"He should have come after you, Savannah. You're the one helping him out of a bind." He shook her gently. "You deserve better."

"Maybe. I gotta go, Tucker. Please. Just let me go."

He hugged her tight and dropped a kiss to the top of her

head. Then he backed up a step and fished in his jacket pocket. He handed her an envelope. "It helps when the Barrons own the bank, but I still pulled some strings to get it here ASAP. Here's a debit card for your checking account. There's thirty grand in there for your travel expenses and bills. If you need more, call me. Anytime, sweetheart. Okay?"

With gentle care, he knuckled her chin up. "*Any*time. Yeah?"

"Yeah."

"Good luck, Savannah." He didn't wait for her to reply. He headed for the door and slipped out.

"I'm gonna need it," she murmured. One thought kept running through her head. *Idiot. Idiot, idiot, idiot. I'm such an idiot.* If she'd been close to a wall or the breakfast bar, she'd bang her head. How could she have *slept* with him? She *knew* what he was. Who he was. Who his father was. And she'd had about enough.

She schlepped to the bedroom, found her duffel and an empty suitcase in the closet. While an outsider might think there was no rhyme or reason to her packing, she was quite methodical. She knew what she needed to take. She'd leave the rest to keep up the charade.

Thirty minutes later, she was getting into the backseat of a cab, after a five-minute fight with the doorman, who insisted he call the hotel's limo. She'd won the argument.

"Where to?" the cabbie asked, looking at her in the rearview mirror.

"Clark County Fairgrounds. Rodeo barn parking lot."

She had just enough cash in her pocket to pay the cabdriver. Kade had loaded up Indigo and left early that morning. She hitched the new trailer to her new truck, loaded her new horses in the trailer and pulled out. The fuel tanks were topped off but she wanted an ATM. She'd need a big chunk of cash before hitting the road, headed south. The San Antonio Stock Show and Rodeo was her next stop.

She located a truck stop on the outskirts of Henderson and pulled in. She could stock up on Diet Cokes, Snickers and salt-and-vinegar potato chips. She hit the ladies' room and ATM, grabbed her drinks and snacks, and got in line to pay. Within ten minutes, she was ready to go. The truck came with one of those fancy navigation systems. She'd punched in her destination, and it spit out her itinerary. Without the trailer, she could probably make the trip to San Antonio in eighteen hours. With the trailer, she'd need to stop and spend the night somewhere. Considering her late start, it would probably be either Phoenix or Tucson. She'd drive until caffeine didn't work any longer, then she'd find a rest stop. She could let the horses out for a bit of exercise, and grab a nap in relative safety.

That's when she had her first epiphany. She now had three hundred dollars in her pocket, thanks to the ATM. She had a debit card tied to a bank account with thirty thousand available. Well, twenty-nine thousand seven hundred. She could afford to stay wherever she wanted. And wasn't that a kick in the seat of her pants.

She merged onto US 93, accelerated to highway speed, set the cruise control and clicked on the radio. The DJ introduced Cole Swindell's "Ain't Worth the Whiskey" and the opening notes filled her truck.

"Ha! The country music gods are smilin' on me tonight," she announced to the empty cab. As soon as Cole started singing, she was singing along. At the top of her lungs. She didn't care that Chase and his father had shown their true colors. It was time for her to move on. All the way to San Antonio. If she got lucky and stayed on the circuit, she could mostly avoid Chase until she sat across from him in some attorney's office signing the divorce papers a year from now. She raised her Coke bottle in a not-so-silent toast, considering she was still singing—only slightly off-key. When the next song came on, Savannah launched into it, as well. The music gods were happy tonight and sending her way every great breakup-he-done-me-wrong song on the playlist.

The lights of Las Vegas faded to a dull glow in her side mirrors. The truck's headlights swept down the highway. This was her life. A million stars overhead, wide-open spaces, good music and the rodeo. To hell with Chase Barron. And his kisses. He'd left her alone after both old man Barron and the maître d' humiliated her. She was done with him. So. Done. So done she ignored the ache in her chest. She knew better than to dream, knew better than to fall for a sweet-talkin' man. She wasn't her mother.

Fourteen

Chase let himself into the apartment quietly. After shutting and securing the door for the night, he breathed in relief. The automatic lights in the living room cast a soft glow. The rest of the place remained shrouded in darkness. He'd hoped Savannah would be there waiting for him.

She wasn't. The couch was empty. So was the kitchen. He didn't bother checking his office. She wouldn't be in there. He headed to the bedroom, a slow smirk appearing. He'd acted like a jerk, but the talk with his father had been worth it. They'd come to an agreement. Of sorts. Barron Entertainment was still his. Cyrus would butt out of his personal life. If he didn't get Savannah pregnant in two years, he'd cut her loose with a small settlement. Since he planned to divorce her in a year that was an easy stipulation to accept.

He felt his way to the bathroom, slipped inside and shut the door before he turned on the light. Once he got into bed, he'd wake Savannah, make love to her by way of apology for all she'd had to put up with tonight, and then they'd have breakfast in the morning before she headed off to… wherever she was off to for her next rodeo appearance.

Chase was halfway through brushing his teeth before he realized his bathroom counter was all but empty. He pulled out drawers. Empty. He looked up in the mirror. The short satin robe Savannah wore was still hanging there. He spit and rinsed, wiped his face and opened the door.

A rectangle of light slanted across the bed. The empty bed. He flicked on the bedside lamp. Her phone wasn't charging on the nightstand. Her boots weren't lined up next to the chair where she sat to put them on in the morning. Chase tore open the closet door. Most of the clothes Tucker had bought for her were still hanging there. He sorted through the hangers carefully. She'd taken a few things. A fringed leather jacket. A couple of skirts. All the jeans. Every pair of boots.

The drawers holding her underwear, T-shirts and sleep stuff were empty. Prowling through the apartment, he flipped on every light in the place. Getting progressively angrier, he searched for a message from Savannah. And found none. What did she think she was doing, running out on him like this? His cell pinged and he dug it out of his pocket. Maybe she'd left him a text. The current text was from Tucker. He ignored it to scroll through messages and emails. Still nothing from Savannah. He swiped his thumb across the screen to load Tucker's message.

Situation in security office. Next time you ignore your wife to have dinner with your old man, try to do it away from cameras.

What the hell? Rather than call Tucker, he stormed out and headed down to the executive floors. Five minutes later, Chase threw the security room door open and stood there with his hands on his hips, not bothering to hide his anger. The people scanning the monitors briefly looked up. With no exceptions, their gazes slid guiltily away. His focus narrowed on Tucker, and four people standing with him, their eyes downcast.

"Tuck?"

"Not now, Chase. I'll brief you shortly."

Someone cleared a throat behind him and Chase glanced back. Four burly security guards stood in the hallway, waiting. He stepped farther into the monitor room to let them enter. Each one escorted out one of the people—two women and two men—who'd been standing with Tucker.

"Short bathroom breaks only until I get some overtime people in," Tucker announced to the people left at the monitors. Then he gestured for Chase to precede him into the hall and closed the door behind them.

"You just fired four people?"

"Yeah. I did."

"You wanna explain why, cuz?"

"Not really, because even if I do I'm not sure you'll get it through that thick head of yours."

Chase bristled. "What the hell?"

Tucker brushed past him and strode down the hall, turned a corner and, at the end of the second hallway, pushed open the door to his office. Chase followed him and shut the door.

"What's going on, Tuck?"

"That little stunt of yours, Chase."

"What little stunt?"

"At Barron House. Ring a bell?"

"There was no stunt." He was confused. Why would Tucker fire employees whose job it was to watch security monitors?

"Savannah got a boatload of disrespect. From an employee and then from your father. What did you do? You ignored her, and merrily sat with your old man and enjoyed your steak."

"So?"

"Jeez, Chase. You truly are clueless when it comes to

women. You didn't see Savannah's face. But those jerks in the monitor room damn sure did. And when I walked in, they were laughing and cracking jokes. About. Your. Wife!"

Chase had never seen his easygoing cousin so angry. He opened his mouth to placate Tucker but the man kept going.

"Instead of going after her, you smile and make nice with Cyrus, sit your ass down at his table and proceed to eat hearty."

"Okay?" Chase still wasn't following.

"Savannah was with me when I stopped in at Security to delete that footage. She stood there and listened to them crack jokes about her and your relationship to her. Thirty minutes later, your *wife* took a cab. With a suitcase and her duffel." Tucker must have seen something in Chase's expression because he softened his tone. "You hurt her, Chase, and she was so upset she was trying to access the wrong elevator when I caught up to her. Then she was witness to the idiocy of our security staff before I could escort her to your rooms. Me, Chase. Not you. Not her husband."

"Oh." Tuck was right; he'd totally messed up. "I'll fix it."

"Seriously?"

"Yes, Tucker, seriously. I have to keep her loyal for a year. I'll do what it takes."

Chase left before Tuck could respond. He rode up to his apartment in the private elevator, thinking. He had stepped on his poncho where Savannah was concerned. He'd sleep on it and come up with a plan.

The next morning, Chase discovered that breakfast was boring without Savannah. That should have been his first clue his life was veering off track. He grabbed his phone and texted Tucker.

Where's Sav headed next?

Tuck's reply came a few moments later. You don't know?

Hello, not her travel agent.

His phone rang in lieu of a text. Tucker's gruff voice exploded in his ear. "No, but you *are* supposed to be her husband."

"Ow. Low blow, cuz."

"It was meant to be, Chase."

"So…where's she headed?"

"San Antonio."

"Cool. I like it there. Wanna go?"

He could picture Tucker rolling his eyes as his cousin replied, "No. Someone has to take care of your business."

Laughing, Chase teased back, "That's why I pay you the big bucks."

Three hours later, he was packed, his calendar cleared. Reservations had been made for a suite in a five-star hotel on the Riverwalk, and he was on board the corporate jet winging to South Texas. He figured he had a day and a half before Savannah arrived. He had a lot to do.

Late Sunday night, Savannah had stopped in Kingman, just over the Nevada-Arizona state line. As she drove, it occurred to her that she wouldn't have stall space in San Antonio until Tuesday evening. She could drive easy instead of pushing it. And since money wasn't a problem, she planned to find stables for overnight boarding and a comfortable hotel to sleep in.

Her conscience twinged a little bit at the thought of spending lots of Chase's money, but only a little bit. Chase Barron was a jerk with way too much money. Her truck and trailer were rolling advertisements for Barron Entertainment, so by golly she would stay first-class from now on, just like the other competitors with big sponsors.

She knew a place just outside Kingman where she could stable Red and Cimarron and park her trailer. She pulled into the Best Western Wayfarer's, got her own room and called the stables. Luckily, she arrived before midnight so the owner was awake and had stalls available. She drove there, got the horses settled and fed, unhitched the trailer, and headed back.

Monday's travels got her to El Paso. The sun was just over an hour from setting as she off-loaded the horses and she decided to give them a workout. Rather than dragging out their tack, she tied off the lead line on Cimarron's halter to use as reins and swung up onto him bareback. The paint pranced sideways, testing her seat. She squeezed with her knees and the horse settled. With Red on a halter rope, she rode out into the field behind the barn.

This was what she loved about the life she'd chosen—on the road, a good horse between her legs, the sky above. Her heart should have been light but it wasn't. Try as she might, she hadn't been able to put aside the hurt from the scene Sunday night. And Chase hadn't bothered to call. Or text.

She rubbed at her left ring finger and noted there was a small rash within the dark circle left by the ring. She needed to get some clear fingernail polish to coat the ring. She'd heard somewhere that it helped seal cheap metal. Her mood shattered now, she rode back to the barn, dismounted and rubbed down both horses. She tossed in a block of hay, poured a measure of grain and made sure they had fresh water.

After a solitary dinner at a Mexican restaurant down the street from the Holiday Inn, Savannah showered, flopped onto the bed with the TV remote and resisted the urge to call Tucker. Doing so was a really bad idea. Tucker had been nice to her, but not only was he Chase's family, he was Chase's second in command. Putting him in the middle of things was way more high school than she was comfortable with.

She found an action-adventure movie starring a hunky actor and settled in to watch. She fell asleep somewhere between a big explosion and the steamy kiss between the star and the beautiful girl he rescued. Savvie didn't turn off the TV and she blamed that fact for the sexy dreams she had, the images leaving her hot, achy and frustrated when she woke up, despite a cold shower, followed by a hot shower. She found herself squirming a lot on her drive to San Antonio.

As she queued up in traffic to turn into San Antonio's AT&T Center, Savannah was rocking out to Luke Bryan's "That's My Kind of Night." In fact, she was singing along and bouncing in her seat so hard she didn't notice the knot of people who surged forward as she pulled up to the horse check-in station. She grabbed her purse and the folder with the horses' veterinary health certificates, put on her Stetson, hopped out of the truck and froze.

Chase recognized the truck and trailer as it idled in line. He'd been hanging around since Monday afternoon and when Savannah hadn't shown up, he'd...*panicked* was too strong a word. He'd been concerned, and as a result, he had Cash's security company locate her by the GPS installed in the truck. When he realized she was taking her time, he was relieved. This gave him more time to set up for her arrival.

And set up he did. He'd already secured her two stalls, feed and hay. He also started the rumor in social media that he and his bride were using her rodeo appearances as an extended honeymoon. The paparazzi were salivating. Any picture of him was a guaranteed paycheck for the freelancers.

Watching as the truck inched closer, Chase felt unaccustomed anticipation build in his gut. Nothing so wimpy as butterflies; the sensation was more like F-16 fighter jets dive-bombing. Though disconcerting, it was still fun—like what Christmas used to be when his mother had been alive. Savannah was doing something inside the cab: bouncing around, waving her arms. He wondered if she was singing along to the radio. That was kinda cute.

As soon as she stopped and climbed out, he headed in her direction. He didn't let the look on her face deter him as he shoved up in her space, took her in his arms and kissed her hard enough to knock her hat off.

Chase eased back on the kiss and whispered against her lips, "Smile, kitten, we're on *Candid Camera*." Then he claimed her lips again and kissed her like a starving man—or a man still celebrating his honeymoon.

Her fists balled against his chest. Was she pushing him away or resisting an urge to grab his shirt and pull him closer? He couldn't decide. He prolonged the kiss for several more long moments before easing back, letting her catch a breath. He stepped to Savannah's side as a rodeo official appeared. The woman wore a huge grin and pantomimed fanning her face.

"Sugar, I gotta admire your tenacity t'hit the circuit, but dang. If that man was my husband, I don't think I'd get out of bed for a year."

"Yeah, easy for you to say," Savannah muttered under her breath, but loud enough for Chase to hear.

Laughing, he hooked his arm around her neck. "That's why I'm here. We might be newlyweds but I love that my woman wants to do things her way, wants to make her mark in her chosen career. I'm proud of Savannah, and I plan on being at the Thomas and Mack Center in Vegas come December. I'll be cheering when she wins the championship."

He didn't miss the crowd snapping pictures with their cell phones and cameras. He planned to tie her up tight in his web so she was stuck with him, just like their agreement stipulated. Chase had a plan.

Fifteen

Chase didn't give Savannah a chance to protest. He rushed her through check-in, off-loading and feeding the horses. Then he locked up her truck and trailer, herded her to the Ford Explorer he'd leased for the week and swept her off to their five-star suite on the Riverwalk. He had kept the location secret, though that was always subject to change. It all depended on Savannah.

"I thought we'd go out to dinner," he suggested after she'd showered and shed the funky horse-sweat smell.

"Feel free to go without me."

"Kitten." He put a whole heap of *pretty please* and *don't be mad* in that word.

"Don't. Just…don't."

He choked back a laugh. Her lip curled and her nose scrunched as she glowered at him.

"Kitten." This time, his amusement leaked through, along with a dribble of *I think you're cute*.

"No. Won't work. Just…go out to eat. And don't come back. Better yet. You stay in, I'll go out and get a room in another hotel."

"Sweetheart, I'll bet a week's salary that the lobby is swarming with media."

"Then why are you suggesting we go out to eat?"

"Because we can go out the back way, catch a river taxi, have a great dinner and talk."

She crossed her arms, and Chase reminded himself to breathe so he didn't hyperventilate. He loved her breasts, and when she was standing like that, they were plumped and peeking at him through the V of her shirt. He wanted to cup them, kiss them—wanted to kiss her in lots of places, actually. Maybe room service wasn't such a bad idea. He shifted the fly of his jeans and didn't hide the motion.

Her skin flushed. He watched the pink tinge climb from her chest to her neck before it flooded her cheeks. Getting her to blush was almost as much fun as making her mad.

"Fine. We'll go out. What's the dress code? I wouldn't want my lack of taste and sense of propriety to reflect badly on you and your father." She spit the words out, hissing like the wildcat he often compared her to.

He was even more turned on. "There's a Mexican café down on the river. I think you'll like it. And you're dressed fine. Put your boots on and grab a jacket. It's chilly at night on the water."

He waited while she rooted for clean socks, sat on the bed to pull them on and shoved her feet into a pair of boots. She grabbed the fringed leather jacket from the closet and shrugged into it. Then she stood there, thumbs hooked in her front pockets, glare on her face, her breasts still peeking at him from the V of her shirt. He contemplated how angry makeup sex was always fun.

With a shake of her head, she marched across the suite to the door. "Whatever you're thinking, hoss, ain't gonna happen."

He perked up at that slip. *Hoss.* That was infinitely better than many of the names she'd probably tagged him with in the past few days. "After you."

Thirty minutes and a leisurely water taxi ride later, they

were seated on the patio of Cantina Cactus. He ordered her a top-shelf margarita on the rocks with extra salt, and a Corona for himself. When the waitress returned with their drinks, Savannah ordered dinner in a clipped voice, ignoring him. He added his order, then leaned back in his chair. He'd debated their seating arrangement and opted to sit across from her.

There were several reasons—he could see her face, and she was basically cornered by the railing surrounding the patio at her back. Mainly, though, she wouldn't be able to see anything he might do beneath the table, like logging into his fake Twitter account and tweet using the #FindChase hashtag. He'd resorted to the ruse to both avoid the paparazzi and to use them as needed. He hoped he didn't have to employ such antics tonight but... One look at Savannah's face, he figured his thumbs would be getting a workout.

After their meal arrived, Savannah rolled a flour tortilla and waved it. "Are you sure you want to do this in public?"

"Do what, kitten?"

"Don't call me that."

"Kitten."

She threw up her hands, still clutching the tortilla. "Gah! What do you want, Chase?"

He composed his expression to what one ex-girlfriend called his dreamy-eyes-and-dimple face. Something flickered in Savannah's eyes so he hoped it was working. "I want you, sweetheart."

"No, you don't."

"Okay, look. I screwed up."

"Ya think?"

"Yes, I think. Which I wasn't doing at the time. Look, darlin', things get intense with my dad. There's a long history there, and I didn't mean for you to get caught in the middle."

"Yes, you did."

Her voice was so soft he wasn't sure he heard her. "Excuse me?"

She raised her chin, and he admired the stubborn tilt. "Yes, you did. You dragged me into the middle the moment you put this ring on my finger." She held up her left hand, fingers splayed.

"I was up front, Savannah."

"So was I. And I made a mistake."

Chase stiffened. If she called off the marriage, he was up a creek full of excrement. "A mistake." He enunciated those words very carefully and there was no question mark at the end when he said them.

"Hands off. I didn't stick to my rule. That was my mistake. I slept with you. I won't be that stupid again."

"Excuse me? Sleeping with me was a mistake? Really? And how many times did you get off?"

Pink colored her cheeks, and she broke eye contact. He'd flustered her. That was good, and his anger receded a little. He couldn't lose control. Not if he wanted her back in his bed—and not just to sleep. Reaching across the table, he clasped her hand, tightening his grip slightly when she tried to pull away.

"Kitten, listen to me. Saturday night was *not* a mistake. Not for me. Yes, twenty-four hours later I totally screwed up. This whole marriage gig is new to me. I'm not used to looking out for someone else. I'll make it up to you."

Savannah raised her eyes to gaze into his. "Don't do this. Don't be nice and apologetic. I don't want to like you. I just want to get through the next twelve months."

"Is everything okay with your food?" The waitress appeared with a water pitcher.

Chase glanced up at her. "Everything is fine, thanks." After the woman wandered off, he realized the moment had passed. He'd have to activate Operation Twitter. "Eat up, kitten, before your dinner gets cold."

Following his own advice, he shoveled several bites of

his chiles rellenos into his mouth. After a sip of his beer, he dropped his hands to his lap and started typing. Time to pull in the big guns.

Savannah stood on the balcony of their suite watching the traffic on the Riverwalk. Water taxis cruised, leaving gentle waves in their wake. Pedestrians thronged and a mix of music floated up.

She'd managed to choke down only half her tamales before the paparazzi found them. She'd had to pose with Chase, a smile on her face, and then eyes closed in pretended bliss while he kissed her—his way of bribing them to go away. They didn't go far, and the restaurant staff sneaked the newlyweds out through the kitchen.

Savannah's feelings were all over the map where Chase was concerned. She didn't trust him. Couldn't trust him for so many reasons.

He was a player. Egotistical. Self-centered enough to be a narcissist. Yet when he smiled—the smile that played peekaboo with his dimple and lit up his eyes—she could fall in love with Chase Barron. Way too easily. And if she did, he'd only break her heart. She was a means to an end. A convenient wife in inconvenient circumstances.

"Kitten?"

She hadn't heard the door behind her open but Chase was suddenly there, his arm circling her waist and pulling her to him. The hard length of him nestled against her bottom. She didn't realize how chilly she'd been until his heat surrounded her.

"You should go to bed," she said briskly.

"As soon as you come with me."

"I'm sleeping on the couch."

"Savannah." He swept her hair off her neck before his lips began to nibble. She stiffened, but he just held her tighter. "I said I was sorry, Sav. I meant it. But we're still married. We're still good together in bed. Why deny ourselves that pleasure?"

"It's a bad idea, Chase."

"No, it's not. In fact, I want you to see a doctor tomorrow."

Her head jerked up and connected with his face.

"Ow. Damn, woman. You tryin' to kill me?"

She twisted and turned but now he had her back braced against the railing. She hadn't bloodied his nose, thankfully, but she was still wary. "Why do I have to see a doctor?"

"Birth control. I'm clean. You said you hadn't dated in a long time—"

Heat suffused her face, and she pushed against his chest with her palms. "I don't want to talk about this."

"Sav, it's okay. I figure you're clean, too. I'm always careful, but with you? With you, I want it all. I want to feel you surrounding me, with no barrier between us. That's all I'm sayin'. Okay?"

Her agreement came out a little breathier than she would have preferred. This man got to her—in all the wrong ways. She didn't—couldn't—fight when he dipped his head and his mouth sought out hers. His tongue teased, asking for entrance, and she parted her lips even as she parted her legs so he could stand between them, his hot, hard desire evident as he rubbed against her center.

"Come to bed, Savannah," he murmured against her cheek when he broke the kiss. He backed away just enough to sweep her into his arms.

He carried her inside to the bedroom and settled her on the bed. "Be right back," he whispered. She heard him out in the living area shutting and locking the balcony door, closing drapes, checking the security bar on the front door. Then he was back, shedding clothes as he approached her.

"Seeing you lying there, it's like Christmas. I get to unwrap you and find the present beneath."

Her heart melted even as her brain jumped up and down trying to get her attention. She ignored the logic and went for emotion. Tonight—*just* tonight—she'd take what he had to offer. He'd make her feel cherished and wanted. He'd soothe her loneliness with gentle but demanding hands. He'd make love to her, even if it was only sex in his mind. She could live with that. Yes, for a year, she'd take what he offered. And when the time came, she'd walk away and hope her heart survived.

Sixteen

That week in San Antonio passed like a dream. Savannah's times remained top-notch, and while Chase didn't hover, he was around. A lot. He hung out in the contestants' hospitality room. He took her to dinner. They held hands. He made her laugh. And his kisses curled her toes despite her best intentions. He made love to her at night in ways sweet and sometimes dirty, but always satisfying.

She'd broached the subject of his work, but he waved away her concerns. "I can work anywhere I have a laptop, sweetheart."

And it seemed that he could.

Then it was Sunday. She won the barrel racing and picked up her check from the rodeo office, but even more importantly, she added points to her total. Chase was in the mood to celebrate, so they did. They went to New Braunfels, ate, and then partied and danced at Gruene Hall to a live band. Savvie never considered herself much of a dancer but Chase could boot scoot with the best of them.

They returned to the hotel, ordered up late-night appetizers, fed each other, drank beer, laughed and fell into bed happy. Chase made love to her slow and easy, much like their night had been, and she fell a little more in love with him.

He followed her to Bakersfield, Beaumont, Wichita. To Helena, Minot, Abilene. She participated in a few all-girl rodeos along the way but Chase didn't stray. She didn't hide her face in checkout lines because they'd faded from the tabloids. Paparazzi occasionally popped up, but there was nothing juicy about an apparently happily married billionaire and his cowgirl bride.

Savannah relaxed. And that was her first mistake. They'd been together for almost six months. Chase was off in the Bahamas wheeling and dealing over some big new resort. She'd been on her own for a week and was settled in her hotel in Reno, gearing up for the weekend and the rodeo. While the hotel wasn't a Barron property, it was luxurious, and she was treated like a VIP. Like so many of the big hotels in Reno, it had a casino and restaurants. After her experience in Vegas, she shied away from those. She wanted a comfortable place where a cowgirl could sit and eat a burger, drink a beer and maybe listen to some county music on a jukebox.

The hotel doorman directed her to Riley's Saloon and got a cab for her. "Hard to park, and if you have more than a beer or two, you'll want to take a cab back. Local cops have a no-tolerance rule."

She'd learned to tip doormen and cabdrivers. Hers passed over his card, told her to call when she was ready to go back to the hotel and tipped his baseball cap to her. She walked into Riley's to the sounds of Toby Keith's "I Love This Bar." Perfect.

After her eyes adjusted to the lower lights, she looked around. There were a few tourist types, but it was mostly locals and several tables of rodeo cowboys. A couple of the guys nodded or waved, and one stood up. He motioned her over to the empty chair at his table. Jess Lyon was a cowboy's cowboy and a cowgirl's dream come true—ruggedly handsome, broad shouldered, a hint of bad boy in his grin. Savannah had known him forever.

Full from her burger, mellow after two beers and comfortable in her surroundings, she leaned back in her chair. Jess's arm was draped across the top and her shoulders brushed against it. Carrie Underwood was singing about taking a smoke break, and Jess leaned in to speak directly into Savvie's ear.

"Heard a rumor, sugar."

"Oh?"

"Yup. Seems someone's photo just got added to the NFR site under barrel racing's leaders."

She squealed and, without thinking, turned in her chair, grabbed his face and laid a smacking kiss on his lips. Then she grabbed her phone from her hip pocket and started Googling the National Finals Rodeo site. There she was. She was hot on the trail of the top leaders. She thumbed over to her contacts list and hit Chase's number, all prepared to give him the good news.

Her call rolled to voice mail. Disappointed, she left a message amid shouted congratulations from the cowboys in the bar. Celebrating, she stayed later than she'd planned, drank more beer than she should have and ended up accepting a ride back to her hotel with Jess. He left her at the front entrance in the doorman's solicitous hands, driving away to her shouted thanks.

Reno was another conquest. She walked away with a first place and a hefty check. Her life was good and next up was Cheyenne Frontier Days. Chase had promised to meet her there. While she hated to admit it, she missed him—and not just in her bed. She missed his boyish grin and the mischievous twinkle in his eyes. She missed holding his hand as they walked and the sound of his voice. She'd called him several times—getting voice mail—but she left messages telling him that she missed him and was looking forward to reconnecting in Cheyenne.

Tucker had leased a condo for them in Cheyenne and made arrangements to board Red and Cimarron at a nearby ranch. She had a week off and once Chase arrived, she planned on taking some vacation time with him.

After arriving in Cheyenne and settling in, Savannah went to the grocery store to stock up and was pushing her basket toward the cashier when one of the tabloids caught her eye.

She sucked in a sharp breath, then lost it in a whoosh as she caught the two pictures on the cover. One was of Chase, standing with a model-thin woman in a backless dress. Chase, with his hand resting on the small of her naked back. Chase, smiling his sexy grin into the lens of the camera. The other photo featured Savannah. In Riley's, kissing Jess.

Oh, no. Nonononono. This was bad. Very, very bad! She didn't hesitate. She grabbed all the copies and dumped them into her basket. She checked out, numb to everything around her. Getting the grocery bags to her pickup was a struggle. Getting in her truck was harder. Driving while panic blurred her vision was almost impossible.

Finally back at the condo, she dragged her purchases inside and left them on the kitchen counter. She called Chase. Voice mail. Again. She managed to leave a choked "Call me, please!" before she cut the call and dialed Tucker. Voice mail. She left the same message. How could things go so wrong?

Chase ignored his phone and glared when Tucker's rang. Wisely, his cousin didn't answer, either. He shoved the tabloid across the coffee table. "Wanna explain this?"

Tucker glanced down, then met his gaze. "Not me who was out with Diane Brandenburg."

"I wasn't out with her. And I damn sure didn't kiss her."

"Jealous?"

"Of what?"

"The fact your wife was kissing another man."

"Wife in name only, cuz, as she's proved."

"You claim being with Di was innocent. Has it occurred to you that Savannah is innocent?"

"I didn't kiss Di."

"And Savannah was in a bar, sitting at a table with eight other people. Savvie is not the type to make out in front of an audience."

"How do you know?"

Tucker stared at him, his expression incredulous. "This *is* Savannah we're talking about, Chase. Not even Cash could turn up dirt on her. She's had a couple of semiserious boyfriends—one in high school, one in college." His cousin studied him for several long moments. "You really like this girl."

"No, I don't," Chase answered quickly. From the arched brow he got in return, maybe too quickly. "It's business, Tucker. Always has been." He muttered a few cusswords under his breath.

"Ah, so all that spending time with her, holding hands, kissing for the cameras was just…work."

"No, it was to make a point to my father. And the minute I was out of sight, she didn't bother to stay in touch." His phone pinged again. Irritated, he jerked it out of his pocket and scrolled to Voice. He had over thirty messages. All from the same number. Savannah's. "What the hell?"

He checked the times and dates. The calls went all the way back to the week she was in Reno, including the night she was in that bar with that cowboy Casanova. Well, this would be good. He hit Playback and put it on speaker.

"Chase! Chase! Guess what! Jess just gave me the news. I made the NFR leaderboard. I'm on the website. So excited. Everyone here is thrilled. Me, too. Miss you. Call me when you get this! Bye!"

He refused to meet Tucker's disapproving gaze as they listened to the next message. "Hey, baby. A little drunk but I'm back at the hotel. Jess gave me a ride. He'd like to meet you 'cause he says you make me happy. You do, you know." She giggled. "I shouldn't admit that. Miss you, hoss. Bunches."

They listened to each voice mail she'd left, ending with her final two, the choked "Call me, please," left several minutes before. It was the first call he'd deliberately ignored. The last message was a soft sob and a whispered "I'm sorry."

"Yeah, that definitely sounds like a woman playing you for a fool, Chase."

"Shut up, Tucker. Why the hell didn't I get these calls when she made them?"

"Good question. I'll try to find out."

Two hours later, Chase landed at the Cheyenne Airport and drove directly to the resort where Tucker had leased the condo. Savannah's truck was parked in front of one of the rustic redwood buildings. He didn't bother stopping at the office to grab a key. If Savannah wouldn't let him in, he'd kick in the door and pay for the damages.

He parked his rental SUV, left his bag in the vehicle and marched up to the door. It was jerked open as he raised his hand to knock. Savannah's eyes were red rimmed and puffy. She'd been crying. Her expression shifted from hopeful to guarded then back. He did the only thing he could think of under the circumstances. He opened his arms, and she fell into them.

"I'm so sorry, Chase. So-o-o sorry. I didn't know a reporter was there. It was just some of the rodeo crew."

"Shh, kitten, s'okay."

"Nonono. I kissed Jess. I did. But it didn't mean anything. I was just excited when I got the news. He's a friend. Just a friend. He was there. I was excited so I grabbed him. That's all. He has a fiancée. I promise. Just a friend."

"Savannah." He moved her inside and got the door shut

behind them. "Easy, honey. Deep breaths. And please don't cry." He managed to get her to the couch and settled in his lap before her breathing was under control. In normal circumstances—with any other woman—tears had no effect on him. Savannah's tears ripped into his heart with sharp kitten claws. He didn't want to make her cry. Not ever.

"I called," she hiccuped. "That night. You didn't answer. I kept calling."

"Glitch in the system. I didn't know you'd called, sweetheart. None of the times. And I was busy and didn't think to call you." He kissed her forehead. "Congrats on making the top twenty, kitten. Sorry I wasn't there to celebrate with you."

She sniffled and wiped her nose with her sleeve before taking a very deep breath. Twisting her head, she glanced at the pile of glossy papers on the coffee table. "What's going to happen?"

"Nothing. Tucker is doing damage control in the media, and I've already discussed the situation with my family."

"Uh-huh." She stiffened slightly. "I... Who..."

"She's a model, Sav. Diane Brandenburg. She was there on the island for a photo shoot. We weren't *together* together. Just casually at that cocktail party."

"Promise?"

"Promise." He didn't hesitate to answer, even though he'd considered inviting Di back to his room. Doing so would have created more trouble than any pleasure he might have gotten. That was what he'd told himself, anyway, because the alternative—that he wanted to be only with Savannah—was too big to contemplate. While Di was all sleek and built for fast sex, Savannah was curvy and comfortable. Running his hand along her side and hip, stroking down her thigh and back up, was soothing. And sweet. And felt like home.

Seventeen

Savannah awoke tangled in the blankets. After making love—several times—she and Chase had fallen into exhausted sleep, bodies pressed together, legs entwined, her head on his chest. From the position she found herself in upon opening her eyes, she figured neither of them had moved.

"Mornin', kitten."

"Howdy, hoss." She smiled against his warm skin. "Want some coffee?"

"Can you make it from here?"

"Don't think so."

"Damn. You gonna let me kiss you before I brush my teeth?"

A giggle escaped her and her shoulders shook with repressed laughter. "Maybe your morning breath cancels out mine."

"Let's find out."

Chase tightened his arms around her back and urged her higher in the bed. His mouth found hers and he kissed her deeply. He tasted of sex and chocolate mints and she wondered if she could find a coffee flavor to match because that would be heaven to wake up to every morning. Not that she was addicted to coffee. Or to Chase.

He broke the kiss but didn't let go. In fact, he nibbled along her jawline until he reached her ear. He sucked her lobe in before kissing the soft spot behind it. Then he trailed down her neck, along the crest of her shoulder before dipping to her breast, which had her moaning in the back of her throat and arching into him.

"Want you, kitten."

He didn't give her a chance to answer as he rolled her onto her back. While he laved her breasts, his hand smoothed down her belly and cupped her. "Spread, darlin'."

She shifted her legs and his fingers dipped into her heat. Arching her hips, she sought his touch. Shivering in anticipation, she concentrated on breathing and absorbing the absolute pleasure of their lovemaking.

"Please," she gasped, wanting him—all of him—inside her.

He obliged, shifting his weight to rest between her legs, teasing her for a moment before sinking in. Their sighs of completion echoing one another, they lay still as if stunned by the enormity of their feelings—both physical and emotional. Then he moved, slowly lifting his hips as he slid out before gliding in deep. She hooked her heels around his waist and hung on as his tempo increased. He might be on top but she could still ride him, and she did. When they tumbled over the edge, they did it together, the circle complete.

The next week passed in similar fashion. They made love upon awakening, sharing coffee and breakfast before another round of sexy times in the shower. Then they braved the outdoors. They went sightseeing. They went horseback riding. Chase discovered he enjoyed the horses. The ranch had always been his home, but he'd never been one for the great outdoors and all the activities that went on there. Cord, Chance and Cash had done the whole hunting, fishing and riding thing. Clay was the scholar and was almost ten years older. While he'd wanted to emulate his oldest brother, Chase didn't hang around Clay much. He'd retreated into books—adventures and tales of derring-do.

Now, atop a horse, surrounded by the Rocky Mountains, and in the company of a beautiful woman, he believed he'd come into his own. Tucker had ridden hard on him, reminding him that if Savvie had to be monogamous during the term of the contract, he should, too. He didn't want to admit that he had no desire to stray.

As they rode into a mountain meadow, Chase and Savvie startled a herd of elk. Reining their mounts to a stop, they watched as a magnificent bull elk threw back his head and trumpeted a challenge at their intrusion. Chase laughed, understanding the animal's territorial stand. He'd felt the same when he first saw the picture of Savannah kissing that cowboy.

They skirted the meadow, found another trail and followed it, leaving the bull behind to protect his cows. A sense of contentment stole over Chase, and he urged Red closer to Cimarron so he could reach over and snag Savannah's hand.

"This is nice."

Her concerned expression softened as she smiled at him. "It is. Not sure I could live up here. It's beautiful but…" She glanced around, then up, taking in the towering peaks. "I guess I'm an Oklahoma girl born and bred. The biggest mountains I want to spend time in are the Wichitas or the Arbuckles. I *like* the wide-open spaces."

He squeezed her hand in agreement. "I've turned into a city boy, and I don't go home much. Maybe I should. My granddad used to say that once you got red dirt on your hands, it soaked in and got in your blood, became such a part of you that you'd never be happy away from it."

"Are you happy?"

"What do you mean?"

"Living in Las Vegas. Traveling like you do. I mean to Hollywood. Nashville. All those exotic places you go."

They rode in silence as he contemplated her question. "I was. I love what I do, Savannah. Barron Entertainment is my red dirt. I'm good at running hotels, picking places to put them and watching them get built. I like dabbling in the true entertainment side—movies, and the new record company. Radio and TV. All of it."

"Is this okay?"

He didn't like the hesitation in her voice. "Is what okay?"

"This." He still held her right hand so she dropped the reins in her left and used it to wave between them. "Us. You spending this time here with me instead of doing work stuff."

Something warm spread through his chest. She was worried about him. He liked that. "Yes, kitten. This is very okay. Tuck is my second in command. He can deal with most situations. I've picked good people to work for me. And truthfully?" He leaned closer to make sure she was gazing into his eyes when he spoke again. "There's no place I'd rather be."

That was the truth. He didn't just feel content, he felt complete when he was with Savannah. Was he falling in love with her? Was that a good thing or bad? How did she feel about him? He studied the expressions flickering across her face. He liked the one that settled in place.

"I think that's the nicest thing anyone's ever said to me." She squeezed his hand and murmured something that made his breath catch. He wasn't positive, but it sounded like she'd added that she was falling in love with him. He inhaled, relaxed, tugged the hand he held to his mouth and kissed the back of it.

Happy, they rode in silence, turning by mutual agreement back toward the stables. This was the last day of their alone time. The rodeo started tomorrow, and Savannah would be focused on her events. Chase had several deals in the works and really needed to spend some time going over paperwork and discussing things with his staff. He'd fit that in around watching Savannah compete. Something else he'd learned—he enjoyed the heck out of watching his wife do her thing. He'd had to pull some major strings to get tickets in a box where he could see all the action. Instructing Tucker to add a line item to the budget to become a major sponsor of next year's Frontier Days would take care of that situation.

Two days later, the rodeo was in full swing. Savannah was in her element and having a blast. As good as her rodeo run was, her personal life was even better. The absolute craziest thing had happened. She'd fallen in love with a Barron—the biggest playboy in the Barron barn, in fact. And while she didn't have much experience or a great track record with the men she had dated, she'd almost bet that Chase felt the same about her. He didn't say the words but there was something about the way he looked at her, especially when he thought she wasn't paying attention, the way he touched her, the way he made love to her at night. Despite her best intentions, Chase had captured her heart.

He'd sent her a text right before her first run of the day wishing her luck and complaining that business had come up that he needed to take care of. He apologized for missing her competition and promised to contact her as soon as he knew what was going on. She'd received a second text a couple hours later asking her to meet him for dinner before the rodeo concert that night. Chase's cousin Deacon Tate and his Sons of Nashville band were the featured performers and Chase had gotten them fantastic seats. It always helped to have family connections.

She'd had a great day, once again coming out on top in the barrel racing. She was quickly working her way up the ranks of the top twenty riders on the Wrangler National Finals Rodeo list.

Now, showered, primped—she'd put on a filmy skirt and blouse—and ready for some fun, she was all but floating when she walked into the restaurant. The hostess beamed a huge smile her direction as she approached.

"Hi. I'm meeting—"

"Mr. Barron, right?" The girl cut her off. "He's waiting for you in the lounge."

"Oh! Thanks." She returned the smile and headed in the direction the hostess pointed.

The bar was separate from the dining area, down a hallway decorated with Western art. Savannah could hear music, the clink of glasses and the clack of balls on a pool table. She stepped through the door and glanced around. The place was a fusion of roadhouse bar and upscale cocktail lounge. It shouldn't have worked but it did.

The corners were shadowy, the tables and booths lit by candles in old-fashioned lanterns. She scanned the area, looking for Chase. He wasn't sitting at any of the tables, and she was about to walk through and check each of the booths when two men standing at the bar moved aside. She caught sight of Chase's profile and headed toward him. She was halfway there when the whole scene coalesced in her brain.

He wasn't alone. A woman stood with him. Against him, actually, pressed between his spread thighs as he sat on a leather-seated bar stool. Her hands rested on his shoulders, and she was smiling. She wore a formfitting dress with no back, and Chase's hand rested on her bare skin, his fingers inside the draped material.

The woman turned and looked right through Savannah, who recognized her. It was the model photographed with Chase in the Bahamas. Frozen to the spot, Savvie didn't know what to do. She couldn't breathe, couldn't move, could only watch as the beautiful model leaned closer and kissed Chase, as Chase tightened his arm around her back, his whole hand disappearing inside her dress. As he looked right at Savannah while he kissed Diane Brandenburg, his expression one of smug conceit.

Tears burned her eyes, muting the scene with blurry watercolors. Too bad she couldn't dull the sharp pain in her chest, the sense of betrayal. She watched Chase move his head, whisper something to the model. Savvie stood there while the woman tossed her perfect blond hair over her shoulder so she could see Savannah. She saw that pair of eyes, so brilliantly blue she could tell the color in the half-light. She heard the low, throaty laugh that was both sexy and dismissive.

Chase didn't move when the woman nibbled on his ear and whispered something back. He just watched, one corner of his mouth quirked. Sardonic. That was another word her English professor had used that Savannah had never known the true meaning of. Not until that moment.

The music from the jukebox stopped playing as the moment stretched out. Her phone rang. She ignored it, her brain still incapable of controlling her muscles. The woman moved, turning in Chase's embrace. She slid an arm around his neck and cocked her hip to press against his groin. Her lips were curled in a cat-ate-the-canary smile that didn't reach the ice blue of her eyes. A part of Savannah's brain wondered how a woman could betray another woman like this. Then she understood. She was the interloper here. She was the one who didn't belong.

The room had grown silent and nobody moved, as though the moment had been frozen in time, a photograph capturing a momentous occasion. Heart breaking, Savannah inhaled. She would not cry. She'd already shed too many tears over this man. No more. Straightening her shoulders and raising her chin, she pasted a proud smile on her face—a smile that cost her everything to manufacture and hold in place. All she had left was her dignity. She refused to give Chase the satisfaction of seeing her fall apart.

She turned her back. Placed one foot in front of the other until she was out of the room. Until she was down the hallway and past all those people lined up to eat and laugh and have a good time. Until she was outside under the summer sky. Until she was safely inside her truck. Driving. Then inside the condo. Staring at the bed where she and Chase had made love less than twelve hours ago.

Savannah wouldn't sleep in that bed. What if he'd brought that woman here? Had sex with her in that bed. She couldn't bear it if she buried her face in the pillow she'd slept on last night and smelled someone else's perfume. Her phone rang again.

This time her fingers worked and she retrieved it from her purse. It was Tucker. She should have turned the phone off but she didn't. Obviously a glutton for punishment, she answered.

"Savvie, hi. I've been trying to reach you. Chase is stuck here in Vegas and still in the emergency meeting. He asked me to step out and call you."

She didn't say anything so he continued. "He's sorry about missing Deke's concert but says you should go without him. Deke wants to meet you and will be watching for you."

She still didn't speak.

"Sav? Are you there?"

"I can't believe he's got you doing his dirty work, Tucker."

His voice turned cautious as he asked, "Sugar? Is everything all right? What's going on?"

"I know what his business is, Tucker. I just saw him with that model. Di whatever-her-name-is. Tell him nice try, but I won't be falling for his lies anymore. Tell him not to bother coming back here. I'll keep my end of the bargain so long as he doesn't contact me again."

Savannah dropped the phone from her ear and tapped the end call button. Then she turned off her phone. No longer hungry, she wanted only to get numb. The ache in her chest made it hard to breathe. She wanted to get mad at Chase, but how could she be angry at him? She knew who and what he was. She should be furious with herself. *She* had let her guard down. *She* had let him worm his way into her bed and her heart. This was all her fault. She knew better but she did it, anyway.

"You, Savannah Wolfe, are an absolute, complete idiot." Announcing it to the empty room didn't help. There was a six-pack of beer in the fridge. Maybe if she drank all of them, she could take the edge off the pain. She and alcohol weren't exactly friends, but maybe if she killed off enough bottles, she would stop missing him. Maybe fall asleep. Without dreams. Because dreams just messed up everything.

Eighteen

Chase was desperate to get back to Cheyenne. He had no idea what Savannah thought she'd seen, but he had to get to her, talk to her, fix things. Tucker had talked to her at 7:30 p.m. It was now 2:00 a.m. and the plane was still twenty minutes from landing. He'd tried calling her cell and left so many voice mails that the last time he called, the message said her mailbox was full. He called the condo phone. It just rang.

He'd been stuck in a meeting of other casino managers, the Clark County district attorney, and a police task force that included the FBI, US Marshals Service and lawyers from the Justice Department to discuss a fraud ring working the casino. He'd walked out during a break, informing the authorities there was an emergency with his wife. Luckily, no one had tried to stop him, otherwise he'd be in jail for assaulting a federal officer.

Just after 3:00 a.m., he was pounding up the walkway to the condo's front door. Savannah's truck was parked in its spot. That was a plus. He put his key in the door. The first lock clicked and he pushed. Nothing budged. She'd thrown the dead bolt. Fine. His key fit both locks. In moments, he was inside.

The TV flickered on some infomercial and Savannah was curled up on the couch, huddled under a throw blanket. Why wasn't she in bed? Gazing down at her, he noticed her thick eyelashes were matted and the skin around her eyes puffy. She'd been crying. Even in sleep her breath hitched. Kneeling beside her, he carefully moved her hair off her face so he could see her better in the low light.

Savannah erupted off the couch, pushing and shoving, reminding him of the first time they'd met. He gathered her close before she could get any momentum, and with a quick twist, settled on the couch with her in his lap, her legs trapped by one of his, her arms encircled by his. She squirmed and fought.

"Shh, kitten. Shh."

"Get out." She didn't scream, which might have been better. Instead, her voice carried the cold disdain of a dead relationship.

"No."

"Then I'll leave. Let me go."

"No. You aren't going anywhere until we settle this."

"Settle this? Settle what? I saw you, Chase. I saw you tonight in that bar with that woman. Kissing her."

"Whoa, whoa, whoa. What bar and what woman? Honey, I flew to Vegas yesterday. I texted you."

"Oh, yeah. You texted. Told me you had some work and you'd be back in touch. You definitely did that. What I want to know is why. I never pegged you as being cruel."

He breathed deliberately to keep his temper in check. First, he had to get to the bottom of things. Then he'd go pound on someone. "I'd never hurt you, kitten."

"Don't. Call. Me. That." She hissed and snarled, renewing her efforts to get free. He was truly glad she worked with her hands so her nails were short and rounded. Harder to claw his eyes out that way.

"Savannah. I can't fix what's wrong if you don't talk to me."

"Fix what's wrong? You can't fix this. You leave my bed—our bed—lie to me, meet that bimbo, then make sure I see you? How is that fixable? Oh! And then you have your cousin call me to make up some excuse. What happened? You texted me instead of her about dinner? Except you didn't seem surprised to see me, and you made damn sure I saw you lay a big, fat wet one on her."

"Dammit, darlin'. Back up. What are you talking about?"

"You texted me, telling me to meet you for dinner before the concert. So I did. Only you were in the bar with that...that skinny skank from the Bahamas. The one you said means nothing to you. Only you were all over her like stink on sh—"

"Savannah! Look at me." He took a chance and cupped her cheek, easing her face around to look at him. "I didn't text you a second time."

"Yeah. Right."

"Honey, I didn't. When I landed at McCarron Airport, my plane was met by the Feds, and I was escorted to the Clark County Courthouse. I spent all day and most of the freaking night with a bunch of attorneys, the FBI and more cops than I ever want to see again. I don't know who you thought you saw—"

"Shut up, Chase. I saw you. You sat there on that bar stool with that model between your legs, your hand in the back of her dress stroking her butt."

"Model?" He searched his memory, hit on a name. "Di Brandenburg?"

"Yeah, her. You said something to her and she turned around to look at me like I was...pond scum or something. Then she whispered in your ear and the two of you kissed. You. Kissed. Her! Looking at me the whole time."

"Aw hell, kitten." A headache bloomed behind his eyes as he rested his head against her shoulder. "I'm going to kill him."

Savannah didn't breathe for a minute. Her voice squeaked when she asked, "Him who?"

"Cash. We're identical twins. Most people can't tell us apart."

She opened her mouth, probably to dispute his assertion, but then snapped it shut. She studied him hard. His hair. Eyes. Nose. Mouth. Then his eyes again. Her gaze stayed there, unblinking, before she closed her eyes and kept them that way for a few minutes.

"Your eyes. Your eyes are different."

No one had ever noted that difference and he was curious what she thought she saw. "How so?"

"Even when you were angry, back when we first met and you threw me out? You weren't...cold. Mad, yes. But there was this look, this...it was..." She shrugged and struggled to find a description.

"It was what?"

"You looked resigned, but there was humor there, like the world is a big joke and you're the only who gets it."

"Okay..." He stretched out the word. "And?"

"And last night...your brother. There's something in his eyes. Hard. He has hard eyes."

"I'm gonna kill him. For real." Chase gazed into her eyes. "I'm sorry, kitten."

"Why would he do that to you?"

"Don't know, but I suspect Dad put him up to it. Whatever the reason, I plan to find out." His gaze dropped to her mouth and he placed a gentle kiss on her lips. "First, though, I want to make love to my wife."

Chase made one phone call to Tucker's brother, Bridger—who was second in command at Cash's security company—and got Cash's location. He seemed surprised when he opened his hotel room door to find Chase standing there. Pushing inside, Chase studied his twin as he shut the door and sauntered across the room to the coffeemaker. He poured a cup without offering one to Chase.

"You're a jackass."

Cash swallowed a sip of coffee while watching him over the rim of the cup, but made no comment. They stared at each for several minutes before Chase broke the silence.

"What the hell, Cash? Why did you set up Savannah like that?"

"It's for your own good."

"My own good? You have no clue what's good for me."

"Then I'm doing it for the good of the family."

Stunned, Chase stared at his brother. It was like looking into a mirror, but seeing only the dark side of their personalities. "Family. Gotcha. So the old man put you up to this."

"Somebody has to look out for you. This woman is an inconvenient complication in your life. She's only after your money."

"Yeah? You're wrong, Cash. Not everyone is like our old man."

"You think I'm wrong? I plan to prove it to you."

"Stay away from Savannah, Cash. This is your only warning."

Chase hated the expression on his twin's face. Ugly, twisted and angry. What had happened to Cash to put that look in his eyes?

"You gonna choose that bimbo over your family?"

"I love her."

He hadn't meant to say the words. Not out loud. And definitely not to Cash or anyone else in his family. Savannah should have had those words first, not the angry man facing him. Chase knew what they all believed. But Savannah wasn't what they thought she was, wasn't *who* they thought she was. She was sweet and funny. Warm. Loyal. Every bit as special as his three sisters-in-law. He knew as soon as those words were out of his mouth they were true. He did love Savannah, and he wanted her in his world far longer than the year they'd agreed to. He wanted her for a lifetime.

"You love her? What the hell do you know about love, Chase? How many women have you bedded, then kicked out to chase the next one? Dad damn sure gave you the right name. This one isn't anything special. She's just one more notch on your bedpost."

"You're wrong. She's the one, Cash. Like Cassidy is for Chance. Like Jolie always was for Cord. Like Georgie and Clay."

"Jeez, Chase. When did you become whipped like them?"

"Jeez, Cash, when did you become such a bastard?"

"We only have one of those in our family."

"Yeah, our old man."

"No, our ranch foreman."

Chase rocked back on his heels. "Wow. You went there. What the hell is going on with you, Cash?"

"Nothing."

"That's bull. You've been on a mission to be a complete jackass since Chance hooked up with Cassidy."

"Someone needs to worry about this family."

"And your way of doing that is to keep all of us single and miserable?" He rubbed his fingers through his hair, leaving it tousled. "I... Dammit, Cash, you seem like a stranger lately. You're my brother. My *twin*, for God's sake."

"You're the one who married a stranger." Cash looked unapologetic and angry, his hands fisted at his sides and his shoulders tensed, as though he wanted to throw a punch.

"She's not a stranger now. Would you be happier if I'd married Janiece? Talk about a gold digger. That woman spends money like it's dirt, and that whole deal was some business thing concocted by Dad. I would never love Janiece."

Chase's cell vibrated in his hip pocket and he pulled it

out. Savannah. He very suddenly craved the sound of her voice, the touch of her hand in his. "Someday, Cash. Someday it will happen to you. Someday you'll find the woman you love and I hope to hell you aren't stupid enough to lose her. We're done here. My wife is calling."

He turned on his heel and headed for the door, his phone to his ear. "Howdy, kitten. I'm on my way."

"You okay, hoss?"

He wasn't, but he wouldn't admit that to her. She'd worry even more. "S'all good, darlin'. I'll be there shortly and will meet you behind the chutes. Gotta give my girl a good-luck kiss before she rides."

Silence stretched between them, then he heard her breathe. "Am I? Your girl?"

"Yeah, kitten. You are."

Nineteen

Chase had insisted they go out for brunch and explained his reasons. "Kitten, you can bet there were photos taken last night in the bar. It's just a matter of time before they hit the tabloids. We're going out for breakfast. I'm tweeting our location—"

"Wait! What?"

He blushed all the way to the tips of his ears, a look Savannah found oddly endearing. "I…sort of have a fake Twitter account and hashtag."

"You have a hashtag?" She didn't know whether to laugh or worry about the guy's need for attention.

"Yes. When I want to be seen, I type—" he held up two fingers on each hand and made a hashtag of them "—hashtag FindChase."

Her eyes widened, once she understood the implications. "Wait! You set me up. In San Antonio. And other places."

He had the good grace not to lie. "It worked, didn't it?" He leaned down and kissed her. She meant to break away, until his arms wrapped around her and he deepened the kiss. By the time he finished, she was on her toes, one leg hitched around his hip, her arms clenched around his neck as she held on for dear life.

"Damn, kitten. Keep that up and I'll have you for breakfast."

Laughing, she pushed away and got her bearings. "I'm hungry." As his gaze grew heated, she quickly added, "For food."

"Tweeting comes in handy. Like now. I'll *leak* our location. Somebody will ask about last night. I'll explain it was Cash. Then I'll kiss you."

"Uh-huh. And why will you kiss me?"

"Because I like kissing you?" He offered his boyish grin—the one with a hint of dimple—and a wink. "Technically, it's a photo op. We're still newlyweds in love."

"What if they ask about the skinny skank?"

He choked back a laugh but it erupted as a snort. "That *skank* is one of the world's highest paid models, wildcat."

"So?"

"If the subject comes up, I'll reasonably point out that the photo allegedly showing me with her was actually Cash, and that they're having a secret affair." He waggled his brows and it was her turn to giggle and snort.

"Turnabout is fair play, and payback is hell."

"My thinking exactly."

Brunch had played out as expected and then he'd kissed her goodbye, sending her off to the rodeo grounds. Unable to leave well enough alone, she'd called him. She had to make sure he was okay. His brother had cut him to the quick. The experience—and profound sense of betrayal—left her feeling shaky, too. She wanted assurances from Chase, wanted him to understand why she needed them.

She was riding Cimarron, warming him up in the practice arena, when she noticed Chase standing at the gate. She slowed the horse's canter to a trot, then a walk as she approached. He opened the gate and she rode through before stopping and dismounting.

"Howdy, kitten." Chase's voice held a hint of something sad.

"Howdy, hoss. You got a kiss for me?"

"Always, baby." He dipped his head and brushed his lips across hers.

Need blossomed within her. And desire. This man had worked his way under her skin in a way no other had. By mutual consent, they started walking, Cimarron trailing along as she led him by the reins.

"How bad was it?"

Chase's expression firmed, the skin around his eyes tightening. "About like I expected."

She slipped her hand into his and he laced their fingers. "I'm sorry, Chase."

"No, I'm sorry. I saw your face last night. I..." He cleared his throat. "I've been a lot of things in my life. I've done a lot I'm not proud of." Hesitating, he tugged her to a stop. "I wouldn't set you up like that, Savannah. If I was going to step out on you, I'd be honest and tell you."

Her chest grew tight, and she worked to keep her expression bland, obviously failing as his eyes softened. "I'd tell you, and I wouldn't do it in public. It's not going to happen, sweetheart. I'm not sure what's going on between us, but whatever it is, it's good. I like it. I wouldn't hurt you like that."

"Okay."

His smile was tentative and a little sad. "I don't blame you for not trusting me, kitten. I'll work to change your mind."

"Look, Chase, I... I don't get why your brother did what he did. I know we don't fit together. I'm not the type of woman your family would pick. I get that. But he hurt me, and he did it on purpose. It shouldn't have bothered me, given our arrangement, but I'm gonna be honest here." She paused to inhale.

Chase prompted her to continue. "Okay."

"I know we have an agreement. I know you plan for us to go our separate ways after a year. I know that it's convenient to hang out with me, to—" She had to breathe again. "To sleep with me."

Throwing back his head, Chase laughed. There was a hint of self-deprecation hiding behind his obvious humor. "Kitten, there is *nothing* convenient about you."

Savannah didn't know how to take that. "Okay, fine. I'm inconvenient. Whatever. But just so you know, I don't sleep around. In fact, I can count the number of guys I've been with on one hand. I don't sleep with just anybody. But I slept with you. You remember that, Chase Barron. And you remember that I normally don't give second chances. I don't know if you just have bad luck or bad karma or bad…something. I won't be made a fool of. So no more chances. Don't blow what time we have left."

She shook free from his grasp, turned on her boot heel, tugged Cimarron's reins and stalked away. Chase watched, enjoying the angry sway of her hips far too much. Eventually, his brain lassoed his libido and he considered what she had—and hadn't—said. He'd admitted to Cash that he was in love with Savannah. Up until the moment she dropped his hand and walked away, he believed she was falling in love with him. Now he wasn't so sure.

Don't blow what time we have left.

She'd implied that she'd keep to their original agreement, that she'd divorce him after their year was up. That's what he wanted, too. Wasn't it? Given his family history, he was a bad bet in the marriage game. But something about Savannah called to him. She wasn't pretentious. She wasn't naive so much as guileless.

I can count the number of guys I've been with on one hand... But I slept with you. You remember that, Chase Barron.

Her words reverberated in his brain. She was the last

person on this earth he should be involved with—much less be contemplating a long-term relationship with.

Knowing all of that didn't matter. He didn't care that she was wrong for him, because being with her felt too damn right. He had six months to change her mind. Less, actually. He had until December, when she returned to Las Vegas to compete in the Wrangler National Finals Rodeo. He was positive she'd be there. She'd be on his home turf, and he could make his move. He didn't need another chance. He was going to take the one he had and run with it.

Forget Operation Seduce Savannah. He was now all about Operation Rest of Our Lives, for better or worse.

His phone beeped with a text. He glanced at it. CALL ME!!! It was from Tucker, a man who never used all caps and thought exclamation points were for preteens texting about boy bands. His mind on ways to win his inconvenient cowgirl, Chase meandered to the arena and up to his box. Once seated, he texted Tucker back.

Little busy here. What's so important?

His phone rang almost immediately. He answered with "Not a good time, dude."

"Gonna have to make it a good time, cuz. The Feds are not happy you pitched a hissy and stormed out last night."

"Didn't have a choice, Tuck."

"Gonna enlighten me?"

"Cash."

"What about him?"

"He was here with Di Brandenburg."

"So?"

"Pretending to be me."

"Oh, crap. Savannah saw."

"Yeah."

"S'all good now?"

"Pretty much." Chase couldn't keep the smile out of his voice.

"Dang. Then this sucks. Sorry to burst your balloon, Chase, but I need you back here ASAP."

"No. I have plans with Savvie."

"I don't care. And neither do the Feds. This is a big deal, Chase. The fraud ring isn't just hitting us here in Las Vegas. They hit the Barron Crown in Scottsdale last night. Palm Springs. Miami. They've all been targeted in the past few months."

"Why didn't we know?"

"No clue. Justice Department is wondering if we aren't helping them. Some sort of money laundering scheme or something."

"Well...hell."

"Look, I can probably stall them for a few days, but you need to get your butt back here as soon as you can."

"I'll fly back tomorrow. I want tonight with Savannah."

"Uh, Chase? What's the deal there?"

"It's the real deal, Tucker."

"You sure?"

"More than I've ever been. Being with her? It feels right, Tucker." Chase brushed his fingers through his hair and leaned forward, an elbow on his knee. Lowering his voice, he added, "Cash didn't take what I had to say very well."

"I can imagine."

"He set it up, Tuck." Anger leaked into his voice. "My own twin planned it out to hurt Savannah."

"That's low, cuz."

"Yeah." Silence stretched between them, though the arena came to life around him and crowd noise covered what he said next. "Something's wrong, Tuck."

"Yeah. The Feds are crawling all over us."

"I meant Cash, cuz. He's not..."

"He's not who you thought he was? You know, Chase,

for a businessman as smart as you are, you sure wear blinders where your family is concerned. If your old man weren't my uncle—"

"What about Cash?"

"He's got a mean streak, Chase. He's always had it, even when we were kids. You got all the sunshine and rainbows. And Cash? Cash got the thunder and lightning."

Opening and closing his mouth several times as he attempted to form an answer, Chase finally gave up. "Not gonna discuss that now. Tell the Feds I'll be there tomorrow morning. Get with Bridger and find out what's been happening at our other properties. And get the accountants lined up. The Justice Department has wanted a piece of us ever since Clay won his first election."

Savannah took Chase to the airport the next morning. After dinner and dancing at one of the cowboy bars, they'd spent the night making love. She didn't want to say goodbye, afraid she'd lose something important if they were apart. They stood on the tarmac, Chase delaying getting on the plane as if he didn't want to go any more than she didn't want him to leave.

"Gonna miss you, kitten. And remember, if I text, I'll use our code word."

She was pretty sure she blushed to the roots of her hair. "*Purr* is not much of a code word, hoss."

"But you purr so prettily when I make you come."

Now she was positive her face was scarlet. "Shut up."

Chase laughed, a deep rolling sound from his chest. Wrapping his arms around her, he lifted her so they could kiss, then swung her around and around until she was giggling and dizzy. "Put me down, you big goof."

He did, though his hands lingered on her waist, and he smiled down at her. "Can you make it home for a visit after Frontier Days?"

Savannah stilled at the word. *Home*. His home. The

apartment in Vegas. Where he'd thrown her out of his bed, and then taken her to the heights of passion in that same bed. Moments passed and Chase squeezed her waist. She stammered out a breathless "Yes. I'll try."

He kissed her again, slowly, like she was some delicacy to be savored. She melted against him, her fingers curling in the lapels of his jacket. She rolled up on the balls of her feet to get closer to him, clinging just a little as he started to pull away. Part of her wanted to say the words, but she clamped her jaw shut as soon as she'd said, "I—"

"I?" Chase kissed the tip of her nose as she dropped back to stand flat-footed. "I what, kitten?"

She scrambled to fill in the blank. "Miss you. I will miss you." *A lot. A whole,* whole *lot.*

"Good. That means you'll be thinking about me. Turnabout is fair play, because I think about you all the time."

The flight attendant appeared in the doorway of the executive jet. "Sorry to interrupt, Mr. Barron, but the pilot says there's some weather moving in. We need to take off now to have any chance of missing it."

"I'll be right there." Chase turned back to Savannah. "Really gotta go, kitten. If you can't make it to Vegas, I'll see you in Dodge City." He flashed her a lopsided grin with a hint of dimple and a wink. "Provided Dodge City has an airport."

She sputtered in support of Dodge. "For a man born and raised in Oklahoma, that's just mean. Dodge City is awesome."

"It is when you're there." He glanced over his shoulder and waved at the flight attendant. "Gotta go, babe. Call me."

"Ditto. You, me."

They kissed one last time until Chase broke away. He paused at the door to the plane and waved. Savannah backed up, but waited, waving at him until the plane taxied away.

* * *

Savannah didn't go to Vegas between rodeos. Chase had to fly to Miami. He didn't join her in Dodge City. Or Caldwell, Idaho. Something related to his business always came up. Savannah would have been angry or hurt, but Chase called her constantly. He even bought her an iPad so they could Skype, and she could respond to his sexy emails. And oh, boy, did he send sexy emails. She would read them and blush, and then the ornery cuss would tag her on Skype just so he could see her face.

Deep down, Savannah knew he wasn't avoiding her, despite evidence to the contrary. Even Tucker vouched for him. So she did what she'd always done. She drove from rodeo to rodeo. She competed. She mostly won, sometimes lost and learned she could call Chase when she was feeling down. He never failed to take her call. If he was in the middle of a meeting, he took a moment to talk to her, and then set a time when they could Skype.

September rolled around and that meant the Pendleton Round-up. Like Calgary and Cheyenne, Pendleton was one of the big ones. It was an important rodeo with the stiffest competition. Winning at Pendleton was a big deal, but she was so lonely, she could barely get out of bed.

Staring at the mirror in her hotel room, she reminded herself of her idiotic tendencies. "He's a busy man, Savannah. He runs a huge corporation. And you're just his…" She stopped speaking as she considered what exactly she was. What had he said all those months ago when he proposed this? A marriage of convenience. "That's all you are, girl. Just a convenient wife. Yeah, he likes the stuff we do in bed. He probably even likes you. But forever? Nope. When the year's up, he'll be done with you, ready to move on."

She made good time in the afternoon run. Her evening run was even better. She was in Cimarron's stall, brushing him down, when she looked up. Chase stood in the stall door, a half smile on his face and something she couldn't describe in his eyes.

"I remember standing in a stall like this in Vegas, watching you worry over a horse. Watching you straighten your shoulders when the world tried to slam you to the ground." His quiet voice washed over her, filling the empty spaces that had opened up in his absence. He stepped in, closed the gate behind him. He took the curry brush from her hand, tossed it into the bucket in the corner of the stall. "I've missed you, kitten."

Savannah fell into his arms. "You're here. You…" She cupped his cheeks and kissed him. "You're really here." She closed her eyes as she laid her head against his shoulder, hoping to stem the relieved tears forming there.

"I'm really here. And if my brother Chance hadn't warned me about making love on straw, I'd show you just how excited I am. But you have a big, comfortable bed in your hotel room, yeah?"

"Yeah." She grinned at him as his eyes grew hooded and that dang dimple came out to play.

"Yeah."

Oh, the things her man could say with only one syllable.

Twenty

Vegas. She was in Vegas. Savannah's emotions were as crazy as a Tilt-a-Whirl. She'd made the National Finals. As a top-fifteen money winner, she was one of the last cowgirls standing in the race to the All-Around Cowgirl Championship. She'd done it. Being here was exciting, the culmination of everything she'd worked for since her first win, at the rodeo held in conjunction with the Western National Stock Show in Denver last January. October and November had been nuts—totally crazypants with back-to-back rodeos as she pushed to make the cut for the NFR.

Vegas. Yeah, but. She was in Vegas. In Chase's home. Well, his apartment atop the Crown Hotel and Casino. With a whole rack of her clothes in the closet, most of which still had the price tags attached. All of which she'd stared at for almost an hour, trying to decide what to wear. Chase wanted her to go with him to Barron House for dinner with an associate and his fiancée.

"I want to show you off," he'd said.

Which made her panic. She almost broke out in hives just thinking about the Barron House. She couldn't stall any longer—not if she was going to be on time. There was no way she'd be late—even fashionably. So her emotions had run away to the carnival and were currently riding every scary ride on the midway.

Savannah twisted off her wedding band and grimaced. No matter how often she cleaned her hands, the black mark continued to encircle her ring finger. She tried not to let it bother her. She really did. But after their wedding, especially when their relationship went to new levels of commitment, she'd figured he'd buy her a real ring. Except he hadn't. In fact, he hadn't bought her any jewelry at all—not that she wore much, but still. It was the principle. Drying her hands and slipping the cheap ring back on her finger, she tried not to think about waking up the morning after their completely Vegas-style wedding and having to face Chase's father. Then there was that scene with the maître d' at the restaurant—the one his father had witnessed.

She smoothed her palms down the coffee-brown microsuede skirt she'd chosen to wear. Paneled, it hugged her curves yet still swirled around the pair of custom-stitched boots on her feet. She'd dithered—and wasn't that a fun word to describe the near-panicked freak-out she endured while picking out an outfit to wear. She eventually breathed through it and chose a cashmere sweater the color of butterscotch to go with the skirt.

With the addition of a turquoise-and-silver squash blossom necklace and a fringed shawl, she figured even the snooty maître d' would be impressed. The still-vivid memory of that encounter plagued her all the way down in the elevator.

With more confidence than she felt, Savannah wended her way through the main floor of the hotel to reach the restaurant. She slowed when the front entrance came into view. If Chase arrived first, would he wait for her? Or would he already be seated at his table with the couple? Was she late? She glanced at her watch. No. She was a few minutes early. Breathing deeply, she controlled her emotions. She was Mrs. Chase Barron. She could do this.

Approaching the host stand, she plastered a smile on her face, all the while rehearsing what she was going to say. *Good evening, I'm Mrs. Barron. Is my husband's table set up for our guests? Good evening, I'm Mrs. Barron—*

"You have some nerve."

The cutting voice interrupted her thoughts and her forward momentum. She'd been so wrapped up in getting through the next few minutes, she'd totally tuned out everything around her. But when she looked up, she found herself face-to-face with Cyrus Barron. She scrambled to collect her thoughts. Was he supposed to be there for the meeting? Had Chase told her and had she blanked it out?

"Excuse me?"

"You heard me. You have no class and no sense of propriety. Parading around pretending to be married to my son."

"She is married to your *son*, old man. I don't recall inviting you to dinner after the meeting this afternoon."

Chase. He'd come up behind her and even now ignored his father to smile at her, his eyes warm and appreciative as he took in her outfit. He dropped a kiss on her mouth, careful not to smear her lipstick.

"Don't kiss that woman in public."

Chase narrowed his eyes at his father's derogatory emphasis on the word *woman*. "Don't go there, old man." He stepped in front of Savannah, partially shielding her, acutely aware that his father had bushwhacked her.

"We're done, Dad. You don't get to do this to my wife. You don't get to do this to me."

"Shut up, Chasen. You listen to me, boy—"

"I am not your *boy*. I am the CEO of Barron Entertainment. I run this hotel and ten others. I oversee radio and television stations and a whole group of other entertainment enterprises. I make this family a ton of money. I've worked my butt off to get where I am and you will respect me as the corporate officer who made that happen even if you don't respect me as your son."

His anger made him reckless and he pressed closer to his father. "I get it now."

Cyrus's eyes widened, but he leaned toward Chase. "Get what?"

"Why our family sucks. Two things are gonna happen now. Either you apologize to Savannah and return to your table, or I will have you escorted out by Security and banned from this property." To emphasize his statement, Chase eased Savannah to his side, his arm around her shoulders in a show of support.

"You've made your bed, boy." He flicked his gaze over Savannah. In a voice as cold and insincere as he was, Cyrus added, "My apologies."

Chase turned Savannah into his chest, both arms around her. He rubbed the top of her head with his chin and murmured, "My old man is a jackass, kitten. I'll make sure you're never alone with him again. Okay?"

"Okay."

Holding her hand, he brushed past the maître d', who stood there as still as a statue. "I have two guests coming. Mr. Brown and his companion. Show them to my table when they get here."

"Yes, sir. Of course, Mr. Barron."

He seated Savannah at their table, ordered wine for her and a Scotch neat for himself. After the waiter disappeared, he took her hand and pulled it onto his thigh under the table. "Breathe, kitten. You're fine." He let his appreciation for her beauty bleed into his expression. "And gorgeous." He fingered the sleeve of her sweater. "Soft. Like the woman wearing it."

And there was the pink tingeing her cheeks that he so enjoyed. No one had ever spoiled this woman, had ever told her she was beautiful and cherished. He had plans to do both for a very long time. But the waiter came back with the drinks just as the other members of their party arrived, interrupting him. After a round of introductions and then everyone ordering dinner, Chase settled in, his arm around the back of Savannah's chair while he turned his attention to Jason Brown. Brown fancied himself a corporate raider, and the man had his eye on one of the Barron properties. If the price was right, Chase would do business, but that *if* was a huge question mark at the moment.

Savannah, still shaken from her encounter with her father-in-law, did her best to entertain Heather with the last name she couldn't remember. During introductions, she'd learned that Heather and Jason's wedding was imminent. During their meal, she discovered that Heather couldn't speak or eat without waving her left hand. The huge diamond nestled in a pile of big diamonds glittered in the light cast by flames dancing in the nearby fireplace. Savvie was duly impressed—what woman wouldn't be? Still, she was getting fed up with Heather flaunting her ring.

Chase and Jason were deep in a discussion about cost overruns and acceptable losses. Savannah tuned in to them. Even though she didn't really understand the terminology, the men's conversation was infinitely more interesting than Heather's incessant wedding chatter.

"What about yours?"

Savannah jerked her attention back to the other woman. "Excuse me?"

"Your ring?" Heather huffed out a breath to indicate her irritation. "I was asking about your wedding ring." She made a dismissive gesture by flicking her bediamonded hand toward Savannah's left hand.

Glancing down, Savannah just managed to hide her wince. The dark circle left on her skin by the cheap metal was clearly visible again.

"Considering how much the Barrons are worth, I figured you'd have double the number of carats as I have in my ring. At a minimum."

Embarrassed, Savannah struggled to hold on to her composure even as Jason chastised his fiancée.

"Seriously, Heather? We discussed this." Jason turned to Chase, who kept his gaze focused on Savannah. "I'm sorry, Chase. Heather and her sorority sisters have this whole mine's-better gamesmanship going on. I've cautioned her that not everyone is as concerned about quality or quantity as she is."

Savannah couldn't meet Chase's intense stare, wishing the floor would open up and swallow her.

Heather huffed out a breath, ignoring Savannah and focusing on her fiancé. "But look at her hand, Jason. That ring is just...cheap." The woman pitched her voice just loud enough that the large group seated nearby, and Cyrus Barron, turned to watch.

Chase reached over and clasped her left hand. He lifted it, staring intently while he rubbed his thumb over her ring finger, before raising her hand to his mouth for a kiss. Then he turned the intensity of his stare on Heather.

"I'm a very lucky man, Ms. Martin. My wife is a cowgirl. She has her priorities straight. Savannah is also sentimental. There's a story behind this ring and she wears it to remind me what's important." He raised his free hand and their waiter appeared immediately. "Add twenty-five percent to the tab for your tip, Kirk."

He pushed back from the table, still holding Savannah's hand for a moment. Then he released her so he could hold her chair as she stood to join him. "I think we're done, Jason. Ms. Martin, I wish I could say it was a pleasure."

Chase didn't wait for a response from the couple. He tucked Savannah's hand into the crook of his elbow and walked out of the restaurant with her. Cyrus caught up to them.

"When are you going to come to your senses and end this travesty of a marriage?"

"Shut up, old man." Chase's hand clenched around hers as she stiffened beside him.

Smirking, Cyrus shook his head. The smirk morphed into a coldly deliberate sneer. "You won't win, Chase."

Savannah could breathe again at Chase's next words.

"I already have."

Twenty-One

Savannah was floating on air—or would be if she wasn't riding Cimarron. She'd done it! Champion All-Around Cowgirl! She even had the belt buckle to prove it. And the saddle. And the prize money. The endorsements. The trailer. Not that she needed one, considering Chase's generosity. She couldn't wait to see him, to fall into his arms for a big hug and a searing kiss. He'd be proud of her, proud *for* her. Ever since the night he'd stood up for her, taking on his father on her behalf, their relationship had deepened. Tonight, they were both winners.

Chase talked about *when*. *When* they went here, *when* they did this or that. He spoke in future terms and never with an *if*. Convinced he wanted a future with her, believing he shared the same feelings for her that she held for him, she'd let her guard down. She'd opened her heart and welcomed him with open arms and unconditionally. She loved him. She'd admitted that to herself in Cheyenne after the thought of him being with another woman left her devastated and so angry she couldn't breathe between the sobs.

In the months following, he'd done everything in his power to show her how much he cared. He'd gotten her to trust him. And she was ready to be honest and tell him how she felt about him. Coming out of the arena after accepting her awards, she'd expected him to be behind the chutes waiting for her. He wasn't.

She pulled her phone from her hip pocket. No text. No missed call. Concern now colored her excitement. Dismounting, she led the big paint horse to the competitors' holding area. She could put him in a stall while she searched out Chase. She knew he was here. She'd seen him before her last run, had seen him in his box cheering as she rode into the arena to collect her prizes when she was announced the winner.

Standing, unsure of what to do or where to go, Savannah was surprised when one of the candidates for rodeo queen sauntered by with an insincere smile on her face. Great. Just who she wanted to run into. Twyla Allan, the same girl who'd been draped all over Chase back at the Clark County rodeo right after her marriage.

Twyla stopped and with a catty look on her face asked, "Looking for that gorgeous hunk you claim is your man?"

Something about the other girl's demeanor worried Savannah, but she nodded her head, unable to stop the gesture.

"Saw him back that way, headed toward the competitors' lounge."

"Oh. Uh, thanks." Savannah walked away but glanced back over her shoulder to find Twyla watching her go, a hand on one hip, her eyes smoldering and a smirk crinkling her lips. Something was wrong. Like the chick knew something Savannah didn't. That was bad. Very bad.

All but trotting, she jogged past the holding pens. People clogged the area behind the chutes and she ended up playing running back as she dodged and cut between cowboys, officials and others. She waved off shouted congratulations with a distracted smile and hand flick. The closer she got to the area under the arena where the hospitality room was located, the more panicked she became.

One of the bigwigs with Wrangler jeans caught her, staying her forward progress with a hand on her arm. He wanted to talk about a sponsorship. Accepting his card, with a promise to call, she rushed on. The leather soles of her boots slipped on the incline leading from the staging area floor up to the first level, where hospitality was located. She reached the landing and made a sliding turn. When she regained her balance, she stopped dead at the sound of Chase's laughter. His deep, sexy, only-for-her laughter.

He stood twenty feet away, surrounded by paparazzi he'd most likely tweeted to get there. A curvy, blonde cowgirl stood on his left. She had her arm around his neck and his hand rested comfortably on her hip. The Stetson on her head was tipped back, and she was laughing at what Chase was saying. The camera flashes lit up the hallway as though it was the Fourth of July. A second woman stood tucked against his right side. Her thick hair was a dark chestnut with red highlights. She was as gorgeous as the blonde, and her hand was splayed across Chase's abs.

Savannah's stomach cramped and she had to bend over, her hands braced on her thighs. Two women. Both beautiful. And definitely cowgirls from the way they were dressed. Real cowgirls, not the kind who would shop in Leather and Lace.

Somebody tapped her on the shoulder, and she jerked upright. Twyla.

"Just wanted to check to make sure you're all right, hon."

Yeah, Savannah just bet she did. She straightened without looking at the girl with the tiara attached to her cowboy hat. "I'm fine, Twyla. Just a little light-headed from all the congratulations."

"Sure, whatever. Anyway, I see you found your *husband*."

She didn't need to see Twyla's face. Savannah heard the sneer in the way she said that last word. "I did, and now you can get lost." She didn't add the name she wanted to call the pushy, two-faced witch.

"Now, why would I want to do that? You think you're all that because you conned Chase into marrying you. What you see is what you get, and I get to watch you getting it." Twyla cackled, her glee evident.

What you see is what you get. She'd believed him in Cheyenne, that his brother had masqueraded as Chase. But what if the twins had pulled a double switch? What if Chase had actually stayed in Cheyenne for the rendezvous with Di and Cash had been here in Vegas dealing with those federal officers? Oh, yeah, they could have pulled that off.

She blanked her face. No way would she give Twyla the satisfaction of seeing her crumble. She was Savannah Wolfe and she would keep her chin up. No freaking matter what. Her brain whirled. Should she confront him? Should she just walk up as though she had no problem he was all but making out with two beautiful women? Should she walk away, go back to the hotel and eviscerate him in private?

The decision was made for her when the blonde turned and saw her standing in the hall. The woman leaned closer to Chase and whispered in his ear, her eyes never leaving Savannah. That's when Savannah knew. That's when she saw the same look on the blonde's face as she'd seen on Di Brandenburg's. That's when she knew she'd been played for a fool. Frozen in place a moment too long, she watched Chase's head turn. Saw him recognize her. Saw the moment he understood he'd blown it with her. She watched him shake off the women, watched him take a few steps in her direction, fighting through the throng of reporters.

That's when her muscles thawed and her brain took over. She pivoted and ducked back down the ramp. By the time she hit level ground, she was sprinting. Cimarron. She'd leave him. He was safe in the pen. She'd call Kade later to come pick him up. Him and Red. She didn't want them. She didn't want the trailer. The clothes. Nothing. At the moment, though, what she wanted was to get away. Needed to get away. Someone called her name. She kept running.

Chase lost sight of Savannah in the crowd. People were staring, but that didn't matter. All he cared about was getting to Savvie, explaining to her. The look on her face had gutted him. She believed he'd betrayed her. He had to talk to her. Tell her he was an idiot. That what she saw wasn't what she thought it was.

"Chase! What the hell, bud?" Chance grabbed his shoulder and forced him to stop.

Cord stood next to Chance, breathing hard. "You almost knocked Jolie down. Not cool, dude."

A moment later, Clay pushed through the mass of people, sheltering Georgie against his side, while he made a path for Cassidy and Jolie. "Want to explain what that mad dash was all about?"

Chase stared at his brothers and their wives. He knew Savannah had seen him with them. Knew she'd leaped to the wrong conclusion. And he knew why. He'd never introduced her to his family. To anyone besides Tucker. Just as he'd been thoughtless about that cheap ring he'd put on her finger, he'd never considered taking her home to Oklahoma to meet his brothers and their wives. To meet Miz Beth and Big John, the caretakers who'd all but raised the Barron boys. He'd made her his wife but he hadn't made her part of his family. He'd planned to remedy that, but he'd waited too long.

Cassidy sidled up beside Chance. "Why did she freak out like that, Chase?"

The question was a legitimate one. He'd told no one but Tucker about Cash's sabotage attempt in Cheyenne. Why he'd felt the need to protect his twin was beyond his comprehension at the moment. Cash had done despicable things to all of them.

Hunter Tate, Clay's chief of security, appeared, along with several of the Tate brothers and a man Chase vaguely recognized as part of Clay's security team. His oldest brother was a US senator and had been campaigning for the presidency before following his heart to marry Georgie, Clay's former director of communications. The football scrum of Barrons and Tates put the three ladies in the middle and moved outside to the parking lot, where they had a modicum of privacy.

Jolie fisted her hands on her hips and did her best to look tough. The ER nurse got right to the point. "Just say it, Chase. Rip the Band-Aid off fast."

Chase watched Clay shrug off his leather jacket and drape it around Georgie's shoulders. She was still recovering from the illness that threatened her life. The tenderness in that gesture floored Chase. He wanted that with Savannah. Inhaling deeply to fortify his resolve, he laid it out for his family.

"Chance knows most of the story. The beginning, anyway. Dad decided I needed to get married. He picked out Janiece Carroll. Tucker got wind of things." He glanced around the group and realized Kade had joined them. The ranch manager did not look happy. "Since I was supposed to be out of town, Kade arranged to have Savannah stay in my apartment. Only I came home early. And kicked her out."

He dropped his chin at that admission. "In my defense," he told the pavement, "I'd just gotten burned by those two singers in Nashville."

"So you made amends by marrying her?" Kade's voice betrayed his tightly held anger.

"We made a deal. She needed help. I needed a wife. It was convenient for both of us."

"Convenient?" Cassie brushed a slap against the back of his head. "What were you thinkin'? Oh, wait. You weren't thinking. Duh."

"This doesn't explain why we're standing here in the middle of a parking lot on a chilly December night, little bro." Cord always cut to the heart of the matter.

"I discovered I liked her. A lot. And then I fell in love with her."

No one said a word. He couldn't even hear them breathing. He glanced up. Every one of them wore the same shocked expression. "You heard me. I fell in love."

He went on to explain about Cash. About his father. The ring. His idea to have them all there when he presented her with a real ring and asked Savannah to spend the rest of her life with him. He finished up with "And in true Barron fashion, I've totally screwed up everything."

"Ya think?" Cassie rolled her eyes. "Dude, you really shot yourself in the foot this time. We need to fix this."

Chance reeled her into his side with an arm around her neck. "No, sweetheart, *Chase* needs to fix this."

Twenty-Two

"Where would she go?" Chase considered the question, not realizing he'd voiced it aloud until Cord snorted.

"You're asking us? Like we'd have a clue because we know her so well."

He glared at his brother. "Yeah, stick that knife in and twist, Cord. My fault I didn't introduce her to y'all. My fault she didn't realize who Cass and Jolie are. My fault." His voice rose with each sentence he uttered and he finished by throwing his hands in the air.

"Where's her old truck?"

Clay focused on Kade. "What?"

"She left Cimarron in a holding pen. Big Red is in his stall. The trailer hasn't moved. I had Security check, and her new truck is gone. That surprises me. I figured she would have left it and taken a cab."

"What are you sayin', Kade?"

"I'm sayin' that I know Sav. She'll walk away from everything you gave her." He shoved his thumbs in the front pockets of his jeans. "Let me ask you this. What's in your apartment? The stuff she owns, I mean."

Chase considered, mentally walking through the closet. "Her clothes. Her…stuff."

"All of her clothes? Her duffel bag?"

He searched his memory again. Thought about what she'd taken the first time she tried to run. "Ah, hell." He stared at Kade. "She kept the stuff she arrived with in that duffel."

"Yup. And she keeps that duffel in the truck. She'll walk away with exactly what she walked in with." Kade's eyes hardened. "And she'll walk away from the money she won this year. She'll consider the winnings payback for your sponsorship."

"Ah, hell."

Tucker's phone pinged and he glanced at the screen before accepting the call. He held up a finger as he listened. "No. Don't do anything. Just keep an eye on her. We'll be there shortly." He returned his gaze to Chase. "She's in the parking garage at the Crown."

Chase breathed around the tightness in his chest. "She's gone home."

Kade growled in frustration. "No, you idiot. She doesn't have a home. Except that damn ol' Ford pickup of hers."

Hunt stepped closer, his phone in his hand. "SUVs will be here in a minute. We'll load up and head her off."

Chase had VIP parking and his Jag was close. "I can't wait."

Savannah finally found her old pickup. Breathing heavily, she leaned against its rusty fender and bit her lip to stave off her tears. Her hands shook even though she pressed them against the hood. Her nose burned and her vision was blurry. This corner of the hotel's parking garage was cloaked in shadows. No one could see her. No one would know that Chase's betrayal shattered her heart into so many pieces she'd never find them all.

Stiffening her spine, she pushed off the hood and stood straight. She was better than that. Stronger. She wasn't her mother. She didn't need a man to define her. Support her.

Take care of her. She'd been taking care of herself since she was twelve. Wiping her sleeve over her cheeks, she squared her shoulders.

She was done with anything bearing the Barron name, including the prenup, checking account and her winnings, all bought and paid for by Chase. She couldn't keep any of it and walk away with her pride intact.

She had to dump the contents of her purse to find the keys to the old Ford. She unlocked it and transferred her belongings from the new truck. She'd leave the key with the security guard at the exit. Settling in behind the steering wheel of her Ford, she inserted the key in the ignition and turned it.

Nothing happened.

No click. No whirr. No grinding chug. Nothing. And didn't that just sum up her life? She had nothing but a couple pairs of worn blue jeans, some old shirts, a pair of boots she didn't pay for but was keeping because she didn't want to go barefoot and a heap of a truck that wouldn't even start.

In the distance, she heard the rumble of life on the Strip. Closer, tires squealed as a driver took the circular ramp too fast. She got out, popped the hood. Everything looked okay. She jiggled the wires on the battery. Back in the driver's seat, she cranked the ignition. Nothing. Just like her. Her mother had been right—she was a loser. At least Chase had listened and not paid her old lady a cent. Savannah slumped, her forehead resting on the steering wheel as she let the tears fall.

Tires screeched right in front of her, and she looked up to see Chase's Jaguar blocking her truck. She had just enough presence of mind to slam her door and lock it. He stalked to her, but she couldn't decipher the expression on his face. Anger. Hurt. Concern. At the moment, anger was the primary emotion.

He jerked the door handle and his face clouded. "Open the door, Savannah."

"No."

He jerked again, then pounded on the window. "Open the damn door, Sav."

"No!"

More vehicles arrived. Black SUVs. People climbed out. She watched, slightly disconnected from the scene. Chase continued to bang on the window and shout.

"Open the door or I'll break the window."

Three women appeared—the blonde, the auburn-haired beauty and a third woman with short hair. They were accompanied by three men. Savannah blinked. She recognized Senator Clay Barron. His arm encircled the short-haired woman. Savvie swallowed hard. She vaguely remembered some news reports about Clay stopping his presidential campaign to be with his fiancée while she fought cancer. Savannah's gaze tracked to the other two women, and the men with them. She didn't recognize the men beyond the fact that they had to be Barrons. Chase's brothers?

"Dammit, Savvie! Swear to God I'm gonna rip this door off if you don't open it right now."

What was going on? She popped the lock, and in less than a breath, Chase had jerked the door open and pulled her out. He gripped her biceps and shook her.

"What were you thinking? Why did you run away?"

Her gaze remained glued on the two women. "I saw you."

"I know, kitten. But you didn't *see*."

"Yes, I did."

"No, you didn't. You saw what you wanted to see, not what was really there." He inhaled sharply and backed up, tugging her with him. "This is not the way I wanted to do this. Not the way I planned. At. All." He pointed to the women. "My sisters-in-law. Cassidy Barron. She's married to my brother Chance. That's Jolie. She married Cord and is the mother of my favorite nephew."

Cord snorted. "CJ is your only nephew, bud."

"You didn't see her back at the arena, but that's Georgie, who is Clay's wife."

"Uh-huh."

"Uh-huh? That's all you have to say?" He stormed away several steps and turned back. "You didn't trust me, Savannah. How can I do this if you don't trust me?"

She gulped, and as she often did when nervous, rubbed her thumb against the cheap metal of the band on her left ring finger. She opened her mouth to defend herself, but Chase didn't give her the chance.

"Look, I know I screwed up. Royally. From the beginning. I take responsibility for that. But I also made you a promise. And I asked you to trust me. At the first sign of trouble—perceived trouble—you cut and run. Do you really believe I'm such a bastard that I'd throw women in your face?"

She hung her head. "I'm sorry."

"Ah, Savannah." His voice broke as he gathered her into his arms. Stroking her back, Chase murmured against her hair, "I'm the one who's sorry, kitten. I'm a jerk. I admit that. I should have introduced you to my family. I should have gotten you a real ring. I should have taken better care of you. I..." He cleared the lump in his throat. "I'm the world's biggest idiot but I swear I never meant to hurt you."

He loosened his arms and dropped to one knee. "I didn't do this the first time I asked. But you deserve this." He dug in his pocket and pulled out a velvet box. Snapping it open, he removed the rings nestled inside. "I'm asking you for real this time. In front of my family. I love you, Savannah Wolfe Barron. Love you with my whole heart. Will you marry me again? I want you. Now and forever. I want you to have my last name. I want to live with you. Love you.

Fight with you. Make up with you. Because I can promise, me being me? I'm always gonna screw up somehow."

Everything faded into the distance as she focused on him. His expression said it all—soft, pleading eyes, hesitant smile. She cupped his cheeks, bent to kiss him.

"Yes," she whispered.

Chase surged to his feet, grabbed her and swung her in a circle. Then he removed the old ring, slipped it in his pocket, and placed the new engagement ring and wedding band on her finger.

"I love you, hoss."

"Not as much as I love you, kitten."

And he did. He loved his inconvenient cowgirl with his whole heart.

Epilogue

"You sure about this, cuz?"

Chase gazed at Tucker a full minute before rolling his eyes. "Seriously? You ask me this now?"

Tuck clapped him on the back, sloshing the coffee in his cup. "Better now than later."

He watched his best friend's expression morph from teasing to serious. "I'm happy for you, Chase. You know that, right? She's good for you."

"Yeah, I know. She's… I don't know how to explain how she makes me feel."

"That's good, because really? Dude, we're guys. We don't talk about that stuff." Tucker shuddered dramatically. "Feelings. Ugh!"

Laughing, Chase glanced around to see his brothers entering the family great room. A huge Christmas tree filled the corner near the massive fireplace. Miz Beth had outdone herself. For the first time in a long time, Chase was happy to be in Oklahoma to celebrate the holidays with his family, especially since Cyrus had chosen Hawaii and a female companion over being here. For the first time in ages, this felt like home. And he had Savannah to thank for that.

"Welcome to the ranks, little bro." Cord wrapped an arm around Chase's neck and gave him a short, strangling hug.

"Glad you found her," Clay added. "And didn't let her get away."

Chance studied him a moment. "It's good to see you happy, little bro."

Looking at Clay, Cord and Chance, Chase realized one face was missing. Cash. His twin. They'd parted on angry words last summer in Cheyenne, and Cash had avoided him since.

More laughing male voices crowded in. Tucker's brothers had arrived, stomping in from the kitchen. Barrons and Tates. One big, dysfunctional family where blood always tied them together. His sisters-in-law appeared, laughing at something. He watched as they picked out their husbands in the crowd. Georgie, still looking wan but getting healthier every day, didn't have to go far. Clay was beside her immediately, tucking her under his arm.

CJ, his nephew, hit Cord like a mini tornado. Jolie had eyes only for her men—Cord and CJ. By the time she reached them, Cord had his son up on a hip as he reached for his wife and pulled her in for a kiss.

Cassidy, all sass and hair tossing, sashayed to Chance and rolled up to her tiptoes to kiss him. He held her a moment, then turned her so her back rested against his front, his arms crossed over her chest.

"Savannah's almost dressed," Cass announced to the room at large. She turned to Chase, her eyes twinkling with mischief as the doorbell rang. "You should get that, Chase."

Suspicious, Chase prowled to the front door. He opened it and discovered a lavender-haired Liberace in a fur coat standing there with Kade. Kade got his big foot wedged in the door before Chase could slam it shut.

"No. Not happening!" Chase was adamant. Laughter spilled out from the other room. Almost all of his family was here. But a moment of isolation stabbed through him. He wanted Cash to be here, too, despite everything.

Kade urged the Liberace impersonator inside and shut the door behind them. "Dude's not licensed in Oklahoma, but since y'all are already married, doesn't matter. He's gonna say the words again." He glanced around. "Where's my girl?"

"Up here." Savannah's voice floated down from the landing at the top of the stairs, arcing over the foyer.

Chase couldn't breathe. Her black hair fell in thick waves around her face, over her shoulders and down her back. Brown eyes shining, her face glowing with happiness, she stepped down. She wore a long skirt that looked like lace, only…it wasn't. The cream-colored crocheted skirt brushed the toes of her boots. She lifted it to descend, and Chase saw that her Western boots were the color of red dirt. A matching leather belt cinched her hips and he recognized the heavy silver buckle—her All-Around Cowgirl Championship buckle. A silk blouse the color of the Oklahoma sky caressed her curves and his fingers itched to mold the material to her skin.

"Beautiful." That's what his mouth said, but his brain? His brain was shouting, *MINE!*

He met her at the bottom step and took her hand. Together, they returned to the great room. With family gathered around, Liberace read the words that would renew their vows. Chase took them to heart this time. For better or worse. In sickness and in health. Until death did them part. His inconvenient cowgirl was now the most important person in his life. He looked around the room, his gaze connecting with each of his brothers and their wives. Chase understood now, understood where his big brothers found the strength to stand up for themselves and the women they loved.

Movement near the arch leading to the kitchen caught his attention. Whoever stood there didn't come into the family room, but Chase knew who it was, knew the shape of that shadow as well as he did his own. Cash had come home, after all. Chase sent a look and a barely perceptible nod that direction. No one else saw, but his twin would.

"You may now kiss your bride."

Chase gathered Savannah into his arms and she tipped up on her toes as he lowered his head to kiss her. "I love you." They spoke simultaneously, their words and breath mingling. And he realized some things the moment she melted into his arms for the kiss that sealed their lives. He did need a wife, so long as it was this woman. And blood wasn't what tied a family together. It was love.

* * * * *

Pick up all the RED DIRT ROYALTY *novels from Silver James!*
These Oklahoma millionaires work hard and play harder.

COWGIRLS DON'T CRY
THE COWGIRL'S LITTLE SECRET
THE BOSS AND HIS COWGIRL
CONVENIENT COWGIRL BRIDE

Available now from Mills & Boon Desire!

* * *

MILLS & BOON®

PASSIONATE AND DRAMATIC LOVE STORIES

Give a 12 month subscription to a friend today!

Call Customer Services
0844 844 1358 *

or visit
millsandboon.co.uk/subscription